A NEW DAWN BREAKS

J. A. FRANCES

A NEW DAWN BREAKS

Troubador Publishing Ltd
Unit E2 Airfield Business Park,
Harrison Road, Market Harborough,
Leicestershire LE16 7UL
Tel: 0116 279 2299
Email: books@troubador.co.uk
Web: www.troubador.co.uk

ISBN 978-1-80514-508-0

British Library Cataloguing in Publication Data.
A catalogue record for this book is available from the British Library.

Printed and bound by CPI Group (UK) Ltd, Croydon, CR0 4YY
Typeset in 11pt Minion Pro by Troubador Publishing Ltd, Leicester, UK

FSC www.fsc.org
MIX
Paper | Supporting responsible forestry
FSC® C013604

For Bea and the family

Part I: 1919-1922

ONE

Now the War has Ended

Glasgow
January 1919

A dapper figure in regulation dark jacket and pinstripe trousers stood by an upper window overlooking George Square. Casual observers might have taken him for a lawyer or accountant; acquaintances were led to believe he was a middle ranking civil servant. Only a very few associates knew of his true role in the shadowy world of the security services.

From his vantage point he could survey the whole scene, watch with grim satisfaction as workers in their thousands came streaming into the city centre to hear the government's response to their demands. Throughout the week Glasgow had been gripped by industrial unrest, with increasing disruption as shipyard workers and engineers laid siege to power stations and picketed tram depots. The intention was obvious; to force municipal employees to join the strikers, and exploit the chaos that must inevitably ensue.

So the extremists had crawled out of the woodwork again: he had always known they would. Earlier attempts at mob rule by radical socialists had been nipped in the bud, but the spirit of revolt had never been fully crushed. Time and again he had given warning of his misgivings, and his reports had been ignored or dismissed. The consensus seemed to be that Fraser Dunlop was obsessed with non-existent communist plots. Well, now the boot was on the other foot. Even the most sceptical of government ministers could scarcely deny the existence of Red Clydeside. And the secretary for Scotland, Munro, was running around like a headless chicken, declaiming that bolshevism was rife in the land.

There was a polite cough behind him. "Excuse me, sir," murmured a voice.

Dunlop swung round, frowning at the interruption. "Yes, Armstrong," he said testily, "what is it this time?"

"I thought you might like these." The man held out a leather case. "The field glasses will give you a better view."

For a moment Dunlop was taken aback. If this was an attempt at an olive branch… "Very thoughtful, I'm sure." He made an effort to stifle his irritation. "Thank you, Armstrong."

It was not that the fellow was obstructive, or even outwardly critical: it was the hint of mockery in his attitude, like the servility of a valet sneering at his master behind his back. And to claim that he had been sent up from London purely to help out with the present situation was barely credible. In all probability this interloper had been foisted on him to assess his handling of the crisis. Was it with a view to recommending a long overdue promotion? Dunlop rather doubted the possibility. There had been rumours of department cost cutting since the end of the war. Was he being considered as surplus to requirements? That could mean a transfer back to the police service. His lips wrinkled in distaste. But there was still a card to be played on that score. He could only hope it would be enough.

"Anything else?" His subordinate was still hovering.

"Latest report, sir. Indications show that a crowd of over forty thousand can be expected in the Square. That includes demobilised soldiers and unemployed workers, as well as actual strikers."

"Good. They'll soon get short shrift. Government can't be held to ransom. By the by, is there any information about the meeting of the War Cabinet?"

"Just in, sir. That's why I'm really here."

Dunlop gritted his teeth in exasperation. "God's sake, man. Have you no sense of priorities? Out with it."

"Of course, sir." Armstrong smiled faintly. "Cabinet has received and considered the Lord Provost's message in reference to the proposal for a general reduction in working hours." He paused for effect.

"I'm well aware of that. What was the outcome?"

"As you anticipated, sir. Ministers have unanimously rejected the demand for the imposition of a maximum forty hour working week. Employers must be permitted to set their own terms of employment."

"That goes without saying, Armstrong. What about my suggestions for dealing with civil unrest?"

"Largely accepted, sir. As you can see from the window, the City Chambers is protected by policemen, and the Square itself is ringed with heavy reinforcements, both mounted and on foot."

"Excellent. What about the position of the army?"

"The War Office has the matter in hand. Soldiers based in Glasgow are confined to barracks to prevent any attempt to suborn them by friends in the crowd. There are ten thousand reliable troops outside the city who can move in at a few hours' notice. I believe there's even a squad of tanks available as well."

"It's on the cards they'll be needed. When the mob hears the answer to their demands there'll be a riot."

"Are you sure of that? Perhaps they'll be overawed by our show of strength and simply disperse. They can't all be red revolutionaries."

"Perhaps not. But it just goes to show how clever the real instigators have been in whipping up fears of unemployment. This bid for a forty-hour week is no more than a ploy to delude the masses. Their real object is to cause confusion, stir up violence and anarchy so they can set up a workers' state – just like in Russia."

"So you keep telling me. Do you really believe that those responsible are the same people who sought to take control of the shipyards and munitions works during the war?"

"There can be no doubt of it. You will recall that the shop stewards on Clydeside attempted to exploit craft resistance to essential changes in work practices. This Clyde Workers Committee, as they called themselves, gave us no end of trouble before we could bring them to heel. And then we made the mistake of assuming there was no further cause for concern. The ne'er-do-wells were allowed back to their old stomping ground, to lie low while they plotted and schemed. They think this is their opportunity – with Russian paymasters calling the tune this time."

"And that is your considered opinion?" Dunlop could only stare at the sudden change of tone. Before he could react, Armstrong was quick to follow up his advantage. "In that case I would have to say that Whitehall feels your views are somewhat misplaced. And has done so for some time. Agents in the field can sometimes overlook the bigger picture. Would you not agree?"

Dunlop stiffened at the rebuke, then rallied. "But – look at the evidence, man," he protested. "The rabble out there, baying for blood. And you yourself admit that the War Cabinet agrees about the danger."

"Perhaps not quite so much as you imagine. The Prime Minister did not feel the situation was serious enough to warrant his return from the peace conference at Versailles. Doubtless a few hotheads might try to stir up violence. But we're well equipped to deal with such an eventuality. George Square will go down as no more than the last whimper of the wounded beast. There'll be no Petrograd on Clydeside. You may rely on that – Dunlop."

There was a sharp intake of breath. Daring to question what was obvious? Insulting him to his face? Was Armstrong showing up his true colours at last? He could only wonder as he choked back his resentment. "May I remind you that dissent has already spread to Edinburgh and Leith," he said coldly. "Not to mention messages of support sent by workers in other areas. And you can't deny near mutiny among the troops in France over the pace of demobilisation."

"Mere pinpricks, Dunlop." Armstrong smiled blandly. "They'll soon fizzle out. And in the wider context bolshevism is on its last legs."

"Are you serious?" He could hardly believe such complacency. "Well then, what about Germany? There's a communist regime in Bavaria. And fighting in the streets of Berlin. So much so that the new government had to flee for safety."

"Try to keep up with the times, Dunlop." The words were laced with irony. "This Spartacist revolt, as they term it, is as good as over. The rebel leaders have been captured and shot out of hand. The regular army and *Freikorps* are just damping down the last embers. Don't you read the newspapers?"

Dunlop glowered, but chose to ignore the barb. "What about Russia? The soviets are still committed to worldwide revolution."

"Mere posturing. They're in no position to offer any material help. Quite the contrary, I should think. There's civil war, open revolt against the Bolsheviks in their own back yard. Or hadn't you noticed? And the Reds are heavily outnumbered, what with counter-revolutionary forces advancing on a dozen fronts. It's only a matter of time… Need I say more?"

Dunlop shook his head. The man seemed to have an answer for everything. Wearily he turned away to stare through the window.

"You know, Dunlop, I've nothing against you personally. You've done good work in the past. But you've been stuck in your own little groove for too long. I shouldn't be telling you this, but it has already been decided to run down the Glasgow office. If I were in your position I'd put in for a transfer. Before it's too late."

Transfer? That meant all was not lost. He spun round. "Whitehall, you mean?"

Armstrong chuckled. "Alas, no. I was thinking of Ireland."

"Ireland? Why there?" He could not hide his disappointment.

"Because Ireland is a powder keg just waiting to explode. You know the Sinn Feiners swept the board at the recent election – with the exception of Ulster, that is. And then refused to take their seats at Westminster. They've set up a sham parliament of their own in Dublin."

"But we've got half of their MPs locked up. They can't do us any harm in jail."

Armstrong sighed. "Do I have to spell it out, Dunlop? We smashed their pathetic little rising in 1916. And executed their leaders, who are now conveniently seen as martyrs for Irish independence. Already there's growing civil disobedience. Many parts of the countryside are almost ungovernable. And that's far from all. Remember the prewar paramilitaries – the Irish Volunteers? We believe they've been reformed, and are drilling with weapons looted from arms stores. The Irish Republican Army – that's their new name. Last week they ambushed and killed two policemen in County Tipperary. It could be the signal for the start of guerrilla warfare."

"And you need people like me to ferret them out?"

"Exactly. I look forward to receiving your application. Give you a chance to redeem yourself." With a meaningful look he strode away.

Dunlop bristled with indignation. To be put in his place by this jumped-up pen pusher was the final humiliation. Savagely he wrenched open the leather case and snatched out the binoculars: the urge to hurl Armstrong's offering after him was almost irresistible. Fortunately, the moment passed. It would be nothing but a futile gesture. Contenting himself with an angry glare, he set himself to study the scene from his window.

By this time the Square was well-nigh packed, a sea of faces from one end to the other. Here and there speakers could be seen clambering onto makeshift platforms to harangue their audience. His attention shifted over to the police guarding the City Chambers. Silent and impassive they might appear to a casual glance, but he was well aware the bobbies would be winding themselves up to react to the slightest provocation. He saw the line part a little to allow passage for a group of figures. This would be the delegation sent to hear the decision from the Lord Provost in person. No doubt they would be left to kick their heels awhile before he condescended to receive them. And when they emerged with the news…

Surely all was not yet lost. A rampaging attack on the building, even if repulsed, would prove that he had been right. The press would have a field day, exposing poor judgment on the part of his superiors. Lessons would have to be learned: no longer could Glasgow be ignored with impunity. In the meantime, his hireling had been well briefed; it was high time for him to be about his business. As if in response to the wish, his eye caught a ripple in the crowd.

* * *

Iain Baird pushed through the scrum surrounding the statue of Gladstone in front of the City Chambers. Blast Robertson! Trust him to insist on a meeting at the most inconvenient time. But that was typical of the man. There had been no word of him for months; and now his old mentor had suddenly reappeared, announcing his return with a curt note pushed through his letter box the previous evening. What the hell did he want this time? Whatever the reason, his presence was an added complication. He had his instructions, and Dunlop would be far from pleased if there was any hitch in carrying them out.

A muttered oath gave little comfort as he cursed his misfortune. Stan Robertson was a wily bird; that was why he generally lurked in the shadows, pulling the strings while others danced to his tune. And he expected no less from the raw journeyman he had befriended, singled out and inducted into the Party. That was why he had expected his protégé to accept his offer to accompany him on a passage to Russia when the strike movement on Clydeside crumbled away after the government crackdown back in 1916. To be fair, Stan had taken his refusal in good part, contenting himself with a warning of likely retribution on the part of the authorities, and he had been imprisoned on trumped up charges as a conscientious objector. Were he ever to guess how his pupil had obtained his release… Robertson would show no mercy. Personal relationships counted for little in the mind of a dedicated revolutionary. The cause was everything. And disloyalty was a mortal sin.

But surely his secret was safe. Only Dunlop knew of his role as a double agent. Would the spymaster undo his efforts after springing him from a ten-year sentence of penal servitude? There was no guarantee, especially if his usefulness was considered at an end. The bastard had already shown the mailed fist by having him clapped in jail for a couple of months after the failure to capture Robertson. He pulled a face at the recollection of the fracas at the railway station where he had been overpowered while his companion made good his escape. That treatment was unlikely to be repeated, even though wartime regulations had not yet been lifted. All the same, it would be foolish to put the issue to the test. Dunlop might stop short of betraying his activities to the Party, but the spectre of postwar unemployment loomed large. The sudden end to the war had meant immediate cancellation of government contracts, with thousands of skilled workers thrown on the scrapheap. Only a favoured few could hope for a transfer to the shipyards where wartime losses of merchant shipping were still to be made good. And he was to be among their number – chargehand back at Deuchar's, with confirmation of his company house. That Dunlop had been behind the move he had little doubt: that the arrangement could be terminated at a moment's notice, none at all.

A ragged cheer went up. That would be for the deputation making its way into the City Chambers – Gallacher, Kirkwood, Shinwell and the others. Just as well he had turned down the invitation to join them: Dunlop had other ideas for him. The police were under strict instructions that public transport was to be kept running at all costs. Any attempt to block the passage of trams would result in swift retaliation. One line ran along the south side of George Square: the hint could not have been made clearer. He glanced at his pocket watch. Stan was late. That gave him an excuse to make a start before he turned up, thus avoiding any need for explanation or argument. It would be easy to claim later that they must have missed each other in the crush.

As he moved off, Iain went over in his head the rough plan he had already sketched out. An ideal spot for his purpose would be where the tracks veered off the Square, passing the corner of the municipal buildings within full view of the police cordon. Close enough to provoke a reaction, but hopefully not before he had time to accomplish the task he had been set.

Dunlop was counting on a show; disabling a tramcar to hold up the traffic should fit the bill nicely. His original thought had been to leap on board, push the motorman aside, yank out the controller's handle and throw it into the crowd. But then the thought occurred that it might be simpler to cut off the electricity supply from the overhead wires. The pole carrying the current to the transmission could be disconnected by pulling on a cord: he had seen it done often enough at the terminus when power had to be transferred from one cable to another for the return journey. Cut the rope – and the pole would hang helpless.

The persistent clanging of a bell drew his attention towards an approaching tram, crawling along at a snail's pace as it fought its way through the press of numbers encroaching onto the track. He pushed forward, reaching his objective as the car began to turn the corner. Lunging for the rear platform, he swung himself on board and dashed up the spiral staircase. Luckily there were no passengers on the upper deck – no interfering busybody to get in his road. It was the work of a moment to undo the rope from its hook on the rail, then drag on it to wrest the fillet at the end of the pole from the overhead wire. Next, taking a clasp knife from his pocket, he stretched out as far as he could, and began to saw on the cord. As the last strands parted, he felt a wild surge of exhilaration. Now the vehicle was dead, a useless lump of metal – at least until a long ladder could be fetched to attach a new rope.

"What the hell dae ye think ye're playin' at?" An angry face appeared from the front of the tram. It was the conductor, come to investigate the sudden loss of power.

Iain was gathering up the length of hemp he had just cut. "Bloody scabs!" he snarled. "I'm daein' what you should be doin'. Stickin' up for workers' rights."

"We'll see about that." The man began to advance along the passageway between the seats. "Gimme that rope."

"Nae chance!" Iain leaned over the side. "Up here, lads," he shouted. "Catch it." The coil was dropped to the onlookers below. "It's a trophy o' war. See ye burn it." Immediately it disappeared into the crowd.

"Grab the bugger, Jackie," called another voice. He felt a tug on his shoulder. Instinctively he whirled round, drawing back his fist and letting fly with all his strength. There was a howl of anguish as his assailant fell back. But there was no time for more. Already the driver was rushing to the aid of his crewman: out of the corner of his eye he could detect movement in the police lines, batons being drawn, and a troop of horsemen coming into view from the rear. The result had been achieved; only a fool would linger. He fairly skipped down the stairs; then suddenly pulled up short. Confronting him at the bottom, wagging a finger in admonition was – Stan Robertson.

"Trust you, ya dummy. Couldnae wait five minutes but ye had to be off, chargin' round like a bull in a china shop." He shook his head wearily. "When will ye ever learn?"

"Stan!" Iain chose to ignore the rebuke. "Where the blue blazes did you spring from?"

"Never mind that." Robertson jerked a finger. "Look ower there." Even as he spoke, a squad of policemen broke into a charge, evidently with the intention to cleave a path to the tram. "Get yer arse out o' it. Unless ye want to be lifted by the bobbies, that is."

The advice was not to be ignored. Iain allowed himself to be hustled out of harm's way, slipping down a side street before officers could arrive in force to block the escape route. His companion set a brisk pace; not a word was exchanged until Robertson decided there was no further danger of pursuit and called a halt.

"That was a rare stramash ye kicked up. No' the sort of thing that's expected o' a body wi' a start back at Deuchar's next week," he added slyly. "Ye'd be a marked man if they ever found out it was you."

For a moment Iain was taken aback. Was there anything the man did not know? "You're a sharp one, Stan." He gave a sheepish grin. "I dinnae ken how ye manage it. Especially when ye're never around for months at a time."

"Ye shouldnae be surprised. Ye ken fine I like to keep up wi' what's goin' on. Just a friendly interest in old comrades, ye might say. You seem to have landed on yer feet after that spell in jail. Near enough a'body paid off at the Ordnance, yet you get taken on back at the shipyard. Somebody must like ye."

"Nothin' like that, Stan." Iain recovered his wits. "It's just that I'll be a shop steward again. They've orders on their books, so they'll no' want to upset the apple cart."

"Aye. Likely that'll be it. Shall we walk on? I could dae wi' a wee daunder. Nae sense in hangin' around here. Ye've caused enough mayhem already."

They fell into step together. "By the by, I hear ye stand high in the Party these days. And ye're a leadin' light in the CWC as well. Gallacher's right hand man, so I'm led to believe."

A wary look came into Iain's eye. It was true he had helped Willie Gallacher, acknowledged leader of industrial militancy on Clydeside, to rebuild the revolutionary Clyde Workers Committee in the last year or so of the war, and that on his release from prison he had been swept back into the movement to play a leading part in preparations for calling a general strike. What no one must ever know was that he had done so with the full knowledge and approval of the government's security services.

"I wouldnae go that far," he mumbled. "I only did my bit."

"Ach, ye're ower modest, laddie. Gettin' over a hundred thousand to come out must have taken some organisation."

"Aye, well." He breathed a little more easily. "I'm just disappointed we couldnae go as far as I would hae liked."

"Ye don't say. What else could ye have done?"

"Demanded a thirty-hour week. That would hae shown we mean business. But the moderates wouldnae wear it. The Trades Council insisted it was forty hours or nothin'."

"So ye had to compromise. I can understand that."

"Maybe. But that's no' all. We could've done more to stop the traffic. Bring Glasgow to its knees."

"How so? Ye had pickets a' ower the place."

"Pinkston, ye mean? That's the main tram depot. Aye, we laid siege to it. Much good it did. Didnae stop the trams runnin'. I was all for marchin' in and occupyin' it, but the rest o' them thought that wid be too provocative."

"So ye felt stymied. Is that why ye took it intae yer heid to cut a dash in George Square? Did ye get permission for this stunt?"

"From the Party, ye mean? Well, no – no' exactly. It wisnae discussed."

Robertson sucked his teeth. "Iain, how many times must I tell ye? It's discipline that wins wars. Once a plan is decided, ye stick to it. There's nae room for lone wolves doin' their own thing."

"And I would agree wi' ye, Stan. But maybe there's scope for a body to gie a wee nudge. Ye've said yersel' that activists need to be ready to adapt to changing situations," he added artfully.

"And ye suppose this was one o' them?"

"Don't you? Ye ken fine that the bosses would never agree to the forty hours. Yon meetin' was just a smokescreen to buy time. Only the power o' the masses can force the capitalists to make concessions. I was just stirrin' things up a bit."

"Ye've certainly managed that. Cats among the pigeons, and nae mistake. There'll be fights breakin' out a' ower George Square by now. Maybe the polis will be driven back, though I hae my doubts. In any case I hear the army's to be brought in. Ye'll hae sodgers patrollin' the streets."

"All the better. At least it'll show up the class enemy in their true colours."

"And the good citizens will rise up in protest? Grow up, son. That cock winnae fight. It worked in Petrograd, but it'll no' happen here. The war's over. Nae war weariness or discontent in the army to exploit. There's nae chance o' an insurrection in Scotland now. We need to look at different paths to achieve power for the people. D'ye suppose this demonstration will change anythin'?"

"But what else can we do to bring about the workers' state?"

There was no immediate response. Robertson appeared to consider his reply carefully before he spoke. "Can ye guess where I've been these past months?" he asked, as though changing the subject.

"I've nae idea."

"Russia. And I've met Lenin again. The soviet leader, in case ye've forgotten."

"Oh aye." Iain was non-committal. "That would account for no' seein' ye for so long." Stan had been in Petrograd when the Bolsheviks had seized power, and had returned with the promise of Russian weapons to arm the workers. Evidently he had been there for a second time, to find refuge and lie low until the heat died down at home.

"Ye don't sound very impressed."

"It's no' that. But we were countin' on a shipload o' rifles and they never came. What did they offer ye this time? I dinnae see how we can expect any help fae Russia. No' when the Reds are bein' driven back on all sides by the Whites." The newspapers were full of the civil war in Russia, with gloating reports that the Russian Revolution was all but over as White counter-revolutionary forces marched on both Moscow and Petrograd.

"And ye believe everythin' ye read in the press?" It was almost a snort of derision. "Come off it, Iain. Ye should ken better than that. It might seem things are no' goin' too well at the minute, but we'll win through in the end. D'ye want to know why?"

"I'm sure ye're gonnae tell me."

"That I am. It's true the soviets have had some setbacks. But the enemy is disunited – a real ragbag o' monarchists, nationalists, social democrats, and God kens what else. They hate each other even more that the Bolsheviks. Stands tae reason they'll no' cooperate wi' each other – coordinate their attacks, like. That'll gie the Red Army the chance to pick them off one by one. You'll see."

"Aye, maybe. But—"

"And there's a lesson in that for us here. Unity means strength. We need to stop squabblin' amongst ourselves and set up a broad movement o' the left if we're to get anywhere."

Iain spun round in amazement. "Man, ye've surely changed yer tune. Ye used to say that only the Socialist Labour Party had the answers. Ye couldnae thole anyone else's ideas."

"Well, times change. And that's how Lenin sees the way ahead. Direct action – strikes and demonstrations – can only take us so far. We need to gain control o' the apparatus of bourgeois government in order to destroy it. That means takin' part in elections for Parliament." He held up two crossed fingers. "It's like the blades o' a pair of scissors. Between them they'll cut up the fabric o' the capitalist state."

"That's all very well." Iain voiced the obvious objection. "How the hell can a tiny party like us ever hope to win seats?"

"Simple. We join the big battalions." His companion stared at him blankly. "D'ye no' get it? We affiliate wi' the Labour Party."

"But—" He gaped like a stranded fish.

"Hear me out. Ye'll find it makes sense. Once we're in, they'll no' be able to get rid o' us. The cuckoo in the nest, ye might say. We'll be the activists, we'll set the agenda. We'll snatch control o' the organisation, we'll select the candidates for the House o' Commons. Anyone in our way will be swept aside. Lenin himself telt me we maun shake Labour wi' one hand so we can choke the life out o' him by the other."

"But can Labour ever win?" Iain found his voice at last. "They didnae do very well at the election."

"That was just government propaganda. Folks were rushed intae votin'. Taken in by a slogan o' who had won the war. Wid ye credit it? Forbye that, thousands were turned away because they didnae get the chance to register.

Things will be different next time round – once the true cost o' the war sinks in. It'll be our job to mobilise the masses to cast their vote. Then there'll be hundreds o' new Labour MPs." He grinned at Iain. "You could be one o' them. How wid ye fancy that?"

Iain frowned, then laughed. "Very good, Stan. One o' your best."

"Ye think it's a joke? Far from it. We're gonnae need reliable men where it really counts. Think about it. That's all I ask." He offered his hand. "And now I must be away. I'll be in touch. See if ye can stay out o' trouble. Ye'll be nae use in clink. Gie my regards to yer lass," he added, almost as an afterthought.

Iain watched him disappear round a corner. The idea was laughable. Yet Robertson evidently thought it was possible. He shrugged his shoulders. Ah well, time would tell.

* * *

The short winter afternoon had almost run its course before Iain decided he might as well take himself home. Robertson had given a broad hint that he should quit the scene without delay, but curiosity had induced him to linger. Surely he was entitled to witness the march of events, savour the outcome of his exertions. Joining a swarm of demonstrators making their way towards a rally on Glasgow Green, he learned that the police had more or less cleared George Square, though not before suffering a bloody nose. At one stage a baton charge had been repulsed with a fusillade of lemonade bottles looted from a delivery van. And there was also news of the strike leaders deputed to wait upon the Lord Provost. Kirkwood, on hearing the commotion outside, had dashed from the municipal buildings to remonstrate with the officers, but had been clubbed down before he could register a protest. Gallacher had apparently tried to rush at the Chief Constable, but had been struck senseless. Now both of them were in custody, bloodied and bandaged, the victims of police brutality. This was all grist to the mill. Dunlop could have no complaints at the results this time.

As daylight faded, an eerie hush fell over the city streets. Most of the remaining marchers were dispersing, melting away in dribs and drabs. No doubt passions had cooled, snuffed out in the chill night air. Many would now be fearful, stunned by remorse at their bravado, anxious about the inevitable retribution for daring to confront the forces of law and order.

Buttoning up his jacket and pulling down his cap, Iain fell into step behind a group of shadowy figures. There was security, as well as anonymity, in numbers. Should a police squad be lying in wait for stragglers, he was ready to dodge away, leaving those around him to fend off the assailants.

A sudden commotion made him look up sharply – shouts up ahead, followed by the sound of breaking glass. His momentary alarm gave way to a grin of satisfaction. Some hotheads were smashing shop windows. With any luck there would be looting as well to add to the account. And that was not all. Through the gloom appeared the outline of a tramcar, motionless in its tracks: others in the crowd had apparently taken the hint, and copied his example. At this rate there might be dozens of vehicles abandoned with their wires cut. Chuckling to himself, he trudged on. Never mind that Morag would not yet be home. With the fire banked up, and a glass of whisky to toast his success, he would be quite content to await her return. Afterwards he might even persuade her to celebrate with a visit to the picture palace.

But would she agree? There was no guarantee of that. His mood changed as bitter thoughts brought a scowl to his lips. At one time an evening out would have been rounded off with a night of passionate lovemaking. But that was now firmly in the past, never to be repeated. He had scarcely touched her in the last six months – not since the second miscarriage, and the stern warning from the hospital that any future attempts to start a family might well have fatal results. How ironic that she had ensnared him in the first place, yet could not give him the son he craved. Now he was stuck in a childless marriage. Other women found him attractive, and there was some solace to be gained in brief couplings, but that was no answer to the heartache that had come to bedevil his life.

His feelings deepened. It was perhaps not Morag's fault that she was barren, and he would have forgiven everything had she responded to his entreaties to give up her work – nanny to Elizabeth's child, to the boy he had fathered. She was little more than a skivvy, nursemaid to his own flesh and blood. The situation was intolerable, an affront to his manhood. Was it meant as an act of revenge on her part, to pay him out for daring to take his brother's girlfriend in the heat of the moment? No doubt her employer had spun her some gruesome tale which she had chosen to believe. She never made accusations to his face, but it was clear there was some invisible barrier between them.

If only he could have some contact with his own son, it might at least help to ease the pain. As the biological father, it was only natural he should have the right to some consideration. But apparently no one else shared his view. Elizabeth had married his kid brother to give the lad protection: Alastair was now his legal guardian. Had he perished in the Spanish flu epidemic at the end of the war things might have been different. But against the odds he had pulled through, after lying at death's door for several days. On the other hand, he was away from home for the foreseeable future, sent overseas to a sanatorium in Switzerland to regain his strength. Morag had told him he might be gone for six months or more. Could something be gained by his absence? That was a question he had been asking himself, without as yet reaching any conclusion.

Lights twinkled from countless windows in high tenements as he reached the familiar surroundings of Govan. Wearily he turned into Brighton Road, towards the company house Dunlop had secured for him when he made his pact with the devil. The cold was seeping into his body: now the excitement was over he realised how drained he felt. A stiff dram and seat by the fire had never seemed more enticing. But if Morag came home in one of her moods… At the foot of the close some sixth sense made him look upwards. There was a light shining from the top floor flat. It could only mean she was back early. Usually she was last to return, lingering with her charge till the last minute. Another night of sullen silence, he thought gloomily. Either that, or a slanging match if he so much as opened his mouth. Surely there must be something that might induce her into a better frame of mind. Slowly he began to drag himself up the flight of stairs, racking his brain for a solution. At the top landing he swore in exasperation: he could think of nothing to convince her. Gritting his teeth, he stabbed the latchkey into the lock.

"Morag!" he called out, pushing open the door. "I'm back. Fair famished, as ye might expect. But we gave them a run for their money." Pitching his cap onto a peg on the rail, he crossed the hallway to confront his wife.

"Morag?" He glanced round, almost in disbelief. The kitchen range stood cold and cheerless; the fire laid but not lit. There was no sign of preparations for his evening meal. Yet the light bulb, burning in its socket, was proof positive that Morag had been home. Had she gone out again? But her coat and hat had been hanging on an adjoining nail in the lobby. For a moment he was puzzled. Then he heard movement in the other room – the creak of a bed. And – were his ears deceiving him? Surely it was the faint sound of sobbing. His jaw dropped as she came out; her face was puffed, her eyes red and bleary from the tears.

"I'll see to yer tea now," she muttered, making a movement as if to slip past him.

"Never mind that." He blocked her path. Standing before him was a picture of dejection, sunk in the depths of misery. This was a turn up for the book, and no mistake. Normally, when she had fault to find, she would fly into a tantrum, swearing like a trooper and spitting like a wildcat. A show of grief was a weapon she rarely used. "If I've done somethin' to upset ye –," he began.

"It's nothin'. Let me get on."

"Nothin'? Why, ye're shakin' like a leaf." He grasped her by the shoulder and propelled her towards the armchair. "Sit ye down. Bide here while I put a match to the fire. Then I'll see about a dram to calm yer nerves."

Mechanically she obeyed, watching stonily as the flames crackled into life, meekly accepting the glass that was thrust into her hand. The fiery liquid made her retch and choke, but the afterglow brought warmth to her body. Wordlessly she drained the tumbler and handed it back to him.

"Feelin' better?" She nodded dumbly. "That's dandy." He fetched a kitchen chair and placed it opposite her. "Maybe now we can get to the bottom o' this. What am I supposed to hae done this time?"

"It's no' you. At least no' directly." She swallowed hard. "It's wee Eddie and Miss Elizabeth."

"Eddie an' his maw?" He caught his breath. "Are they no' well? Come down wi' the flu like yon namby – I mean that brother o' mine?"

"No. It's nothin' like that. It's just that – that they're leavin'. Goin' back to Edinburgh to stay wi' her parents."

Iain whistled. "Ye don't say. That would explain things, right enough."

Her head jerked up. "Just what d'ye mean by that?" she snapped. "They'll be gone in a fortnight. And I'll never see Eddie again." Tears rolled down her cheeks. "Miss Elizabeth wanted me to go wi' them. But I couldna dae that. I could never bring mysel' tae abandon ye."

Now his mind was racing. He stretched over to take her hands in his, a wan smile of thanks on his lips. Mechanically she brushed them away. He was left in silence to ponder how this startling new state of affairs might best be handled. There would be no need for further attempts to keep her at home, give up her charge. No longer would he suffer the humiliation of a wife in service, at the beck and call of the hated upper class. And surely her pain and disappointment would soon fade, especially if some cause could be found to fill her time – something more appropriate to her status as the wife of a good socialist.

He gave a start as another thought suddenly struck him. Was there some deeper force at work? Was his son to be spirited away to remove the possibility of any contact between them? Who could be responsible for the deed? It came to him in a flash – Elizabeth's father! Only a devious lawyer would go to such lengths to deprive him of his natural rights. Sir Edward Lixmont had much to answer for – a debt to be repaid should opportunity present itself.

Morag was still staring at him. He shifted uncomfortably in his chair. That look of accusation – as it was all his fault. "Have ye nothin' else to say?" he growled.

A strange gleam came into her eye. "I've been thinkin'" she began tentatively. "I suppose ye widnae consider the pair o' us movin' to Edinburgh. You could easy get a job there, and mebbie we could find ourselves a wee flat."

His brow darkened. Christ, would she never give up? It was an effort to keep himself in check. "Why would I leave Glesga?" he demanded. "I've a start back at Deuchar's next week – a skilled man wi' real prospects. There's years o' work in front o' us in the shipyards. Where wid I get a chance like that ower there? Besides," he laughed harshly, "the Lixmonts wouldnae thole it. They'd move heaven an' hell to keep me out o' their hair."

She pursed her lips, barely able to conceal her dismay. It had been a forlorn hope even to challenge him. The force of his argument was unanswerable. "What am I to dae while ye're out at work?" she asked bitterly. "I couldna abide just gawpin' at these four walls a' day."

Iain breathed a sigh of relief. The thought occurred to him that he had almost overlooked perhaps the most important consideration. Dunlop would raise Cain at the slightest hint that his catspaw might be lost to him. And if his wife was ever to find out about his role as an informer… But there was no point in dwelling on that; as things stood, the prospect was highly unlikely. Morag knew when she was beaten. Now he could afford to be generous, offer some olive branch to sweeten the pill. Perhaps there was a way to repair their relationship after all.

"Aye, I take yer point," he conceded. "Right enough, it widnae be fair on you. Tell ye what." He snapped his fingers. "Why no' do what ye did before? Go back an' work wi' Mrs Barbour."

"Mary Barbour? But—" Her jaw dropped. "D'ye mean thon time when I was in the housin' association? Ye're haverin', man. That was during the war, wi' the evictions an' rent strikes. She'll hae nae need o' me now."

"Don't you believe it. The rent restrictions winnae last much longer. Then we'll be back to the old days wi' graspin' landlords squeezin' honest folk for a' they're worth. Forbye that, I hear she's involved in a wheen o' other things besides housin'."

"Is that so? And just what might these be?" She was mocking him. But was there also a glimmer of interest as well?

He chose to ignore the sarcasm. "It's true. She's taken up health issues like providin' public baths and better medical care for them that cannae afford doctors. I'm even told she's goin' to stand for the council next year – Labour candidate in Govan. That'll take a muckle organisation if she's to get in. She'll be cryin' out for bodies like you to volunteer. Ye'd no' need a wage. We can manage fine on what I earn."

There was a long silence. Morag was wrestling with her feelings; he could read it in her face. "It widnae cost anythin' to go an' see her," he added slyly.

His words seemed to have an effect. "Well," she temporised, "I suppose it would get me out o' the hoose. And it would be in a good cause. As ye say, it widnae dae any harm to pay her a visit."

"Guid lass. Ye'll no' regret it."

Aye, but—" Her lips trembled. "I'm no' sure if it would be enough. There, I've said it."

For a moment he was taken aback. What nonsense was this? Then he rallied. "What in blue blazes d'ye mean by that? How no'?"

"Can ye no' see?" she hissed. "I want a wean to care for. It's a woman's right."

"So that's the way the wind blows." He leaned back in his chair. "And just how dae ye hope to achieve that? Find some other stuck-up bitch wi' a sprog that needs nannyin'?"

Morag flushed at the barb. "It's nothin' like that," she said quietly. "I ken ye're disappointed we cannae hae a bairn. And it's a' my fault. But have ye ever considered adoption? There's any number o' poor souls in need o' a good home"

"So what?" he snarled. "That might suit you. But it'll no' dae for me. It wouldnae be my ain flesh an' blood."

"Is that so important?"

"Aye, it is."

"So there's no hope—" she faltered.

Her obvious distress made him pause. "Sorry," he mumbled. "I didna mean to bite yer heid off."

"But—"

"Bide a wee. Gie me a chance." He stroked his chin, as though in search of inspiration. Eddie might be lost to him, but perhaps there was another answer. "Tell ye what!" he suddenly exclaimed. "I've just had a notion. Maybe there is a way to gie both o' us what we want."

"I dinnae understand."

"It's been starin' me in the face. Why did I no' think o' it afore?"

"What has—?" Now she was thoroughly bewildered.

"I could gie ye a son." He made an effort to contain his excitement. "Suppose I could get somebody else to oblige me as a favour. I'd be the faither. Then we simply adopt the nipper. Kill twa birds wi' one stone, ye might say."

Morag goggled helplessly, dumbfounded at the audacity of his suggestion. "But what if it's a girl?" she stammered. It was all she could think of saying.

"We'll cross that bridge when we come to it." Iain brushed aside her feeble protest. "Trust me. Ye'll see it makes sense. Naebody need ever ken." He rose to his feet, stooped to give her a peck on the cheek. "I'll be awa out now. There's a meetin' o' the strike committee to decide what's to be done next. They'll be expectin' me." That was a lie, but it was as well to escape further questions. "Never mind about my tea. I'll get somethin' when I'm out."

It was hard to conceal a smirk as he turned away. His spouse scarcely noticed as she slowly began to digest the implications of his proposition.

TWO

Facing the Future

Edinburgh
September 1919

"Are you sure you can't stay, Hugh? The chap's train is due in a few minutes."

"Sorry, dad. I must be off soon. Time and tide, you know. I've a train of my own to catch. Thanks for the lift, by the way."

Sir Edward Lixmont nodded, and then frowned as he looked round the main concourse. On a cloudless Saturday afternoon, it was inevitable that the Waverley Station would be crammed with trippers determined to make the most of the good weather at the tail end of summer, and he was concerned that his daughter and grandson might wander off and become lost in the crowd. Elizabeth would be mortified were she to miss her husband's return from convalescence in Switzerland. His brow cleared as he caught a glimpse of them on a nearby platform, apparently passing the time in a game of hide and seek round a huge stack of luggage. Reassured, he turned back to his son. He had a shrewd idea that the boy would go to almost any length to avoid an encounter with a brother-in-law he evidently still regarded as a rank outsider. Hugh grinned back faintly, as though daring him to make a comment.

"I must say I don't like it, son. Can't you give me any more details? All you've told me is that you're leaving for Ireland."

"'Fraid not, dad. I don't know much about it myself."

"Then why in heaven's name did you volunteer for the job?"

Hugh Lixmont stifled a yawn. "We've been through this all before, dad. They closed down the depot at the end of the war, and tried to use the excuse of my old war wound to have me pensioned off. Pension?" He laughed mirthlessly. "I'd be practically destitute."

"I do understand, but there are other things you could do."

"Dad, I'm a soldier. And that's all I know. I went down on my knees and begged them for a posting – India, Egypt, even Palestine. I'd take anything."

"But Ireland? I suppose you realise you'll be stepping into a quagmire."

"I wouldn't put it quite like that."

"No? From what I read in the papers Ireland is almost ungovernable. There's a campaign of civil disobedience – the king's writ barely runs outside Dublin Castle. Sinn Fein has set up its own parliament, and the IRA is drilling openly in the countryside with looted weapons."

"All the more reason to see that law and order is restored."

"I appreciate that. But what about the ambushes and attacks on police stations? These can only escalate, and before you know it, you'll be in the thick of a full-scale guerrilla war. Hit and run tactics, never really getting to grips with the enemy. How long do you think the British public will be prepared to tolerate that state of affairs?"

"As long as it takes. We have to win. It's as simple as that. Ireland is part of the British Empire, and that's the way it must stay," he added stiffly.

His father sighed. "Have it your way. I've said my piece. There's no need to get on your high horse. I promised your mother I would raise the subject. She apparently has visions of you ending up with a bullet in the back."

"Point taken. Mama always did have a vivid imagination. I'll keep my wits about me, never fear. Is that why she didn't come to the station to wave me a fond farewell?"

"Do be serious, Hugh. She didn't want to be seen to give way in public."

"Good old mama. Always concerned about her image, isn't she? I noticed the pair of you in deep conversation after breakfast this morning. Was it about me?"

"Only partly. We were discussing the future – for the whole family, that is."

His son pulled a face. "You mean the plans she's got mapped out for your future," he chuckled. "I thought it was all cut and dried. You're a successful KC, with a knighthood to show for it. You've done well serving your country in wartime. No doubt you'll be a county court judge in a year or two – if you don't blot your copybook, or the family doesn't disgrace you again."

"What d'you mean by that?" His expression hardened. "If you are referring to Elizabeth and her child—"

"Nothing of the kind." Hugh was quick to make amends. "It was only a joke. Besides, it's all water under the bridge now."

"Well, let it pass." The flash of annoyance faded. He could ignore a thoughtless remark. "Since you ask, things may not be as straightforward as you seem to believe. Your mother rather enjoyed lording it over her committees while the war lasted. The last thing on her mind is a return to being merely lady of the house."

"Then what is she suggesting?"

"She happened to mention that in her humble opinion elevation to the bench might be something of a backwater. It would stunt my abilities, as she puts it. And, thinking things over, I must admit she may have a point."

"How do you make that out?"

"Well, I found the small contribution I was able to give to the war effort very fulfilling on a personal, as well as professional level. I'd like to continue on these lines, and help out with postwar reconstruction. I won't be able to do much of that as a judge. Rebuilding the community, ensuring the general welfare of the people – there's nothing more important than that."

"You're beginning to talk like a damned politician. You're not going to join that rogues' gallery, are you?"

"That's my Hugh. You don't mince your words." He refused to take offence. "No, it's not like that. At least not in the conventional sense. I'm not about to stand for Parliament, if that's what you mean."

"What, then?"

"I've been sounded out about a seat on the town council at the next election. I've almost decided to accept the nomination."

"You'll be a Tory? I can't picture you as a socialist."

Lixmont grimaced. "Quite right. And I'll not be a Liberal either. If I stand at all, it'll be as a Progressive."

"Progressive?" It was clear his son and heir knew little or nothing of local affairs.

"The Progressive party," his father explained patiently, "likes to see itself as taking little or no part in the hurly-burly of mainstream politics. We believe in stable and fair-minded administration through representatives who have greatest knowledge of local needs. Such individuals are the best guardians of the public purse in ensuring value for money in the provision of services for the benefit of all."

"Is that so? Can't say I'm all that interested, but I wish you well." He held out his hand. "I'd best be on my way."

"Just a minute, Hugh" Now the mask dropped. "Can't you tell me anything before you go? I see you're not in uniform. Are you still in the army? At least tell me that."

"All right, dad." He hesitated before going on. "For what it's worth, I do still hold the king's commission. It's just that the powers that be insisted that I didn't draw any attention to myself. As to rank, I haven't yet been informed."

"But your duties? Surely you can give me a hint."

"All I know is that it's some kind of liaison with the RIC."

"Royal Irish Constabulary? Then you'll be assisting the civil power if there's an emergency?"

"Something like that. I'll be briefed when I reach Dublin. Till then… Oh, look. There's Elizabeth waving to you. The train must be coming in. Give them my regards. Goodbye."

A brief handshake and he was gone. There was a lump in Lixmont's throat as he watched him disappear from view.

* * *

Elizabeth Baird (née Lixmont) checked her appearance in the mirror above the fireplace as she waited for her husband to join her in the sitting room of their new home. It had been an inspiration on her part to persuade her father to take the lease on the terraced house in Comely Bank on the western fringe of the city. Not that he had taken much convincing to allow the married couple to set up on their own: the merest hint of possible squabbles in the family villa in Trinity was enough to send shivers down his spine. And the location she had chosen was ideal – just far enough away to discourage her mother from making her presence felt on a daily basis, but close enough to appease her with weekly visits from her daughter and grandson. A neat solution to a tricky problem – or so she had assumed.

Now she was not so certain. How Alastair might react had scarcely entered her thoughts when the arrangement was made. But on his return… It went without saying she had written to tell him of their good fortune, but it was clear he had expected a much more modest property. He seemed utterly bewildered on their tour of the house, tugged along by an excited Eddie while she droned on about her plans for each room. It was not long before she had realised her mistake. Tact would be required to make him see sense and accept the realities of the situation. There was nothing to be gained by rushing her fences.

Poor Alastair! What an ordeal it must have been for him – the long, wearying journey from Switzerland. And then to be whisked off to take tea with her mother. His head must have been spinning from the barrage of questions about life in the sanatorium. Mama never could resist the temptation to ferret out every detail. Thank goodness her father had the wit to draw proceedings to a close as soon as decently possible, drive them back, and leave them to their own devices. Now they could have a proper homecoming. The maid had been given the evening off, and Eddie bathed and put to bed. She tried to curb her impatience. Alastair was taking a long time in reading his bedtime story. No doubt the thrill of seeing his stepdad again made him slow to settle. But what did it matter? The whole evening stretched before them.

Drawing the curtains, she switched on the standard lamp before plumping herself down on the settee. Damn! There was that magazine she had promised to read – and give her honest opinion to its editor. Or was it the owner? She could not quite remember. Politeness demanded at least a token effort, especially as an appointment had been fixed for the following Monday. With a gesture of irritation she snatched it up and began to thumb through the pages. It was obvious there was little to be said in its favour, with an uninspiring title and articles that seemed dull as dishwater. Rumour had it that the rag was on its last legs, and the most casual of glances was enough to prove this could not be far from the truth. At best the publication was badly in need of a complete makeover if it was ever to achieve any success in campaigning for women's rights. But was it worth the bother?

"Penny for them. Mind if I come in?" The paper slipped from her fingers. In an instant she had leapt up and dashed into his arms. "Here, steady on. You'll have me over," he gasped.

"Sorry. It's just that I've dreamt of this moment for so long." She relaxed her grip. "Let's sit down. We have the whole house to ourselves."

He picked up the discarded magazine. "What's this you've been reading?

I see it's called *The Lady Voter*. Are you taking up with the suffragettes again?" He smiled, to show it was meant as a joke.

Her eyes danced. "Not this time," she grinned. "I'll tell you about it later. But come and take the weight off your feet." She nudged him onto the sofa. "What do you think of the place, then?"

"It's fabulous. There's no denying that. I know you wrote and told me, but I never suspected anything like this."

"Thought you'd like it. Eddie just loves his new home. You'll have noticed it lies right next door to Inverleith Park. He can chase round to his heart's content, and he likes nothing better than to sail his boat on the pond, and feed the ducks and swans. And it's very convenient for the Academy. You know he's just started school there."

Alastair's face clouded over. "That's just it. How can we afford the school fees – not to mention the lease on this house? I know I haven't a bean. I suppose this is all your father's doing," he added moodily.

"That's not fair! Daddy went out of his way to help us while you were ill. Don't you understand, dearest?" she went on more gently. "That's what families are for – to support each other through times of trouble."

It was some moments before he ventured to reply. "Sorry, Elizabeth. You're quite right. I must sound like an ungrateful beast."

She squeezed his arm. "You could never be that."

"But he must have spent a small fortune on sending me to that sanatorium. How can I sponge on his generosity any further? I need to be able to stand on my own two feet."

"And you will. But these things take time. Learn to walk before you run. You're not fully recovered yet. The first priority is to get your strength back." She smiled as she pulled him towards her, cradling his head against her bosom. "Now that we're comfortable, would you care to hear a story? It's really quite amusing."

"I'd love to. Fire away."

"Remember the paper I was looking at when you came in?"

"Of course. What of it?"

"Well, I happened to bump into its owner last week. It was at an art exhibition, as I recall. We were both admiring the same picture and got to talking. He happened to mention this woman's journal. Its circulation was apparently dropping like a stone and he couldn't work out the reason why. Well, it ended up with a promise on my part to go over the latest issue and give him my opinion. I'm afraid I rather agreed to call at his office this Monday. He even hinted that if anything could be done to save it there might be a place for me on his editorial team."

Alastair sat up at that. "And would you accept it? If he made an offer, I mean."

"I don't see why not. I'm at a loose end at home, now that Eddie's away during the day. And it would bring in a salary. Not much, I admit. But it's a start – and it would help pay the bills."

"You'd have me be a kept man? My own wife?" he said bitterly.

"Please don't take it that way, Alastair. It's just that I feel the need for some outlet to stretch myself, an outside interest to make use of what little abilities I might possess."

"I've no wish to hold you back, if that's what you really want." He forced himself to concede the point. "But try to consider things from my side. You say I'm not up to holding down a job. In that case, what's to become of me? Left to kick my heels here while you're at work? Don't my feelings come into it?"

"Of course they do. And I have been thinking about your future. You could go back to university, finish your degree. Then the world really would be your oyster."

University? He gaped at her like a stranded fish. "But that would involve more expense – what with the fees and the cost of books."

"It's not impossible, you know. I read somewhere about government grants for ex-servicemen to enable them to complete their education."

"I'm not sure I would qualify on that score." He seemed determined to find objections.

"At least you could try. And there would still be time to enrol before the start of term next month."

"You make it sound so easy." He caught her expression of dismay. "Sorry. I shouldn't have said that. I know you have my best interests at heart."

Elizabeth could have wept with frustration. Things were not turning out as she had planned. And there was something else on her mind – an item of news that would be certain to upset him. She had intended to wait a few days before broaching the subject. But some sixth sense warned her that any delay might be unwise. Oh well, better to be hung for a sheep…

"Alastair, dearest," she began, "there's something I was meaning to show you." She went over to her writing desk and returned with two letters. He could see that one of them had been slit open; the other, bulkier, was still intact.

"This came for you a few months ago." She settled herself down, handing him the slimmer envelope. "It's from Broomburn – from your Mr McIntosh. I'm so sorry," she went on sadly, as he fished out the enclosure. "There's no easy way to put this. Your old teacher, Mr Ogilvie, has passed away. He was carried off in the last wave of the influenza epidemic back in February."

Alastair stared dumbly at a folded sheet of paper. "We didn't want to disturb you," she hastened to explain. "It might have affected your recovery. In any case the funeral was over by the time the letter arrived. As you can see, it had to be redirected before it reached us here. I wrote back to Mr McIntosh, of course, to inform him of your situation and offer our condolences. He was laid to rest in the kirkyard at Broomburn."

"And I missed the memorial service." There was no disguising the despair in his voice.

"You mustn't blame yourself. It couldn't be helped." She took his hand in hers. "I'm sure he would understand."

"But don't you see? I owe everything to him – him and my mother. He coached me nearly every day for two years to win that scholarship. And if I hadn't won a place at Fairhill Academy I'd never have gone to university."

"That's to your credit. You gave him pride in your achievements. From what I can gather it set the pinnacle on his career." She hesitated a moment. "There's nothing to stop you going to Broomburn, you know. Put some flowers on his grave. I'm sure he would appreciate the gesture."

"I suppose so." He brightened a little. "Yes, there's always that. I think I'll take your advice."

"I'm so glad. When will you go?"

"No time like the present. Monday might be best. And it'll give me a chance to pay a visit to my sister as well."

"You do that. Would you like me to come too? I can always postpone my appointment."

"Bless you, my dear. I don't know where I'd be without your commonsense to keep me on the straight and narrow. There's nothing I'd like better. But I can manage on my own. No need to disappoint this editor chap."

She nodded her agreement. "As you wish, dearest." It would serve no purpose to insist on accompanying him. "Here's the other letter for you. I haven't opened it because it only arrived a few days ago, after I found out you were coming home. It seems to be from a lawyer in Glasgow."

Frowning, he accepted a paper knife and sliced through the seal. A thick sheet of foolscap was revealed, crackling as it was unfolded. Elizabeth watched anxiously as he scanned the contents.

"Not bad news, surely?"

"No. Nothing like that. It's just that I'm totally stunned. According to this letter Mr Ogilvie has left everything to me. His entire estate. It comes to nearly a thousand pounds."

Her face lit up. "That is good news."

"Is it?" he muttered feverishly. "I must write back. How can I accept this? I haven't done anything to deserve it."

"That's nonsense!" The sharpness of the rebuke made him wince. "How can you say that? He had no other relatives. He chose you as his beneficiary as an investment in the future. That's where he thought his legacy would do most good. Are you going to insult his memory by rejecting it?"

The force of her argument was impossible to deny. He quailed before the onslaught. "I hadn't thought of it like that," he confessed lamely.

"Well, then?"

"I suppose – that is, maybe I could put some of it to take my degree. Do you think that would be a proper use of the money?"

"Very fitting. I've no doubts on that score." She beamed at him. "In fact I feel that's what he intended you should do."

"And the remainder could go towards Eddie's school fees, and helping out with household expenses."

Elizabeth was careful not to smile. "I think that's a splendid idea." It would do no harm to give him a sense of his own worth.

"Good. Then consider it settled. Broomburn on Monday. Afterwards I'll tackle the university authorities about matriculation for next session."

"Steady," she laughed. "Don't let your newfound enthusiasm run away with you. You've had a lot to take in today. You must be dog tired. Why don't you go up now? It's high time you had a proper rest."

"You could be right." He kissed her on the forehead. "I'll do that. What about you?"

"Presently. I'll just see to things down here first."

A few minutes later she paused by the bedroom door. Alastair was sitting motionless on the bed, staring down at the little blue box on his lap. Her eye caught the glint of gold, sparkling in the glow from the bedside lamp. It was his most prized possession – the medal he had won as dux of Fairhill Academy. He was quietly sobbing.

Silently she stole away.

* * *

"Have you not finished yet, Alison?" The owner and publisher of *The Lady Voter* appeared in the doorway of the inner office. "Our guest is due in a few minutes. It would never do to create the wrong impression."

"And just what do you mean by that?" A woman in early middle age rose from her desk to glare at her employer.

"It means, my dear," he said mildly, "that I expect you to help keep the premises neat and tidy. I'm fully conscious of the fact that you are my secretary and personal assistant, but in these straitened times we must all rally round as best we can."

"Including acting as your maid-of-all-work?" She gave a little toss of her head. "Not only do I have to sort out the papers you strew all over the place, but I'm expected to sweep the floor as well. You'll be telling me to wash the windows next."

"If you wouldn't mind, Alison." He flashed his teeth to show he spoke in jest. "Well, perhaps not quite that. But you know how we're fixed. I've had to let the cleaner go. We can't afford her any longer, even on a part-time basis. It's asking a lot, I realise that, but I'll try to make it up to you somehow."

Alison Brodie could have wept with frustration. Not for the first time she damned herself for a fool. Why did she continue to endure the slings and arrows in this poky little office? Was it her fault the subscription list was dropping like a stone? It had all been so promising when she joined the magazine, she thought bitterly. But that had been before the war, when the suffrage campaign was in its heyday. Then the publication had its own suite of rooms in the New Town, with a team of dedicated correspondents and an enthusiastic editor who really knew his business. There had even been plans for a launch into the mainstream, with a weekly issue on sale at bookstalls and newsagents.

In the nature of things, the outbreak of hostilities had put an end to such ambitions, as interest in women's rights faded, and staff drifted away to do their bit for the war effort in various shapes and guises. But what really made the difference was the untimely death of the owner. His heir, a nephew, had promptly decided to take over himself, forcing the existing editor into premature retirement. Lacking any journalistic experience, he had struggled to keep their heads above water. Now they were reduced to a couple of basement rooms in Stockbridge, with only the two of them to work up copy on a bi-monthly basis. And the bills were mounting up, especially those of the printer whose final demands for payment now threatened court action.

Yet she could not find it in her heart to walk out on Nick Norman. Perhaps it was his matinee idol looks – and he could be a real charmer when he put his mind to it. She knew she was no great catch, and her frequent visits to the picture palace were generally unaccompanied. But she could dream. Nick had a reputation as a ladies' man. The evidence was plain to see, but none of his companions seemed to last long. Perhaps one day he would come to appreciate her loyalty and devotion. If only he would open his eyes… With a gesture of vexation she brushed aside the thought.

"I don't see why you invited this Baird creature here," she muttered sullenly. "What does she have to offer us? Or we to offer her, for that matter?"

She swept her hand round the dingy office, with the faded notice in the dusty window announcing the name of the publication, the rickety desk and chairs, the battered filing cabinet and solitary ancient typewriter. "What do you think she'll make of all this rubbish?"

"Oh, I don't know. Time will tell." He gave a shrug.

"But does she have any training as a journalist?"

"I would doubt that."

"Then, why—"

"Let me enlighten you. Her father is one of the richest lawyers in Edinburgh. And from what I can gather he dotes on his only daughter. We badly need an injection of capital. If I can butter her up, offer her a job – say as assistant editor." He shrugged. "I'm sure you can work it out."

There was a footstep on the stairs outside. "Hark, there she is now." A face peered in at the window. "Quick, the door. And not a word."

Elizabeth Baird waltzed into the room, stretching out her hand as a smiling figure advanced to greet her. Rather flashily dressed for an editor, she could not help thinking, but he carried it well and was undoubtedly good looking.

"Good of you to come, Mrs Baird." He bowed over her gloved hand. "My name is Nicholas Norman, in case you had forgotten. But everyone calls me Nick. And I hope you will do the same. I believe your name is Elizabeth. Will you allow me to call you that?" She nodded assent. "Much more friendly, don't you agree?"

Alison Brodie pulled a face at her employer. Soft soap already. The man was shameless.

Nick chose to ignore the gesture. "Won't you step into my office, Elizabeth? Make yourself comfortable in the easy chair." Alison made a move to follow them in. "No, not you, my dear. We mustn't drag you away from your other duties. Perhaps you might make us a nice cup of tea."

"Not for me, thanks," Elizabeth called back. "I'm due to take morning coffee with a friend later on."

"As you wish." He turned towards his secretary. "Did you hear that, Alison? See we are not disturbed." The door closed, almost in her face.

Elizabeth frowned slightly. "Why did you do that? Shut out your assistant, I mean. Don't you trust her?"

"Oh, it's nothing like that. But she is sometimes inclined towards tittle-tattle. And after all, this is a private conversation."

"I see. Well, as you please." She took off her hat and gloves.

He settled himself in his chair. "I must say, Elizabeth, I really like your outfit. It sets you off to perfection, if I may be so bold."

"Why, thank you, kind sir." She pretended to simper. "But surely you didn't invite me here just to offer compliments."

"By no means. But I find a few initial pleasantries help to break the ice. Particularly when they happen to be true."

"Really?" Her eyes twinkled. She caught a whiff of eau-de-cologne. He would be asking her out to lunch next.

"I trust you found no difficulty in locating our little lair," he went on.

"None at all. I live along the road at Comely Bank myself. It's only a ten-minute walk."

"Now that is fortunate." He saw her grope in her bag and produce the copy of the magazine he had given her. "Ah well, to business." It was almost a sigh. "And what did you think of our publication?"

"Do you wish me to be frank?"

"Of course. I wouldn't have it any other way."

"Very well, then. Since you insist. I found it rather tedious."

"Ouch!" He gave a wry smile. "That was a sore one. Is it truly as bad as that?"

"I'm afraid so. Take the name, for example."

"What's wrong with it?"

"*The Lady Voter*? It sounds tired and dated. No doubt good enough to pass muster in the staid old days before the war. But times have moved on since then. You need a sharp, punchy title to attract new readership." She noticed his lips tighten. "I hope I haven't caused offence. But you did ask for my honest opinion."

"No, no. Not at all," he hastened to reassure her. "I was just a little taken aback. But I do appreciate your views. Please go on. How did you find the content?"

"Not much better." She saw no point in softening the blow. "The articles were insipid. The whole tone is far too complacent. It looks as if you're only interested in women who have already won the vote. What about those who were left out?"

"Point taken." He held up his hand in mock surrender. "I suppose you mean people like you. The bright young things," he added with a grin.

She laughed at that. "Yes, if you like. Though I wouldn't describe myself in exactly these terms."

"Why not? I can't think of anyone who fits the bill so admirably. Shall I tell you something?"

"Only if it's about the matter in hand" Flattery was all very well, but… Some sixth sense prompted her to cut him short. "Shall we get down to brass tacks? After all, my time is limited."

"Of course, dear lady. Just as you wish." There was a pause as he cleared his throat. "I fear I have a confession to make."

"You do surprise me. Please continue."

"Thank you." He appeared not to notice the inflexion in her voice. "I suppose I had better come clean. The truth of the matter is that we simply can't afford top notch writers. That's why we have to put up with second rate hacks. As a matter of fact, some of the stuff is culled from other publications, suitably doctored of course, so it's not easy to tell what's been cribbed."

She nodded. "I might have guessed as much. Is that why the print is so small that it's difficult to read, and there are hardly any illustrations?"

"Right first time. We have to cram as much as we can into as few pages as possible. Saves printing costs."

"Anything else I should know?" she asked drily.

"Well, it's issued on a subscription basis only. And subscribers have been dwindling."

"So it's not in general circulation? Not for sale on the newsstands? Well, I don't wonder at that. How many would buy it?"

"Fairly few, I have to admit. In any case we don't have the cash to make the attempt."

"This is worse than I had imagined. I suppose you have debts to be paid off. Perhaps the best option might be to cut your losses."

"Close *The Lady Voter*, you mean? That's the last thing I would wish to happen."

"What's the alternative?"

"Look, let me explain the situation. Then you might think differently."

"I doubt it." Then she weakened. "All right. Convince me."

"You won't regret it, I promise you. It's like this. You will have worked out that I'm fairly new to this game. I had no experience of any form of journalism, let alone a suffrage magazine. My uncle died a couple of years ago, and left it to me in his will. In fact I was recuperating from a war wound when the solicitor's letter reached me." He pointed to his shoulder. "A Jerry bullet hit me here. The bone was so smashed up that they decided to invalid me out. There's little sign of it now, but the arm is pretty useless. I can't lift anything heavy."

"Oh! I had no idea. I'm so sorry."

He gave a wan smile. "No need to mention it. I just thought you might care to hear the background. Well, I had nothing better to do, so it crossed my mind that I should try to carry out the old boy's legacy. I haven't had much success, as you can see, but others were dependent on me for a living. Do you think it was so terribly wrong of me to stick it out in hope of better days to come?"

"I suppose not. But don't you get the point? You're doomed to failure unless you make radical changes."

"And that's precisely why I asked you here today. A fresh face, bursting with new ideas. You know exactly what the younger generation expects. Won't you give us the benefit of your help? Tell me exactly what we have to do."

"Well, since you put it like that—"

"I do."

"In that case I'd start by getting rid of all these stodgy articles you seem to favour. That's the surest way to turn people off. We need to lighten the load, make use of features you find in the most popular magazines. That's not to lose sight of the campaign for equal rights, of course, but readers expect to be amused and entertained. Sugar the pill, so to speak."

"Hmm. I see what you mean." Then he looked away wistfully. "But that would be a huge task. I doubt I would be up to it."

"Why do you say that?"

"Isn't it obvious? I have no resources. I couldn't possibly succeed. Not on my own." He hesitated, as if a thought had just struck him. "Would you be interested in becoming my assistant editor? I couldn't pay you much, but—"

"You feel we could do great things together?" She smiled at him. "Well, I'm prepared to give it a try. But on one condition."

"Name it."

"We put an end to this subscription only malarkey. From now on every issue has to go on sale to the public. Maybe just in the local area to begin with, but we can build on that."

"Oh! I had thought of something rather more modest. To do what you suggest would involve a heavy investment – far more than I could possibly lay my hands on. But I can see that you are right. It's all or nothing." He shook his head mournfully. "I suppose I'll have to give Alison notice. And tell her that the next edition will be the last one."

"Now that would be a shame." His show of concern was almost laughable. But two could play at that game. Why not take him at face value – at least till he proved otherwise? "Suppose the necessary funds could be made available. How much would be required? Just for argument's sake, you understand."

"I really have no idea." He shrugged his shoulders. "I suppose a couple of thousand might be enough to get us started."

"Good." She was not fooled by the seemingly casual remark. "I'll go and see my father. He may be able to help. Would that be agreeable?"

"Of course, dear lady." He could hardly contain his glee. "I'd be forever in your debt."

"You may count on that. Two thousand, you said. And not a penny more. No doubt there will be papers to be drawn up. My father will see to it. Shall we say next Monday? That should be enough time to complete the arrangements." She rose to her feet.

"Just as you wish, Elizabeth." He came round the desk. "Allow me to show you out."

There was a faint sound of retreating footsteps. His assistant had only just time to scuttle back to her place. "Alison!" She looked up enquiringly. "Mrs Baird is just leaving. The door, if you please!" He turned to his visitor. "Bless you. I feel we are on the brink of a very productive relationship."

He escorted her into the tiny courtyard, watching as she ascended the area stairs to the roadway. At the top she looked back, gave a little wave, and was gone. Behind him there was a snort of derision. He whirled round.

"What's gotten into you now? I suppose you've been earwigging – as usual."

His secretary ignored the accusation. "So she fell for it? You managed to reel her in?"

"That's right." He chuckled. "Hook, line and sinker. The old war wound story – it never fails."

"But that's simply not true," she protested. "You told me you were exempted on health grounds."

"So what? What if I did dress it up a bit? I don't see why you should be so particular. You ought to be grateful. I've just saved your bacon."

"That's as may be," she sniffed. "But there's still work to be done. You coming in?"

He followed her back into the office. "You know, Alison, we'd both be out on the street if something hadn't turned up. Now it just has. I think this calls for a small celebration."

"Oh, aye. And what did you have in mind?"

"Nothing much. A bite of lunch wouldn't come amiss. And perhaps a glass or two to toast our new partner. Ten bob should cover it. You could let me have it out of the petty cash."

Wordlessly she delved into her desk drawer. He managed to evade the look of fury as she counted out four half-crowns. "Thanks," he mumbled, sweeping the coins into his hand. "You won't mind holding the fort, will you? I should be back in an hour or so."

Angrily she thrust a sheet of paper into the typewriter. Fat chance of his return that afternoon. She knew him only too well. In her exasperation she banged away at the keys with a good deal more force than was strictly necessary.

* * *

"You cannot possibly be serious, Elizabeth."

"Never more so, daddy," replied his daughter promptly. She had anticipated his initial reaction. But he would come round in the end, if past experience ran true to form.

"Let me get this clear," he went on. "Earlier this morning you had an appointment with some magazine owner. He offered you a post as assistant editor if you made an investment in his publication. Is that correct?"

"Not quite, daddy. I only hinted at a contribution after he had made the offer. I fully admit the whole organisation is a bit of a shambles, but I think it could be saved." She reached over to squeeze his arm. "Won't you let me try?" she pleaded. "It would mean so much to me."

Sir Edward Lixmont grunted. It was only an hour ago that Elizabeth had brazenly marched into his chambers to whisk him off to lunch. She would brook no excuses, she had insisted. They rarely had an opportunity for a quiet *tête-á-tête* these days. Now they sat facing each other in a crowded restaurant.

"What do you know about publishing?" he grumbled. "Another of your fads, I suppose."

"No, it isn't. I may lack experience, but I can learn. I know what women like to see in a magazine. And I've bags of commonsense."

"Have you? What about those notions you had about teaching and nursing? They didn't last long, did they?"

"That's not fair, daddy," she said quietly. "I did make a success of nursing during the war. You must admit that."

"Well, yes – possibly." He gave a wry smile. "Caught me out, haven't you? I'm sorry Elizabeth. You're quite right. You did do well."

"Is it a go, then?"

"Not so fast, young lady. You haven't convinced me yet. What do we know about this fellow – Nick Norman, I think you said? Some kind of interloper, is he? I've never heard of him. In fact, with a name like that he sounds rather like a music hall turn."

"Very funny. A man can't help what he's called. For your information he inherited ownership of the magazine, and he's trying to carry it on."

"That's all very well. But a suffragist journal? What appeal would that have in this day and age?"

"You'd be surprised. Equal rights for women are all the rage. There's so much still to be done. See here, daddy. Mr Norman has his faults, but who doesn't? Never fear, I'll keep my beady eye on him. I'll insist on an equal partnership, so he'll not be able to do anything without my say so."

"Hmm. We'll need to go into that. You should have given me some notice of your intentions. An opportunity to at least think things over would have been appreciated. I suppose you didn't want your mother to hear. She would have been quick enough to pour cold water on your scheme."

She grinned back at him. "How well you know me, father. Please don't tell mama – about the investment, I mean. She ought to be pleased that I've found something worthwhile to occupy myself. Time hangs rather heavily with Eddie away at school."

"I expect she'd be better pleased if the pair of you decided to add to your family. As would I."

"God's sake, daddy! Be reasonable. Alastair has only just come home. And he's far from fully recovered. It all takes time, you know." A note of anxiety came into her voice. "You won't mention the money to him either, will you?"

"I haven't agreed to give you anything yet," he said drily.

"But you will, won't you?"

He frowned portentously, then his brow cleared. "Anything for a quiet life," he sighed. "I suppose I must humour you, or I'll never hear the end of it. But there is one condition."

"Of course. Whatever you wish."

"You will not enter into any legal partnership. Do you realise you would be jointly and severally liable for any debts incurred? You could lose far more than your investment."

Her face fell. "Then what is the alternative?"

"Two thousand, you said. I'm willing to advance that sum by way of a loan, at a gentle rate of interest, and repayable after two years. That way it might be possible to rescue something if the business flops."

"I see. And you feel there's no other way?"

"It's the best I can do. I'm not prepared to have you pouring money into a bottomless pit. If you agree, I'll have the loan papers drawn up for his signature."

Elizabeth nodded. "So be it." Perhaps her father was right to be cautious. There was always the prospect of further capital should the venture prove successful. She watched him make a note in his pocket book.

"By the by," he continued, "were my ears deceiving me? Are you keeping secrets from your husband?"

"Oh! I suppose you mean the money. It's just that I don't want him to think I'm sponging off you. You know how touchy he is on that subject."

"And you've no objection to sponging off your father, as you term it? Charming, I'm sure." He glowered, then broke into a broad grin. "I won't breathe a word."

"Thank you. Actually, there's more to it than that. It turns out he's been left a legacy. His old teacher, as it happens. Alastair has been informed he's to inherit the entire estate. It comes to just about a thousand pounds."

"Aha! I thought there was something else. Good for him. The chap deserves a bit of good fortune." He looked at her shrewdly. "You believe he would insist on helping you out?"

"No doubt of it. And that's the last thing I would want him to do."

"Why not? Has he any other plans for his windfall?"

"As a matter of fact, he has. He's decided to go back to university and finish his degree."

"Really? That's excellent news. It's about the first sensible thing I've heard today. Tell him he has my full approval. Much better than pottering around at home."

"Alastair would never do that. As luck would have it, I saw him off on the train this morning. He's away to Broomburn to visit his mentor's grave and see his relatives."

"Broomburn, you say?" His eyes narrowed. "Do you think that was wise? Allowing him to go off on his own while he's still recuperating?"

"I don't see why not. I did offer to accompany him, but he said he felt fine." Suddenly a tinge of dread stirred within her. "You know something, daddy. Come on, out with it."

Her father hesitated a moment. "It may be nothing. But he's bound to hear the bad news in the village. And in his present state of nerves—"

"Why do you say that? What bad news?"

"Your Uncle Robert phoned me last week. You will remember that he is managing director of the coal mines in that area."

"Yes – but I don't understand how that might involve him."

"He informed me that his company is in severe financial difficulties. Now that the government has rejected nationalisation of the coal industry, the owners of less productive mines have apparently been hung out to dry. With dwindling output and huge losses stacking up, the only solution seems to be a programme of pit closures."

"And that would mean Alastair's relations being thrown out of work?"

"I'm afraid so. Almost everyone would be affected."

She thought for a moment. "Yes, I realise that. But what I can't quite grasp is why Uncle Robert should contact you. Surely there are company lawyers to handle the legal side of things."

"Ah, but there's the rub. It's true we generally don't have much time for each other. It was far from a social call, as you might well imagine. Semple wanted to consult me on a personal basis."

"But why would he seek your advice?"

"I'm not sure I can divulge that. Client confidentiality, you understand." Then he relented. "This is in strict confidence. It must go no further – not even to your husband. Promise?"

"Cross my heart."

He flashed a warning look. "Mind, I mean it."

"Sorry, daddy."

"Very well, then. To cut a long story short, it seems that shareholders have been complaining about being misled, and are trying to hold Semple personally responsible. He could be ruined if they sue him."

"That's dreadful. What did you say?"

"I told him to hang on as long as possible. The government still holds power over prices and wages. And there's always the possibility of a further subsidy to keep the industry going."

"But isn't that clutching at straws?"

He shrugged his shoulders. "It was the best I could do. And now, young lady," he said, rising to his feet, "it's about time I was off. You stay and finish your coffee. I'll settle the bill on my way out. That's what you really intended, isn't it?"

She forced a smile as she accepted his peck on the cheek, but her face clouded over as soon as her father had gone. Poor Alastair! How would he react to the discovery that his kinsfolk were about to lose their livelihood? He must not be allowed to brood. The sooner he threw himself back into his studies, the better it would be for everyone.

THREE

Voices from the Past

Glasgow
August 1920

Human Remains found in Lanarkshire pit.

Iain Baird sat suddenly transfixed, the colour draining from his face as he scanned the short paragraph tucked away near the foot of an inside page in a month-old newspaper. Surely it had not come back to haunt him… that vision of a stocky figure calling for help, striving in vain to hold back the floodwaters. And to his shame he had panicked and fled, abandoning his father to a watery grave. Must it forever be on his conscience? A groan of anguish escaped his lips.

The image faded, leaving him trembling. People in the reading room were looking up, staring at him; he glared back defiantly, as though daring anyone to make a comment, before dropping his eyes once more to focus on the closely typed print. It appeared that the skeleton of a man had been discovered during an operation to pump water from a long disused mine shaft, and subsequently removed for burial in the local kirkyard. Surely the result of some tragic accident many years previously, the report went on, but now the mortal remains could be laid to rest. The mine owners were to be congratulated on their sensitive handling of the affair, and especially for their generosity in defraying the cost of the interment.

Iain scowled. Trust the buggers to come up smelling of roses, he thought bitterly. The article, though short on detail, seemed to admit of little doubt. But was it just possible that the reference might be to some other pit? No names were given. And why would anyone wish to reopen old workings which had been sealed as a tomb? There had to be some way to find out the truth of the matter. If he knew for certain, it might help him lay the ghost of his father once and for all. A visit to Broomburn was out of the question.

Mining communities had long memories; his reputation was bound to ensure a hostile reception. The cold shoulder was the least he could expect; more likely it would be insults and abuse, even physical violence to drive him away. No, that would not do at all. An alternative might be to send a letter to his sister in the village asking for information. But there had been no contact with Mary for years, not since the day of his mother's funeral, and there was every chance she would ignore his plea, especially if her lump of a husband had anything to do with it. In his frustration he slumped back in his chair. It was all so unfair. Was his misfortune always to be held against him?

Feverishly he cudgelled his brain for inspiration. If there was nothing to be done in Broomburn, it could be that an answer lay closer to home. Perhaps his wife might hold the key. Had she defied his wishes and kept up a relationship with her former employer? Knowing her, it was a distinct possibility. Handled the right way, she might be persuaded to write and make a few inquiries. That milksop of a brother was bound to have been summoned to act as a pallbearer at the funeral if the body in the mine was that of their father. It seemed the best option open to him. At least it was worth a try. It was in a more hopeful frame of mind that he carefully tore the offending article from the page and slipped it into the grubby pocket book he had been using to take notes, before rising from his seat and striding from the room.

It was still raining outside. Cursing the foul weather, he buttoned up his jacket and pulled down his cap. The Saturday half day meant rest for the working man, but apparently not for the party faithful: activists were expected to devote their free time to spreading the word at street corners and factory gates. As though that was not enough, Stan Robertson had sprung yet another burden on him – one he had neglected till now. According to his mentor, the Bolshevik leadership in Russia had decreed a change in policy: the goal of worldwide revolution was henceforth to be achieved through the exploitation of industrial unrest. To this end it was considered essential for a record to be made of strikes and workplace grievances in each locality as an aid in planning future strategy. Stan was away at the minute – rumoured to be in attendance at a big conference of socialist groups in London. But that had been several weeks ago. There was no knowing when Robertson would appear again, and heaven help him if he had nothing to offer. That was why he had decided to give up a wet Saturday afternoon to thumb through copies of old newspapers in the public library.

A passing tram caught his attention, clanking and grinding along the tracks. He sprinted after it, and with a final spurt managed to grab the rail and swing himself on board; before the conductor could utter a protest, he had disappeared into the saloon. The lower deck was crowded, not a seat to be had. But that came as no surprise; no one in his right mind would brave the elements on the open top on a day like this. Standing room only: he joined the row of passengers hanging onto leather straps in the gangway. At least the conductor was making no attempt to pursue him for the fare: he could just catch a glimpse of a uniformed figure on the rear platform, perhaps wisely deciding it would be foolhardy to brave the jostle and scrum within.

Oblivious to the chatter around him, random thoughts tumbled through his head. Robertson was a hard taskmaster, but Dunlop had been far worse. Still, that now seemed to be in the past. There had been no word for well over a year now – no impossible instructions, not even a single message berating him for lack of effort. To all intents and purposes, the bastard had simply vanished into thin air. His contact at the shipyard could tell him nothing, in fact discouraged further enquiries: he would be informed if his services were required at some stage in the future. A furtive visit to the safe house behind the Trongate confirmed his suspicions: the building was shuttered and deserted. This was all to the good, but… could there be a downside? Rumours of a trade recession were growing by the day. That would mean a slump in orders for new vessels – and inevitable consequences for the workforce. With Dunlop gone, his position as a shop steward would not save him – quite the reverse. He could almost picture the glint in the manager's eye as he was handed the fateful redundancy slip. But why worry about that now? He already had concerns enough to occupy his mind.

The rain had eased to a fine drizzle as the tram set Iain down at his stop on the Copland Road. Now that it was only a short walk home, niggling doubts began to grow at the prospect of confronting his wife. Morag could be a queer kettle of fish – so unpredictable. Would she even listen to his proposition? It would take all his powers of persuasion to bring her round.

"Baird! Iain Baird!" So engrossed had he been with the problem that he failed to notice the man lurking in a close on the other side of the street. "Ower here, ye gowk!"

His head jerked up. There was no mistaking the bark. It was Stan

Robertson. His heart sank. That was all he needed. "What the blue blazes are ye doin' here?" he called out as he crossed the road.

"Waitin' for a prize ninny." Robertson grinned and stretched out a hand. Iain winced at the power of his grip. "I chapped on yer door but there was naebody at home."

"Aye, well." He shook himself free. "It's likely Morag wid be out. She's workin' for the election – Mrs Barbour, ye ken."

"Just so. And what about you?"

"I've done my bit. Though there's no' many folks around in this weather."

"That's true. And you havnae been out in it either. Otherwise ye'd be drookit. And ye're far from that."

"The rain's just about off now." He caught the raised eyebrows and went on hurriedly. "But ye're right. You're a sharp one, Stan. Since ye must ken, I've been at the library – finishin' off that list ye wanted."

"Just as well." The frown relaxed. "I'm glad ye've no' been neglectin' yer duties. I could take it now, if it's a' the same to you."

"Well, maybe it's no' quite the whole kit an' caboodle. I was countin' on another week or twa."

"What the hell d'ye mean by that? Ye've had ample time as it is. Besides, I need it for the meetin' on Monday. That's why I've been standin' here for the best part o' an hour."

"But—"

"D'ye hear what I say? Hand it ower."

Iain flinched at the venom in his voice. With a gesture of resignation, he produced a slim dog-eared notebook from an inside pocket. "Here ye are. What's this about a meetin' on Monday?"

"Aye. I was goin' to tell ye. It's to update the members wi' the result o' the London conference." He began to flip through the pages. "I see what ye mean. There should be far more than this." He looked up. "Can I no' depend on ye for anythin'? I'd hazard a guess that—" A sliver of paper fluttered out. Robertson stooped and caught it before it reached the ground.

"What's this?"

"Nothin'. That is—" He gave a sickly smile. "I forgot it was there. It's nothin' for you to bother about."

"I'll be the best judge o' that. There are nae secrets where the Party is concerned." He peered at the contents.

Iain could only watch anxiously. "See what I mean?" he muttered.

"No' really. Why wid ye cut out somethin' about a mine accident lang syne?" He frowned at the obvious look of distress. "There's mair to this than meets the eye. Come on, out wi' it."

For long seconds the younger man hesitated, but there was no escape. "It's probably my faither," he blurted out.

"The body in the mine?" Robertson thought for a moment. "But ye cannae be certain?" Iain nodded. "Then ye'd best go and find out. That's my advice. It's the only way to set yer mind at rest."

"But I cannae go back to Broomburn."

"Why ever no'?"

"For fuck's sake—" The flash of anger died on his lips. Stan would grind him down. He always did. "Ye never rest till ye ken everythin', don't ye?" he said bitterly.

"It's for the good o' the Party. That's all that interests me."

"A' right, then." He sighed. "Ye mind I telt ye my faither was killed in an accident doon the pit. And that afterwards I couldnae thole bein' a miner. That's why I came to Glesga."

"Aye. But what of it? I can see ye're upset, but—"

"What I didna tell ye was that I got the blame. For no' getting' my faither out, I mean. I gave the alarm, and everyone else escaped. But that wisnae enough. They needed a scapegoat. So they picked on me."

"And that's the true story?"

"It is. Ye do believe me, don't ye?"

"What I believe is neither here nor there. What matters is that, according to your account, the result was that the village more or less cast ye out. Is that no' the case?"

"That's about the size o' it. I darena go back."

"Now that is unfortunate. It could make things awkward – for you."

"What the hell d'ye mean by that?"

"Later. After the meeting. I've a lot to think through now."

"Because of me, ye're sayin'?"

"Exactly. Here, ye can hae this. I'll hang on tae the book." He handed back the slip of paper and made to turn away. "Monday. Eight o'clock. The usual place. Mind ye're no' late."

* * *

"Anybody there?"

As he fully expected, there was no answer. Thank God she had been out when Robertson had called. The unexpected encounter in the street had been bad enough. But to return home and find them squabbling like a pair of rabid cats, or maintaining an icy silence… well, that would have been too much to bear. He shuddered at the prospect of having to act as peacemaker. Morag never could be bothered to conceal her dislike of the man.

It had been a narrow escape. A stiff dram to steady his nerves would not come amiss. Crossing over to the kitchen press, he found the whisky bottle, uncorked it and took a generous swig. The warm afterglow gave him comfort. Now perhaps he could forget Stan for the moment and concentrate on what was uppermost on his mind. No doubt Morag would be out of sorts – wet, tired and hungry. Were she to find a sympathetic welcome on her return, with the fire banked up, and the table laid for tea, then she could hardly fail to be impressed. And a glass of sherry to revive her spirits would surely have the desired effect.

Or would it? Even as he bustled around on his self-imposed task, the thought occurred that this attempt to curry favour might be taken as evidence of some guilty secret. Morag had never spoken openly of the subject, but the generally strained atmosphere was a constant reminder of her attitude towards his stated ambition to father a son and heir. He had always counted on the appearance of a baby boy to mend their relationship: all would be forgiven once her mothering instincts were reawakened with a lusty infant to suckle. Finding partners willing to meet his needs presented little difficulty, especially with the mention of payment for adoption, but as yet there had been no outcome – at least so far as he was aware. Could it be that conscience was robbing him of his manhood? That would be too awful to contemplate, but… The click of the latch gave him a start. Hastily he pretended to fiddle with the place settings as his wife entered the room.

"So ye're back." He greeted her with a sickly smile. "Ye're a wee thing late, are ye no'?"

For a moment she stared blankly, then shook her head in disbelief. "Name o' the wee man!" she exclaimed. "I've seen it a' now. The new age o' miracles, right enough."

His face reddened. "What the hell d'ye mean by that?" he spluttered.

"You – daein' housework. Ye've never troubled yer heid wi' that afore."

"Well, I jaloused ye'd be soaked through in a' that rain. I just wanted to gie ye a wee hand wi' the tea things."

"Really? In that case I'm sorry to disappoint you. We werena outside at a' this afternoon."

"Oh! Where were ye then?"

"Where d'ye think? At Party HQ, of course. We were puttin' the finishing touches to Mary's election address. It's due at the printers, ye ken." She sniffed suspiciously. "By the by, I saw yer coat hangin' in the lobby. No' exactly wet through, either. Somebody else no' out in the rain, I'm thinkin'."

He quailed before her piercing glance. The implication was all too obvious. Then he felt his hackles rise. Damned if he would let the insinuation pass. "Now you just listen to me," he hissed. "It's no' what ye might suppose. And I can prove it. I've been at the library ever since dinner time."

"Ye don't say." She was clearly sceptical. "Nae doubt ye'll be tellin' me ye went inside just to keep dry."

"No' quite. I was goin' through auld newspapers."

"And why in heaven's name wid ye do that?"

"If ye must know, it was because Stan Robertson asked me to make a list o' industrial disputes in this neck o' the woods. Said it would come in useful for plannin' future action."

"Still got a bee in his bonnet about socialist revolution, has he? I thought ye hadnae seen him for months."

"Aye. But now he's turned up again. In fact he was waitin' for me at the foot o' the close no' an hour syne. Fair put the wind up me, as ye might imagine. Just as well I'd some stuff to gie him. Otherwise, I'd never have heard the last o' it."

"You an' Stan Robertson. He only has to wag his little finger and you come runnin'. I telt ye nae good would come associatin' wi' the likes o' him."

"Aye well, mebbies ye're no' wrong. Leave it at that." This was no time to provoke another argument – not if he was to stand any chance of gaining his purpose. "Look, I've somethin' here to show you." He drew a flimsy scrap of paper from his hip pocket. "Take a gander at this. It was in a month-old copy o' the *Record*."

Frowning slightly, she took it from him. He watched intently as she studied the contents. Suddenly she gave a little gasp of dismay.

"Aye, that's right." He nodded grimly. "I see it's gotten to ye. Are you thinkin' what I'm thinkin'?"

"I – I'm no' sure." She felt her head spinning. "Just what are ye sayin'?"

"Why, is it no' plain as a pikestaff? It's my faither they found. And buried him in the kirkyaird."

"But – ye cannae be certain o' that. There's nae mention o' names. Or even the place."

"Does that matter? Who else could it be?" There was a pause. "Still, ye might have a point. It's best to ken for definite."

"You could go to Broomburn. Find out for yersel'."

"Broomburn? Are ye daft? It would be like pokin' my heid into a hornet's nest."

"What, then?"

"Mebbies I've an idea. That brother o' mine wid ken. Nae doubt he would have been asked to be one o' the pallbearers – principal mourner, like as no'." He scowled at the thought.

"And you believe that should have been you?"

"It's my right. I'm the eldest. But I ken fine they would never stand for it." He breathed deeply. "Ah well, what's done is done. Nae sense in dwellin' on it."

"But ye cannae let it be, can ye?"

"It's like this. I was hopin' ye might be able to find out where yon pipsqueak bides in Edinburgh. That is if ye dinna ken it already." He gave her a sharp look. "You could write to his wife. The pair o' ye used to be thick as thieves. Ask her about it. What d'ye say to that?"

Morag hesitated, as though undecided how to respond. "It's quite true," she confessed. "I do know the address. And we have written to each other now an' again."

"Is that so?" Somewhat to her surprise his tone was quite mild. "I suppose ye'd be wantin' to learn how the lad was gettin' on."

"Aye. It's as ye say. Can ye blame me for that?"

"Maybe no'. Have ye said anythin' about me?"

"Of course not. Your name has never been mentioned."

"Just as well." He shot her a warning glance. "Strange that I've never seen any letters come through the door."

"That's because we arranged to use Mrs Barbour's office. I didna want to take the risk o' you flyin' off the handle."

"Very considerate o' you, I'm sure." He glowered, then checked himself. "Well, that's as may be. Then we're nae further forward – unless, of course, she's already spilled the beans."

Morag dropped her gaze. "Miss Elizabeth did tell me," she said quietly.

"And you didna see fit to let me ken? That's a rare thing to dae – keepin' secrets from yer husband."

"It's no' what ye might think," she protested. "Ye ken what a temper ye've got when ye're roused. Ye might have done somethin' ye'd regret. And forbye that, I did make a promise to Miss Elizabeth."

"So that yon sod could hide behind mama's skirts?" He could not resist the sneer. "Was that it? Well, ye've let it out o' the bag now. So ye might as well gie me the rest."

She sighed, and gave a reluctant nod. "I suppose it canna dae any harm now."

"Course no'. I'm no' likely to fly off the handle, as ye term it."

"Very well, then. Ye're right. It was yer faither. Mind you, there's no' much more that I do ken. It seems Alastair went to the funeral and came back in a dreadful state. Miss Elizabeth was really worried. He was down in the dumps for ages after it. And… I'm afraid there was a lot o' ill feelin' in the village."

"About me? Aye, like as no' it would bring back auld memories – wi' me in the firing line, as usual."

She looked at him anxiously. "You do understand, don't ye? We were only thinkin' o' your best interests."

"If ye say so. I'm no' bitter, if that's what ye mean. But what I dinna get is why they went to the trouble o' drainin' that shaft in the first place. It must have cost a pretty penny to bring in the gear they'd need. And more to the point, why did the miners let them dae it? Chances are they'd have been out on strike at the very notion."

"I dinnae ken anythin' about that. There was nae word o' trouble at the mine."

"Still, it is queer. Unless—" Suddenly he snapped his fingers. "Got it! Now I ken why. The Duchess is about played oot. Openin' up the auld Broom face wid be the only way o' savin' the pit. Nae wonder they didna kick ower the traces. It was that – or the dole."

"So what if ye're right? Does it make any difference?" She made as if to turn away. "I'd best see to yer tea."

"Haud on a minute, Morag. There's nae hurry."

"Somethin' else botherin' ye?" she said wearily. "Well, what is it now."

"Nothin' really. It's just that I cannae help feelin' that maybe I've been a bit hard on ye. A few days in Edinburgh wid dae ye good."

"Pay a visit, ye mean?" She could hardly grasp what she was hearing.

"Aye, why no'? It's what ye always wanted. I'm sure the wee chap would be glad to gie ye a big hug."

"But – ye've made out that ye dinnae want anythin' to dae wi' them."

"A body can a'ways change his mind, can't he?"

"I – I dinnae ken. That is – I'm no' just sure that's a good idea. There's ower much to do here – what wi' the election comin' on, an' such like." She brushed past him. Why the sudden change? It sent a shiver down her spine.

Iain was left to reflect on her apparent confusion. For Alastair and his wife, he cared nothing. But little Eddie… now he was his own flesh and blood.

* * *

Sir Edward Lixmont rose from his seat, and once more began to pace up and down the confines of his hotel room. It was galling to have to contain his impatience, especially when the purpose of his visit was shrouded in mystery. Why had he been summoned to meet his son here in Glasgow? And why the insistence that he come alone, and on a Sunday? The telegram delivered to his office had been explicit on one point, if on no other: on no account was his mother to be informed. So why the need for secrecy? True, Hilda was a notorious gossip, but it went against the grain to invent an excuse that would stifle her curiosity. On the other hand, if this was something connected with the troubles in Ireland, perhaps the least said the better.

There as a tap on the door. It swung open before he had time to react. "Hugh! Where did you spring from?"

"Sorry, I'm late, dad." There was a soft click as he closed the door. "Bit of a rush. The meeting went on longer than I had expected."

"No need for excuses, Hugh." They shook hands warmly. "Just glad you're here. Come and sit down. Give yourself a chance to catch your breath. Whisky?" He produced a flask from his portmanteau. "As you see, I always come prepared."

"Thanks. They told me downstairs where to find you, in case you're wondering." Hugh Lixmont settled himself into an armchair. "Just a smidgeon, though. I can't stay long."

"You look tired, Hugh. Here, this'll buck you up." They touched glasses and each took a sip. "Feeling better now?"

"A little. How are things at home? I'd be intrigued to hear how you managed to keep mama away. She can be rather overpowering at times."

"I simply explained that there was client in Glasgow who required an urgent consultation before leaving the country. And today was the only available date."

"And she was satisfied with that?"

"I believe so. She was certainly relieved it was not your Uncle Robert looking for more legal advice regarding his damned coalmines. I was able to reassure her on that point."

"Good. I don't think I could face the mater just now. She'd start by lecturing me on the dangers of service in Ireland, and end up by turning on the waterworks to badger me into resigning my commission."

"Well, you can understand her position. I gather from the newspapers that things aren't going too well over there."

"That's an understatement. You were spot on with your assessment last year. But now the situation is worse than you could ever imagine. British rule is close to collapse unless we do something radical – and soon."

"Is that why you're in Glasgow? You said something about a meeting. And I see you're in mufti."

"That's so as to avoid drawing attention to ourselves. And the conference couldn't be held in Dublin or Belfast. Too many prying eyes and ears. It's no exaggeration to say we don't know who we can fully trust anymore."

"Are things really that serious? You didn't ask me over just to tell me that, did you?"

Hugh smiled faintly. "Not exactly." Then his voice hardened. "For far too long we've handled them with kid gloves, turned a blind eye to their outrages. Sinn Fein and the IRA have made a mockery of the rule of law. First it was attacks on police stations, then the murder of RIC officers and so-called collaborators. Before long they'll be killing British soldiers. Well, that's not going to happen. We're going to fight fire with fire. They'll learn that every atrocity will be met with instant reprisals."

"Here, I say." Lixmont half rose to his feet to protest. "Isn't that going over the score? It sounds like an Italian vendetta. People at home won't stand for naked retaliation."

"I'm not so sure about that. In any case the government will deny any wrongdoing, or at least muddy the waters. And our press can be relied upon to emphasise IRA brutality and praise for our forbearance in the face of heavy provocation."

His father subsided. "I see you've got it all worked out. Is that what your meeting was all about?" Hugh nodded. "Then why are you telling me this? I would have thought secrecy was paramount."

"Of course. But I know I can trust you not to blab. I've no intention of revealing the details, but I feel you've the right to some information. What I have to say involves you – in a personal sense, that is."

"I – involved?" He gasped in astonishment. "How can that be?"

"Hear me out. I've a bit of background to explain first." He held up a warning finger. "This is for your ears only, mind."

"That goes without saying – but I still don't understand."

"You will. Would you be surprised to hear that for the past months I've been attached as a liaison officer to the Royal Irish Constabulary Special Reserve?"

"The Black and Tans? I've heard of them. They got their name from the uniforms they wear."

"That's right. Police tunics and army trousers. Don't ask me why they were kitted out in that rig. As you may be aware, they were formed as a sort of counter-insurgency force, with recruitment restricted to the British mainland. That was to ensure there could be no doubt about their loyalties. However, between you and me they're a pretty rum bunch, too prone to go on the rampage and ask questions afterwards, as far as I'm concerned."

"But surely they could be subjected to proper military discipline?"

"Given time – perhaps. But we don't have that time. For the moment we're putting our hopes on a new outfit composed of former British army officers. We'll see how it goes. It's called the Auxiliary Division, in case you're wondering. I might even try to wangle a posting there myself."

"It seems to me that we're only sinking further and further into the mire. Don't you think that sooner or later we'll have to open negotiations?"

"Could be. But if we do, it must be from a position of strength. A hard crackdown first, put them in their place. Only then can we contemplate making concessions."

"Hmm. How long will that take?"

"Does it matter? Look here, I really don't have much time. Best if we could cut to the chase..." He leaned forward. "In my line of business we receive requests for assistance from time to time when armed support is required."

"I see. Go on."

"Well, about a fortnight ago I had a visit from a chap – name of Dunlop. I knew him slightly, been able to help him out several times in the past." He paused to drain the remnants of his whisky. "It was to be a raid on a deserted farmhouse a few miles outside – well, never mind the name. The local IRA commander was supposed to be in hiding there. I lent Dunlop six good men to bring him in."

"And was the operation successful?"

"I'm afraid not. Quite the reverse. They walked straight into an ambush." He gave a hollow laugh. "Shows how far we can trust so called informants."

"My God! What happened?"

"They were waiting for us. Dunlop was in the lead – gunned down before he could even draw his own weapon, so I was told. Two of my men were wounded. We had to pull back. By the time reinforcements could arrive the birds had flown. They found Dunlop in the yard, half his face blown away."

Lixmont nodded sympathetically. "I can understand how you must feel. But I still fail to see—"

"You will in a minute. The point is that it fell to me to write the report and go through his effects." He pulled a slim package from his coat pocket and pushed it across the little table between them. "Including this. It was found on his body. Here, take a look for yourself."

"What is it?"

"A sort of personal diary. Highly irregular, of course. Some of the entries go back years. It seems he was based in Glasgow during the war, tasked with the suppression of sedition."

"A member of the security services, you mean?"

"That's about the size of it."

"So? Very interesting, no doubt. But how on earth can it concern me?"

"Brace yourself, dad. Your name is in his book."

There was a gasp of astonishment. "Impossible! Is this your idea of a joke?"

"Not a bit of it," chuckled his son. "But there's no cause for alarm. You're not under suspicion, or anything like that."

"Then how? Why?"

"It appears that Dunlop blamed you for scotching his little scheme to have your precious son-in-law drafted back into the army."

"But why would he want to do that?"

"Because Baird was identified as a red revolutionary – in fact one of the leaders beavering away behind the scenes. Sending him back to the front was the easiest way to get rid of him."

"Well, that certainly clears up one mystery. I've often wondered who was responsible. But why would this Dunlop imagine Alastair Baird posed any real threat?"

"Ah, there's the nub. He was denounced by his own brother. Can you believe that?"

Lixmont frowned in distaste. "Can't say I'm really surprised. From what I know of him, he's only out for himself."

"Agreed. He's the type who'd do anything to save his own skin. Jailbird, you know. Serving ten years as a conchie. Turns out he was sprung from quod on condition he became a double agent."

"Is that what it says in Dunlop's notes?" His son nodded. "Well, it certainly proves he's an unsavoury character. But we knew that already."

"Of course. But I didn't ask you here just to rake up ancient history. I hear that my sister is worried this fellow is capable of making trouble for the family – over your grandson, I mean."

"How the devil—"

"Did I know about it? Mama wrote and told me. She must have wormed it out of Elizabeth."

"Your mother takes too much upon herself. I thought I had been able to set her mind at rest."

"Apparently not. Are you absolutely certain there's no danger?"

"You know I could never claim that. But there's been no sign of the scoundrel – not to my knowledge at any rate."

"You admit there is a possibility – however remote? In that case it would be wise to take precautions. The contents of this notebook should be more than enough to warn him off."

"Threaten to report him to the authorities, you're saying? What good would that do? If he was working for them, they wouldn't want the fact advertised. They'd probably deny any knowledge of the man, and impound the evidence on grounds of national security."

"I wasn't thinking of the authorities. His comrades would know what to do if they suspected him of treachery."

"Betray him to his own side? I couldn't be a party to that."

"Dad, we live in uncertain times. Sometimes you have to fight dirty to protect what is right and good. But it's up to you. I'll leave the book. Do with it as you will. Now I must be off. I've a boat to catch."

"Here, I say—"

But his son was already making for the door.

* * *

"You're back early." There was a hint of surprise as her husband tramped into the room. "I thought yer meetings usually went on for hours."

"No' this time," he growled.

"Well, sit ye down by the fire while I put on the kettle."

"Dinnae bother. I need somethin' stronger."

"A dram? Just as ye like." For once she was determined not to be drawn into yet another fruitless quarrel. "I'll maybe join ye wi' a wee sherry."

Iain Baird stared suspiciously as his wife rose from the kitchen table, but forbore to make any comment. Instead, he contented himself with an indeterminate grunt as he settled into his armchair and began to unlace his boots.

"I've just been goin' over these canvass returns." She handed him his whisky. "Things really seem to be takin' off. Better than we dared hope. I ken it's no' a foregone conclusion, but—"

"Dinnae count yer chickens. It's three months to the election."

Morag sighed. This was going to be hard work. "Mrs Barbour told us we should hae a wee break. Recharge the batteries afore the final push, she said. I've got a whole week off."

"Is that a fact?" He hardly bothered to conceal his lack of interest.

"Aye, it is. And I thought I might take up yer notion o' a visit to see wee Eddie. If ye've nae objection, I'll write to Miss Elizabeth an' see what can be arranged."

He shrugged his shoulders. "Dae what ye like. I can fend for mysel' while ye're away."

"Iain, why are ye actin' the dismal Jimmy?" She slipped into the chair opposite. "Is it somethin' that happened at the meeting?" There was no reply. "Care to tell me about it? It might help to get things off yer chest."

For some minutes he appeared deaf to her appeal, gazing stonily into the flames.

"Iain! Speak to me."

He stirred at last. "I hear ye. Maybe it will at that. Cannae dae any harm, I suppose. Ye're bound to hear about it anyhow – sooner or later."

"Go on, then. I'm listening."

He spat into the flames. "Well, it's like this. Ye mind me tellin' you last year about the Russians settin' up an organisation for a worldwide socialist revolution?"

"The Communist International?"

"Aye. Comintern for short."

"A load o' claptrap, if ye ask me. And just how was the workers' paradise to be achieved?"

His eyes narrowed at the implied mockery. "There's nae need for that," he admonished her. "It'll be by industrial action, as well ye ken. And by harnessing the votes o' the masses to seize control o' the levers of power in the capitalist state."

"Gettin' a majority in Parliament, ye mean? Fine words, but dae ye imagine yer extremists could ever manage that? It's the moderates that'll win through, no' them that preaches revolution. Fu' o' hot air, an' no' much else," she added with a sniff. "The working classes are well aware that support for the Labour Party is the only way to improve their lot."

"Reformism? A few crumbs from the rich man's table? That never worked in the past. And it'll no' work now?"

"Then what's your alternative?"

"Oh, we're no' as hidebound as you might think. Thon big conference in London last month was to work out a new road for the future. That's why Robertson was away."

"And now he's back to tell ye what was decided."

"Exactly. In the past we've spent ower much time bickering amongst ourselves, instead of concentrating on the class enemies. There's nae room for lots o' left-wing societies arguin' over tiny points of dogma."

"I widnae disagree there. What answer did they gie ye?"

"It's no' hard to work out, Morag. The solution is to bury our differences by creating a new party – the Communist Party o' Great Britain. Any organisation can join, so long as it agrees wi' affiliation to the Comintern."

"So that it can dance to the tune o' the Bolsheviks in Moscow? Be a puppet for Lenin an' his cronies?"

Iain shook his head ruefully. "Och, I wouldnae put it like that. The Comintern is there to help wi' advice, no' tae dictate from on high. Gie it a chance. By the by, Robertson said the new party will be applyin' for affiliation to the Labour Party. We'll be the cuckoo in the nest, so that when Labour gains enough seats in Parliament—"

"Labour believes in peaceful methods," she protested. "It would never tolerate those that preach violence in its ranks."

"I wouldnae be too sure of that. It claims to be a broad church. Is that no' the case? Once we build up membership among the masses, Labour will be forced to come to terms."

"Does that mean you'll put up your own candidates for MP?"

"Aye – why no'? We'll form electoral pacts at local level, so that we'll no' be treadin' on each other's toes."

"And you really imagine that would work?"

"Maybe no' everywhere at first. But Stan says that the coalfields gie us the best chance o' winnin' seats at the next election. What wi' a' the trouble and strife in the mining districts—"

"It should be a pushover, ye're sayin'?" She looked at him shrewdly. "And you've to devote your energies to traipsin' round the highways and byways to drum up support? Nae doubt he minds that ye started out as a pitman."

Iain's brow darkened. "He does. But there's more to it than that. He wants me to stand for Parliament."

"You – an MP?" She whistled. "I never saw that comin."

"Neither did I. Communist candidate for Mid Lanark." There was a sardonic laugh. "Can you believe it?"

"You dinnae seem very happy. I should have thought ye'd be overjoyed at the prospect."

"Well, I'm no," he snapped. "Are ye no' forgettin' something? Broomburn is slap bang in the middle o' the constituency. And I'm to put my heid into the lion's den."

"Sorry. I didnae realise. Did ye no' explain the situation to Robertson?"

"That my name's mud in the village? That the Party wouldnae stand an earthly wi' me as candidate? Aye – I tried to."

"And what was his reply?"

"Well, I couldnae speak up when he announced it at the meetin'. It fair floored me, I can tell you. But I got hold o' him after everyone else had left."

"I understand. Was he sympathetic?"

"What d'ye think? He telt me that the decision had already been taken at the highest level. Damned me for no' being grateful for the chance. Said he'd gone out on a limb to get me nominated. Any change now would reflect badly on him."

"I see. His reputation comes before anything else."

Iain nodded. "That's about the size o' it. He had the cheek to let on that it was a test o' my loyalty to the Party. I'd just hae to mend my fences – there was nae alternative."

"Did ye expect any different? As I've telt ye often enough, ye're just a tool to be used – and tossed aside when ye've served yer purpose."

"I suppose ye're right. But – I cannae just up sticks and leave him in the lurch."

"More fool you, then."

"Look, it's no' just as simple as that. He promised that if I had a stab at it and didnae get in, there'd be somethin' else for me."

"Did he say what?"

"No' exactly, but—"

She cut him short. "Thought so. It's your funeral. I've said my piece. Leave it there. Why no' just go out and drown yer sorrows? I've a letter to write, and I'd like it to catch the next post."

FOUR

Swing of the Pendulum

Edinburgh
July 1921

Alison Brodie gave a nod of approval as she stepped back from the table. It had been a herculean task, stretching far into the evening, but it was over at last. Copy and illustrations for the bumper autumn number had been arranged, marked and neatly laid out. Now all that remained was to gather up the proofs, ready to be sent off to the printer in the morning.

"That's about it done now. Thanks for your help." She turned towards her companion. "If this doesn't wow the punters, nothing ever will."

"I agree. There's a lot riding on this issue." Elizabeth Baird smiled. "And any success will be largely due to you. But for your efforts, I don't know where we'd be."

It sounded unconvincing, but there was nothing to be lost in making the gesture. The simmering resentment of a devoted employee towards a favoured newcomer had scarcely abated since her first day in the office. For the most part their relationship had been one of studied politeness, try as she might to put Alison's fears at rest, but there was no telling when it might flare up into open warfare. And the attitude of the magazine's owner did little to help matters. He seemed not to care for the strain he was placing on his secretary's loyalty, exploiting her goodwill far beyond the call of duty. The woman was worth her weight in gold; massaging her bruised ego was a small price to pay to keep the peace.

"We did it together." Alison was honest enough to acknowledge the help of the assistant editor. "Trust our lord and master to stay well clear when there's any real work to be done." She thumbed her finger at the closed door of the inner office.

Elizabeth laughed. "Just like a man. I'll go and tell him he can come out now. We've finished."

"No, don't bother. You get off. I'll chase him out. Enjoy your day off. And please give my congratulations to your husband on his achievement."

"Thank you. I'll pass on your good wishes." Her heart swelled with pride at the thought of the impending graduation ceremony. Alastair was to be capped with First Class Honours in History – a well merited award for almost two years of dedicated study.

"Just a minute!"

Elizabeth paused in the act of gathering up her coat and hat from the hallstand. Her eyes narrowed as Nick Norman appeared in the doorway, brandishing a bottle of champagne and two glasses.

"Time for a little celebration, I think. You won't mind." He motioned towards his office.

The two women exchanged glances: Alison shrugged her shoulders while Elizabeth reluctantly laid aside her coat.

"Not you, Alison, I'm afraid." He barred her path. "I've business affairs to discuss with Elizabeth. I'm sure you could do with an early night."

Alison's face was a picture. There was a gasp of disbelief, followed by a glare of pure vitriol. Her cheeks crimsoned with rage as she turned on her heel.

Elizabeth bit her lip in vexation. "That's a bit rich, isn't it? You've really upset her, Nick. There's no need to treat her like a common skivvy, you know."

"Never mind her. She'll be over it by tomorrow. Let's enjoy a glass of champagne."

She frowned at that, but after a moment's hesitation allowed herself to be ushered into the inner room. He was swaying slightly, his voice a little slurred. Her nose wrinkled in distaste as she caught the smell of whisky on his breath.

"Make yourself comfortable while I do the honours." He indicated the large settee recently installed on his instructions – and without bothering to think of consulting her beforehand.

She gave him a sharp look, but made no further objection. That he was up to something she did not doubt. Now if this was to be another half-hearted attempt at seduction…

"There you go." He handed her a filled glass before easing himself down beside her. Instinctively she edged away. He appeared not to notice. "Well, bottoms up. Here's to us."

The liquid was harsh and warm – almost undrinkable. She set her glass aside after the first sip.

"I think this is much better than sitting at opposite sides of a desk. More informal, don't you agree?" He flashed an oily smirk at her.

"If you say so." Trust Nick – true to form as usual. Turning on the charm like some smooth-tongued salesman when he saw profit for himself. "You said something about business affairs."

"Yes. But first I wanted to show my appreciation for all your hard work over the past – what is it? Nearly two years. In that short space of time you've completely revitalised our magazine."

"I wouldn't go that far."

"No, I really mean it. You came up with the new title: *Bright Horizons*. And the strapline: *Women on the march, Breaking the mould*. Now that was inspired. It's given us a whole new purpose that resonates with today's readership. Look what it's done for our circulation."

"Good of you to suggest that. But others have been just as important – Alison, in particular."

"Ah. But no one else had the wit to think ahead, plan for the future. You did."

"I'm sure I don't know what you're talking about. See here, Nick. You didn't ask me to stay behind just to mouth platitudes. Kindly come to the point. Then perhaps we can both get off home."

"*Touché*. Smart girl," he chuckled. "There's no pulling the wool over your eyes. Though I did mean the compliment I paid."

"Understood. Please get on."

"If you insist. I think you have worked wonders, but there's no getting away from the fact we are still just a provincial mag. It's a cutthroat market out there. We either expand, or wither on the vine."

"Become a national heavyweight, you mean?" It was hard to take him seriously. "And just how do you intend to manage that?"

"Well, obviously not overnight. Look, I've been mulling things over. These offices are no good – far too cramped. And nobody knows we are here. We need bigger, more prestigious premises. I've had my eye on a property in the New Town where we can really showcase our presence."

"But we've only just had this place refurbished. And taken out a lease on rooms on the next floor." High time he was brought down to earth. "Is all this to go to waste?"

"Blame Alison. She was always complaining about having to work in such dingy surroundings. You know it was only to be a temporary measure to keep her quiet."

Elizabeth could only marvel at the cool effrontery of the man. The business was still mired in debt, and he was calmly hinting at further expenditure – and on a massive scale. Her father would have kittens when he heard of this; he had already made scathing remarks at how money seemed to run through Nick Norman's fingers.

"Think big, Elizabeth. The sky's the limit. And I've never known you to duck a challenge. All that's required is a fresh injection of capital."

"A mere detail, of course." It was only too obvious where this was heading. "And just how do you propose to raise the funds?"

He affected not to hear the note of sarcasm. "Well now, I've been thinking it out. You know we're due to repay your father's loan in a month or two. It would be useful if you could persuade him to write it off."

"Hmm. I'm not at all sure he would agree, but even if he did, that wouldn't take us very far."

"I was coming to that. What we need is another fifteen or twenty thousand. That would do the trick. Then we could really spread our wings."

Elizabeth gulped. "And you honestly expect him to entertain such a proposal?" The enormity of the sum was staggering.

"Why not? Sir Edward is a rich man. And the investment would be repaid many times over in a few years. I'm sure his daughter would find little difficulty in convincing him of the merits of our case. If she was only willing to try," he added with a sly grin.

"That's impossible, Nick," she snapped, stung by his attitude. "My father would never consent to an undertaking of that size, especially with no guarantee of success. Despite what you appear to believe, the risk would be just too great. I wouldn't even make the effort."

He pouted at that, like a small child denied a new toy, then forced himself into a dry laugh. "It was worth a try. Though I do think we're missing out on a grand opportunity." He appeared to reflect. "Maybe you're right. At least there's no need to fall out over a trifle. Let's just sit and chat about something else. I see you've hardly touched your wine."

"It's not really to my taste, to tell you the truth. And the hour is late."

"You don't care for my company?" He pulled a face.

"It's not that, but I did promise my son his bedtime story. You look a bit tired yourself. It's been a long day." She thought she put it rather well. He was clearly tipsy, but there was no need to cause offence by drawing attention to it.

"Don't go yet. You weren't like this last year when you needed a shoulder to cry on."

She paused in the act of rising from her seat. "What – what do you mean by that?" It was little more than a whisper.

"Come off it. You know well enough. It was when you told me your husband couldn't come up to scratch anymore."

Elizabeth gave a little gasp. Bitterly she recalled her moment of weakness in confiding in him. But what else could she have done? He had caught her at a low ebb following the final verdict from the consultant. Alastair was making good progress towards a clean bill of health, but the ravages of war and influenza had left a permanent mark. While there was no impediment to physical relations, given due care, it was highly unlikely he could ever father a child. Oh, Nick had made all the right noises with his expressions of sympathy, but now she understood. He was only biding his time. This was behind the hints and innuendo she had hitherto dismissed as office banter. Now drink had emboldened him to take a step further.

"I just thought you might require some companionship," he went on. "We could console each other, if you know what I mean."

"How dare you?" Bristling with indignation she sprang to her feet, "Think of yourself as God's gift to women?" she sneered. "Well, that cuts no ice with me. Even if you were the last man on earth."

"Sorry you feel that way." He shrugged his shoulders. "Most women are only too happy to jump into my arms."

"In your dreams!" His conceit beggared belief. "Look at you – an ageing Lothario. Why don't you just curl up and sleep it off." She turned her back on him and made for the door.

"You will speak to your father, won't you?" he called out after her.

She spun round. It was so unexpected. His tone had altered – firm, insistent, almost harsh. Was this some kind of threat? There was a glint in her eye as she retraced her steps to confront him. "I thought I had explained that he would never stand for the idea," she said primly.

"That's a pity. I hoped you'd see sense." There was no trace of banter in his voice now. "I suppose your husband must wonder what you get up to – spending all those late hours in the office, if you catch my drift."

"Alastair and I have no secrets."

"No? I find that hard to believe. And I would wager you've never told your parents of the situation. How would Lady Hilda react to the news about her son-in-law? What would her fine circle of friends make of it?"

For long seconds Elizabeth stood speechless, numbed by what she was hearing; then a cold fury seized her as the implications sank in. "So it's blackmail now," she hissed. "I never thought even you could stoop that low."

"Sticks and stones," he murmured.

"You think so? Do you really imagine you can bully me by threatening my family?"

"I hope it won't come to that."

"On your own head be it." She seemed to tower over him. "You haven't thought this out very well, have you?"

"What – what do you mean?" For the first time there was a quaver in his voice.

"What do you suppose would happen to your precious rag if I just walked out? You know very well who pulled it up from the gutter. You've admitted as much yourself."

"Here, I say. Isn't that going a bit far?"

She brushed aside his feeble protest. "And then there's my father to consider. Did you think of him? He's not without influence, especially now he's on the town council. He could make things pretty hot for you if he found out about your little game."

"No need for that." He made an attempt at an ingratiating smile. "It was really only a jest on my part. Just the drink talking. You know I'd never do anything to hurt you."

"I know nothing of the kind." Now she held the advantage, Elizabeth was not to be denied. "What about the account books you keep in that safe behind you?" she continued remorselessly. "I've little doubt some of the items wouldn't bear close scrutiny, despite that shady character you've dug up to audit them. The charge would involve embezzlement, would it not?" She drew herself up to deliver the crushing blow. "You might cause a scandal for me and mine, but you would languish in a prison cell – probably for years to come."

A low moan escaped his lips; he fell back, utterly deflated. "How did you know about the books?" he whimpered.

"I didn't know for sure. But I do now. The expression on your face is enough to confirm it. You must take me for a complete idiot. All those odds and ends on your expense account? They must add up to a pretty penny."

"Are you going to tell your father?"

"I haven't decided – yet." She wagged a finger at him. "Were I to stay my hand, it would be for the sake of the magazine, not your worthless hide. And there would be strict conditions."

He looked up with renewed hope, like a condemned man suddenly granted a reprieve. "Anything."

"First of all, you will give up the office chequebook into my keeping. In future all expenditure will require my approval. And I mean all – down to the last farthing. Secondly, the books will be audited by my father's accountant. That way we'll stay on the straight and narrow. Lastly, you'll work normal office hours. No more sloping off at lunchtime – and not bothering to come back. Is it a deal?" He could only nod his agreement.

"Then I'll be off. You've got off lightly. But if you ever try such a stunt again, I won't be answerable for the consequences."

Elizabeth left him to his own devices. As she made her way homewards, she could take a quiet satisfaction in finally putting Nick Norman in his place. He would hardly dare to threaten her again. But as to the promise of an honest day's work – how long would that last? On the other hand, he did have a point about the benefits of expansion, though hardly on the magnitude that he appeared to envisage. A modest advertising campaign to boost circulation might be possible if daddy could be persuaded to renew the loan, and perhaps even add to it. Then there was Alastair. Her face clouded over at the reminder of her folly in sharing a confidence with the likes of that wastrel. Now her conscience began to nag away at her. Should she admit her fault, and beg his pardon? But that would only upset him. And nothing must be allowed to cast a shadow over his big day. Her confession could always be postponed to a more suitable occasion.

* * *

"Why are you so obviously determined to spoil my day? Today of all days, when your husband has just graduated." He threw up his hands in mock surrender. "Very well, then. I suppose I must indulge you – again. Anything for a quiet life."

Sir Edward had retreated into his study. The family was engaged elsewhere – or so he had assumed. His wife was busy superintending the preparations for the celebratory tea to be held in the garden, while his son-in-law had gone off with his grandson to the nearby park – to let off steam, as he put it. The graduation ceremony with its pomp and ritual had been a memorial occasion, and he had enjoyed the principal's reception for the favoured few; but now they had returned to familiar surroundings, he felt in need of a short rest. Apparently even this was to be denied him. Elizabeth had seized her opportunity for a word in private, with the clear intention of twisting his arm on behalf of her pet project.

His daughter was not fooled by his apparent reluctance. He had been convinced by the force of her argument, otherwise he would never have given his consent. "Thank you, kind daddy," she simpered, kissing him lightly on the forehead. "You won't regret it, you know."

"I sincerely hope not," he replied drily. "You say you've managed to put a curb on that bounder?"

"Nick Norman, you mean?"

"Who else? That's the only reason I'm prepared to advance you another couple of thousand. I won't pry into the details, but I expect you to live up to your promises."

"No need to worry on that score, dad. Nick knows which side his bread is buttered." She gave him a broad smile. "I'll leave you in peace now."

"Don't run away just yet. Since you're here, there was something else on my mind. I wanted to ask about Alastair. Has he said what he intends to do with his degree?"

She pulled a face and subsided back into her chair. "You know he's set on secondary teaching?"

"And he has all the relevant qualifications – more than most."

"That's just the point. There seems to be a dearth of suitable posts on the go. He's sent in several applications – and heard nothing. I thought there would be no difficulty in snapping him up."

"Well, what can you expect in the present economic climate? There's a trade depression, and the government is demanding cutbacks in expenditure. Education must bear its fair share."

"But can you do anything for him? With your contacts, that is."

"Possibly – but you know how he feels about accepting favours. In any case do you think he's up to the rough and tumble of school life?"

"Has he fully recovered from his illness, you're saying?" She thought for a moment. "He claims to be perfectly fit for the job. But to tell you the truth, I have my doubts."

"Hmm. I've an idea. But it'll require careful handling."

Elizabeth was intrigued. But before she could question him further there was a knock at the door. The maid came in and gave a little bob of the head. "Excuse me, sir, miss. Her ladyship says that everything is ready, and will you both come at once."

"Right on the button! Agnes, you may tell your mistress we'll be down directly." He rose to his feet. "Come along, Elizabeth. You'll have to contain your curiosity a little longer."

And he refused to be drawn for the full duration of the meal. Corks were popped, toasts proposed, and the cold collation voted an outstanding success. Only after coffee had been served did he tap his glass for attention.

"I do hope you're not going to make one of your interminable speeches." His wife sighed wearily, and raised her eyebrows as though in supplication.

"Hardly that," he protested. "I merely feel this could be an ideal opportunity to look to the future. That is, of course, if you've no objection, Hilda."

"None at all." She frowned at the note of sarcasm. "I've no problem with a family discussion, so long as it's sensible. But does Eddie have to stay and listen? He's been good as gold all day, but he must be getting bored by now."

"Have you something to suggest?"

"Hugh used to have a collection of toy soldiers. If I'm not mistaken, it's still in his room, in a tin box under the bed." She turned to her grandson. "Would you like to play with Uncle Hugh's soldiers, Eddie?"

The boy's face lit up. "Yes, thank you, granny. I'd like that very much."

"Go with Agnes, then. She'll help you set them up." She glanced round and motioned to the maid. "We're just going to have a little talk, Eddie. Then we'll come in and see how you're getting on." They watched in silence as servant and child disappeared into the house.

Elizabeth was the first to speak. "That was a good idea, mama. But we can't stay very long. It'll soon be Eddie's bedtime."

"Time enough." Her father was not to be rushed. Why don't you tell your mother how well the magazine is doing?"

"I'm sure mama has no interest in my humdrum affairs."

"Indeed I do not. You know my views on your association with a feminist publication. But naturally my feelings are of no consequence," she added with a sniff.

Elizabeth flushed. "*Bright Horizons* is designed to appeal to a wide variety of readers. It is neither radical nor extremist in its views. If you were to glance through a copy—"

"You can't imagine that I would approve of anything in its content." Her lips curled in disdain.

"I suppose you think I shouldn't soil my hands." She felt her hackles rise. "Letting down the side as usual. Is that it, mama? I should be a society lady like you?"

"Ladies, ladies!" The head of the household belatedly recognised his mistake. The subject was obviously a red rag to a bull, so far as his wife was concerned. Hastily he sought to rescue the situation. "We can't have all this bickering, you know. Can't you at least make the effort to get on with one another at family gatherings?"

Elizabeth lowered her gaze. "Sorry, daddy," she said quietly. "It just slipped out." She looked up at her mother. "I apologise, mama. I shouldn't have spoken like that."

"Hilda?"

"I – I suppose I may have overstepped the mark. I'll try to be more careful in future."

"Good." Not for a moment did he believe that peace had broken out. It was only a truce between mother and daughter, but at least a full-scale altercation had been nipped in the bud. "And now I think we should move on." He turned to his son-in-law. "Alastair, you haven't had much to say for yourself. I gather you're still determined on a career as a schoolmaster."

"Yes, that's always been my ambition, ever since my time at the village school in Broomburn."

"That would be with Mr Ogilvie. You thought a lot of him, didn't you?"

"I still do. I owe him so much – more than anyone else, apart from my mother. But for them I'd probably have been sent down the mine, like almost all of my schoolmates."

Lixmont nodded sympathetically. "He encouraged you to broaden your horizons, coached you to win a scholarship to a prestigious school, did he not?"

"That's so. But there were other hurdles to be crossed before I could even think of going on to university. As you might expect, funding was the greatest obstacle. He steered me through the applications for fee and maintenance grants. And don't forget it was his legacy that enabled me to complete my degree."

"Hmm. There could have been other ways. But let that pass. You believe that the best way to repay his kindness is to follow in his footsteps."

"Not just that. Mr Ogilvie was never more than a parish dominie. His aspiration for me was to aim higher."

"To advance the cause of learning in a senior school, you mean? Now that is interesting. I quite understand your desire to honour his memory. From what you've told me, he was a man ahead of his time."

Alastair smiled. "If you are suggesting that he wished the benefits of education to be open to all, to be seen as a pathway to a more egalitarian society, then I'm in full agreement. But as for being ahead of his time, John Knox wrote and preached something similar nearly four hundred years ago."

His father-in-law chuckled. "I stand corrected. But we've made some progress since then. Ogilvie would have been pleased with the provisions of the recent Education Act, would he not?"

There was a loud snort. He frowned at the interruption as his wife raised a pointing finger. "Rome on the rates!" she hissed.

"Spare me your trite observations" He ignored the icy glare. "That remark is hardly original. I'm surprised at you, Hilda. I should have thought you would welcome the inclusion of Catholic schools in the state system."

"You know very well what I mean," she snapped. "We pay for the papists to have their children educated, while they control what is taught in their schools. They appoint their own teachers, and we provide their salaries."

"Really, Hilda," he admonished, only half in jest, "I had no idea you had such sectarian leanings."

"Stuff and nonsense, Edward! I'm as open minded as anyone else. It's just that I expect an even-handed approach. If they wish to peddle their own dogma, it should be at their own expense." She lapsed into an injured silence.

"Catholic schooling is only one part of the 1918 Act. I think we'll leave it at that." There was no point in pursuing an argument he could not possibly win. "As I was about to say, the Act also embraces the vision of secondary education for all, coupled with the raising of the school leaving age. You would agree these are worthy ideals, Alastair?"

"Of course, sir. But what has been done to achieve them? So far, virtually nothing."

"True enough. I admit that circumstances have not been favourable. Savings have had to be made. But this economic downturn must end soon. And when it does—" Abruptly he changed tack. "By the way, how have your applications been going? Any sign of a vacant post?"

"I'm afraid not." He gave a faint grin. "But we live in hope."

"Hmm. Early days, I know. But have you considered other options. Worst case scenario, and all that."

"If nothing suitable crops up, you mean? No, I haven't got that far yet."

"Perhaps you should. There may be an alternative that might just fit the bill."

"Good old daddy!" Elizabeth had been listening intently. "I knew you had something up your sleeve."

Her father threw her a sharp glance. Why did women always have to butt in? A wrong word now might ruin everything. He hesitated a moment, weighing how best to express what was on his mind.

"Suppose there was some other way to pay tribute to your mentor, make the case for progressive reform."

"I don't understand." Now Alastair was thoroughly perplexed. "You're surely not implying I should teach teachers in a training college, are you? I can't think of anything else."

"No, not that. Though I have no doubt you would make an admirable tutor," he added hastily. "Hear me out. You may, or may not, be aware that the government department in charge of Scottish education is now permanently based here in Edinburgh, with only a token presence left in London."

"Yes, but—"

"And is now led by George Macdonald. An eminent archaeologist in his own right, before he turned to public service."

"I still don't see—"

"Let me explain. I have had some dealings with Macdonald, in my capacity on the city council. He tells me that many of his officials have been reluctant to transfer from Whitehall to Edinburgh. Consequently, he is on the outlook for bright young men to help staff his office here. I happened to mention your name, and qualifications. He seemed interested, and I have every confidence you would be a prime candidate for an appointment to the administrative grade, should you care to apply."

For long moments Alastair sat tongue-tied, as he wrestled with the implications. It was a tempting prospect, one he could never have envisaged. But then his brow cleared. There could be only one reply.

"Please do not think me disrespectful, sir. I am grateful for your efforts on my behalf. But to accept your offer would smack of patronage. I must make my own way, by my own endeavours."

Lixmont sighed and shook his head. "That stubborn pride of yours, Alastair. It can amount to an indulgence if taken too far. Can I not persuade you? Even in a junior position you would be working on the formulation of policy, contributing your ideas for the betterment of the nation's children. Close to the centre of power, you would have more influence than the headmaster of a large school."

"Even if that were true, sir—"

"You are a man of principle, I know." He snapped his fingers, as though a thought had just occurred. "Tell you what. Let's make a bargain. If you obtain a teaching post before the start of the new term, then well and good. If not, promise me you will at least consider my proposition." He extended his hand.

Alastair took it. "Yes sir, I think I can promise that. It would be churlish to refuse."

"Good. Then that's agreed." He turned to his wife. "What's your opinion, Hilda?"

"I'm surprised you bother to ask, Edward." She made a show of folding her napkin. "My opinion is that it's high time we went indoors." With that she swept from her chair, leaving the others to follow in her wake.

Her husband chuckled. "Yes, I suppose we'd better go in, if only to rescue Agnes from playing at soldiers."

"You go on ahead, Alastair," said Elizabeth. "See he hasn't made too much of a mess."

He nodded his agreement. "I'll do that. Your wish is my command," he added lightly.

Elizabeth waited till he was safely out of earshot. "Thank you, daddy. I'll make sure he does the right thing."

"I was counting on it. But don't go overboard. Just a quiet word now and again."

"Of course, daddy." She took his arm to escort him across the lawn and into the morning room through the French windows.

"Hurry up, you two." The voice came from the top of the stairs. "My grandson would like you to review his troops."

It was an impressive sight that met them as they entered Hugh's room. Eddie was on the floor, drawing up the last of his men in columns of four, while Hilda and Alastair looked on in admiration.

"Look at that." She pointed to the display. "All these uniforms from every part of the empire. It reminds me of the late queen's diamond jubilee."

"You were never at the procession in London," scoffed her husband.

"No. But I saw the colour plates in the illustrated magazines. You should be proud of your son, Elizabeth."

"That goes without saying." She stooped to ruffle the boy's hair. "But all good things must come to an end. Help Agnes to pack everything away, Eddie."

"Must you?" Her father had dropped onto his hands and knees. "Look, there's only a few more to arrange."

"It is rather late, daddy."

"I suppose so." Reluctantly he rose to his feet. "Shall I telephone for a taxi, Elizabeth?"

"No need for that. We'll walk up to Goldenacre. It's not far, and there should be plenty of cabs at this time of night."

"Perhaps that won't be necessary." Alastair was standing by the window. "I can see a taxi coming. It's slowing down. Yes, I was right. It's pulling up outside your gate."

"I wonder who it could be," said Elizabeth. "Never mind. If we're quick—"

"There's someone getting out. He's paying off the cabbie. Good heavens, I do believe it's your brother, Elizabeth. Yes, it's Hugh right enough – Hugh Lixmont."

* * *

"Here you are, Hugh. Get this down you." He handed his son a stiff dram, before turning to his wife. "What about you, Hilda?"

"Just a very small sherry, Edward. I feel we've already had too much. Still…" Her voice trailed away.

For some minutes they sat in silence, nursing their drinks: no one seemed inclined to make conversation. That their son was out of sorts was only too apparent. No, there was more to it than that: his father knew him well enough to read the signs. He was inwardly seething with anger, and not trusting himself to speak. Why the sudden appearance, without the hint of a warning? Not as a belated guest to the party – that was clear enough. He had been plainly surprised to find the whole family gathered there. Now the others had departed, leaving him to face his parents.

"How are things in Ireland, Hugh?" asked his father, in an attempt to break the ice. "There's a bright spot on the horizon, don't you think? I mean what with the truce being signed."

"Truce!" It was a snort of derision. "Surrender, you mean." Hugh found his voice at last. "These craven poltroons – Lloyd George and the rest – have simply given in. We had the IRA on the rack. They knew they could never take us on in open warfare. And they can't keep up a sustained guerilla campaign. They're short of both men and guns. Another few months and we'd have had them."

"But surely the prospect of peace is to be welcomed?"

"Glad you think so. I don't agree. Not on these terms." His suppressed feelings came tumbling out. "The Paddies will have everything they want. Ireland will be divided into two. The only thing left to decide is the exact border between north and south. Our troops are already confined to barracks. And when we finally pull out, what do you think will happen to those who remained loyal to the crown?"

"I hadn't thought of that. But surely with goodwill on both sides—"

"Don't you believe it. There'll be reprisals against those who backed the wrong horse. And we'll have abandoned them."

"But what about you, Hugh?" His mother had her own anxieties. "How will you be affected?"

"Oh, there's no need to worry on that score. I shan't be returning to the firing line. I've been sacked."

"Sacked?"

"It amounts to that. My services are no longer required by His Majesty's Government. Hence my contract has been terminated – with immediate effect. I have been given a month's leave in lieu of notice. Then it's Civvy Street for me."

"But surely—"

"Circumstances alter cases. Apparently there's no need for my role in negotiations with the Fenians. We mustn't allow ourselves to suspect their intentions. That's what I was told."

"So that's what this is all about." Light dawned on his father. "I can well understand your bitterness. No chance of another posting?"

"None."

"They must have given you something. A pension, perhaps?"

"Not a bit of it. No award, or token of recognition. It's as though they're determined to expunge our efforts in Ireland from the record." He allowed himself a rueful smile. "Still, it's an ill wind. I have been graciously permitted to retain my army rank, if not to wear my uniform. I can style myself as Captain Lixmont."

"Captain? But you've been a major, and then a colonel."

"These were only temporary appointments, so they don't count. Captain was my substantive rank. That's as far as they were prepared to go."

"A poor recompense. Don't you agree, Hilda?"

"Poor! Is that all you can say? I think it's monstrous" Her growing indignation found an outlet. "That a gallant officer could be treated in such a disgraceful manner beggars belief. And that after years of dedicated service, laying his life on the line in defence of his country."

"A scandal indeed. But Hugh's not alone there. Think of the thousands of servicemen who found themselves at a loose end after the war."

"And ended up knocking on doors, trying to sell insurance, or bootlaces, or some such thing. You're surely not thinking of that for Hugh, are you?"

"Of course not. But I do have contacts, you know. There are ways and means."

"Here, I say." Their son raised a hand in protest. "Before you start organizing my life for me—"

"I'm sorry, Hugh. That was a little presumptuous of your father." Hilda was equal to the situation. She rose to give him a peck on the cheek. "We're just glad to have you back safe and sound." She turned to her husband, oblivious to his look of blank astonishment. "I'm going to check that everything's in order in Hugh's room. Then I'm off to bed. Don't keep the boy up too long. He must be exhausted after his journey."

Lixmont gave a rueful shake of the head as she left the room. "That's your mother for you. Always has to have the last word." He refilled their glasses. "Just a small nightcap, man to man, eh?"

"Thanks, dad." He took a sip. "Sorry if I spoke out of turn. It's just that this has come as a real shock. No warning of the chop, barely a day's notice. I've been a soldier ever since the cadet corps at school. I don't know what else I could turn my hand to."

"Don't trouble yourself about that, son. The army demands qualities of leadership and drive that can be put to good use in other walks of life. But there's no need to go into that now. Deciding what's best for you will keep for another day."

"No time like the present. You sound as though you had something in mind. Don't make a mystery of it."

"Well – if you're sure. A thought has just occurred. You can thank your mother for it."

"How on earth—?"

"It was when she mentioned insurance."

"Flogging insurance? Surely you can't be serious."

"Perhaps not." He chuckled. "Let me explain. I don't think you're cut out to undertake legal training. But there could still be a niche for you in the family firm. Although I'm not directly involved, we have established a financial arm – advising clients, investing their spare cash for them."

"But I know nothing about money." He laughed harshly. "Except how to spend more than I earn."

"Nonsense. You can always learn from the other brokers. The first principles shouldn't take long to pick up. And the position can be quite lucrative, I believe. You would be entitled to a share of the profits made in the dealing room. If you did well, in the fullness of time there would be every prospect of a partnership. Think it over for a few days. Let me know if you're interested, and I'll set up a meeting with the line manager."

"Thanks. I'll do that." He drained his glass. "By the way, just out of idle curiosity, have you had any trouble from that bounder?"

"Bounder?" Then recognition dawned. "I suppose you mean young Baird's brother."

"Who else? The bastard who—"

"All right. No need to go into chapter and verse." He took a deep breath before going on. "As a matter of fact I did have a run in with him. I was going to tell you."

"Thought as much. I guessed he might come sniffing around. So the notebook came in handy after all?"

"How do you know I made use of it?"

"How else could you get rid of him? I don't imagine you tried to buy him off."

His father nodded. "You're right, of course. Blackmailers always come back for more. But I'm not proud to have to resort to such underhand methods."

"No need to reproach yourself. I bet mama thought you did the right thing."

"Your mother knows nothing of this. And must never find out. So don't you go letting the cat out of the bag."

"As you wish, dad. But how—?"

"Baird never came here. He went to Elizabeth's house."

"He informed her of his intentions? A letter, perhaps?"

"Not a bit of it. He meant to catch your sister on the hop. But we knew he was coming."

"How was that?"

"You remember that Eddie's old nanny is Baird's wife. She sent Elizabeth a wire to say he was on his way from Glasgow."

"Good of her to do that. I mean, going against her husband to take the family's side."

"Well, she was very attached to the lad. And she's not blind to Baird's faults. She paid a visit to Elizabeth last year, and let it be known they couldn't have children, and that Baird was becoming obsessed with fatherhood. She said he was determined to have what he considered to be his rights."

"I see. Does that complicate matters?"

"Possibly. But I trust not – thanks to you."

"All in the day's work." He waved aside the acknowledgment. "Please go on. What happened next?"

"Not much to tell. Alastair took the boy out of harm's way, and Elizabeth made a telephone call to the office. I was able to forestall him when he arrived."

Hugh grinned. "I would have liked to have been a fly on the wall at that encounter. Was he surprised to see you?"

"Well, he certainly wasn't overjoyed to find me waiting for him. I refused to invite him into the house. After a bit of grousing, he accepted that I was empowered to represent the family, and agreed that a turn in Inverleith Park might offer some privacy."

"Very wise. You wouldn't want Elizabeth to be hovering in the background. She might butt in and spoil everything."

"I wouldn't put it quite like that. I simply saw no need to involve her in what must have seemed a distasteful task."

"I stand corrected. What were his demands?"

"Just as you might expect. Regular access to Eddie, including occasional visits to stay with him and his wife in Glasgow. In return he would promise not to reveal that he was the boy's biological father. He would represent himself as a favourite uncle."

"Very generous of him. And if you refused?"

"He would create a scandal. Write to the gutter press and expose his true parentage."

"He believed that the publicity would bring ruin to the family. And you would do anything to avoid that. How did he take it when you produced the notebook?"

"I didn't have it with me. He might have made an attempt to snatch it away. But I was able to give him enough factual detail to prove I knew all about his shady past."

"And what was his response?"

"Oh, at first he tried to stonewall. Denied any knowledge of Dunlop. The evidence, if it existed, was obviously forged. But when he saw that wouldn't wash, he changed tack a little. His argument was that I was wasting my time. The authorities would never admit to employing him as a double agent."

"True," murmured his son.

Lixmont frowned at the observation. "I took your advice. I told him I wasn't thinking along those lines. How would his friends in the Communist Party react to the news? And how would it affect his chances as a candidate for Parliament?"

"Parliament? My, Baird is going up in the world."

"Yes. Communist candidate for the constituency of Mid Lanark. I've been doing a little research of my own since you passed on Dunlop's notes."

"That was time well spent. Did he now realise the position he was in?"

"I thought so. But he made a last attempt to brazen it out. If I denounced him, he would claim it was a capitalist plot to discredit the Party. I told him to go ahead. He would know his associates best. If they were bound to take his word on trust—" He smiled to the recollection. "I could read it on his face. He knew full well doubts would be raised, suspicions sown, and his past activities would be investigated."

"And he caved in?"

"Not in so many words. There we were, standing eyeball to eyeball. Then he swore, shook his fist and stomped away. I think we can say it's checkmate."

"You're convinced he's shot his bolt? We've seen the last of him?"

"Yes. Aren't you?"

"Perhaps. But this is more than a family affair now. If he's been selected to stand for Parliament at the next election, he must stand high with the leadership of the CPGB. He'll not want that to be put at risk."

"Then what are you saying?"

"We have documents that clearly incriminate him. Working as an agent for the class enemy? The Communist Party of Great Britain will take a very dim view of that. He knows he's not safe till that book is in his hands. So guard it well."

FIVE

Red Clydesiders

Broomburn, Lanarkshire
October 1922

"Rouse yersel', laddie! This is our stop." Stan Robertson lowered the window and leaned out to open the carriage door. "And try no' to look like a dismal Jimmy," he added, glancing back. "Ye've been a wet blanket ever since we left Glesga. It's no' yer funeral, ye ken."

The train, gasping and wheezing, had pulled into a wayside halt on the branch line. With a sigh of resignation Iain Baird heaved himself to his feet. Many a true word spoken in jest, he thought ruefully, as he lumbered after his companion. All very well for Stan to insist that this was his opportunity to close the book on the past with the promise of a golden future under socialism. But that was typical of the Party leadership – blinded to everything except the class war. The individual was merely a cog in the machine, expendable on a whim if the cause demanded it. His superiors had decreed that his presence at the meeting was necessary, and would brook no argument from a subordinate.

He peered round suspiciously as Robertson slammed the door shut, and the engine started up in a gush of steam and smoke. The place was deserted – not a soul in sight. No one was waiting on the platform, and they had been the only passengers to alight. His gaze shifted to the track leading to the mining village less than a mile distant. Still not a sign of life. But that gave scant assurance. Was this an omen – the calm before the storm?

"What's up wi' ye now? Ye're like a cat on hot bricks?"

"Sorry, Stan." Iain sought to make amends. "Just a bit nervous, I suppose."

"And why would that be? Did ye expect a welcomin' committee?"

The younger man winced at the jibe. But that was Robertson all over

– mocking him with gallows' humour. What did Stan know, or care, about the memories evoked by the journey? His last appearance in Broomburn had been eight – no, nearer nine years ago. That was to attend his mother's funeral. On that occasion his visit had been barely tolerated. What would be his reception this time – with old wounds reopened by the discovery of his father's remains?

"I was just thinkin', Stan." He screwed up his courage to make a last despairing appeal. "Does it make any sense for me to show my face in the village? It would just be a distraction, as I've telt ye umpteen times. After all, the main thing is to drum up support for workers' control o' the coal mines. Why take the risk o' spoilin' that?"

He was rewarded with a frosty glare. Then Robertson made an effort to curb his obvious annoyance.

"Aye, that was the original purpose o' the meetin'," he conceded. "But things have moved on since then, as fine ye ken. The Tories in London have kicked out Lloyd George and set up their ain government. But it cannae last. There has to be a general election, and the date could be set any day now. That's why it's important to publicise your nomination. And where better to start than in the heart o' the constituency."

Iain bit his lip. It was hard to challenge the facts. Backbench Tory MPs, disillusioned with the postwar Lloyd George coalition, had defied their own leaders and brought down the government. Without support, the Prime Minister had been forced to resign, and had been replaced by Bonar Law as head of a minority caretaker administration, tasked with making arrangements for the country to have its say. With the Liberal Party hopelessly split, and the Tories under new, untried leadership, it seemed an ideal opportunity to capture the working class vote for socialism. The Left confidently expected to hold the balance of power in the next parliament: the dream of an absolute majority was not out of the question. And the Communist Party was determined to win a substantial number of seats in its own right, stressing its role in preventing any backsliding on the part of the more moderate Labour Party.

"I appreciate what ye're sayin', Stan." He had one last card to play. "But surely it would be better to announce my candidacy somewhere else – like Hamilton. That's where the nomination papers have to be lodged, and that's where the count will take place."

"No. The decision's made. And that's final. Ye hae to grasp the nettle sometime. Better here and now."

It was a crushing blow. Further protest might well lead to having his loyalty questioned, perhaps even expulsion from the Party. Not only would he lose any chance of a political career; his present position would be snatched from him. He had been only too glad to accept the offer of paid employment when the shipyard made him redundant at the start of the year – with a salary provided from funds supplied by Moscow. But there was a downside. Stan had emphasised how difficult it had been to argue the case for a deputy. The implication was clear; total obedience was expected. His paymasters would tolerate nothing less. A single word from Robertson would mean ruin. The prospect of years of enforced idleness was too awful to contemplate. What other employer would be likely to take him on, with his reputation as a shop steward and troublemaker? He knew when he was beaten, and had to make the best of it.

"Just as ye like, Stan," he muttered sullenly. "What happens next?"

His mentor frowned at the hangdog expression. "See here, Iain," he said gruffly, "this is nae time for half measures. Ye hae to show a brave face, act like I telt ye. Why spoil it for a daft bee in yer bonnet?"

"Aye, but—"

"Nae buts." He drew a breath. A word of encouragement would not come amiss. "Listen to me, laddie. Ye've worked wonders, travellin' around the countryside to sow the seeds."

"Maybe that's so. But never here. No' in Broomburn."

"Gie me strength. Ye've spent these last two years, near enough, exploitin' miners' grievances, spreadin' the gospel o' workers' control, recruitin' hundreds o' new members for the Party. And ye've encouraged militancy – unofficial strikes and sabotage in the pits. Ye ken the result o' that?"

"Aye. Retaliation by the masters. Lockouts and police brutality."

"Exactly." Robertson chuckled. "When will they ever learn? They're playin' right into our hands. It's amazin' what a bit o' disciplined political organisation can achieve."

"Ye really think so?"

"Of course. The day o' union leadership toadyin' up to the bosses is nearly over. Nae wonder they're runnin' scared, now that real socialists are gettin' intae positions of power and influence. It'll no be long afore we turf the rest o' them out."

"And then?"

"Fine ye ken. The next step is Parliament – the last bastion o' capitalism. So ye see how important it is to win a majority in the House o' Commons. Maybe no' this time. This is just the start. You'll be one o' the first Communist MPs."

Iain pulled a face. "I wish I could share your confidence," he grumbled.

"Do I have to go over it again?" Robertson bristled with impatience. "Ye'll mind the present MP is standin' down?"

"What of it?"

"That means there'll be a clear run for new candidates. No' much chance o' personal loyalties gettin' in the way. I doubt if the Liberals or Tories will put up a show, no' wi' thousands o' new voters on the register. And if there's only one candidate on the Left, then we'll be home and dry."

"Naebody else to queer the pitch? Ye're sayin' ye've fixed that? How the hell—?"

"Did I manage it?" He tapped his nose. "I've no' been neglectin' yer interests these past months. I've been in touch wi' the executive o' the LMU."

"Lanarkshire Miners Union? Ye never let on about that. How did ye get on wi' them?"

"Just dandy, since ye ask. The county union is prepared to take you on as their candidate. That'll go a long way to ensure success at the polls. Labour would be daft to put up a rival. They'd only be blamed for tryin' to split the vote."

"Then it's a foregone conclusion?" He did not sound fully convinced. "In that case why d'ye insist I come to Broomburn? I still dinnae see the point."

"Oh, ye don't, dae ye? Well, let me spell it out. The union has set out their conditions before makin' any official pronouncement. Ye have to prove ye're worth backin'. They want a fighter as MP, no' a body that hides at the first sign o' trouble. This'll be yer test."

"So that's to be the way o' it?" He could see now how Stan had woven his web. There was nothing for it but to run the gauntlet. His head drooped in a gesture of resignation.

"Get a grip on yersel'. It's no' as bad as ye might think. It was a piece o' luck there was naebody here to see ye."

"How would that make any difference?"

"Use yer loaf, laddie. It gies us the element o' surprise. Forbye that, I've taken precautions."

"Precautions?"

"Aye. There's a van comin' to drive us to the village hall. I doubt there'll be a big attendance for a lecture on the evils o' capitalism."

"So what?"

"That's to our advantage. The union's district organiser will chair the meeting. Just as well he's on our side. He'll mention the change o' subject, and then sing the praises o' a worthy candidate to be the next MP. Only at the end o' his spiel will he gie out yer name. That'll be your signal to make yer appearance."

Iain gave an involuntary shudder. "They'll slaughter me."

"No, they winnae. No' if you play yer part like we agreed. The union man will have primed a few trustworthy souls to start cheerin' for ye. Everyone else will wonder what the hell's goin' on. That'll gie ye a chance to say a few words – then slip away afore anyone can catch their breath. The chairman will declare in your favour, close the meetin', and then report back that ye won them over."

"And the union will wear that?"

"Guaranteed."

There was a long silence. Maybe it was clutching at straws, but Stan's plan of action did seem to offer a glimmer of hope. Dusk was falling; they would reach their destination under cover of darkness. "I'll do it, then," he muttered at last.

"Good. Trust me. Just gie it yer best shot."

The honk of a motor horn announced the approach of a grocer's van.

"Right on cue," chuckled Robertson. "There's our transport. You hunker down in the back out o' sight, and we'll smuggle ye intae the village hall by the back door."

The journey was uneventful, and mercifully short, even though the driver took a detour to avoid the village square where a passing vehicle might attract attention. It was no joke to sit in a cramped position on a hard floor, and Iain was not sorry when the van pulled up in the gloom at the rear of the building, and he could tumble out to stretch his limbs before being hustled through a narrow door and into a dimly lit lumber room. There he was left to his own devices while Robertson disappeared to check that all was in order. Nothing was to be left to chance, he was assured.

Time passed. It was unnerving to be kept waiting in solitude, amid dark shadows cast by a single electric bulb, knowing that his audience was congregating just a few yards away. The growing hum of voices from behind the partition wall was proof enough of that. He tried to ignore the distraction, pulling out a grubby paper from an inside pocket. But it was impossible to concentrate on the speech he was expected to make; his eyes were drawn inexorably towards the closed door which, as he remembered only too well, gave directly onto the stage at the far end of the main hall.

"Glad to see ye're makin' good use o' yer time."

He spun round in alarm, then scowled to hide his relief. "Christ's sake, Stan. I wish ye wouldnae come in like that. It fair gies ye a turn."

"Did ye suppose it would be anyone else?"

"No, but ye shouldnae sneak up on folk. Especially when they dinnae ken what's goin' on."

"That's what I'm here to tell ye. I've had a chat wi' Yardley – that's the union wallah. He says it's a' arranged. There's a bigger crowd than I would've expected, but they seem docile enough. I doubt there'll be a problem." He held up a finger. "Hush, now. They're about to start."

The buzz had died away. The union official was opening the proceedings: his words came through quite clearly. He was full of apologies at the change of agenda, but the matter was urgent. A national election could be declared any day now, and it was vital to select a candidate who would carry the fight into Parliament. There followed a litany of praise for a young man, a former miner who knew the conditions in the coalfields, and would make an ideal choice. It was for the meeting to support the recommendation of their union and endorse his nomination.

"And now," Iain heard him conclude, "it only remains to introduce your candidate. I give you—" He paused for effect. "Iain Baird!"

That was the signal for Robertson to throw open the door. "Ye're on, laddie." Iain felt himself propelled onto the stage.

Slowly, hesitantly, he shuffled forward into the limelight. Every eye was on him: the sea of faces sent a shiver down his spine. As he tried to gather his thoughts, a feeble cheer went up from a few individuals – quickly suppressed as they found themselves surrounded and hustled away. A sudden cry of rage behind his back made him jump: he gasped at the sight of Stan Robertson struggling in the grasp of four or five brawny pitmen. He shot a despairing glance at the chairman: the official could only wring his hands in apparent disbelief. In vain he cast round for a means of escape.

"Baird! Iain Baird." An imposing figure was pushing his way through. Iain's heart sank. Though he had aged, there could be no mistake. It was Cha White – his father's best friend.

"Dinnae fash yersel'", the man called out. "Naebody will touch a hair o' yer heid – unless ye gie us cause, that is. A wee birdie telt us about yer wee scheme. That's how we had time to organise a warm welcome for ye – you an' yer sidekicks." He glowered malevolently at each of them in turn.

Iain could only goggle helplessly. Robertson had recognised the futility of resistance, and now stood quietly in the hands of his captors. Yardley cowered away behind his makeshift lectern.

"Ye creep in here like a thief in the night, try to fool us intae choosin' you for our MP," he went on, barely able to contain his suppressed anger. "That Geordie Baird could spawn a son like you. He must be turnin' in his grave."

"That's no fair." Iain found his voice. "I only want to put things right," he protested. "But you wouldnae let me. Ye've hounded me since the day my faither died."

"Hounded you!" White brandished his fist. "You'll never be accepted here," he hissed. "No' as long as I live and breathe. You're nothin' but a snake in the grass. That's why we decided to ask the local Labour Party to put up its own candidate. In fact he's here now. Come an' show yersel', Rob."

There was an immediate outburst of applause from the body of the hall. Striding forward was Cha White's son. Iain gulped in astonishment; this was the man his sister had married. He had always looked down on his brother-in-law as a dimwitted oaf, destined to spend his life down the pit. What did this numbskull know about politics? What possible challenge could he provide? It almost beggared belief to regard him as a threat.

The older White held up his hand for silence. His sardonic smile seemed to read Iain's thoughts. "At least he's an honest man. And you're no' fit to lick his boots." He spat out the words, before jerking his thumb towards the exit. "And now you lot can bugger off. Afore we change our minds. See ye dinnae come back. Or I'll no' be responsible for the consequences."

* * *

Glasgow
November 1922

Some were saying the crowd was close to a hundred thousand, others put the figure at twice that number. Whatever the truth of the matter, there could be no doubting that a vast throng had flocked to the city centre, braving the elements on a snell Sunday evening in late autumn. Unlike other occasions, however, this was not a massive display of protest against injustice: this demonstration was to register success at the polls, and renewed hope for the future. Two huge red flags, clearly visible in the glare of arc lights, adorned the entrance to St Enoch's station. Spilling out from the railway yard into Argyle Street and surrounding thoroughfares, the immense assembly was imbued with all the fervour of a revivalist gathering, joining the choir of the Christian Socialists in lusty renditions of popular songs, hymns and psalms, followed by the *Red Flag* and *Internationale.* Every now and then a cheer would go up as one or more of their heroes managed to struggle through to the station vestibule. Did their new MPs not deserve a rousing send off as they left to perform miracles – or at least make their presence felt at Westminster? The citizenry was out in force to see that they got it.

The election had come, and gone. The result, if not an absolute triumph for the Left, at least marked a sea change in national politics. The legacy of the Great War had bitten deep: the parties of the Right had no answer to the problems of housing shortages and heavy unemployment. Labour was now the largest party in Scotland, with 29 MPs returned, ten of these from Glasgow alone, and a similar number from neighbouring mining constituencies. The Prime Minister himself, Andrew Bonar Law, had almost suffered the ignominy of defeat in his own Glasgow seat. So now eighteen of these Labour members were about to board the night train for London, to carry the fight against poverty into the heart of government.

And he had no part in it. Iain Baird stared dejectedly at the scenes of jubilation from the shelter of a shop doorway. His humiliation was complete; the stigma of failure clung to him like a shroud. Why had he been dragged here to view the spectacle, if not to rub his nose in the dirt?

He turned to his companion. "Let's get out o' here, Stan," he muttered. "We've seen a' there is to see."

"All in good time, laddie. The show's no' quite over yet."

Iain lapsed into silence. It went without saying that it was all Stan Robertson's fault – a calamitous error of judgment, if nothing worse. But for the folly of that trip to Broomburn, Rob White would never have been put up to blight his chances. He had been ridiculed, mocked and jeered; the miners' union had withdrawn its offer of support; and at the polls the workers' vote had been hopelessly split. And to add insult to injury, the Liberal candidate had stood down, allowing the Tory to come through and win by a whisker. The bourgeoisie uniting to defend its interests against the common foe? Should Stan have anticipated that? Perhaps not, but he had flounced out of the count without a word of commiseration, only to reappear days later, with a knock on the door and curt order to fetch coat and hat, and come with him.

The older man seemed to read his thoughts. "Penny for them," he said quietly. "But ye'd be wrong. I brought ye here for a reason. It's no' meant as a punishment."

"No?"

Robertson ignored the glance of disbelief. "Your trouble, Iain, is that ye wear yer heart on yer sleeve. This is no' the end o' the world, ye ken."

"Really? It didnae sound that way last week. Ye stormed out o' the town hall in Hamilton as soon as ye heard the result. Ye didnae even stay for the speeches."

"Aye well, it was a disappointment, right enough." He paused a moment. "Maybe I was a bit hasty. There's been a deal o' soul searchin' these past few days."

"So ye admit losin' the vote wisnae my fault?"

"In the grand scheme o' things the Party didnae achieve the result that was expected. It's obvious our time has not yet come. We need to reconsider strategy in the light o' recent events."

Iain scowled as he recognised the formula. Mistakes made during the election campaign would never be admitted. Rather than that, it was policy to deflect attention away from any shortcomings on the part of the leadership, and thrust the blame elsewhere. Thank Christ the Party had failed miserably in almost all seats it had contested. One solitary Communist MP and two near misses in industrial towns on the outskirts of Glasgow was a poor return. Accordingly, it was all the more difficult to hold him to account for his own showing. It was small comfort to escape being cast as the scapegoat, but perhaps the best that could be expected. Wisely he decided to leave things at that.

"What about the Labourites that were elected?" he ventured to ask. "Most o' them are on the left o' their party – ILP, are they no'?"

"Independent Labour Party?" Robertson was openly contemptuous. "They might think they're the leadin' lights o' the Labour movement, but they're just reformists for a' that, tinkerin' on the fringes o' capitalism. There's no' many o' them claim allegiance tae Karl Marx. Mair likely the Bible, or Burns."

"How d'ye mean?"

"Well, it stands to reason. That lot ca' themselves the Clyde Brigade. Look at what they're sayin'. Take Maxton, for example. I heard him in Bridgeton just afore I came to pick ye up. *Socialism in Our Time:* that's his byword. Moral opposition to the government will show them up. Peaceful persuasion will win the day. Some hope!" he sneered. "The only difference between the ILP an' the rest o' Labour is that they think it'll happen quicker."

His companion nodded glumly. It was true enough. The sentiments of the new MPs owed more to Scripture than Bolshevism, more to the Scottish Covenanters of yore than to Soviet communism.

"And I'll tell ye somethin' else," he went on. "The ILP is only strong in the west o' Scotland. Everywhere else it's the constituency parties and trade unions that rule the roost. So ILP members o' Parliament will be a tiny minority. They'll need to toe the Labour Party line – or be muzzled and ignored."

"Ye believe that?"

"I'm no' sayin' a voice in Parliament winnae be useful. If they stick to their principles, that is. But I hae my doubts. The House o' Commons is like a gentleman's club. Labour will crave acceptance. Most likely they'll bend to the wind, allow themselves to be sucked intae the system. Respectability will be everything. The capitalists are no' daft, ye ken. Every so often they'll throw out a bone, so the PLP can salve its conscience. That's how they conquer and survive. And the workin' class is fobbed off wi' vague promises – sometime never, that is."

"PLP?"

"Parliamentary Labour Party, ye ninny. Ye should ken that."

"Of course." He gave a sickly grin. "Just jokin'. But there must be an answer, Stan."

"Aye, there is. But it's no' through a talkin' shop. No' on its own. Anyone wi' an ounce o' sense knows that. Words must be backed up wi' action. Violence is the midwife o' the socialist society."

"Ye've said as much often enough. But how is it possible. It's no' as if we're at war, or anythin' like that."

"Agreed. The armed struggle is no' really a starter. But there's other ways o' stirrin' up the revolution."

"Industrial militancy? We've tried that already. What else can we dae?"

Robertson tapped his nose. "That's what ye're about to find out. There's a body I'd like ye to meet. He's expectin' us, so we'd best get a move on." Abruptly he turned on his heel. "Mind an' keep close," he called back, before striding away.

His protégé was left to follow as best he could. The crowd was already thinning as people began to drift homewards, but Iain had to hurry to keep him in sight. Not till they reached the Trongate did his mentor slacken the pace.

"Gie's a break, Stan," he gasped, as he finally managed to catch up. "I might hae missed ye in yon mob."

"Ah weel, ye're here. No' far to go now." He pointed towards the murky gloom of a side street.

"Ye mean we're goin' down there?" It was hard to conceal his dismay.

"Aye, that's right. It's a regular warren o' closes and alleyways. Easy enough to get lost. But just the job for hidin' a body," he added slyly. "Come on."

The prospect was far from inviting, with the inky blackness scarcely relieved by the feeble glow from an occasional street lamp, or chink of light peeping from a window in the high tenements. Yet he dared not hold back. With a muttered oath he plunged after his leader. As they picked their way through a maze of streets his spirits drooped still further: he had almost given himself up for lost when Robertson at last called a halt.

"Here we are, laddie. This way." He felt a tug on his arm, and was steered through an opening and along an unlit passage. "Bide here a minute." There was the sound of a fist banging on a door, followed almost immediately by the creek as it swung inwards.

"Is that our young friend, Stan? You are most welcome, *Kamarad*." A flickering paraffin lamp gleamed in the darkness.

Iain peered suspiciously as a shadowy figure beckoned them inside. This must be the man of mystery he had been summoned to meet. His heavy foreign accent betrayed his origins. "Russian?" he queried.

"Eastern European, at any rate," came the response. "We should leave it at that. You have a sharp mind, young man. Come and make yourself comfortable." He led the way into a small, dingy apartment. "You will see we only have oil lamps. No gas or electric light. That is because we do not wish the authorities to learn we are here." He gave a short laugh. "Otherwise, your police might take an interest."

"This is Peter Petrovsky, Iain." His mentor made the introduction. "He is a representative of the Communist International." Iain winced at the strength of the handshake he received.

"I have heard so much about you, comrade. Please to sit." Petrovsky indicated a couple of chairs on either side of a small table. "Find a place for yourself, Stan," he added carelessly.

Robertson had to make do with a stool by the fireplace. "Comrade Petrovsky is on a visit to give us the benefit of his advice and experience," he said as he perched down uncomfortably.

"Yes, yes. Have you told our young friend?"

"Not yet, comrade. I was leaving that to you."

"I thought it was agreed that you would explain. Please to do so now. We are wasting time."

"Aye." He frowned at the implied rebuke. "Iain, ye ken that the World Congress o' the Comintern is meetin' in Moscow. Weel, I'm to go there. And you're to come wi' me."

Iain's jaw dropped. His eyes widened in disbelief.

There was a dry chuckle. "Rather more than that, comrade. Tell him, Stan."

"Ye see, it's like this, laddie. You'll no' be comin' back wi' me." He went on hurriedly. "It's a rare honour, ye ken. There's no' many get the chance o' advanced study an' trainin' at the Lenin Institute. Just those picked out for the top. A body wid be plain daft to turn down the offer."

"But why me?" He tried to grapple with the implications. "I'm fair gobsmacked."

"Your talents have not gone unnoticed. Is that not so, Stan? The struggle will be long. In consequence it has been decided to prepare a new generation for leadership. You are one of the first to be selected."

"Is there a choice?" It was all he could think of saying.

"But of course. The Party is always democratic." The Russian agent leaned forward. "But you have to choose now. Time is short. Preparations for the journey will be necessary. And you must be off within the week – both of you."

"Christ! That soon?" He blew out his cheeks. "How long would I be away?"

"Who can say? At least one – maybe two years. But perhaps the idea does not appeal. Or a position of authority on your return."

"It's no' that, but—"

"Ah. I think I understand. You have a young wife. And the thought of a long separation…" He spread his hands. "But that need not be a problem. She can come with you. Women have equal status in the Soviet Union. I am told she is a socialist, though possibly not yet schooled in the principles of Marxism-Leninism." He smiled broadly. "We shall teach her. What do you say?"

Iain felt his pulse quicken. He was being pressed for a reply. Sweat gathered on his brow. To be torn from familiar surroundings, spend years in an alien culture, endure a harsh climate, face unknown privations… it was enough to put the wind up anyone. Yet what was the alternative? To defy the wishes of the Party meant instant oblivion. He would become a non-person, condemned as a social reactionary. What chance of making his way in the world if that was to happen?

"Come, come." There was a note of impatience the voice. "Is there anything else you need to know?"

"No." For long seconds he hesitated, wrestling for an answer. Would a couple of years really be so bad? A carrot had been dangled before him: the prestige of graduation from the Lenin Institute would guarantee rapid promotion. And Morag would be there with him. With her at his side, free from the influences that were tearing them apart, they would make a fresh start. He screwed himself to reach a decision.

"I'll do it. I'll go to Russia."

"Good." A hand stretched out to seal the agreement. "Go home now. Tell your wife the good news."

* * *

"For the umpteenth time – no! Can ye no' take a tellin'?"

Her husband managed to stifle his growing impatience. "It'll be a grand opportunity. If ye'd only listen—"

"That's enough o' that," she snapped. "Ye've said yer piece. And I'll no' hae it."

Morag Baird bristled with indignation. Iain had been like a bear with a sore head ever since he had lost the election. In his present frame of mind it came as little surprise that he had scorned her offer of an olive branch – a suggestion that they bury their differences, if only for a day, and go and watch the departure of the Clydesiders, as the new Labour MPs were being called. Yet he had jumped fast enough when his master came calling – disappearing without a word of explanation, only to return hours later with the casual announcement that they were to leave for Russia. Russia, of all places! Her eyes glittered. Stan Robertson was at the bottom of this madcap scheme. Damn the man!

"But I promised we wid go." Now he was almost pleading. "I stayed behind wi' ye last time. And see what happened as a result."

That gave her pause for thought. Robertson had indeed tried to inveigle her man into a trip to war-torn Russia, to witness the unfolding of the revolution as he put it. Iain's refusal to go with him had led to imprisonment as a conscientious objector. She pursed her lips. Be that as it may, such considerations could not be allowed to affect her judgment.

"It cuts nae ice wi' me. That was back then. Times have changed now. Ye're no' likely to be locked up if ye bide at home."

"I widnae be so sure o' that." He gave a feeble grin. "Ye ken ye'd be welcomed wi' open arms. Look at yer friend – Helen Crawfurd, I mean. Ye'll mind o' her from the old days o' the rent strikes. Well, she was a delegate at the Comintern meetin' in Moscow a couple o' years back. Even spoke wi' Lenin."

"That's as may be." A flicker of annoyance crossed her face. Helen had indeed been a close colleague in the Women's Housing Association, fighting against grasping landlords during the war. But their paths had diverged when she became a founder member of the British Communist Party. "I dinnae see much o' her these days. She has her own furrow tae plough. Ach! What's the point o' arguin'? Let's agree to differ. You go if ye want to. I wouldnae stand in yer way."

"But we should go thegither." He was nothing if not persistent. "I telt them we would."

"Them?"

"Aye. There was another body besides Stan. Chap fae Russia. He said it was all about firsthand experience. We could learn how to do things by seein' what's goin' on there."

"How to build the socialist utopia?" She gave a hollow laugh. "Is that what ye mean?"

"Go on, then. It's easy to mock." He waved a hand in reproach. "Look, we both want the same thing. Right? I ken things are no' perfect ower there, but gie it time. There's bound to be setbacks along the way."

"I suppose that's your excuse for the famine in Russia. Millions dyin' o' starvation in the countryside, while the peasants are robbed o' their food at gunpoint. Is that what ye ca' socialism?"

"That's no' fair!" This was going too far. "Ye dinnae believe all ye read in the capitalist press, dae ye? It's a' part o' the conspiracy against the first workers' state. In case ye've forgotten, there's been a civil war in Russia – a war instigated by bourgeois reactionaries, and aided and abetted by foreign intervention. Nae wonder there's been some dislocation."

"Spare me the sermon. If that's what ye call the dictatorship o' the proletariat, then I want none o' it. Ye'll never convince me that good can come from violence."

Iain bit his lip in frustration. It was useless to argue further on the rights and wrongs of Soviet Russia, but perhaps there was another way.

"Your place is at my side. That's a wife's duty. You refuse to come wi' me. Well, I'll no' try an' force ye. But have ye considered the future? The pittance ye get frae Mary Barbour will no' go far. And I'll no' be able to support ye. I'll need every penny for board and keep in Moscow. So when the rent man comes round…" He shrugged his shoulders.

"I'll be out on the street?" She smiled grimly. "Thanks for yer concern. But I wouldnae worry ower much about it."

"Is that a fact?" It was hard to resist a snort of derision. "How d'ye make that out?"

There was no immediate response. Morag allowed her attention to wander round the shabby apartment. Try as she might to keep the place neat and tidy, she could never bring herself to regard it as home. She shook her head wistfully. It was far removed from the roomy flat they had enjoyed in Govanhill, but of course that had gone when Iain had been laid off at the shipyard. And this was the best that his new masters could provide – a down-at-heel room and kitchen in one of the poorest areas of Glasgow. With something of a sigh, she turned back to her spouse.

"Listen to me, Iain," she said quietly. "I've somethin' to tell ye. There's nae need for me to stay here. Ye see, I've a standin' invitation to go back and work for Miss Elizabeth – anytime I like. Here's my chance to take it up."

"Ye'd move to Edinburgh?" He gasped in disbelief. "Go back to be a nanny?"

"No' exactly. Wee Eddie would be at school most o' the time. I'd be more like a secretary – helpin' Miss Elizabeth wi' her business. Typin' and such like. The job wouldnae be much different from what I'm daein' for Mrs Barbour."

"And ye'd live wi' them? Ye seem to hae it a' worked out."

"That I have. So if ye're done, I'll be away to my bed."

Head held high, she brushed past him. He made no move to stand in her way: it was as if the ground had been suddenly cut from under his feet. His mind went blank as he slumped into his chair.

Alone in her room, Morag threw herself down on the coverlet. She felt drained, utterly washed out from the stress of the confrontation. What was the point of it all? Iain had never shared a bed with her, not since they had moved from Brighton Street. Rather than that, he preferred to make do with a truckle bed in the kitchen alcove. To avoid disturbing her when he came home late – that was the lame excuse. She had done her utmost to be a good wife to him, so far as her condition allowed. But he would never be content to accept that. Too dispirited even to turn down the bedspread or kick off her shoes, she lay motionless as the tears began to trickle down her cheeks. What hope for their marriage now?

"Morag!" There was a thump on the door. "We're no' finished."

Her heart jumped at the sound of his voice. What on earth could he want now? She decided to say nothing, pretend to be asleep. Surely he would go away and leave her in peace.

There was a loud crack as the door suddenly flew open; electric light flooded into the room. She made an attempt to sit up: there he was, lurching towards her, tugging at his belt, fumbling with the buttons of his flies. God in heaven—!

"So ye'd betray me, wid ye? Take yersel' away to Edinburgh? Poison the laddie's mind against me? Well, we'll see about that."

Before she could raise a hand to fend him off, he was on her, pinning her down, pawing at her bodice. She could smell the whisky on his breath, see the malice in his eyes. Blind panic gave her strength. She managed to free an arm, jam an elbow into his throat. Caught unawares, his grip loosened, allowing her to roll aside. It was only for a moment, but time enough to cast round for a weapon, snatch up the heavy brass candlestick on her bedside cabinet. He came at her again, but this time she was ready for him. In desperation she swung her club to deadly effect, striking a solid blow to the side of his head. There was a howl of pain as he reeled back, lost his balance and crashed to the floor.

How long he lay there he had no means of knowing. Dazed and bleeding, he drifted in and out of consciousness. He dimly recalled a face peering anxiously at him; someone kneeling by his side, probing his wound, feeling his wrist. Later there was a distant click of a door closing. He groaned feebly as he tried to struggle to his feet. Christ! His breeks were down round his ankles. Feverishly he pulled up his trousers, fumbled for his belt buckle. His head was spinning as he staggered through to the kitchen. Not a sign of her. Where the hell had she gone?

He forced himself to think. Her coat and hat were missing from the peg – a single glance told him that. There would be money in her purse… He snapped his fingers. Of course! She let out that she would go and live with the Lixmonts. That was it. And it was up to him to stop her. But how? Once in Edinburgh she would be out of his reach. The family would protect her – and had the means to do so. But there might still be a chance. She would probably be at the station to catch the first train in the morning. He only had to waylay her at Queen Street and… Bugger it! He punched his hand in exasperation. Any attempt would probably provoke a scene; perhaps the police might be called. And Robertson had emphasised the need to lie low, not draw attention to himself before they left for Moscow. Bad enough to have to confess failure to control his wife: he could just picture the scathing remarks. No, best to let sleeping dogs lie – for the present. On his return… well, that would be another matter.

Part II: 1925-1929

SIX

Unexpected News, Unsettling Events

Edinburgh
January 1925

Sir Edward smiled faintly as he was relieved of coat, gloves, hat and scarf, and allowed himself to be steered towards the most comfortable armchair in the room. The walk from Trinity across the frosty wastes of Inverleith Park had been invigorating, though now he would not be sorry to rest and recover from his exertions. Thank God his little subterfuge had been successful. His wife had declined to accompany him to his daughter's house in Comely Bank – as he well knew she would. Catch Hilda venturing out on foot in the depths of winter, he chuckled to himself. She would insist in coming by motor car, but he had been adamant. It was Shanks pony, or nothing. No doubt there would be sharp words on his return, but that could not be helped. What he had to share with Elizabeth was not for prying ears. Easing himself into the chair, he patted his breast pocket, as if to reassure himself that the missive was still there.

"This comes as a happy surprise, daddy. We don't often have the pleasure of a visit on a Sunday afternoon – at least not at this time of year. Now you must take something to warm you up." She fussed over him while her husband took the hint to pour a welcoming glass of sherry.

"True enough." He gave a rueful grin as he accepted the sherry. "I told your mother I could do with some fresh air. Much better than a snooze after the Sunday roast, don't you think?" He caught her eye. "Well, yes. There is another reason."

"Thought as much. Can't it wait awhile? I was in the middle of something. Nothing important – only a minor revision for the mag. But it must go to the printer first thing. I'm sure Alastair can entertain you for a few minutes."

"Of course." He looked round. "And I was hoping to say hello to my grandson."

"Oh, he's gone out for a ramble with Morag. I asked her to take him. Truth to tell, she's been looking a bit seedy these past few days. Probably overdoing things. I'm surprised you didn't meet them in the park. Oh well, never mind. They'll not be long. And now I must dash."

Her father half rose from his seat as she swept out. "Come and join me, Alastair. We haven't managed a proper chinwag for some time."

"Thank you, sir. I'd like that."

"I wish you wouldn't keep calling me 'sir'. After all, you are part of the family."

"Old habits die hard." He forced a smile as he took the chair opposite.

"True." There was no point in pressing the issue. "What shall we talk about?"

"What about your council work? You must find it stimulating."

"Well, it has its moments, I must admit. Most of my time seems to be taken up with providing legal opinions for various council committees. Unpaid advice, of course – they know what they're doing. I'm hardly ever in my own chambers these days."

Alastair nodded sympathetically. "And your son – Captain Lixmont, I mean? How is he getting on? We don't see much of him here."

"Hugh?" He frowned at the recollection. "Well, he has his own life to lead. Though I have to say he seems to have made the best of things since he left the army. Elizabeth has probably told you he's now a partner on the financial side of the firm. Heavily into investment trusts, or so I'm led to believe."

"Is that good? I'm afraid I know next to nothing about stocks and shares."

"Nor do I. But I do know when someone sails a little too close to the wind. Encouraging people to invest in foreign concerns of which they know little or nothing? Dealing in mergers and takeovers rather than putting capital into developing companies at home? It smacks of sharp practice."

"But if that's where the profits are to be made—"

"Oh, he's certainly coining the money. No question of that. He's recently bought himself a substantial property in the Grange. I only hope he's not pushing the boat out too far. It could have consequences – and not just for himself."

"I understand, sir." There was an awkward silence. Lixmont gave him a shrewd glance. He was far too acute an observer not to notice there was something on the boy's mind.

"You seem preoccupied, Alastair," he said gently. "Care to tell me? A trouble shared is a trouble halved, you know."

"Is it so obvious? Sorry to be such a wet blanket. It's just that I've had a letter from my sister in Broomburn. She tells me that they're about to emigrate to Canada."

"Canada?" That meant his kith and kin had decided to join the exodus – the thousands of Scots taking the opportunity to escape hard times by moving to a new life in the dominions overseas. "It must have come as a shock to you, Alastair. Were any particular reasons given?"

"Only one. The main colliery in the area is played out. Exhaustion of the coal seams; that's the official explanation. We knew the mine had been running down for years, but it's still a heavy blow. The remaining pitmen have been paid off and issued with eviction notices. And that includes my brother-in-law, Rob White. They sail from Greenock next month."

"I see. Well, as it happens, I do know something of the background. You will recall that my wife's brother is managing director over there. According to him, they have been hanging on by the skin of their teeth ever since the end of the war. But for the government subsidy the mine would have been closed down long ago. And now that imports of cheap German coal have been restored, any further extraction would not be worth the candle. The shareholders forced Semple's hand – or so he tells me."

"Was the situation really so hopeless?"

"Apparently. But look on the bright side. The coal industry lurches from one crisis to the next. The government can't go on giving handouts year after year. The employers demand longer working hours and wage cuts as the only answer to the problem. The unions threaten a national coal strike. Need I go on?"

"No. I hear what you're saying, but—"

"Canada may prove a blessing in disguise. The mines there are crying out for skilled men. There's a huge untapped potential just waiting to be exploited. A rosy future for those willing to take their chances."

Alastair heaved a sigh. "You make it sound attractive. Perhaps we should all emigrate. It would certainly make things simpler." Too late he recognised the slip. "Sorry," he stammered, "I didn't mean to say that."

His father-in-law looked up sharply. Evidently there was more to this than met the eye. He hazarded a guess. "Problems at work, Alastair? You don't often mention what you're doing at the SED."

"Not very much, since you ask." There was a trace of despondency in his reply. "Scottish Education Department? I seem to be constantly banging my head against a brick wall. I don't mean to sound ungrateful, but I often think I would be more use as a classroom teacher."

"Sorry to hear that." Now he was genuinely concerned. "I had no idea. Can you explain why? Might do you good to get things off your chest."

"Well, since you put it that way." The younger man paused to marshal his thoughts. "The intention of the 1918 Act, as I understand it, was to deliver the promise of secondary education for all. Yet the Department appears determined to thwart that objective. It's a case of taking one step forward and two back. The system is worse now than it was before the war."

"Surely that's an exaggeration. I admit there's had to be some retrenchment, but that's inevitable during a recession. After all, you can't spend what you don't have."

"Perhaps. But hear me out. The SED set up so called Advanced Divisions for post elementary education, but these are in existing primary schools or junior secondaries. Only those who win a place at a senior secondary are allowed to benefit from a full five-year course of study. And only they can take the leaving certificate examination. It's for the few, not the many. The vast majority of pupils are to be condemned as failures – early leavers without qualifications. What a waste of talent!"

"Hmm. Have you informed your superiors of your concerns?"

"Many times. But I'm always fobbed off with civil service jargon: *the time is not yet ripe*; *economic conditions are not propitious.* I've been hived off to conduct a long-term feasibility study into raising the school leaving age to fifteen. But nothing will ever come of it. It's simply a ploy to get me off their backs. No wonder I often think of resigning."

"I can understand your frustration. But it would serve no purpose to act in haste. The situation will improve, given time. My advice would be to stick it out. Does Elizabeth know of your feelings?"

"She certainly does." It was a voice from the doorway. Lixmont looked round as his daughter flounced into the room. "And I fully support him," she added, settling herself on the chaise longue. "Sorry I couldn't help overhearing. If Alastair wants to give up his boring job, then I won't stand in his way. We can easily live off my earnings while he finds something that really suits him."

"Your salary from *Bright Horizons*, I presume?" He chose to ignore the veiled criticism.

"What else? The mag is doing very well at the minute."

"Is it? Well, that brings me rather neatly to the main point of my visit." He pulled the envelope from his inside pocket and withdrew the enclosure. "Take a look at this. It arrived in the post yesterday. Perhaps you might care to let me know how your Mr Norman is able to write a cheque for almost five thousand pounds. I thought you were responsible for holding onto the moneybags."

"Of course I am," she snapped. "And what you say is impossible. Is this some kind of joke?" She almost snatched the folded paper from his hand. Then she gulped in amazement. Pinned to it was a cheque for £4972, made out to Sir Edward Lixmont as payee.

"And you will observe", her father continued, "that the attachment is a legal document – a form of discharge for me to sign and return, acknowledging repayment of all loans made to the magazine, together with the interest due. How do you account for that?"

"I – I can't," she stuttered. "It must be a mistake." Then her eyes narrowed. "Here, wait a minute. It's Nick's signature, all right. And it's drawn on our bank. But yes – I thought so. It's a different account number. He must have opened a new bank account. And I knew nothing about it."

"So it would seem. But it still does not explain how he came by the money. I assume the account is genuine and that the funds are in place. He would scarcely risk discovery in such a risible attempt at deception."

"I suppose not, daddy."

"Yet how can he be so flush?" he muttered, half to himself. "That's what troubles me. It's not three months since he came knocking on the door for more capital. And now he's offering to pay everything back, including interest, nearly a year before it's due. Can you shed any light on this, Elizabeth?"

For a moment she looked puzzled, then suddenly the penny dropped. "Of course!" She could have sobbed with relief. "I should have thought of this before. Nick was away in London this past week or so. He's due back at the office tomorrow."

"What on earth—?"

"Don't you see? He went to drum up new finance for his expansion plan – the English edition, you remember? He must have been successful – so successful he can afford to repay your loans."

"How very convenient." He sounded far from convinced. "You realise the implications?"

"That Nick might take himself off to London? What could be better? I'll be left to manage the Scottish end without his tiresome interference."

"Possibly. But that's not the point. If I accept payment, and I don't see how I can refuse—"

"Well, then?"

"It means we have no further hold over him. He can do what he likes with the publication."

"Oh, fiddlesticks! Why would he do anything, daddy? Our circulation is going up in leaps and bounds. We're making good profits. Why would he risk that?"

"I don't know. But you'd better tackle your Mr Norman. Find out what's going on."

"We'll do that, daddy. Morag and I will beard the lion in his den first thing tomorrow morning."

"That would be advisable." He rose to his feet. "And now I'd best be on my way. It'll be getting dark soon. I'll pass on your regrets at missing your mother. Need to oil the wheels, you know."

"Grandpa!" A sturdy ten-year old boy came bounding into the room. "Cook said you were here. We came in by the back door." Remembering his manners, he solemnly shook hands with his grandfather. "We've been exploring the Water of Leith. We got as far as St Bernard's Well," he added proudly. "Auntie Morag says I've to have a glass of hot milk to keep out the cold."

"Then you'd best go and have it." He glanced towards the doorway. Another figure was hovering in the background. "Good afternoon, Morag. How are you? Elizabeth tells me you've been a little under the weather."

"Good afternoon, Sir Edward. It's nothin'. No' worth botherin' about." She backed away in confusion. "Please excuse me." The others were left staring blankly as she disappeared from view.

Five minutes later, after handing Eddie a ten-shilling note for his savings bank, Lixmont belatedly took his leave. That look on Morag's face – furtive, almost haunted. Surely it betokened more than just a slight indisposition.

* * *

"This is where you've hidden yourself, Edward. Whatever are you doing?"

Her husband looked up guiltily. "Just finishing this letter, Hilda. It's for the Ways and Means Committee."

"Just as I thought." She advanced into his study. "Then you admit it? You know my views on keeping the Sabbath."

"Needs must, my dear." He sighed wearily. "It's just that I had forgotten this submission for the committee. And it meets tomorrow. *Mea culpa*, and all that."

"Is that all you can say, Edward?" She refused to be appeased. "You never think of me, do you? It's all very well when I'm left on my own while you gad off to visit your daughter. Then you decide to abandon me all evening while you immerse yourself on Corporation business. And on a rest day, too. It's unforgivable."

"Be fair, Hilda. It was only for an hour or so. I imagined you would be quite happy to listen to the music on the wireless." He gave her a shrewd glance. "By the way, the committee chairman has expressed his gratitude for all the help I'm giving him in what is quite a thorny issue. And he is very influential when it comes to the selection of bailies."

"Oh!" There was a sudden intake of breath. "And your name has been mentioned?"

"I believe it has cropped up." He managed to keep a straight face at her abrupt change of attitude.

"I see what you mean," she said slowly. "Naturally you wouldn't wish to disappoint your colleagues." She bent to kiss his forehead. "Well, don't make a habit of it. I'll bid you goodnight, then."

Lixmont permitted himself a faint grin as the door closed behind her. The honorary title of bailie was sparingly awarded, and then generally only to senior councillors for outstanding service over many years. But it conferred high status, publicly marked by the erection of an ornamental lamppost outside the recipient's domicile. That would certainly flatter her vanity, he muttered to himself as he returned to the papers on his desk.

Half an hour later his task was done. Now he could lay aside his pen and enjoy a well-earned dram before retiring for the night. It had been a ticklish problem, involving the purchase of land for council housing, but he could take satisfaction in finding a neat solution. There could be no objection to the council building properties for rent, so long as the tenants were drawn from the more respectable working class – those who could afford to pay at a realistic rate, which would allow the city to recoup most of its expenditure. It would start to make inroads into the housing shortage, and allow demolition of some of the worst slums. Few could deny that was in the public interest.

He rose from his seat and reached for the tantalus on the sideboard. It had been legislation passed by the late Labour government that had made public ownership possible. About the only thing it had managed to achieve, he could not help thinking, though of course as a minority administration, dependent on Liberal support, it had only lasted nine months. It was a rum do, however, the way Ramsay MacDonald and his ilk had been turned out – vilified in a press campaign for pandering to Soviet Russia. To use a *Red scare* as an election issue to whip up anti-Labour sentiment somehow seemed to be punching below the belt.

His thoughts drifted closer to home as he poked the fire back into life and settled himself into his easy chair. That Alastair was miserable in his post at the SED was now patently obvious: he blamed himself for not reading the signs earlier. Perhaps it was a mistake to have induced him to take up an administrative position. The lad was an idealist, uncomfortable with the compromises demanded in public affairs. But he had the will to stick it out. He would see things through for the sake of his family, if not himself. As for Morag... well, there was a mystery to be unravelled. But he saw no need to press the issue: doubtless it would all come out sooner or later. Other matters were of more immediate concern. He took a pull at his whisky. That fellow, Norman, was up to no good, he felt sure of it. And if it meant a raw deal for Elizabeth...

The sudden jangle of the telephone bell gave him a start. Blast! If this was a constituent ringing him over some triviality... He heaved himself to his feet to go to the cabinet in the hallway.

"Sir Edward Lixmont speaking," he rapped, snatching up the receiver. "Please be brief. The hour is late."

"No need to be so formal, daddy," trilled a voice at the other end.

"Elizabeth? Why on earth—? Has something happened?"

"You could say that. I've found out what's wrong with Morag. I managed to worm it out of her this evening."

"My, that was quick work. Nothing too serious, I hope."

"I'm afraid it is. That's why it can't wait. Morag has had a letter from her husband. He's back from Russia and is demanding to see her. He's even fixed a time and place. Six o'clock next Tuesday at Queen Street Station. She's terrified that if she doesn't turn up, he'll come here and create a scene."

"I see. You were quite right to telephone." He thought for a moment. "On no account must Morag travel to Glasgow. There's no telling what might happen should she fall into that brute's clutches again. I'll go myself and warn him off."

"Thank you, daddy. I knew you'd say that. But there's no need for you to become involved. Alastair insists it is his responsibility to confront his brother."

"Do you consider that wise? The scoundrel has a nasty temper. Things might turn ugly were he to be provoked."

"That's a risk we'll just have to take. I'm afraid he's quite determined to keep the appointment himself."

"A badge of honour, I suppose. Well, I can't fault Alastair for his spirit. I'd like to have a word with him if I may. Could you call him to the phone, please?"

There was a brief delay before he heard the sound of approaching footsteps. "Good evening, sir. Elizabeth tells me you would like to speak to me. I can guess the reason, but with all due respect, nothing could induce me not to keep that meeting."

"Are you sure this is the right course of action?"

"Absolutely. In fact it will enable me to kill two birds with one stone. I had already decided I must pay a visit to my sister as soon as possible. I'll take a day's leave of absence to do that, and then return by way of Glasgow."

"Well, far be it for me to dissuade you from what you consider to be your duty." He paused to take stock. "Is Elizabeth still in the room?"

"No. She's gone to check that Eddie is asleep."

"Good. What I have to say must go no further – not even to your wife." He had hoped it would not come to this, but his son-in-law could not be permitted to put himself in danger without some means of protection.

"If you insist, sir. But Elizabeth and I have no secrets."

"Then in this case you must make an exception. Now listen, Alastair. I have information regarding your brother which may be of some assistance. I have evidence, written evidence, that Iain Baird is, or has been, a police spy, working for the authorities. Were this to be made known to his associates in the Communist Party, things would go very badly for him."

Alastair gasped in amazement. What he was hearing almost beggared belief.

"I can feel for you, my boy. But it's quite true. The proof is in the form of a logbook written by his – handler, I think you might call him. There is no need for you to know how it came to be in my possession, but you are at liberty to inform your brother that you have learnt of the contents. I have already had cause to make him aware of this knowledge on a previous occasion. However distasteful, you must not hesitate to do the same if he refuses to see sense."

"Thank you, sir. But I pray it won't come to that. This has come as a shock. But on reflection I can't say I'm altogether surprised. I can only express my regrets at my brother's foul deeds."

"Don't take it to heart, Alastair. I don't like making threats either. But it's as well to be prepared. Forewarned is forearmed, as they say. Oh, by the way, there's another little snippet of information to might care to hear. You remember your medical for recall to the army back in '18?"

"I do. What of it?"

"Apparently you were denounced to the security services as an agent for the Bolsheviks."

"But that's preposterous. I was nothing of the kind. Oh!" He gave a start. "You're saying Iain was responsible?"

"Yes. He made a false accusation. He was prepared to sacrifice you to save his own neck. I trust you'll remember that on Tuesday. I'll ring off now. Goodnight. And good luck."

He replaced the receiver on its hook and turned away. Was it fair to reveal the full extent of his brother's perfidy? No doubt Alastair was terribly upset. But if the news helped stiffen his resolve… One thing was certain. Iain Baird's hash had to be settled once and for all.

* * *

The two women walked briskly along the road leading through the bustling suburb of Stockbridge. Little was said, each apparently wrapped in her own thoughts. Now that their charge had been delivered to school, inconsequential chatter had given way to an uneasy silence.

Morag Baird was only too aware of the debt owed to her companion. Welcomed with open arms after a desperate flight from an abusive husband, she had found a refuge to recover her sense of self-worth. Over the last two years she had been offered employment to gladden her heart, not only in renewing her relationship with little Eddie, but also in acting as a personal assistant to her sister-in-law, helping out with the magazine. Was all this to be spoiled by the dark shadow cast by the return of her husband? There was relief to be had in knowing that she could depend on the family's protection, but she was far from comfortable at Alastair's insistence on taking up the cudgel on her behalf. She bit her lip in frustration at having allowed herself to be persuaded.

"Cheer up, Morag." They had almost reached the offices of *Bright Horizons* before Elizabeth broke the ice. She felt it her duty to keep a brave face, despite her qualms about Alastair's impending confrontation with his brother. "I can guess how you must be feeling. But there's no need to reproach yourself. I'm not sorry I wangled the story out of you. Or informed my father and Alastair. Families share their troubles. And you are part of the family, whether you like it or not. You could never tackle that man on your own."

"But Alastair—"

"Alastair knows the score. And nothing will stop him once he's decided on a course of action. Besides, I've a notion he's got some wrinkle up his sleeve."

"Ye dinnae believe that, do ye? Iain will eat him alive. And it'll be my fault." She choked back the tears. "I should fight my ain battles."

Elizabeth could feel for her obvious distress. "You really imagine you could talk him round? After the way he's treated you?" She smiled fondly. "You still care about him, don't you?"

"Aye, I dae. Damn him!"

"Leave it at that." She passed over her handkerchief. "Here, dry your eyes. What can't be cured must be endured. The future can wait for another day. In the meantime, we've a bone to pick with our Nick Norman. So let's get to it." She pushed firmly on the swing door and they swept into their place of work.

Alison Brodie was at her post in the reception area, but there was no sign of anyone else. Elizabeth pursed her lips. "Is your lord and master at home, Alison? I need to have a word with him."

"Sorry to disappoint you." She smiled at the woman she had once regarded as a rival. "He's not here yet. But I expect he'll turn up presently." There was a brief hesitation as a mixture of hope and anxiety got the better of her. "Do you suppose it's good news? About the move to London, I mean. I've always wanted to be part of a national publication."

"It's possible." Elizabeth was deliberately noncommittal. Her father's caution had cast doubts in her mind. Why would Nick hand back money before it was due? No matter how much he had raised from other sources, repayment of the existing loans made little sense – not when plans for expansion would be likely to swallow every penny. "Let's just wait and see. Catch it from the horse's mouth."

It was almost lunchtime before their employer deigned to put in an appearance. His assistant editor frowned as she laid aside the set of proofs she had been studying.

"Thought you were supposed to keep normal office hours," she grumbled. "I can see you've obviously been celebrating. Are congratulations in order?"

"You might say that." He rallied at the sarcasm in her voice. "And before you get on your high horse, I only had a snifter. Come into my office and I'll tell you all about it."

"I'm sure it will be worth hearing. Come along, ladies."

"Not you two," he growled, before Alison and Morag could make a move. "There's a few points I have to discuss with Mrs Baird first – in private." He pointed to the door. "The pair of you can cut off to lunch now."

"Is that why you tried to sneak past on your way in," murmured Elizabeth as they watched the others collect their coats and leave the building. "I know that shifty look, Nick."

"Not at all," he protested. "You're imagining things. I only intended to gather my thoughts before going over the details with you."

"Really?" She rolled her eyes in disbelief as she followed him into his sanctum. "Be that as it may, surely your staff should be in on the act as well."

"I thought I'd leave that pleasure to you. You can let them know."

"Why on earth should I do that? It's your responsibility."

"True enough. It's just that I can't stay long. I've a lot on my plate today."

"Is that so?" She took the chair opposite him. "I presume you've been successful in your quest for financial support."

"In a manner of speaking, yes. You know that I went to find backers in London."

"Tell me something I don't know. What happened?"

"Well, amongst others I spoke to the owners of *Women's Life*."

"And they're going to help you set up an English version of our rag?"

"I wouldn't put it quite that way. They're more interested in a Scottish edition of their magazine. That's why they offered to buy me out."

For a moment she was speechless, then chose to laugh it off. "You refused, of course? Good for you, Nick. I knew you wouldn't let us down."

"'Fraid not. It was too good to miss." He shrugged his shoulders. "I am no longer the owner, editor and managing director of *Bright Horizons*."

"I see. Well, that explains a lot. You opened a bank account in London for your ill-gotten gains. Then sent a cheque to my father from there."

"Got it in one. Though I object to your describing it as ill-gotten gains."

"What else would you call it? Never mind." She paused to consider. Nick and his louche ways would be no great loss. "I suppose they'll want the rest of us to carry on without you."

"Sorry." He shook his head. "I can't even offer that compensation. I did my best for you, of course, but they were determined to bring in their own people to run the mag. They may not even decide to keep these premises. They're sending up a team to assess its suitability. They'll be here tomorrow."

Elizabeth's jaw dropped. This went beyond the pale, even for him. "You line your own pockets, and leave the rest of us to fend for ourselves. How much did they pay you?" she asked bitterly. "Thirty pieces of silver?"

"Not quite." He gave a sickly smile. "Ten thousand. And after expenses and your father's loans, there's less than five left."

"But enough to keep you going for a while. What about your staff? Did you even consider them?"

"Of course. I haven't forgotten you." He took three envelopes from his breast pocket and pushed them towards her. "I've made up your salaries to the end of the month."

"Very generous of you," she sneered.

"I thought so." He chose to ignore the barb. "By the way, the new owners have promised to see to any outstanding bills – the printers, freelancers and so on." He rose from his chair. "Just one last thing. You might tell Alison to hand the keys over to the lawyers when she locks up this afternoon. The address is on her envelope."

"You seem to have arranged everything to your satisfaction. You're telling me this is to be parting of the ways."

"I'm afraid so. I must say it's been a pleasure working with you. So if there's nothing else—" He held out his hand.

"You don't get off that easy," she hissed. "We're to be left in the lurch, are we?" In an instant she was on her feet, shaking with suppressed anger. "I always knew you were a wastrel. And now you're a Judas. Stealing away like a thief in the night. You couldn't even bring yourself to face the others. You expect me to do your dirty work for you."

"I – I thought the news would come better from you."

"Coward!" Her eyes flashed. "But for the three of us, you would never have achieved anything. We built up your magazine. We supplied the ideas, and the hard work to carry them out. You did next to nothing, yet you reap the benefit. Is that fair, in all conscience?"

"What else could I do?" He wrung his hands in mock contrition. "It's just the way of the world."

That only served to sting her further. "No doubt you supposed Morag and I would be all right. But what about poor Alison? She stuck with you through thick and thin. She'll be devastated that you've walked out on her. What future does she have now?"

"Times are hard," he muttered lamely. "She'll just have to take her chances."

"And that's all you can say? Typical. You only care about yourself. If I were a man, I'd take a whip to you. But then you're such a pathetic creature, it's hardly worth the effort. Go on, then. Take yourself off. Crawl under a stone. You're not fit to be seen in decent company."

Nick Norman wilted under the ferocity of the attack. There was no defence against the lash of her tongue, the look of scorn and contempt written on her face. Pale and tight-lipped he was only too glad of the invitation to make good his escape. With the shout of 'good riddance' ringing in his ears, he fled for the door into the street.

* * *

Glasgow

Alastair Baird sat in sombre mood as his train pulled into the city's Central Station. Recent events had given him much food for thought. Less than an hour had passed since bidding a tearful farewell to his sister and her family, but at least there was consolation to be had in visions of a better future for them in Canada. There was no such silver lining to be found in contemplating the next stage of his journey. Iain was back from his sojourn in Russia, making his presence felt like some evil genie hell-bent on mischief. He had willingly accepted the task of persuading his brother to keep his distance, though he had grave doubts as to the outcome of any appeal to his better nature. And to follow Sir Edward's advice, to resort to what amounted to blackmail, somehow stuck in the craw.

On the other hand, he had been entrusted with a mission. To return home and tamely confess to failure was unthinkable, especially after the example set by his wife. Only yesterday all her achievements had crumbled to dust. Elizabeth had been cut adrift, sold down the river by that snake oil salesman. Yet far from giving way to despair, she had held her head high, determined to pick up the pieces and start anew, not just for herself but for her companions in misfortune. It made him feel ashamed of his preoccupation with his own trivial problems. His resolve stiffened. Morag and the boy must be protected at all costs. Compared with that, nothing else mattered.

He stepped onto the platform, glancing up at the station clock as he made his way towards the barrier to surrender his ticket. There was no particular hurry; he had ample time to cover the few hundred yards to Queen Street Station before six o'clock. No doubt Iain would be surprised to see him – though there was no telling how he might react on discovering the purpose of his visit. Then a thought occurred. What if they failed to spot one another? It had been over six – no, seven years since last they met. Much could have changed in that time. And amongst the crowds travelling home after the day's work they might easily pass like ships in the night.

In the event he need not have worried. Pushing through the throng milling round the ticket office, book and tea stalls in the station concourse, he hurried towards the platform where the Edinburgh train was due to arrive. If Iain was anywhere, he would surely be here. Suddenly he gave a little gasp. Surely that was his brother, standing by a pillar, his gaze apparently fixed on the track.

"Iain?" He called out tentatively.

The man half turned, obviously puzzled at being addressed by a stranger. Then recognition dawned. "Alastair! What the hell are you doin' here." He peered suspiciously. "Bit o' a coincidence, is it no'? Runnin' intae each other after a' these years, I mean."

"I've been paying a visit to the family in Broomburn to say goodbye and wish them well before they emigrate to Canada."

"Aye, I heard about that. Sad business that they've closed down the old Duchess. I would have gone mysel' to see Mary, pay my respects, like. But you ken the sort o' welcome they wid have dished out."

"Perhaps they would have let bygones be bygones if you were prepared to make the effort."

"I hae my doubts." He laughed harshly. "Anyway, it's a' in the past now. And you're just waitin' to catch the train back to Edinburgh. That's a' there is to it?" There was an ominous glint in his eye.

"No, not exactly. I was hoping for a word with you."

"So ye kent I'd be here? Well, ye'd best be quick. I'm expectin' the wife on the next train. And it's due in five minutes."

"That's just the point. I – I'm afraid she won't be coming."

"No' comin'?" Instinctively Iain clenched his fists. "Aye, I jaloused as much as soon as I clapped eyes on ye." He took a step forward, then managed to contain his temper. " My ain wife couldna bear to face me," he went on bitterly. "Sent my wee brother to try an' deprive me o' my rights."

"Listen, Iain. It's not as simple as that. Could we not go somewhere more private and talk things over?" He gave a wan smile. "Maybe there's a way out of this that's in everyone's best interests."

There was a brief pause, followed by a slow nod. "Aye, right enough, there's nae sense in makin' a scene in public." If nothing else, his training in the Soviet Union had taught him the merits of cool reflection, rather than rushing blindly into action. "I ken a wee howff just round the corner. We'll no' be disturbed there."

And he proved as good as his word. Once clear of the station it was only a minute or two before the older Baird gestured towards some steps leading down to a basement alehouse.

"No' many folk kens about this," he explained. "It's a good meetin' place when ye want some peace and quiet." He pushed open the door. "What's yer pleasure? My treat. Nip an' a pint? That's my tipple."

"Er – thanks." Alastair was momentarily taken aback. "Just a half, please."

"Suit yersel'." He gave his order to the barman, and pointed to a secluded alcove while he collected the drinks.

The younger man looked back uneasily before he took his seat. Iain seemed disposed to be friendly. But that in itself gave cause for concern. He knew his older sibling only too well to be taken in by false bonhomie.

"Here, get this down you." A glass was pushed towards him. "*Slainte*!" He looked up as Iain tossed back his whisky in a single gulp.

"*Slainte*", he muttered in reply, and took a cautious sip of his beer.

"So, how are things?" Iain gave him a sly smile. "Tell us about yer visit to Broomburn. I'm fair dyin' to hear about it."

Alastair reddened at the hint of mockery. So that was the game. His brother was toying with him, like a cat with a mouse. According to Mary's husband he had made regular appearances in the area in recent times, holding pithead meetings, spreading propaganda, recruiting miners for the Communist Party. But there was no point in giving way to anger. He shrugged his shoulders. "As you please. I didn't think you would be interested. But if you insist—"

"I'm all ears. Go ahead. I'll no' say a word."

"Very well, then. Rob White showed me round."

Iain scowled at mention of the name, but made no comment as Alastair launched into a terse description of what he had seen. Most of the pit cottages had already been abandoned, the doors and windows nailed and boarded up; the local co-operative store was closed and shuttered, the kirkyard neglected and overgrown – even to obscuring the headstone on their parents' grave. At the mine itself, the entrance was chained and padlocked; everything that could be salvaged had been removed, and the residue left to rust and decay, a grim memorial to the industry that had once been the lifeblood of the community.

"I suppose Broomburn will be all but forgotten in a few years," he ended sadly. "Just like the ruined dwellings left behind by the Highland clearances. Maybe it'll revert to what it was a century ago – pastureland for a few farmers."

"Could be. At least they'll hae plenty o' choice when it comes tae findin' byres for the coos."

"You think it's a joke?"

"No' I dinnae." His eyes flashed. "Naebody else wid touch thae slums. There's no' been a penny spent on them for years. That's capitalism for ye," he went on bitterly. "They take what they please, then just walk away. What do they care for the poor sods thrown on the scrapheap?"

"You would know about that, of course. I hear you've been seen in the district – on a number of occasions, I believe."

"How the hell did ye ken that? Rob White telt ye, I suppose. Well, it's true enough. But I havnae been to Broomburn. Ye ken what they think o' me there."

"So just what have you been doing?"

"There's nae secret. I've been helpin' wi' the Miners' Minority Movement."

"What on earth is that?"

"Never heard of it, have ye? Nor had the bosses – till we let them ken. Now they're runnin' scared. As are the gutless union leaders who winnae stand up for workers' rights."

"Really?" His brother's rantings were to be taken with a pinch of salt.

"Ye don't believe me? Listen. We're recruitin' members hand over fist in the local union branches – pitmen who want militant action to meet their grievances. My main job is to organise and run Marxist education classes."

"And you really think you can make a difference?"

"Not a doubt o' it. There's a national coal strike on the cards. And when it's declared the rest o' the trade union movement will come out in sympathy. A general strike." He almost gloated in anticipation. "That'll bring the capitalist state to its knees."

Alastair sighed and shook his head. It had all been heard before. "That could never happen," he replied wearily.

"Ye think so? We've already got rid o' the last lot in government – Labour an' the Liberals thegither. Yon letter was enough to bring it down."

"The Zinoviev letter? How do you make that out? Surely the document was a forgery."

"Aye – in a manner o' speakin'." He tapped his nose. "But it served its purpose. And I," he continued proudly, "helped write it. Then they gave me the task o' seein' the press got hold of a copy."

Now his brother was thoroughly perplexed. The affair had been a national scandal at the time of the October election. The Russian leader of the Comintern had allegedly written to the British Communist Party, confirming close links between the soviets and the minority Labour government, as well as passing on instructions to prepare for the ultimate class struggle. The missive had found its way into the pages of the *Daily Mail*, and it was widely believed that its publication had played a significant part in the return of the Conservatives to power.

"But why would you do that to Labour?" he protested. "You must have known it would result in a Tory landslide."

"Exactly. There's nae room for fellow travellers. Labour will never win anythin' worthwhile in Parliament. They only muddy the waters. The proletariat must be made to realise that communism is the only road."

"By means of violence and revolution, I presume?"

"If that's what it takes. As I said, the country will grind to a halt. I fancy that would dae the trick." He took a long pull at his beer, before setting down the glass and leaning forward confidentially.

"Ye ken, Alastair," he went on in a lower voice, "I've spent two years o' special trainin' in Russia – rubbin' shoulders wi' the top dogs, ye might say. And I've been entrusted wi' an important mission. I'm a name now in the movement – known and respected. I've been telt I'm likely tae win a place on the Central Committee o' the Party." His lips twisted into an ugly leer. "That's why naebody will believe ye if ye try to show that book to anyone."

Alastair's jaw dropped. The thrust was all so sudden, so unexpected. To have the wind taken out of his sails… He could only gape like a stranded fish.

"Auld Lixmont put ye up to it. I've nae doubt. He telt ye about Dunlop. Ye were to threaten me wi 'exposure if I didna play ball. Is that no' the case?"

There was no answer.

"Thought as much. He tried it on me once, afore I went to Russia. Cheer up, man, I'm no' blaming you. Maybe we can come to some agreement."

"What – what did you have in mind?" It was all he could think of saying.

"Well, let's see. I'm no' likely to come rampaging through to Edinburgh to demand my rights – no' unless I'm forced to, ye understand. The Party needs me here. I've a wheen o' work on my plate these next few months." He paused to drain the last of his beer. "I'd like ye to take a message to Morag. Tell her I'm sorry for the way I treated her. It'll no' happen again. I'm a reformed character."

"Are you?"

"Aye, I am. Russia taught me to curb my temper. I just want us to meet – anywhere she likes. And I'll no' object if she wants to bring a body along wi' her. I cannae say fairer than that."

There was a long pause before Alastair could bring himself to respond. "Very well, then. I'll pass on your request." It was a doubtful compromise, but perhaps the best that could be achieved in the circumstances. "How will she know where to get in touch?"

"It's still the old address. I got the flat back again. She kens where it is. Only tell her no' to take too long."

"I see. Anything else?"

"Naw." Iain scraped back his chair. "Aye, there is. I'd like a keek at thon book."

"Why?" He was not to be caught out a second time. "I thought you said it was of no interest to anyone."

"Nor it is. But I'm curious to find out what lies they've made out against me."

"Well, that will just have to remain a mystery." He gave a thin smile. "It's in my father-in-law's possession. And I have no idea where he keeps it."

"I'm sure ye could find out – if ye set yer mind to it. Tell him I'd be obliged."

Was this a direct threat? Alastair was left to sit and brood as he watched his brother swagger away.

SEVEN

A Nine Day Wonder

Edinburgh
May 1926

"Hullo Hugh. This is a surprise." He laid aside his newspaper and rose to greet his son. "We don't often see you on a Sunday afternoon. I'm afraid you're rather late if you were expecting lunch."

"No, it's not that." Hugh Lixmont gave a rueful grin at the hint of reproach.

"Just a social call, then? Take a seat. Your mother's having forty winks. I wouldn't care to disturb her."

"No need to trouble yourself." It was a voice from the doorway. Her husband rolled his eyes. Trust Hilda to sniff out anything going on in the house. "I just happened to hear the click of the gate and saw Hugh on the path." She advanced to give her son a peck on the cheek.

"I won't beat about the bush," he said as he sat down again. "I can't stay long. I was just wondering whether this damned general strike is going to take place or not."

"Well—"

"Of course it isn't," snapped his mother. "Mr Baldwin would never permit it. It's a direct threat to the government – a challenge to our democracy."

"Is this true, dad? It can't possibly happen?"

"I think that's a trifle optimistic, Hugh. I don't see how the Prime Minister can prevent it, not unless he's prepared to grant the coal industry another subsidy. And that would involve a considerable loss of face."

"These bloody miners! They make me sick." Hugh burst out in sudden rage. Then he caught his mother's eye. "Sorry, mama. I didn't mean to sound off like that. It's just that I can't stomach the thought of the country being held to ransom by a bunch of bolshie union leaders in the TUC. Their puppet masters in Moscow must be rubbing their hands with glee."

"No need to apologise, Hugh. I quite share your feelings. And I'm sure your father does as well." She looked pointedly at her husband. "What do you have to say, Edward?"

"Well, I agree with you to some extent. But there may still be scope for compromise."

"Really?" She sounded sceptical.

"Yes. Though there's no denying that the miners and coal owners have nailed their colours to the mast over wage cuts and longer hours."

"With the result that a national coal strike began yesterday." His wife was quick to follow up her advantage.

"True, my dear. But as I was about to add, I do not believe that the other union leaders have much appetite for calling out their members in sympathy. It's just unfortunate that they've managed to box themselves into a corner, so much so that they feel obliged to support the miners, possibly against their better judgement. If Baldwin could bring the extremists in his cabinet to heel, and at least offer a fig leaf, then perhaps this fiasco could be averted."

"Fiddlesticks, Edward! You're far too liberal in your views. The fault lies entirely with the trade unions."

"I say, dad." Hugh could see a tiresome argument in the making. "Hasn't the government made preparations to cope with an emergency? You must know what's going on."

His father gave a brief nod. "I wouldn't go that far. But it goes without saying that measures have been put in place to ensure essential supplies are kept moving. And also, of course, to maintain law and order and prevent civil strife. At the same time, so far as I am aware, the unions have done next to nothing to make their own preparations. The obvious conclusion is that, apart from the miners, their heart isn't really in it. They're well aware that in the long run they can't win."

"Well, there's a relief." Hugh blew out his cheeks. "You know how the financial markets can react. I've one or two business affairs that could sink like a stone if this lasts for any length of time." He recoiled at the sight of his father's knitted brow. "Sorry, dad, I didn't mean to put it quite like that," he went on hurriedly. "I bet you're in the thick of things, what with your position on the city council and your experience during the war."

"Tell Hugh about your role in the OMS, Edward."

"Yes, dad. I'd love to hear about the OMS. I believe it stands for *Organisation for the Maintenance of Supplies*."

Lixmont shrugged his shoulders. "If you insist." Taking his son to task was scarcely worth the effort. And the scurry to cover up his gaff was all too obvious. "No doubt you saw the name mentioned in the press recently."

"'Fraid not, dad. I wasn't paying all that much attention."

"At least that's honest. And perhaps not altogether surprising. The OMS has been in existence for some time now, though it was only decided to go public a few weeks ago."

"That would be about the call for volunteers, Edward. Can't you tell us more?"

"I suppose it doesn't matter much at this late stage. Very well, then. The OMS is a semi-governmental agency, with branches throughout the country, reporting to centralised direction from London. It's a network of emergency planning groups, linking together local authorities, business leaders and the civil power. My own responsibility lies with the arrangements for recruiting volunteers prepared to help with essential services." He looked appraisingly at his son. "Have you thought about joining up, Hugh?"

"Me! What good could I do? I've no special skills. I don't see myself humping sacks of grain or driving a bus."

"I wasn't thinking of that. You come from a military background. You've had experience in dealing with civil disorder. Ideal qualifications for the special constables, would you not say? Moreover, you own a large car. That would be an invaluable resource in setting up a flying squad to dash to trouble spots in the shortest possible time."

Hugh thought for a moment. "Sounds like fun. And it would do me no harm with clients were it to be known that I did my bit."

He was rewarded with a cold stare. "Fun? I'd hardly describe it as that. And I don't like to question your motives. But if you're really interested, you might call at the City Chambers tomorrow. Mention my name and they'll arrange for you to attest and be sworn in."

"Fine. I'll do that, dad. And now I must be off."

"Won't you stay and take afternoon tea, Hugh? We don't see nearly enough of you. And the rest of the family will be coming." His mother glanced at the mantelpiece clock. "As a matter of fact, they're due any minute."

"That settles it. I'll nip out through the conservatory, mama, if I may. Please give them my regards." He turned away and disappeared before she could raise any further objection.

"Well, there's your son for you, Hilda." Her husband gave a wry smile. "No time for his sister, especially since she married young Baird."

"He's not really to blame," she sighed. "Oil and water, I suppose. Perhaps it's for the best."

"Excuse me, mum." She looked up enquiringly as the maid came in. "Tea's all laid out in the dining room."

"Thank you, Agnes." Before she could say more there was a loud clang of the doorbell. "That will be the family now. Perhaps you might go and help with the hats and coats."

A murmur of voices in the hallway heralded the arrival of the new visitors. Moments later a sturdy young lad came bouncing into the room.

"Here's little Eddie. Come and give your grandma a kiss." She reached out to enfold him in a warm embrace.

"Not so little anymore, my dear." His grandfather stepped forward to shake him solemnly by the hand. "He'll be starting big school in the autumn."

"Yes, grandpa. And I've something exciting to tell you. Auntie Morag has come with us. She's paying us a visit."

"Here? In this house?" He looked up sharply. Elizabeth and her husband were waiting to greet him. Behind them, distinctly ill at ease, stood Morag Baird. Hastily he remembered his manners. "Come away in, Morag. I'm sure you are very welcome."

Nervously she still hovered in the doorway. He looked anxiously towards his wife. Hilda was sitting rigid, as though unable to believe her eyes. Of course, she had never really taken to that rascal's spouse living in her daughter's home, but really…

"Morag is my guest for a few days, daddy. You know how Eddie dotes on her." Elizabeth could not fail to notice the sudden change in atmosphere. She turned to her mother. "My sister-in-law was reluctant to accompany us, but I insisted. If you have any objections, mama—"

"I don't want to cause a fuss." Morag thrust herself forward. "I can leave. Or take tea wi' the servants."

"You'll do no such thing." The master of the house felt it was time he exerted his authority. "My wife was just a little surprised at seeing you again. You know the family will always have reason to be grateful to you." He crossed over to grasp her hand, before looking back pointedly at Hilda. "Shall we go through? I believe everything is ready."

"As you please." She rose imperiously to sweep past him. Her husband could barely suppress a sigh. It was going to be a difficult afternoon.

"Elizabeth, would you show Morag in? I'll just go and request Agnes to set another place." He beckoned to his son-in-law to wait behind while the others trooped from the room, then deliberately closed the door.

"You wanted a word in private, sir? I think I can guess why."

"Yes, Alastair. We haven't seen hide nor hair of Morag for over a year. And now she turns up out of the blue. Is she all right? I mean, is that brute of a husband mistreating her again?"

"I don't think so, sir. She seems cheerful enough. And what you say is not quite the case. Morag has come through from Glasgow on several occasions – just for a day or so. But she always insisted you should not hear of her visits. Why, I have no idea. Perhaps you should ask Elizabeth. She would know more about the situation than I do."

"Well, perhaps. But not in front of her mother. Has there been any sign of your brother sniffing around?"

"None. I'm convinced of that. He's kept his distance despite the hints he made when you asked me to meet him. You remember his demand over the notebook?"

"I'm not likely to forget it. But we agreed it would be impossible to give him any opportunity to lay his hands on it. That book stays under lock and key. It's the only means of protection we have."

"True, sir. But I've been thinking. It could be that Morag struck a deal with Iain. They did have several meetings, you know, before she left. Perhaps she would go back to him if he promised to keep away from the family."

"You mean she sacrificed herself for Eddie's sake?" He stroked his chin. "It's certainly possible. And it would explain why she was prepared to give up a cosy billet with Elizabeth. Yes, I do believe you may have hit the nail on the head."

"Well, part of the story at least. Morag would have no knowledge of Dunlop's journal. Not unless Iain told her. And I doubt he would do that."

"But can he be trusted? To treat Morag with respect, I mean."

"Who can say?" Alastair spread his hands. "But they do have genuine affection for each other, I'm sure of that. Much though it might be difficult to imagine," he added with a grin.

"Chalk and cheese, I would have said. However, there's nothing more to be done now. We'd best go and join the others before we're missed."

They entered the dining room to a stilted silence.

"Sorry for the delay." He smiled encouragingly as he took his seat at the head of the table. "I see Agnes has used her initiative without waiting to be told."

"So you didn't need to look for her after all," chirped his grandson.

"Caught in the act." He held up his hand in mock surrender. "There's no fooling you, Eddie. Truth to tell, I just wanted to consult your dad about a suitable gift for someone. Can't mention the name, of course."

"But it's not my birthday," protested Eddie. "Not for months yet."

"Why do you suppose it's for you? It might be for somebody else." Then he relented. "All right. We just thought we should mark your promotion to the senior school in some way." He winked at Alastair. "Now, be a good chap and help hand round the cakes and sandwiches. Hilda, would you be kind enough to pour the tea. It should be mashed by now."

It was impossible to resist his bidding, and he was not slow to follow up the momentary distraction. "I believe Elizabeth has some good news," he said casually, accepting the cup of tea passed to him. "Thank you, my dear. I'm sure she's dying to tell you of her latest venture."

"About the lease of the office in Stockbridge, daddy? Yes, all done and dusted. Now the advertising agency really will have the space to grow."

"And the curious thing," chuckled her father, "is that it's the same premises where she used to work on that magazine. It seems the new owners decided to give up the idea of a Scottish edition after all. I was able to arrange a considerable discount."

"You?" For a moment she was nonplussed, then the penny dropped. "You took out the lease in her name. And no doubt at your own expense."

"Well, I helped out. But dash it all, Hilda, look at the way she picked herself up after the fracas with that scoundrel leaving her in the lurch."

"That's as may be. You know my views on married women. Especially those of our class demeaning themselves."

Elizabeth bridled. Had she not laboured tirelessly to rebuild a career from the ruins of *Bright Horizons*? Had not her father himself suggested the solution? Newspapers and periodicals were full of advertisements for goods and services. Why not set up her own agency to provide the copy? She could engage with clients, assess their needs, and then commission the eye-catching captions and illustrations vital for a successful campaign. Jumping at the notion, she had started up in business from her own home and, aided by Alison and Morag, the operation had prospered. Morag was gone, of course, but others had arrived to take her place. And now it was time to expand, to set new targets for herself.

"You're too stuck in your Victorian values to realise that the world is changing, mama," she replied tartly. "Can't you bring yourself to accept that women deserve the same rights as men? And they are capable of running a business."

"Here, I say—"

"Don't interfere, Edward." His wife waved aside his protest. "All very well to think that, my girl. But these are not normal times. Have you considered the effects of this challenge to the country?"

"What do you mean?"

"Just what I say." She could restrain herself no longer. "Look at your visitor here, Elizabeth. What will she be doing? Lining up with the other strikers – shouting slogans and throwing stones?"

"That's enough, Hilda." There was real anger in his voice. "Remember Morag is a guest in this house. And your grandson is present. Hardly an edifying spectacle, I'm sure you will admit."

"Oh!" His wife subsided. "I'm sorry if I let my emotions run away with me. But I feel strongly about this strike and its threat to common decency."

"That's no excuse. You should beg her pardon."

"Nae need for that, Sir Edward. No offence taken." Morag was quite composed as she turned to her hostess. "I dinnae want to cause any unpleasantness, Lady Hilda. It's true I hae every sympathy for the miners. They were driven to this, locked out by the coalmasters for refusin' to accept slave wages. But I'll no' be on any picket line, ye can be glad o' that. I'll be daein' what I can to help them that'll suffer the most – the womenfolk an' their bairns."

"Bravely spoken," murmured Alastair.

"Aye, it'll be a case o' raisin' funds an' openin' soup kitchens. There's a rumour that the government has ordered local councils no' to gie poor relief to the families o' strikers. They'll be near enough starvin' afore this is over."

"And your attitude does you credit." Lixmont tapped the table in appreciation. "Would you not agree, Hilda?"

"Naturally I have no wish to see the innocent suffer distress," she sniffed icily, "but I must say—"

"Leave it at that," he broke in hastily. It was scarcely an expression of regret, but if it put an end to the sniping…

There was an unexpected tap on the door. He almost welcomed the interruption. "Yes, Agnes. What is it?"

"Excuse me, sir." The maid bobbed her head. "There's a – a person at the back door. He widnae give his name. But he's asking for Mistress Baird."

"Someone for me?" queried Elizabeth. "Now who on earth could that be?"

"I don't think it's you, Miss Elizabeth. It's the other Mistress Baird."

"Me?" Morag's head shot up. "I dinna ken anyone here." She hesitated a moment before pushing back her chair. "It can only be Iain," she muttered. "I'd best go and see what he wants."

"Stay where you are, please." Her host rose to his feet. "I'd much rather any interview is conducted in my presence – if you don't mind, Morag." He nodded to the maid.

Moments later a rather dishevelled Iain Baird was shown into the room, nervously fingering the cap in his hand.

Lixmont gave him a frosty glare. "We thought it might be you. You dare to show your face in this house."

Iain flushed, but stood his ground. "No' through choice, that's for sure. I called at yer daughter's place and was telt I'd find the wife here. I've come to take her hame."

"I see. And if she has no wish to leave?"

"That's no' your concern." He looked directly at Morag. "Listen to me, lassie. The startin' pistol could come at any time now. You're needed to help out – like ye said ye would. Ye cannae dae that if ye're trapped here. There's a train for Glesga in less than an hour. It might be the last one. I'm beggin' ye. It's no' for me. Think o' the weans."

"There's no need to for you to go, Morag." Elizabeth was instinctively suspicious. "You're welcome to stay with us."

"No." She made up her mind. "I ken where my duty lies. I'll come wi' ye, Iain."

"But what about your luggage at our house?"

"There's nae time for that now. It's only a bag. Ye'll no' mind if it's left till I can come back for it?"

"Of course not, but–"

"Nae mair to be said." She leaned over to give her sister-in-law a peck on the cheek. "Thank you for everything. I'll no' forget."

Eddie ran round the table to give his aunt a kiss. There were tears in her eyes as she nodded to the others, and followed her husband through the door.

Lady Hilda carefully folded her napkin. "Bring it on, Edward. We'll win, of course."

"Yes," he agreed gravely. "But at what cost?"

* * *

Glasgow

Iain Baird scowled as he stubbed out the embers of his cigarette and heaved himself to his feet. Why in God's name had he been ordered to remain in this damned place? Was all his good work on the Lanarkshire coalfield to go to waste? He would have much preferred to return and help direct events there, but Robertson had decreed otherwise; he was to stay behind and offer his services to the local strike committee. Like as not this was his punishment for daring to absent himself on the eve of the dispute to fetch Morag back. Now he found himself on a picket line, charged with preventing free movement of traffic on the Dalmarnock Road. A motley crew, he could not help thinking, mostly dockers and transport workers, but willing enough, and they looked to him for leadership.

A lorry had been halted, and the driver induced to step down from his cab. Baird trudged across the road: it was his responsibility to check the contents and ascertain that a certificate allowing passage had been obtained from the council of action.

"What do we hae here?" he growled.

The nearest picket jerked his thumb. "Claims it's just supplies for the hospital up the road."

"Ye don't say." He peered over the tailgate of the vehicle. "Looks like buildin' materials to me. Got a permit for them?"

"I dinnae ken anythin' about permits. And the stuff's for roof repairs."

"Ye need a permit fae the strike committee afore ye can pass." He gave the man a searching look. "Aw right, then. I'll believe ye." Taking a wad of papers from an inside pocket, he peeled off a sheet. "Lucky for you I'm empowered to gie ye a certificate. Only two an' a tanner," he added with a sly grin.

"Half a crown? But I'm exempt. Why, it's daylight robbery."

Iain smiled malevolently at the protest. "No' my rules. But ye'll need to fork up if ye want to move."

For a moment the trucker seemed disposed to argue further, but then thought better of it. Sullenly he fumbled for the necessary cash and produced two shillings and a sixpence.

"Thank ye, comrade. Now you can bugger off."

He gave a toss of the head as he turned away to retrace his steps towards the makeshift shelter on the corner of the street. The incident scarcely counted as even a minor victory in the contest to control the distribution of supplies. All very well to have the power to detain single vehicles; but what about a convoy determined to smash through any obstacle in its path? He could visualise the vanloads of police, perhaps an armoured car in the lead and motorcycle outriders on the flanks. His tiny force, supplied only with armbands for protection, would be simply swept aside. What was required was a mass of men, armed with pickaxe handles, together with a barrier thrown across the road to show they meant business. But no. The strike leaders would have it that they stay within the law and offer no provocation. Not that the police would be impressed: they could act with impunity, knowing they would never be held to account. Peaceful picketing? His lip curled. This was no way to fight a war, with one hand tied behind the back.

The sudden trill of a bell caused him to jump aside in alarm. "What the f—?" He swore as a cyclist swept past. "Ye nearly had me ower." His eyes glinted as he watched a familiar figure pull up, dismount and wheel his machine towards the lean-to. The unexpected visitor was far from welcome. No doubt Stan Robertson had come to rub it in, to remind him of his place.

"Well, well. So this is where they put ye, Iain?" His mentor grinned. "Ye look as if ye've lost a bob an' found a ha'pence. I thought ye'd be in yer element here."

"Did ye now?" Iain fumed with indignation. "There's no' much action in this neck o' the woods. No' when the General Council refused to bring out the shipyards an' engineerin' works. And they're champin' at the bit to get involved."

"Nae need to take the huff, laddie. I had my reasons." Robertson tapped his nose. "Ye're right, of course. Ye'd have thought Red Clydeside would have been first in line after what happened during the war. But the high heid yins on the TUC decided to keep them in reserve. Nae doubt to avoid scarin' the horses. They're to be called out next week if needed – maybe." The last word was laced with irony.

"And while they make up their minds, our instructions are to avoid clashes on the picket line," Iain sneered. "We're denied the weapons to fight back against police brutality. Can you no' do somethin' about that, Stan? You're on the Central Coordinatin' Committee."

"Aye, the Glesga Committee. No' where the real decisions are made. And even here I'm barely tolerated. It seems that members o' the Communist Party can make themselves useful at the front, but there's nae room for us in the corridors o' power." He smiled grimly. "Well, we'll see about that. There's more than one way to skin a cat."

"Ye've got somethin' on yer mind, Stan?" His curiosity was aroused. Despite himself, he felt his spirits begin to rise.

"That's as may be. It's the boys on the ground that'll make the difference – no' the spineless gowks on the General Council. They're desperate for peace at almost any price. Look at how they hung on till the last minute to try an' cut a deal. Mark my words, when it comes to the crunch, they'd betray the miners to save their ain bacon."

"So ye're sayin' we're in a fight with the TUC as well as the government? D'ye think we stand a chance?"

"I canna say that. We have to be realistic. The big guns are a' agin us. There's the army to back up the polis if need be. And warships in the ports to guard the docks. As for tryin' to get the message out—" He shrugged his shoulders.

"Well?"

"Think about it. The other side wins hands down. Ye think our voice will ever be heard on the BBC? Then there's Churchill's so-called *British Gazette* spinnin' out lies an' tales o' a Bolshevik plot. And what's our answer? Nothin' but the odd newssheet. How many copies o' the *British Worker* have you seen? There's talk o' a *Scottish Worker*, but I doubt it'll come tae much."

"Ye paint a pretty picture. Why bother to carry on if we cannae win? Ye'll be tellin me next that the Labour Party in Parliament is against us."

"Well, they're no' exactly for us. MacDonald an' his ilk are takin' damned good care to sit on the fence. Wringin' their hands an' deplorin' the violence. That's the grand sum o' their support."

"And it means the game's up, accordin' to what ye're sayin'?"

"Iain, laddie. Have ye forgotten what I keep tellin' ye? The war's no' over till the last battle's won. The pitmen will stay solid, even if a'body else is forced back wi' tails atween their legs. Their martyrdom will be our recruitin' agent. In years to come folk will remember our efforts – and the treachery o' Labour fellow travellers. The proletariat will flock to us as the only way to justice an' socialism."

His companion stifled a yawn. "That's pretty speech, Stan. But ye're no' on yer soapbox here. I wish ye'd keep to the point," he added peevishly. "Ye hinted at somethin' up yer sleeve."

"Aye." He gave a rueful grin. "Sorry if I was runnin' on a bit. Well then, here's the situation. Ye'll have heard about some o' the trams takin' to the streets again." Iain nodded. "Well, we're goin' to put a stop to it. Five hunner coalminers frae Cambuslang are comin' to strengthen the clampdown on the tramway depots at Ruby Street an' Paton Street."

"A mass picket, ye're sayin'?"

"Exactly. And I want you to meet them and—"

"Hi! You there!"

The rest of the sentence was left unsaid. Both men spun round at the sound of a new arrival bearing down on them. An armband showed that he was a courier – the main means of contact between strike HQ and outlying pickets.

"Is one o' you Iain Baird?" he asked breathlessly as his bicycle drew up alongside. "I was telt I'd find him here."

"Who wants to ken?"

"Is that you?" He was rewarded with a curt nod. "Then I've a message." He reached for the wallet on his belt. A folded paper was thrust into Iain's hand. Without waiting for a reply, the rider sped off on his next assignment.

"Anythin' wrong, laddie?"

"I'm no' sure." His brow furrowed as he scanned the writing. "I dinnae quite understand. It's – it's about Morag. It seems she's been arrested. Taken to Govan police station. Nae mair details." He looked up. "The note's frae Mary Barbour. They were due to go out collectin' for their soup kitchen. That's a' I ken."

"Probably some mistake. They'll no' detain her. Ye'll likely find her at hame when ye get back."

"I canna be certain o' that. I'd best go an' see what's up. Ye'll no' mind, will ye, Stan?" he added anxiously.

"Now? Right this minute?" His face hardened. "But ye've obligations here. Is that no' more important?"

"I ken, Stan. But—"

Robertson pursed his lips. It went against the grain to let young Baird off the hook, but the role marked out for him demanded total commitment. Any niggling resentment, any worries over personal affairs, and he might take his eye off the ball – and that would be to court disaster. Second thoughts inclined him towards adopting a more sympathetic attitude. There was time enough. The pitmen were not due before early afternoon.

"Ye ken, Iain," he grunted, "women will be the death o' ye. This is no' the first time ye put yer wife first. I've no' forgotten where ye went last Sunday."

"Ye mean I can go?" He sensed a weakening.

"A' right, then. Ye've one hour – nae mair. Now listen to me. Make sure ye're at Bridgeton Cross by noon. Wait there for the Cambuslang lot. You've to lead half o' them to Ruby Street. Show yer pass, and see they ken what's expected o' them."

"I'll dae that. And then I've to come back here?"

"No. Ye'll stay wi' them. They need to learn how to disable any car tryin' to get out. Now, off wi' ye. Ye'd best take my bike. Ye havnae got long."

With a nod of gratitude Iain seized the bicycle and shot away. Pedalling furiously, he covered the distance in record time. There was an armoured car outside the police station, together with a soldier in full kit on guard at the entrance. Ignoring the sentry's suspicious stare, he jammed his machine against the railings and dashed inside. In moments he was at the public counter, feverishly jabbing the bell to attract attention.

"Nae need for that racket. I heard ye the first time." A florid middle-aged policeman in sergeant's stripes appeared behind the partition. "What hae we here? One o' the opposition?" He pointed at Iain's armband. "Come to gie yersel' up?" he guffawed.

"No, I'm no'! Bloody cheek! Ye've got my wife banged up in here."

"Is that a fact?" The duty officer had seen all before. "And who might you be?"

"Iain Baird. And her name's Morag."

"Mistress Baird." He ran a finger down a page of his ledger. "Aye, she was brought in earlier. Demandin' money wi' menaces. Assaultin' a police officer in the execution o' his duty. She'll be up before the magistrate the morn. A custodial sentence, I wid imagine."

Iain gasped. "Ye cannae be serious. Morag widnae hurt a fly."

"No' my affair. So if there's nothin' else—" He made as if to turn away.

"Sergeant!" The call came from the inner office. "I'll handle this now. Show Mr Baird into the interview room. You needn't stay. I'll be with him presently."

Reluctantly Iain allowed himself to be shepherded into what was no more than a prison cell, with a high barred window, and table and two chairs stapled to the floor. "Bide here. Ye can smoke if ye like." The door closed behind him.

There was nothing for it but to wait impatiently in this rat hole. He sat on the edge of the table and reached in his pocket for cigarettes and matches. But almost at once the sound of approaching footsteps had him on his feet again.

A newcomer came bustling into the room. "Sit yourself down." He motioned to a chair. "Here, let me see to your fag." A match flared.

Iain stared warily for a moment before accepting the light. The man's suit of clothes indicated a detective of some kind. And – there was something vaguely familiar about his features.

"Good to see you again, Baird." Settling himself on the other side of the table, he opened the file he was carrying.

Again? Feverishly he racked his brains. Where the hell could he have encountered this copper before?

"Don't you remember, Baird? I used to work for Mr Dunlop. As did you."

"Ah!" Recognition dawned. This was one of the spymaster's minions – a regular at the safe house where most of their meetings had taken place. Judging by appearances he had gone up in the world since then. "But that was years ago," he muttered. "And Dunlop's dead."

"You heard about that? It's true enough. But the work goes on. And we never forget old friends. You might think you've been retired. But whenever we may have need of your services—" He smiled faintly.

"You want something now?"

"Let's say I might be in a position to do you a favour."

"Ye mean Morag?"

"Precisely. The charges against your wife are indeed serious. But it's possible they might be considered in a more charitable light. For example, had she been collecting willing contributions instead of extorting money—"

"But that's what she was daein."

"I doubt the sheriff would accept her word on that. But let me continue. Suppose a young and inexperienced constable was prepared to admit a possible excess of zeal in jumping to conclusions, and to concede the kick he received might have been an accident when your wife slipped..."

Iain's eyes narrowed. He saw it all now. "You're sayin' the charges will be dropped?"

"Yes, I think that might be managed."

"And in return?" This was pure blackmail, he thought bitterly, all part of a deep-laid plot. Trumped up accusations to ensure his cooperation. He was under no illusions. Saving Morag would come at a high price.

The plain-clothes man leaned forward. "We require information. What plans does your strike committee have to escalate their actions?"

Iain hesitated. "What makes ye think I wid ken anythin'?"

"Don't waste my time, Baird." The sudden harshness made him wince. "We know all about your communist activities." He tapped the folder in front of him. "Don't even think about playing the fool."

"A' right." This was no idle threat. Morag's fate lay in his hands. "I dinna ken much, but—" He breathed heavily. "Ye'll hae heard about the miners marchin' here?"

"We do have some information on that point. Go on."

"They're to form a mass picket at two o' the tram depots. I've to lead half o' them to Ruby Street. Nae trams are to get out."

"That's much better, Baird. Where is the assembly point?"

"Bridgeton Cross at noon. I'm to take them on from there."

"Good." The detective consulted his watch. "Just about time," he grunted. "Wait here."

He was back within five minutes. Iain looked up anxiously.

"All arranged. You'd better be right about this. Otherwise there'll be hell to pay." Then he appeared to relax as he resumed his seat "But you've got more sense than to play us false. You'd best be about your business now. You don't want to be late for the comrades."

"And Morag? What about her?"

"Case of mistaken identity. She's free to go. You'll find her in the lobby outside." Iain slipped from his chair and made for the door. "Just a minute, Baird. A word to the wise. Try and stay out of the thick of it if you can. We don't want you bashed on the head and thrown into a paddy wagon. You're no use to us if you land up in hospital or jail."

* * *

Edinburgh

"Excuse me, sir." The sole occupant of the tiny basement office looked up enquiringly. "Sorry to disturb you, but Mr Harkness would like a word."

Alastair Baird pursed his lips before nodding assent. A summons to attend the great man was a rare occurrence. He laid aside his pen and followed the messenger from the room.

It was all of a piece, he sighed wearily, as he traipsed up the flight of stairs leading to his new chief's grand apartment overlooking Queen Street Gardens. The recently appointed head of section was a stickler for the rulebook, that was for certain. Not for him to entertain any vision of advancing the cause of education for all. He was there to follow, if not anticipate, the wishes of the government minister. Since financial restraint was the order of the day, destroying any possibility of raising the school leaving age for the foreseeable future, then time and resources would be better employed elsewhere. The feasibility study, his project for reform, had been speedily shelved, leaving him to be reassigned to more mundane duties. Now he was charged with checking returns from local education authorities – a role far beneath his status as an administrative officer in the civil service. With some asperity he rapped firmly on the door and went in without waiting for an invitation.

"Ah, Baird. Good of you to spare a minute of your time." Robert Harkness smiled as he glanced up from his desk. He was invariably urbane and polite towards his staff; it was his preferred method of disarming opposition and gaining willing cooperation. But those who worked for him knew well what lay behind the genial exterior. There was a mailed fist for anyone foolhardy enough to press an argument too far – as he had already amply demonstrated.

"You sent for me, sir."

"Yes. Sorry to drag you away up here. I've been going over these accounts you've prepared. A very polished piece of work, if I might make so bold. Highly commended. That's the benefit of concentrating on what serves a useful purpose. Would you not agree?"

"If you say so, sir?" His mouth twitched slightly. "Was there something else?"

He was met with an icy stare. "There is something further. Our lords and masters are not fully convinced of the accuracy of these absence returns from coalmining areas. To put things in a nutshell, the feeling is that schools may be downplaying pupil truancy."

"Do you suppose that's likely, sir? Why would they do that?"

"To show sympathy for the families of striking miners. So that poor relief can still be claimed from the parish. I'm quite sure you realise that, Baird. I'm aware you come from a mining background."

"That is true, sir." Alastair drew himself up. "I have never made a secret of it. My father was a pitman. But it is many years since I lived in a mining community. I left that when I went up to university."

"No matter." There was an imperious wave of the hand. "Be that as it may, you are the obvious choice to undertake the task."

"Task, sir?"

"Yes. It has been decided to instigate an enquiry into this issue of truancy. Snap inspections of selected schools are to be carried out – beginning with those closest to home, so to speak."

"You mean schools on the Midlothian coalfield?" There was a brief nod. "And led by His Majesty's Inspectorate, I presume?"

"Not on this occasion. It is to be directed from this department. And you will act as my first field officer. I know I can rely on your impartial judgment."

"But—"

"The decision is final, Baird. You are to travel to Dalkeith, and from there visit a number of the surrounding pit villages."

"I see. When am I to go?"

"Today. Immediately. You should be back this evening. There will be no need to pack an overnight bag."

"But how am I to get to Dalkeith? There is little public transport available." At least he could feel he was on safe ground here. "Are you willing to sanction a motor car and chauffeur?"

"Out of the question, Baird." The look told Alastair he was clutching at straws. "You can take a train from the Waverley. I believe there is a limited service to the outlying areas."

"I don't deny that. But it's run by volunteers. How many of them really know what they are doing?"

"Really, Baird. The railway authorities would scarcely entrust charge of a railway engine to anyone not competent to drive it. There is no more to be said. Here is the warrant for the journey made out in your name."

Alastair still hesitated.

"Look here, Baird, I can appreciate that this undertaking may be distasteful to you. But you will obey instructions. You do not have to convince me where your loyalties lie. But others may have doubts." He held out the folded paper.

This was a test, no doubt of it. Was he prepared to put his career at risk? How would the family react to what must appear as a mere whim? Without a word he almost snatched the document and turned to leave. His eyes burned with a mixture of anger and shame as he quitted the room. He was still fuming as he made his towards Princes Street and the Waverley Station. So typical of the bureaucratic mindset to focus on trivia when the country was in the grip of a national crisis. But as his temper cooled, other thoughts rose to the fore. Had he gone too far in showing reluctance to accept the assignment? Would he be marked down as somehow suspect? Well, there was nothing to be done about that now – except carry out the survey to the best of his ability.

At the same time, he could not help reflecting on the appearance of relative normality in the life of the city, even though it was now more than a week since the TUC had called its members to take action. Shops were open as usual; there was little evidence of real shortage, even though it could not be denied that coal supplies were few and far between. True, it had been reported that detachments of soldiers had been sent to protect Portobello power station and guard the St Margaret's engine sheds. And the peace was occasionally disturbed by convoys rattling along the main thoroughfares, or strikers making their presence felt in generally good-natured marches and rallies. All in all, there were few signs of distress or anger; citizens were going about their daily business as though little was amiss. There was some comfort to be had in that. He permitted himself a wry smile as he hurried down the Waverley Steps to present his rail warrant at the station booking hall.

Travellers on the main concourse were much less numerous than usual, though it was apparent that some services were running. An obliging ticket clerk informed him that he was in luck – if he lost no time. A train for his destination was on the point of departure. With a muttered word of thanks Alastair dashed towards the platform indicated, through the barrier, and fairly hurled himself into a carriage, past an astonished porter who was about to slam the door shut.

A glance told him the compartment was unoccupied; he took a moment to catch his breath as a whistle sounded, the wheels began to turn, the light dimmed as the coach entered a tunnel. He moved to take a seat when suddenly – an almighty crack rang out, instantly followed by a terrifying shudder. He felt himself thrown forward as if by some irresistible force. Instinctively he threw up his arms, but it was no use: his head struck the panelling on the far side, his legs gave way and he slumped to the floor. As he lay half-stunned, he became conscious of a trickle of blood running down his face. The silence was broken by muffled shrieks of pain and shock. A cry of alarm went up. Gas! Pipes for heat and light must have fractured in the crash. And it would only take a spark…

It was a struggle to react quickly, to pull himself to his knees, fish for the strap to let down the window, stretch out trembling fingers to grasp the door handle. As the door swung open his senses were assailed by the hiss and smell of escaping gas. Coughing and retching, he managed to use what remained of his strength to twist his body and lower himself onto the track below. There was a stab of agony as one foot touched the ground: he had a sprained ankle – if nothing worse. He hirpled away, dragging his useless limb towards the patch of daylight that represented safety – perhaps life itself. But with every step his breath became more and more laboured. His head was swimming, his eyes stinging: he was choking from the poison seeping into his lungs. He tripped and fell, rose and tried to stagger on. Now he could hear the shouts of rescuers, glimpse the beam of electric torches. One more effort… A light shone in his face. Willing hands reached out towards him. Utterly spent, he collapsed into the arms of his saviours.

* * *

The patient's nose twitched; his eyelids fluttered. A jumble of recollections began to filter through his mind: lying on a stretcher, the blare of an ambulance as it sped away, the oxygen mask over his mouth, white coated figures poking and probing. Dimly he became aware of an anxious face peering down at him.

"Alastair, dearest. Thank God you're awake at last." Gently she restrained him as he made an attempt to move.

"Elizabeth?"

"Just you lie still. You're in no condition to sit up."

"But – I don't understand."

"You're in hospital, in case you hadn't noticed."

"I remember now. The accident." He passed a hand over his bandaged forehead. "How long have I been here?"

"You've slept the clock round. But that's all to the good," she said with a smile.

"I see. And you've been with me all this time?"

"Most of it. Though I did manage to get some sleep. The nurses are very kind. And daddy's been a tower of strength – dotting in and out. He should be back soon. Everyone sends their best wishes – mama and Hugh, as well as Eddie, of course."

"Hugh?"

"Yes. But for him we wouldn't have found out nearly so quickly. He was on the spot, more or less, when the crash happened. He recognised you on the stretcher as you were brought out from the tunnel. His first reaction was to commandeer an ambulance and tell the man to drive like the devil. Then he phoned to break the news. So here we are." She caught his look of dismay. "It might have made all the difference, you know."

"I suppose so. I am grateful and I'll tell him as much when I see him next. All the same, I can't help thinking there might have been others far worse than me. Perhaps they should have been taken first."

She squeezed his hand. This was no time to allow him to wallow in a fit of conscience. "Can you remember anything else? If you feel up to talking, that is."

"Not much, I'm afraid. I heard the bang, felt myself thrown across the carriage. I must have been stunned because the next thing I can recall is dropping onto the track and trying to drag myself away. Then I must have collapsed."

"Well, I can fill you in on the rest of the story, if you're interested. Some refuse wagons were left untended in St Margaret's Tunnel – whether by design or accident no one knows. Then the train driver ignored or failed to spot a danger signal and steamed right into them."

"Were there many casualties?"

Elizabeth hesitated. "It could have been far worse," she said carefully. "According to my father, there were only three fatalities. Several more hospitalised, like yourself. But most seem to have escaped pretty lightly. Some had breathing difficulties – effects of gas in the tunnel, so I was told. No doubt heads will roll after this, if it's any comfort," she added brightly.

Her husband grinned faintly. "Don't you believe it. The powers that be will want to hush things up. Even if there is an enquiry, any adverse findings will never see the light of day."

"If you say so, dearest." She looked up at the sound of approaching footsteps. "This must be daddy. Let's ask him." A familiar figure came into the side room.

"Ask me what?" Sir Edward Lixmont gave a broad smile. "I gather you're back in the land of the living, Alastair. Good to see some colour in your cheeks again."

"We were just discussing the accident, daddy. Your son-in-law doesn't seem to think there would be a public enquiry."

"And he may well be right. I doubt the railway company would be happy to admit that the engine driver was a manager from its Glasgow depot. Or that the signalman was a blackleg miner."

"How on earth do you know all that, father?"

"Oh, I hear things in my position, as you might well expect. And this is strictly between ourselves. Not to be repeated outside this room." He wagged an admonishing finger. "But that's by the board. I've been having a word with the quacks outside. They're very pleased with your progress, Alastair."

"Then I can leave now?"

"Not so fast, my lad. You've a badly sprained ankle. Fortunately it's not a break, but you'll still need crutches to get around. The gash on your head is not serious, but you've been concussed. The medics are not too bothered about that, but they are concerned you've been exposed to gas – especially when they learned of your pneumonia. They want to keep you in for another day or two for observation. Make sure your lungs are clear before you're discharged. Hard cheese for you, but it can't be helped."

"Grin and bear it, eh?"

"That's the ticket. If it's any consolation, I had a phone call from your chief at the SED. Very solicitous. He was singing your praises. Said you'll be sadly missed, but they'll struggle on till you're fully restored to health."

"Very good of him, I'm sure."

Lixmont frowned at the obvious irony, but he could make allowances. After all, the boy had been through a harrowing experience. Hastily he sought to smooth ruffled feathers. "I've another item of news I think you'll be glad to hear."

"What might that be, sir?"

"Well, I would hope to be in a position to give a more definite statement tomorrow. But it would appear the strike is on its last legs."

"You mean that the government has accepted the miners' case?"

"Ah! That would be stretching matters a little too far."

"What, then?"

"A compromise solution. With goodwill on both sides, it might work. Let me explain," he went on hurriedly, before Alastair could make a comment. "I have it on good authority that the strike leaders have asked Sir Herbert Samuel to act as conciliator. You will recall that he is, or was, chairman of the Coal Commission – an expert in the field. The TUC is now prepared to accept wage cuts in return for a further temporary subsidy to allow restructuring of the industry, together with a promise of no victimisation. A memorandum to this effect has been prepared and is to be sent to Downing Street. We can only trust that commonsense will prevail."

Commonsense will prevail. The words rang in his ears long after Elizabeth and Sir Edward had taken their leave. This was no compromise. Whether Baldwin and the government would accept their part of the bargain was far from certain. But he had no doubts how the miners would react. They would cry foul at the perfidy of the other unions. Abandoned to their fate, they would soldier on in bitterness and recrimination, till hunger and destitution drove them back on whatever terms the coalmasters might choose to impose.

EIGHT

A Blessing in Disguise?

Glasgow
August 1928

Socialism in One Country. Class against Class: these were the new slogans to be peddled, evidence of a change in policy from Moscow. By all accounts it was only to be expected that the victor in the power struggle to succeed Lenin would wish to stamp his authority without delay. The only surprise was that this was not Trotsky, as had been supposed, but Josef Stalin, a name barely known outside the Soviet Union. He had played a waiting game, keeping himself in the shadows, building up control of the Party organisation behind the scenes, while his arch rival basked in the limelight. Then, like a cuckoo in the nest, he had struck without mercy. The architect of success in revolution and civil war found himself outmanoeuvred, expelled from the Party, and banished to exile in Siberia. Now his deadly foe ruled the roost.

Neatly managed, Iain Baird grudgingly admitted to himself. Here was the sign of a cunning and secretive mind at work, an impression confirmed by the recent *Fraternal Advice* put out by the Comintern. Trotsky's view on the spread of Marxist revolution had been reversed: henceforth defence of what had already been achieved became the overarching priority. Rapid industrial development within Russia itself, together with the collectivisation of agriculture, was essential to ensure the survival of the first communist state. Only when the threat from monopoly capitalism was overcome could the march to world domination be resumed. Meantime, in the interests of ideological purity, communists worldwide were directed to sever all links with more moderate socialists. These were dismissed as reformists, fellow travellers, capitalist lackeys – to be condemned as *social fascists.*

So far as it went, news of the latest events in Moscow had not troubled him unduly. After all, previous twists and turns had made little difference in practice. But that was before the message he had just received from Stan Robertson. The rising star of the CPGB, Harry Pollitt, widely tipped as the next general secretary, was coming up from London, and was anxious to see them both. A matter of urgency, he had been told, and the interview was to take place in Stan's own house.

He glanced at his watch as he left the main thoroughfare to thread his way through the backstreets of Anderston. He had never met Pollitt before, but of course he was aware of the National Organiser of the Minority Movement, and his persistent demands for yet more communist infiltration into the ranks of the trade union movement. With mixed results, it had to be said. Now there were rumours of a separate communist miners' union. A thought struck him. Was this to be his opportunity? Had he at last been marked out for the long overdue promotion he had been promised? To be chosen to organise and lead the challenge, at least in the local area, would be a prize worth having.

For a moment his eyes lit up at the prospect, then almost at once clouded over again. What if it was no more than a pipedream? The Party was notorious for its long memory. And if there was anything held against him… He knew how fickle the leadership could be, especially to those who did not live up to expectations. True, his efforts on the coalfield over the past two years had not been entirely fruitless, but it was difficult to increase recruitment after the pitmen had been forced back to work, seven months after everyone else. Who could blame them, with blacklisting and reduced wages the order of the day? Even to attend one of his pithead meetings carried the threat of instant dismissal. Surely Pollitt must take that into account.

Perhaps so. But there was something else. Heaven help him if any hint of his action during the General Strike should leak out. To put family before Party, to deliver comrades into the hands of the police, would be regarded as the vilest treachery. He shuddered at the recollection of the look Robertson had given him on hearing of the baton charges at the tram depot, and his escape from the scene without a scratch. Nothing more had been said, then or since; but had the seeds of suspicion been sown? At least there had been no further contact from the Special Branch detectives. But what if they should come calling again? He tried to put it out of his mind. Why worry about something that might never happen?

His heart beat a little faster as he approached the dilapidated tenement building where Stan Robertson lived in a tiny room and kitchen flat on the ground floor. Passing down the close, he made an effort to steady his nerves. It would be as well to put on a brave face, act as though nothing was amiss, and hope for the best. Breathing heavily, he reached for the bell pull. But before he could ring, the door suddenly opened.

"I was watchin' out for ye at the window. Come away ben."

"Stan!" He managed a rueful grin. "I'm no' late, am I?" The door closed behind him. "Has Mr Pollitt no' come yet?"

"Been an' gone. He came early, since ye ask. Whizzed up in a taxi, wid ye believe? Kept the meter runnin', then buggered off in it again. Barely stopped ten minutes. The high heid yins hae their perks." He scowled at the thought.

Iain recoiled at the bitterness in Robertson's voice. The usual jaunty air of self-confidence seemed to have vanished. His unease deepened. "Somethin' up, Stan? Ye look as if ye've seen a ghost."

"In here." He gestured towards the front room. "Maybe I have. Ye'll hae guessed that there's big changes afoot. They affect you as well as me." He flung himself into the shabby armchair. "Pollitt couldnae stay. He said I was to tell ye."

"Tell me what, Stan?"

"Brace yersel', laddie. Ye'll no' be seein' me again."

"Jesus! What the hell dae ye mean?"

"Just what I say. It's been decided I would be mair use elsewhere. It seems I've to go an' work for the Comintern. I'll be in London next week. After that, God kens where I'll be sent. Moscow, maybe – or Timbuctoo. I've nae idea."

"Sorry to hear that, Stan."

"Are ye?" He thought he caught a momentary gleam in the younger man's eye. "Dinnae you run away wi' the notion that ye'll be takin' my place here. There's nae danger o' that happenin'."

Iain started. "Christ! Ye cannae believe I'd think that," he protested. "What I dinnae understand is why they're daein' this to ye. A'body kens ye do a grand job here."

"Save yer breath. Yer soft soap cuts nae ice wi' me." His obvious irritation was unnerving. "Can ye no' work it out? The real reason, I mean. It's tae save money, ye dunderhead. The subsidy fae Moscow has been cut, pared tae the bone. There's nothin' left in the kitty to pay my wages – or yours either."

"You're sayin—?"

"That's right. I'm to hand ye a month's pay. And you're to be out o' yer house by the end o' the week – you and yer missus."

"But – it's no' fair." It was hard to take it in. "Did ye no' remind Pollitt o' the work I've done on the coalfield?"

"Ye might be sure o' that." He gave a shrug. "But he didna seem over impressed. It was all ancient history, so he said. It's only the future that counts." His expression softened a little. "Look, Iain, this isnae easy for me. It's no' just yer job. Ye've been purged, expelled frae the Party." He held up his hand. "I ken it's just an excuse. They cannae afford to admit there's nae money to pay ye."

Iain's jaw tightened. He had steeled himself to hear bad news – but nothing like this. Why pick on him? Surely others who had contributed less should come before him in the firing line. His past misdemeanours were known only to himself, he was certain of that – or nearly certain.

"But did ye no' speak up for me? Have I no' proved my worth?" he went on in desperation. "They must ken what I did for the miners – encouragin' the militants to throw stones at the scabs, sabotage pit machinery, derail the trains carryin' coal. Does that no' count for somethin'?"

"I did what I could. But I'm no' exactly flavour o' the month wi' them in London."

"Is that a fact?" His lip curled in disbelief.

"Aye, it is. And it's mainly down to you."

"So just how d'ye make that out?"

"There's a black mark against me – for no' keepin' ye in hand, it would appear. Ye've been soundin' off about the need for a broad left front, for socialists to bury their differences and join forces against the bourgeois tyranny."

"What of it? That's what ye telt me to dae."

"Did I? Well, that isnae the policy now. Ye've been accused o' bein' a Trotskyite. And ye'll have heard what happened to him."

Iain flushed. To be branded a follower of Trotsky was indeed the kiss of death in these changed days. "I think I see it all now," he muttered. Recognition dawned amid his anger and confusion. "Ye had to eat humble pie. And to save yersel' ye were prepared to sacrifice me. Is that no' the truth o' it?"

"And you're as innocent as a new born babe?" sneered Robertson in reply. "There's nothin' on your conscience?"

"I've done everythin' asked of me?"

"Oh, aye. What about the time o' the General Strike? At the tram depot? Hardly yer finest hour."

"Ye cannae hold me responsible for what happened there."

"No? You and I both ken ye ran away. I dinnae ken why ye did it, or why the polis just happened to be there, though I've a fair idea. But there's nae proof. I gave ye the benefit o' the doubt. I held my tongue."

Iain fell silent. So that was why he had been packed off to the back of beyond these past years. That was why he had been denied what he had been promised. A word from Stan would be enough for that.

Robertson seemed to read his thoughts. "What's done is done. Ye'd best take yer money." He pointed to the mantelpiece. "Mind and sign for it."

"Ye're sayin' there's nae mair to be said?" There was no point in protesting his innocence.

"Naw. Bugger off!" Robertson stared stonily into the distance. Iain was left to scrawl his initials into the tattered account book and sweep up the cash. "There'll be somebody along to collect yer keys. It'll no' be me, for I'll no' be here."

The words rang in his ears as he stumbled to the door. That the man he had followed and admired for so long could cast him out like a leper... It was the ultimate humiliation.

* * *

"So ye see, that's the long an' short o' it. I've been shafted." He looked over at his wife. "I suppose ye'll say it's my ain fault. Ye warned me often enough. And I didna pay any heed. Now I'm punished for it."

Morag sighed. It was hard to resist the mute appeal, but this was no time for glib words of sympathy. Thus far she had listened in silence as he poured out his tale of woe. That he had made his own bed was only too plain. More important, the result had produced serious consequences – for both of them.

"I'm no' blamin' ye for bein' taken in," she said. "Or no' entirely. I admit he's done a lot for ye. And he can be verra persuasive. But I've a'ways believed that Stan Robertson had ower much influence for yer ain good. Mind you," she went on, "I widnae describe him as a bad hat. It's just that the cause – whatever that might be – means everythin' to him. At the end o' the day friendship counts for nothin'. Ye're well out o' it, if ye ask my opinion."

"Go on, kick a man when he's doon. Is that a' ye can say? I'm turfed out o' the Party, lost my job an' hoose."

"Sorry, Iain. I'm no' tellin' ye this to show ye up. It's just to remind ye I've got feelings as well. I'll no' mention his name again." She gave a faint smile. "What's done is done. We need to look to the future, work out what's for the best."

"And just what might that be? Any ideas?" He curled his lip. "I cannae go back down the mines. I'll be blacklisted in every pit in Scotland. And I dinnae see mysel' gettin' a start at any shipyard. I was lucky to get taken back after the war. There's naebody now—" He checked himself.

"To speak up for you?"

"Aye, that's right. Leave it at that."

"Pity." She sniffed, as though not fully satisfied. "In that case I was thinkin' ye might be a miners' agent."

"What? Negotiate wi' the bosses? Ye're talkin' havers, woman." Now he could feel on safer ground. "These bloodsuckers widnae wear that. No' wi' my record. Nor would the unions, if it comes to that. They're a' for Labour now."

"And so could you be."

His head shot up. "What the hell d'ye mean by that?"

"Is it no' starin' ye in the face? Ye've been shown the door by yer so-called friends. They've nae further use for ye. But there's nae need to let that be known. Just tell folk that ye've seen the light. Ye've changed yer mind about use of violence as the only road to socialism. Then ye apply to join the ILP."

"Independent Labour Party," he spluttered. "That lot? Ye cannae be serious."

"Why no'? Others have travelled the same path. You're both after the same thing, or so it would appear, but they've a much better chance o' doin' somethin' about it. At least they can raise popular support, win elections. What has your team achieved?"

Iain scowled, then nodded his head. "Aye, I'll gie ye that," he conceded.

"Then what dae ye think?"

"Christ, you're quick off the mark!" He stroked his chin. "There's no' much o' an alternative, the way ye put it," he grumbled. "It goes against the grain, but – I suppose we could gie it a whirl. Nothin' to lose, at any rate."

"Too true. They'd be daft no' to snap up a man o' your calibre. Play yer cards right and ye might find yersel' put up for the toon council. Or even as a Labour candidate for Parliament. There's bound to be an election afore long."

"In yer dreams!" He laughed harshly, as though to drag her back to reality. "Ye're getting' ahead o' yersel', lass. It'll likely never happen. Stick wi' what's goin' on here and now."

"And what might that be?"

"Us. We're due out o' here by the end o' the week."

"I hadnae forgotten. Bide here a minute." She went into the lobby for her hat and coat. "I'll just away out an' hae a word wi' Mary Barbour, see what she has to say. Ye ken she's on the council. She widnae like to see an auld friend put out in the street."

Dare he hope? Iain was left to weigh the chances. At least one thing was certain: he owed nothing to the Party. Not any longer. And if his future was to depend on membership of the ILP, then so be it. To eat humble pie was of little consequence: allegiances could always be shifted elsewhere if things did not work out. It was in a more cheerful frame of mind that he rose to fetch bottle and tumbler from the cupboard. A wee dram would not go amiss while he awaited her return.

Nursing his glass, he allowed his attention to wander. If only it were so simple to free himself from the legacy of that damned notebook, the black cloud that had bedevilled his life for so long. Remove that, and the way would be clear to claim his just rights – access to his son. The Party could do him no further harm, nor could Robertson for that matter. But how was he to convince the boy's family? Old Lixmont might be tempted to brazen it out if he persisted in his demands. But two could play at that game. Eddie was of an age now to be made aware of the true identity of his father. The mere hint of disclosure should be enough to bring his grandfather to heel. It was not as if he was asking for much: to be treated as a favourite uncle as the price for his silence.

His thoughts moved on towards how it might be managed. Careful handling would be required; charging in like a bull in a china shop, as he now realised, offered little chance of success. Try as he might, he could think of no alternative; Morag would have to play a part. Without her good offices he could see no prospect of even arranging a meeting to plead his case.

Thank Christ they had recaptured something of the old relationship, ever since she had shown her gratitude at being rescued from the clutches of the law during the General Strike. Not that it extended to regard him as a knight in shining armour, but close enough to allow him to share her bed from time to time. But it had to be on her terms. Being obliged to wear a sheath was scarcely satisfactory as an outlet for his manhood; somehow it felt alien, like washing feet before removing his socks. She said it was reassurance against pregnancy, with all its dire consequences, and he had had to accept that. He could always find a willing partner elsewhere to slake his lust when occasion demanded. As for the present, Morag might be prepared to offer some consolation to cheer him up. And if the pillow talk afterwards should turn in a certain direction… There was a smile on his face as a rosy image formed in his mind.

"Penny for them!"

"Jesus!" The sudden intrusion made him jump. "I didnae hear ye come in."

"That's obvious. Ye were in a right dwam."

"Was I?" He made an effort to laugh it off. "Aye well, that'd be because I was dreamin' about how yon bastard Robertson kept me in the sticks when I should've been here wi' you."

"Awa' wi' ye. You an' yer blethers." She clucked her teeth in mock displeasure.

"Believe it if ye like." He glanced round at the mantelpiece clock. "Ye've no' been away very long. Did ye no' see Mrs Barbour?"

"Dinnae be daft. Of course I did. And ye'll note that it's been more than an hour since I left. Time enough for the business in hand while you've been snorin' yer heid off," she added with a sniff. "In point o' fact Mary was very glad I called. She wants me to go back and help her wi' her next campaign. The council elections are due next year and she says it's never too early to start."

Instinctively he felt his hackles rise. "Is that why ye went to see her? Ye didnae tell me that," he growled. "Ye ken what I think about you goin' back to work. It's just no' right."

"Needs must. And fine ye ken it. We're goin' to need every penny if you're on the dole. The money you got will no' last long."

"A good month or twa. At least till I can find somethin'." His voice trailed away at the look on her face. It went against the grain, but the cold reality was undeniable. "Aw' right. I cannae stop ye. But did ye get round to askin' about a place to bide?"

"I was comin' to that. Ye put her in mind o' the help ye gave the women durin' the war."

"Did she now? I suppose that would be about the rent strikes."

"What else? She said it was the best thing ye ever did."

Now he was being mocked. Had he not played a leading role in resisting the grasping landlords? The summons to court for arrestment of wages had turned into a show trial; the uproar surrounding the proceedings had produced a famous victory. The government had been compelled to intervene and cancel rent increases for the duration of the war.

"She would say that," he grunted. "But one good turn deserves another. Is she goin' to dae somethin' for us? Or was it just a waste o' time?"

"Ach, ye're ower touchy, Iain. Can ye no' take a joke? Mary wouldnae leave us in the lurch. Quite the reverse, in fact. She's come up wi' a nice wee place no' a mile fae here. No' in one o' the new council schemes they're puttin' up," she hastened to add. "It's on the list to be knocked down, but that'll no' be for some time. It's vacant now, and we can go an' see it the morn. What d'ye think about that?"

Not much, he thought to himself. It probably only meant moving from one slum dwelling to another – probably for the worse since it was due for demolition. But could anything better be expected? He nodded a reluctant agreement. "I'm sure ye did what ye could, Morag."

"Is that a' you can say? At least it's a roof ower our heids till you can find a job. And that reminds me. I ran into Jimmy Maxton at Mary's office – the MP for Bridgeton, ye ken. I was able to have a quick word wi' him."

"I ken who he is. Ye didnae need to spell it out." Maxton was leader of the ILP, at least in its Scottish heartland. Tall, cadaverous in appearance, a high forehead topped with a mop of unruly hair, he could never escape notice. His formidable powers of oratory were well known, whether addressing a crowd on Glasgow Green, or in the bear pit of parliamentary debate. "So ye spoke to the great man? Anythin' interestin'?" he added coyly.

"I should think so. He said he widnae mind a meetin' wi' ye when I told him about yer change o' heart. I fixed it for the day after tomorrow. That suit ye?"

"Do I have a choice?"

"No, if ye ken what's good for ye." She rummaged in her bag and fished out a slim booklet. "Here, hae a gander at this."

Iain frowned as he received the pamphlet. "*Twenty Points for Socialism*", he read aloud. "*By James Maxton*. Is this the new gospel?"

"Ye might say that. It'll dae nae harm to show ye've had a peak at it."

"Ye could be right." He stifled a yawn. "I'm feelin' a bit wabbit at the minute. It's been a hard shift, as ye might imagine. I could dae wi' a lie down for an hour or so. Care to join me?" There was the hint of a twinkle in his eye. "Gie ye a chance to teach me what it says, if ye can spare the time. Just like when we first met – and you roused me to stand up to the bosses."

For a moment Morag looked askance, then she gave a wry smile, shook her head and followed him through.

* * *

Introductions had been made; Iain Baird took his seat opposite the man he had come to meet. There were four in all clustered round the desk in Mary Barbour's tiny office. No doubt Mrs Barbour had remained to act as a witness, or perhaps it was as a referee to pour oil on any troubled waters. In any case she could hardly be expected to vacate her own premises. Morag had insisted on coming with him, possibly with a suspicion that he might fail to keep the appointment. He had indeed voiced doubts that it would probably be a waste of time, but she would brook no opposition. Now, here he was, dressed like a tailor's dummy in his Sunday best. The room was stuffy and oppressive, the stiff collar cut into his neck, and he was irked by the strength in James Maxton's grip.

"You've had an opportunity to look at my proposals for a better society?" The opening was abrupt and to the point, but Iain had expected no less.

"I have that. Best tuppence worth I've read in a long time." He laughed at his own joke, before taking note of the stony faces staring at him in disapproval. "I didna mean it like that." He beat a hasty retreat.

"I see. You think it's cheap as a means of informing the masses, but worth its weight in gold when it comes to action?"

"Aye, that's just right." He could feel the sweat on his brow. The ILP leader was known for his towering intellect; as a master of argument he had few rivals. On this occasion Maxton seemed disposed to let him off lightly, though there was an obvious sting in the tail – a warning to mend his manners if he hoped to create a good impression.

"Ye mustnae mind his snash, Mr Maxton." Morag sailed in to try to redeem the situation. "He's a'ways had a wicked sense o' humour."

"So I observe."

"Aye. But he's studied yer plan – every page o' it, I can tell ye that. As have I. We've discussed it atween ourselves. We're both agreed it's verra interestin'."

"That's a bit vague." He smiled at Morag. "Have you formed any other conclusions?"

"Well, I—"

"On second thoughts I think I'd like to hear your husband's view first." He fixed his gaze on Iain. "We've not heard much from him as yet."

"Gie's a chance." He gasped at being caught unawares. Truth to tell he had scarcely bothered even to thumb through that blasted pamphlet. All that came to mind was a jumble of words and phrases.

"No need to be backward, Mr Baird. You must remember something."

"Of course." Now he was being played like a fish on a hook. He tried to focus his thoughts. "Ye've a lot to say about the causes o' poverty. Underconsumption, I think ye cry it. A'body has the right to a livin' wage. And some industries need to be nationalised. Is that no' it?"

"In essence, yes. Though there's rather more to it than that. Let me try to explain things in a little more detail. Then you can decide whether it's acceptable to you as a path to socialism."

"I – I'd appreciate that." Was this an olive branch? Morag was flashing warning signs at him. "I hae to admit I found some o' it a wee bit hard to understand."

"Then we shall attempt to enlighten you. It is fair to say that the eradication of poverty is at the heart of the issue. At present the fruits of capitalism go to the middle and upper classes. Much of the excess profits are invested overseas, leaving British industry starved of funding. If everyone was guaranteed a living wage, then they could afford to spend on raising their standard of living – to the benefit of the home economy and end of mass unemployment. This is what I term the *Third Alternative* – between the violent overthrow of the state which is the aim of communism, and the gradualism and reformism of the Labour Party."

"And you really believe this would work?"

"Certainly. Naturally, basic industries would have to be nationalised for the public good, as would the Bank of England, to ensure funds were directed where they would be needed most. This could be achieved within a very few years; I have little doubt of that – once we have the majority in Parliament to pass the necessary legislation."

"We?"

"I mean the whole of the Labour Movement. The ILP is affiliated to the Labour Party. We have hundreds of local branches, dozens of Labour MPs in our ranks. Some say we are a party within a party. Though we take the Labour whip, we like to see ourselves as its conscience in parliamentary affairs. Keeping the others from straying from the straight and narrow, you might say," he added with a grin.

"Jimmy." Mary Barbour leaned over towards him. "Ye're wasting time. There's nae need to read him a lecture. Tell the man why he's here."

"Oh!" Maxton knew when he was being gently chided. "Sorry if I wandered away from the matter in hand. It's my besetting sin."

"Go on, then. I thought you told me there might be a job for him."

"That I did, Mary." He turned to Iain. "Well, Mr Baird, what d'ye think? Could you bear to join us in the ILP?"

"That would be just dandy." He perked up at the prospect of paid employment. "And I'd be proud to serve in yer – yer crusade."

"Well said." Was there a trace of irony on the remark? It was impossible to tell.

"Not at all," he managed to reply. "And – thank ye."

"Good. We'll see about your membership card in due course. By the way, I bumped into Wheatley and Kirkwood at a meeting the other night. You'll mind of them from the old days with the Clyde workers during the war. They certainly remember you."

"Oh, aye." Instantly he was on his guard. "And what did they have to say? No' much good, I take it."

"Quite the contrary. They were very appreciative of your efforts in the dilution struggle. First rate speaker, they said. Could hold a crowd in the palm of his hand."

"But? Nae doubt there was a sting in the tail."

"They were a bit peeved when you threw in your lot with the likes of Stan Robertson, I'm sorry to say."

"But all that's finished now."

"That's what I'm led to believe. For what it's worth, I've never objected to card carrying members of the CP joining us. In fact, you could be a positive asset in that regard, showing that we are a broad church, embracing a wide range of view in pursuit of a common goal."

He breathed a sigh of relief. At least there was to be no ill will on that score. "I'll do anythin' I can to help, Mr Maxton. What would my duties be?"

"Duties? Let's see now. I'd like you to prepare talks, address meetings, recruit new members, canvass votes at election times. Oh, and contribute to local papers from time to time, such as the *Forward*, and Wheatley's *Glasgow Eastern Standard*."

Iain gulped. "Is that all?" Even Robertson had never placed such a heavy burden on his shoulders. "You're no' askin' for much."

"I'm afraid that's rather in the order of things." He pursed his lips. "And the worst of it is that we can't afford to take you on as a salaried official."

"Then how—?"

"Are you to make a living?" The MP for Bridgeton smiled blandly. "You must be aware of how the Party has suffered from the fallout after the General Strike, both in membership and funding. We are only now beginning to recover some of the lost ground. But never fear, we'll find something for you where you can earn a crust – and carry out good work for the ILP at the same time."

"Oh, aye. And what might that be?"

"I'm sure Mr Maxton has somethin' up his sleeve," said Morag hastily. "What about the Coop Society? Iain's maw ran the store in Broomburn afore the war."

"I don't really envisage your husband as a storeman or shopkeeper, Mrs Baird. I would suggest his abilities lie in another direction. No, I was thinking of the Trades and Labour Council."

"Trades Council?"

"Yes. There's generally one to be found in each town or industrial area.

They've been set up to look out for the general welfare of the workers in the locality they serve. Union branches affiliate themselves and fund their activities. Mostly it's to arbitrate in disputes between employers and workforce, or in demarcation disputes between different trades in the same workplace."

"And ye suppose Iain would be suited to that?"

"I don't see why not. I spoke to the secretary of the Govan Trades Council." He hesitated a moment. "By a curious coincidence he remembered the name."

"Eh!" Iain's head shot up. "How the hell—?"

"It would appear that he had dealings with you during the General Strike. His name is Rab Youngston, if that's of any use."

"Aye, it is." Now he recalled. "I bumped into him once or twice. He supplied the men for my picket line on the Dalmarnock Road."

"That's what he told me. And it seems it's a mark in your favour. He didn't need much convincing when I asked him to consider you for assistant secretary. It would be daft to turn him down."

Point taken. This was a broad hint there was unlikely to be another offer. The strange thing was that it was difficult to place Youngston. He had barely come into contact with the man beyond the rigmarole of accounting for the certificates of exemption issued to vehicle drivers carrying essential supplies.

"Nae chance o' that." He forced an ingratiating smirk. "And – and thank ye kindly for yer trouble on my behalf, Mr Maxton."

"Jimmy – please. Now that it's settled. You'll have to negotiate your salary with him, of course. I've taken it on myself to arrange an interview for this afternoon. Here's the address."

Iain glanced at the slip of paper before stuffing it into his waistcoat. "Strike while the iron's hot? Is that yer motto, Jimmy?"

"Indeed it is." He rose to his feet. "Here's my hand – Iain. I've every confidence this is the start of a long and fruitful relationship."

"Ye took the words right out o' my mouth." This time he was prepared for the strength of the grasp. "Come awa', Morag. I've a tram to catch."

An hour later he found himself in a side street off the Govan Road, perspiring freely in the bright sunshine of a stifling summer day. He would have much preferred to rid himself of his heavy tweeds for something more comfortable before his interview, but Morag had been adamant: nothing must be permitted to spoil his chances. However, she had mumbled a grudging consent to his plea that he should travel on alone, while she returned home. There was a wealth of meaning in her look as they parted company. He could expect the rough edge of her tongue should anything go awry.

He stared, almost in disbelief, at the scruffy, dilapidated building standing out like a sore thumb in a sea of wasteland – evidently overlooked in a previous bout of slum clearance. The ground floor comprised what remained of a printing shop, long abandoned by the shape of things – the paintwork chipped and flaking, so that it was difficult to make out the address. Once more he checked the note he had been given. No, there was no mistake. Rusting shutters enveloped the premises, but there was a doorway to one side, presumably an entrance to the upper floors. Shielding his eyes, he scanned the upstairs windows, his attention caught by a sudden movement – the twitch of a curtain. He breathed a sigh of relief: at least there was someone at home. Quickly he crossed over and pushed at the door: it had been left slightly ajar, no doubt in anticipation of his arrival. Beyond, in the gloom was a narrow wooden staircase. Gingerly he felt his way up the rickety steps. Another door faced him. He knocked and went in.

"So ye're here after a'. I've been expectin' ye." A squat, middle aged figure advanced to greet him. "I jaloused it might be you when I heard the moniker. Now I ken for certain – I never forget a face."

Iain grunted as they shook hands. "Aye, I mind ye now. Ye've no' changed much." He looked round. There was little enough furniture in the room – an open roll top desk strewn with papers, a padded swivel chair with the stuffing hanging out, a battered typewriter on a small adjoining table. But the abiding impression was of dust and grime: cleaning was obviously not a priority. "Nice place ye've got here."

"No' exactly a palace, as ye'll observe. But that's the way I like it." He pointed to a stack of folding seats in a corner. "They're a' I need when there's a meetin'. Why no' go an' grab one for yersel'?"

"So ye work alone, Mr Youngston?" There was a sharp click as Iain set the chair to rights. "Naebody else to help ye?"

"Ca' me Rab. We dinnae stand on ceremony here." He dropped into the swivel chair. "Naw. I'm a one-man band."

"Then why—?"

"Am I lookin' for an assistant? That's easy. Jimmy Maxton carries a lot o' clout in this neck o' the woods. It wouldnae dae to cross him when he comes callin'." He smiled sourly. "I thought I was the one to ask the questions. So we'll get to business, if ye've nae objections. Have ye been telt about the job?"

"A wee bit. Somethin' to do wi' settlin' workplace disputes."

"Ye could put it like that. We're piggy in the middle. That's why we're rolling in clover." He guffawed at his own witticism.

"What in hell's name d'ye mean by that?"

"Dae ye no' get it? Well, never mind." The banter disappeared. "I wondered why I was asked to take ye on. At first I had the notion ye might be sent to spy on me."

"Spy? Why the devil wid ye think that?" Then the penny dropped. "Ye've got somethin' to hide?"

"That's as may be. Like as no', His Mightiness has his suspicions. But I'm sure you'll be able to convince him otherwise. In fact I'm countin' on it."

"Ye don't say. And why would I be likely to oblige ye?" He tried to conceal his growing interest. "I scarcely ken ye."

"Really? Cast yer mind back to yer days on the picket line – durin' the General Strike, that is. You were responsible for handin' over the cash for every exemption certificate sold."

"What of it? I accounted for every one."

"Is that a fact? What about the extra supply ye requested?"

"God's sake, man. That was to replace the wad destroyed in the police raid, if ye can mind that far back. Ye accepted the explanation then."

"Maybe it suited me to dae that. But it's no' true, is it? I checked up. There was nae police raid on the day ye said."

"Maybe I got the dates mixed up." It was an easy excuse. "Anyway, what does it matter now? Naebody will gie a toss after a' this time."

"Cannae deny that. But I wisnae thinkin' o' blackmail to shut yer gob. Naw, that wid never do. It was just tae show I ken what ye are." He tapped his nose. "It would be in both our interests to rub along thegither. Birds o' a feather, don't ye know?"

Iain shrugged. "Ye're talkin' in riddles. What is it ye mean?"

"Ach, there's nae need to act the daft laddie. The screw is three quid a week. That's what goes through the books. But ye can more than double it – if ye play yer cards right."

"But how—?"

"Haud yer wheesht, an' listen. Our wages are paid through the unions - officially, that is. But there's other ways o' makin' money. Suppose there's a demarcation dispute in a works and we're asked in to adjudicate. We hear the evidence and come down on one side - after careful consideration, of course. The union branch representin' the winners is duly grateful. We're slipped a backhander and nothin' said."

"Ye mean we sell our decision to the highest bidder?"

"That's about the size o' it - so long as it's no' made too obvious. Then again there might be a wage dispute wi' an employer. We examine the case and recommend a settlement - maybe half o' the original claim. The workers might grumble, but they hae to accept. Their boss is relieved at no' havin' to fork out as much as he thought, and shows his appreciation for savin' him money."

"The men widnae be likely to be happy wi' that."

"Dinnae you believe it. It's easy to stuff them. Ye just say it's the most ye could squeeze out o' the auld skinflint, or that it's only for the time being, and ye'll be back wi' a new claim in a few months' time."

"Then everybody's satisfied?"

"Right on the button." Youngston grinned. "Think that might appeal to you?"

A cushy billet, the opportunity of real money at little or no risk to himself: only a fool would turn down what was being offered on a plate.

A slow smile spread over his features. "I'm sure I'll dae my best to live up to your expectations. When do I start?"

NINE

Bitter Pills

Edinburgh
October 1929

Hilda Lixmont felt distinctly peeved as her husband entered the dining room. "About time," she greeted him testily. "Must you bring that paper with you to the breakfast table?"

"Just a glance at the news before I leave for the office. Who could object to that?"

"Fiddlesticks! You've had your nose stuck in it this past half hour. Anyone would think you were trying to avoid me. Now come and eat your kippers before they grow cold."

With a weary gesture of resignation Sir Edward Lixmont laid aside his *Scotsman* as he took his place. Hiding behind his newspaper had merely served to keep her wrath warm, and it was not difficult to guess the source of her displeasure. He braced himself for the onslaught to come.

She lost no time in wading in. "I've a bone to pick with you. What's this I hear of your agreement to allow that scoundrel access to my grandson?"

"Scoundrel? Do you mean Hugh?"

"Don't be ridiculous!" Instantly he regretted his attempt at jocularity; it only added fuel to the fire. "You know very well to whom I refer – Alastair's wretched brother."

"Surely that's a matter for Elizabeth and her husband to decide. If they're prepared—"

"Don't prevaricate! They would never have permitted such an outrage without consulting you beforehand. You even consented to a meeting with that ne'er-do-well to decide on the arrangements."

"How on earth—?"

"You needn't trouble to deny it. Your daughter told me."

"You mean you suspected something was afoot and wormed it out of Elizabeth?"

"That's as may be." She waved aside the accusation. "The worst of it is that you had no consideration for me. Going behind my back," she complained bitterly.

"Look here, Hilda. We didn't mention it because we knew what your reaction would be. I don't like it any more than you do, but facts are facts."

"What facts? The man's a Bolshevik agitator – a red revolutionary. Besides everything else." Her lips curled in distaste. "Ugh! I just cringe at the thought of him in Eddie's company."

"That's not entirely fair. His wife assures me he's a much-reformed character."

"And you believe that?"

"I've never had any reason to doubt Morag Baird's judgment. She told me he's found employment with an organisation that does good works in the local community. And he's left the Communist Party and joined Labour."

"No doubt one's as bad as the other."

"Not exactly. But there's no point in going into that now. It's true there was an interview in my chambers one day last month. Elizabeth and Alastair were also present. I must say he made a good impression – quietly spoken, even humble in putting his case. He regrets his past behaviour and now wishes to make amends."

"Can a leopard change its spots?" Hilda was far from showing any sympathy.

"I think we ought to give him his chance. He only asks for an occasional visit as an uncle – under supervision, of course. Our grandson would not be left alone with him."

"The long-lost uncle," she sneered. "And how is he to explain to Eddie why he hasn't been seen for years?"

"He'll say he's been living abroad. Just recently returned. Incidentally that is true, in part at least."

Lady Hilda shook her head. "I'm surprised you are prepared to associate yourself with this charade. When is the – event to take place?"

"Saturday after next. At Elizabeth's house." He paused a moment. "There is something else you need to consider."

"And what might that be?"

"If Baird is turned away, he might have thoughts of revenge. What's to stop him letting Eddie learn of his true paternity?"

"And how is he to achieve that? In any case my grandson would never believe him. We would simply deny it if asked."

"That might be true of us, and Elizabeth. But what of Alastair? Would he not admit it, if pressed by his brother?"

"Because of that, you feel there's no point in trying?" She shot him a glance of disfavour. Trust Edward to spot the fly in the ointment.

"I'm afraid so. It's not worth the risk. And if it's any consolation, I'm not fully convinced of Baird's *bona fides* either. But I fear there is little choice."

"Have it your own way," she sniffed, with a little toss of the head. "I really can't be bothered to argue."

"Then you agree?"

"I think I'd like to hear what Eddie has to say first. Leave it till then." She made as if to rise to the table, and then thought better of it. "By the way, what was so special in the newspaper? It must be something important to keep you from your breakfast."

"Why this sudden interest in the news?" Lixmont looked dubious. "You're up to something, Hilda." He knew his wife only too well.

"Nonsense! I like to keep abreast of what's going on in the world. Am I right to assume it's some ghastly new ploy from this socialist government? It was bad enough deciding to play up to those murderous Bolsheviks in Russia. What is it this time?"

"Nothing like that." He smiled faintly. "To tell the truth, I've had little to fault with Labour over these past few months in office. Recognizing the soviets as the legitimate authority in Russia was simply acceptance of reality."

"You're too trusting, Edward. We'll come to rue the day they snatched the levers of power into their grubby hands. You mark my words."

"Perhaps you're not wrong, Hilda." It was hardly worthwhile to pursue the issue. "No, it's the situation in America that's the main cause for concern."

"America? Why? What's going on there?"

"Apparently the stock market in the United States has collapsed. There's pandemonium on the New York Stock Exchange. People are desperate to sell off their investments – at any price. Shares have become worthless almost overnight. They're calling the day before yesterday *Black Monday*. You can guess the reason why."

"Really?" She did not seem overexcited. "Why should that be a worry?"

"Grant me patience! Don't you realise the implications, Hilda? It's not just the shareholders who will be affected. Banks will call in their loans, factories will close their gates, and countless thousands will be put out of work. It's a full-scale slump in the making."

She nodded thoughtfully. "I'm beginning to get the picture. But – how could it happen so suddenly? I thought things were going so well in the USA. Hugh told me as much."

"He would! And that's just the trouble. The American economy has overheated. Speculators have poured in millions – no billions, in the expectation of making a quick buck, as they term it over there. They presume shares will always keep rising in price, far in excess of the true value of the assets they cover. But once doubts arise, questions are asked; then it's all too easy to go the other way. There's a stampede for the door, and that's what's happened here."

"So American investors have been ruined? Surely that won't affect people on this country, will it?"

"Don't you believe it. There's many a poor devil in Great Britain who will have bought into the American market. Investment trusts are the usual vehicle, quick and easy to access. They're always touting for custom – until now, that is."

"I see. My God!" Her jaw dropped. "Are you trying to tell me Hugh might have lost money in foreign investments?"

"Almost bound to, I imagine. You know him as well as I do. We can only hope he's not plunged in too deeply."

She drew a deep breath. "So that was why he phoned last night. I almost forgot."

"Hugh phoned?"

"Yes. When you were out at your club. I didn't attach any significance to it at the time. He just left a message to say he would be round this morning. I was asleep when you returned, and it must have slipped my mind. Sorry about that."

"Hmm. I suppose I'd better hang on for a few minutes to see what he wants. Though I have little doubt."

"You mean—?" She broke off. "Why, here he is now, coming up the path."

Moments later Hugh Lixmont was ushered into the room. She could only gasp in dismay at his appearance. Rarely or never had he looked so downcast, so utterly dejected. A dozen questions hung on her lips, but she managed to resist the temptation.

"It's good to see you again, son. Come and have some coffee." She gave him a weak smile of welcome, before turning to the maid hovering in the background. "Agnes, a cup and saucer for Captain Hugh."

"No need to bother. I can't stay long." He waved away the offer as he flung himself into a chair.

"In that case you may go, Agnes. Close the door behind you."

His father eyed him sternly. "Well," he snapped, "I assume this is about this damned Wall Street Crash, as they're calling it. And you've had your hands burned. Am I correct?"

Hugh could only bow his head. "I – I suppose so," he stammered.

"Thought as much. Well, I'm due at the office. You can come with me. We can talk as we go."

"I – I'd rather not, if it's all the same to you, dad. There may be some unhappy punters lying in wait for me there."

"In search of an explanation for their losses, no doubt. I take it you've been investing other people's money in the United States – speculating, I should say. Well, the chickens have certainly come home to roost on that score. There's a price to be paid in terms of your reputation, but that can't be helped. They knew the risks." A sudden suspicion struck him. "You did explain that values could go down, as well as up, didn't you?"

"It might not have come out like that," he was forced to admit.

"Give me strength! You saw fit to ignore the first rule of investment advice. You led clients to believe the bear market would go on *ad infinitum* – a one-way ticket to wealth and riches." He shook his head mournfully. "This is partly my fault. I should have exercised more oversight on the investment branch, kept you on a tighter rein. Instead, you were allowed too much leeway to do as you wished. And this is what happens."

"Sorry, dad."

"Is that all you can say? Why on earth did you not realise the way things were going? The stock exchange there was seesawing for a month and more before this week's disaster."

"Yes. But my agent in New York assured me any fall was just temporary. In fact it was a buying opportunity, before the market started to rise again."

"And you ploughed in even more – funds from your own pocket, as well as from others who trusted your judgment. How much have you lost – personally, that is?"

"Everything." It was almost a whisper.

"Everything?" His mother frowned. "Surely you can only lose what you put in. You'll still have your investment portfolio elsewhere, and that lovely house and big motorcar."

"I'm afraid not. They'll all have to go. Most of the money I put up was on the margin."

"On the margin?" Now she was thoroughly perplexed. "This is beyond me. Can you explain it, Edward?"

"Indeed I can, Hilda." His son shrank from the ferocity of his glare. "It means he paid for the shares received with borrowed money. Now that they are worthless, he will have to sell off other assets to repay his creditors. Do you think you will have enough, Hugh?"

"I – I'm not quite sure. Probably not. No."

"And so you come to me for assistance?"

"Yes. Though I hate to ask. It's that – or bankruptcy."

"It's all you deserve."

"Edward!" It was almost a cry of anguish. "He's your son. Can't you do something?"

His anger cooled a little as he looked from one to the other. "A scandal in the family, Hilda? That would set tongues wagging in your circle of friends. Still, you may have a point. I'm not keen to have the good name of the firm dragged through the mire." He came to a decision. "Very well, then. I'll see what I can do. Hugh had better write a letter of resignation. I doubt the other partners will settle for less."

"That sounds a little extreme, Edward." As usual his wife rose to her son's defence. "Does he really have to leave?"

"Hold on a minute, mama. Father's right. And there's something else you both should know. You're going to cut up rough, but—" He appeared to hesitate.

"Well!" Lixmont was remorseless. "Spit it out. I thought I'd heard everything. But obviously not."

"It – it's just that when things got a bit awkward last month, lenders began to demand collateral for their loans."

"Collateral? In what form?"

"They insisted on a guarantor to ensure repayment if things went pear shaped. I gave them your name, or rather that of the business. It will be responsible for any shortfall I can't manage."

His father recoiled, almost petrified with horror. "I can't believe I'm hearing this. You had the nerve to make us responsible for your debts, without consulting me or anyone else. Why, it's tantamount to fraud. You could go to prison for this."

"I know, dad. I'm afraid I let my expectations run away with me."

"Like a gambler desperate to recoup his losses? Is that it? No wonder you wanted to steer well clear of the office. And you would be foolish to remain here, or at your own house. They'll be swarming round like a hive of angry bees before you know it."

"That's what I thought."

"You'd better make yourself scarce for a few days. Find a hotel to lie low somewhere. It's imperative no one should know where you're going – and that applies to us as well. Phone this evening for news. I'll try to find out if anything can be rescued from the ashes."

He hurried away. In all likelihood Hugh's folly would lead to severe consequences for them all. He might well be asked to step down from his own legal practice, probably be obliged to resign his seat on the town council. Such reckless behaviour was inexcusable. And yet… the bonds of family ran deep. At the door he turned to look back.

"You won't do anything foolish, will you?" There was a catch in his throat as he addressed his son.

"No, dad, I won't do that. I won't take the easy way out."

* * *

November 1929

"There was nae need to come wi' me, Morag. It's gonnae look as though ye dinnae trust me. Surely ye ken I wouldnae let ye down."

"It's no' that, Iain. The family will be expectin' me, as well as you. It was part o' the agreement wi' Sir Edward."

"There was nothin' definite said about that at the meetin'."

"No' in so many words. It was taken for granted. Besides, I'd like to see the laddie as well. It's been ages since my last visit."

Iain Baird scowled, but made no further response as they trudged up from the Waverley Station. It seemed that all his powers of persuasion had failed, all the arguments he could muster against travelling through from Glasgow had fallen on deaf ears. Despite every entreaty, she had remained obstinate, even to the extent of relapsing into a stony silence during the latter part of the train journey. His temper had been sorely tested, but he was all too aware of the consequences of a blazing row: it would almost certainly mean the ruination of his slow and careful planning over the last year and more. As they reached Princes Street he decided on one last despairing effort.

"See here, Morag. That's just the point."

"What is?"

"Ye want to see Eddie. I appreciate that. But if we're both thegither, he'll gang to you. He'll gie me short shrift. I thought the visit was for his uncle to get to know him a bit. Wi' you in tow, that's no' likely to happen."

"Ye've telt me that already," she snapped.

"I ken. But maybe we could reach a compromise."

She stopped to stare at him. "What dae ye mean?"

"What would ye say if I went on ahead? I'll tell them ye'll be round in an hour or so. That'll gie me a chance wi' Eddie. Ye needna worry," he added with the hint of a sneer, "The rest o' them will be there. I'll no' be left wi' the lad on his own."

That gave her pause for thought. "I suppose there's nae objection to that. Ye ken the way to their address? Oh, I nearly forgot." She smiled virtuously. "Ye've been there afore. And got turned away for yer pains."

"Nae need to bring that up," he growled. "That was years ago. And we're wastin' time now."

"That's fine, then. But what about me? What am I supposed to dae?"

"I'll say ye're at the shops. Maybe drop a hint about Eddie's birthday later this month. Ye're buying him a present. Will that satisfy ye?"

"Well—"

"Ye've nae money? Here ye are, then." He produced a crisp slip of paper. She gasped when she realised what it was – a five-pound note!

"Where on earth did ye get that? I havnae clapped eyes on one o' these for donkey's years. Have ye been robbin' a bank?"

"You should be so lucky," he chuckled. "Though I did get it at the bank – from my savings account." It would never do to reveal the true origin of the banknote. "I've been puttin' aside spare cash whenever I could. It's for our future. And this is as good a cause as any."

"I – I had nae idea." To save as much as this from his salary was almost inconceivable.

"It is kosher," he reassured her. "So tak' a daunder along Princes Street. Get him anythin' ye think he might like. Just see it's nicely wrapped. And... if there's any change, spend it on a wee somethin' for yersel'."

He grinned as her watched her disappear into the crowd; then hurriedly crossed the road to the nearest tram stop. It had been a close shave, but the fruits of steady, painstaking effort would taste all the sweeter. He had learned his lesson from previous attempts to demand his rights; persuasion, rather than force, was more likely to pay dividends. The boy's grandfather was the key, as he had always known: convince old man Lixmont of his good intentions, and access to his son would be his for the taking. Nevertheless, it had been a strain on his patience to coax his wife into making an approach to the head of the family. Even then eyebrows had been raised, doubts expressed, according to Morag. But at the end the downy old bird had relented: the interview had gone well. With the present happy result.

And in other fields he had not let the grass grow under his feet. He could take pride in his achievements in the constituency and beyond, creating an instant impression with his speeches and articles. Membership of the ILP was growing once more, in no small measure due to his efforts. Maxton had not been slow to compliment his work, often relying on him to mind the shop, as he put it, while he was absent at Westminster. Behind the scenes was an unspoken, but profitable, relationship with Rab Youngston at the Trades Council, enabling him to trouser far more than his official stipend. It went without saying that care was essential, so as not to throttle the goose with the golden egg; but things were set fair for the future. Youngston had suggested he stand for election to the municipal council, and Maxton had been only too glad to endorse his candidacy for Glasgow Corporation. It only remained to find a safe seat. With these happy thoughts in mind, he alighted from his tram after the short journey to Comely Bank.

Meanwhile, those awaiting his arrival could only resign themselves to what was almost certain to be a distasteful encounter. Sir Edward Lixmont found himself pacing up and down, pausing occasionally to peer anxiously through his daughter's front room window. Already there had been one disappointment that day: his son-in-law would not be at home to lend support. For some reason Alastair had been summoned by his chief at the Education Department – for business seemingly so urgent that his attendance had been demanded at the shortest of notice, and on a Saturday afternoon. As if that was not bad enough, his wife had insisted on coming – to provide backbone, as she put it. A fortnight ago Hilda would have raised Cain to prevent the meeting, had she known about it; now she appeared to accept it with equanimity. That placid look of innocence on her face as she sat thumbing through one of Elizabeth's magazines was enough to give anyone cause for concern.

Now it was a matter of regret that he had failed to take much notice of her rather secretive behaviour over the past week or so – just a vague awareness of unusual comings and goings without any explanation. It went without saying he had been preoccupied elsewhere: his first priority was obviously to clean up Hugh's mess as best he could. Here, at least, he had achieved a fair measure of success – not ideal, but perhaps all that could be managed in the circumstances. The other partners had responded favourably to his plea not to press charges, and had generously agreed to value his son's assets at a fair price, thus avoiding the disaster of a fire sale. These would be sold off piecemeal, as and when opportunity arose. Settling the remaining debt would be onerous, but manageable. It would involve belt tightening for some time to come, but the family – and his good name – would survive. There was relief to be had for that. As for Hugh, he had been packed off overseas to reflect on the consequences of his actions. Perhaps a year or so on short commons in Australia would bring him to his senses.

"Edward!" Hilda glanced up at him. "Stop fussing, for goodness' sake. Come and sit down."

"The man's late," he grumbled. "Keeping us waiting like this."

"Never mind about that. It's all part of his game. No need to get hot under the collar."

"I don't know how you can keep so calm, Hilda." He crossed over to the bay window once more. "Why, here he is now. No one with him, though. I thought his wife was expected."

"No doubt we'll find out soon enough." She allowed her attention to wander back to the reading material on her lap.

Elizabeth herself showed the visitor into the room. "Mr Baird, daddy," she announced.

"Iain, please," he smiled. "After all, you are my sister-in-law."

Lixmont gave him a bleak stare; then inclined his head stiffly, ignoring the outstretched hand. His wife glared up from her seat.

"I trust you had a good journey," he intoned icily. "I was under the impression that your good lady would accompany you."

"That's right." Iain brushed aside the snub. "She'll be along presently. There was a wee bit o' shoppin' to dae. Somebody has a birthday comin' up soon," he went on with a sly grin. "If ye ken what I mean."

"I'm not sure that I do. Shall we get on?"

"Suits me just fine." He glanced round. "Is Eddie about? I dinnae see him here."

"Perhaps you might fetch him, Elizabeth." Her mother laid aside her periodical. "I believe he's upstairs, and Mr Baird is anxious to make his acquaintance."

There was a stilted silence as she departed. Iain was puzzled, rather than alarmed, at his reception. He had expected to be treated with courtesy, if not exactly embraced as a long-lost relation. Obviously there had been some misunderstanding. "Nae need to take me the wrong way." He gave an ingratiating twist of the lip. "I'm just here to see the laddie."

"And so you shall." The lady in the armchair beckoned towards the doorway. "Here is the boy now. Come in, Eddie. Let the – gentleman have a look at you."

Iain's eyes narrowed as they fixed on the youth standing by the door. The lad was sturdy, glowing with health; he had grown and filled out since last they met – briefly, when he had called to fetch Morag on the eve of the General Strike. Though it was to be regretted that his features more closely matched his mother's side of the family, rather than his own.

"Don't be shy, dear." Her husband could only gape at Hilda's obvious determination to seize control of the proceedings. "Come and repeat to this – person what I said to you."

"Yes, granny." Eddie advanced boldly and spoke in a clear voice. "My dad is really my stepdad. He adopted me after he married mama, and I love and admire him."

"That is as it should be. And your true father?" she prompted.

"His name is Arthur Drumore, and he was an officer in the army. He and mama were married just before he went off to fight in the war. He was killed before I was born, and I'm very proud of him for his sacrifice in defending his country," he added with a flourish.

"Very good, Eddie. And was there anything else?"

"Yes. You warned me to have nothing to do with this man who claims to be my uncle. He is a wicked atheist who would try to turn me against everything that is right and decent."

"*Right and decent.* You hear that, Mr Baird?" She turned back to her grandson. "Perhaps you'd like to leave now. The air in here is not quite as it was." Eddie nodded and backed away. "You too, Elizabeth. You can rely on your father and I to do what needs to be done."

For what seemed an age, Iain Baird had stood as though rooted to the spot, utterly dumbfounded by the almost unbelievable turn of events. Now the initial shock gave way to a seething rage. "Ye auld witch!" he snarled. "Ye've poisoned him against me." Then he rounded on her husband. "You put her up to this. We had an agreement. I trusted you."

"Nothing of the kind," she said sharply. "My husband knew nothing of this. He has his way of dealing with threats to the family. And I have mine."

"That's what you think," he hissed. "I'll go to the papers. Tell them a'thing."

"And create a scandal?" She was openly contemptuous. "I don't think so."

"Why you—" Instinctively he clenched his fists.

"Violence? Is that your answer for everything? So be it." As if by magic, a small, metal object appeared in her hand, glistening in the light. "Do you see what this is? A whistle – a police whistle. There are two rather large gentlemen waiting outside the back door. I only have to blow this for them to rush in and take you in charge. So, if that is your wish—"

"A' right. Keep yer hair on." He had just enough grip on himself to realise this was no idle threat. "Did ye think I wid touch ye?"

"No, you would not. Now go over there and behave yourself. I've a few things to say before you leave. In order that that you fully understand your position," she added grimly.

He gave her a savage scowl before stomping over to the settee. "I'm listenin'," he growled as he threw himself down.

"That's better. In the first place no newspaper editor would print anything you might have to say. You've no evidence to substantiate any claim."

"And I suppose you do," he sneered.

"That's as may be. The burden of proof would fall entirely on you. And the penalties for libel can be very severe."

"Ye dinnae get off that easy," he retorted. "I can still make things hot for ye."

"I doubt it. But don't be in too much of a rush to make up your mind."

"Why no'? Ye've already done me down wi' the laddie."

"Just bear with me. It's true Eddie was conceived out of wedlock, but that was not the case when he was born. His father was a lieutenant in the Royal Irish Regiment. They met when he was on furlough in Edinburgh."

"Haud on a minute. Ye expect me to thole that? You blamed my brother for it. He wrote an' telt me."

"That was before we knew the true story. I'm afraid we rather jumped to conclusions. An unfortunate mistake, later set to rights. Alastair has forgiven us, and is now a valued member of the family. May I continue?"

"Aye. I'd like to hear it. Ye should be on the stage."

"Very well, then." She ignored the jibe. "When my daughter discovered she was – with child, she wrote to the young officer responsible for her condition. His name was Arthur Drumore. He immediately accepted his obligations, and she travelled to Ireland for the wedding. They were married on the eve of war by the regimental chaplain. His battalion was cut to pieces at Ypres in October 1914, and Arthur fell while leading a charge. Need I say more?"

"A braw tale. But can ye prove it?"

"Only word of mouth, I'm afraid. The records would be stored in Dublin – if they weren't lost or destroyed during the Troubles there. The regiment itself was disbanded in 1922, after the Irish Free State was set up."

"Very convenient for ye, to be sure. Why did ye no' tell us about this years ago?"

"Why should I bother? I had no idea you were making a nuisance of yourself till quite recently. My husband apparently chose another means of dealing with you." She flashed a glance at him. "With limited success, it would seem."

The unwelcome visitor gave a thin smile as he noted the gesture. "That's right. He couldna fool me. And you're no' likely to dae that, either."

"Just as you please. You can always go over to Ireland and search there. Though I doubt that the Irish authorities would be sympathetic to any request."

"Maybe so." It came to him in a blinding flash. "Since ye're talkin' about evidence, maybe there's nae need to go that far. The laddie was born here, in Scotland. That means there should be a birth certificate. I could go and check at the registry office."

"You could indeed. But why trouble yourself? I have a certified copy of the document in question." She fished in her handbag and drew out a folded strip of paper. "Edward, would you be good enough to show this to Mr Baird? Then he can assure himself that all is above board."

Iain almost snatched the paper from his hand. A sudden doubt assailed him: the old besom had an answer for everything. Anxiously he scanned the entries. The box for the father's name should have been left blank. But now there was writing: *Arthur Drumore*. And next to it his occupation: *Army Officer (Deceased)*.

"Are you satisfied now?" She could not quite conceal a note of triumph.

The words stung him into renewed fury. "It's a forgery," he snarled. "You wrote it. Or got somebody to dae it for ye."

"Not at all. You can always check the records at Register House." She smiled patiently. "By all means take it with you. You can compare it with the original."

"Maybe I'll dae just that. But first I want to hear it fae yer daughter. Fetch her back."

"I'll do no such thing." Her scorn rang out loud and clear. "I'll not have her disturbed further. You've done enough damage already."

"Well, then – my brother. I'll get the truth out of him. Where is he?"

"He was called away to a conference, I'm sorry to say. There's no point in awaiting his return. In fact," she continued, "our business is complete. You should take yourself off quietly – if you've no desire to be marched to the nearest police office, that is. My two associates will follow you – at a discrete distance, of course. Just to make certain you catch your train, you understand."

"Think ye've won, ye bitch?" He could scarcely contain his anger and frustration. "We'll soon see about that."

"Here, I say—" Lixmont moved forward to intervene.

"Stand back, Edward. Don't sully your hands." She put the whistle to her lips.

Iain was sorely tempted, but for a second time just managed to restrain himself. He would not give her the satisfaction of having him run in. "Ye havnae heard the last o' this," he muttered as he tramped away. But he knew it was a feeble gesture. There was absolutely no consolation in slamming the door behind him as he left.

"Phew!" Sir Edward Lixmont blew out his cheeks. "I thought it was touch and go back there."

"But virtue brings its own reward," she chirped. "We're done with him now. Are you not going to offer me your congratulations?"

"Congratulations? I only wish I could be so certain. But at least now we know why you've been dashing around these past few days."

"Well, I had to check the facts to my story – those that could be disproved, at any rate. Or rather I engaged an Inquiry Agency to do most of the work."

"And your two – private detectives, I suppose we must call them? Did they come from the same agency?" She nodded agreement. "Was Elizabeth informed of your intentions?"

"Just as much as was necessary for her to play her part. She was only too happy at the thought of being rid of that scoundrel once and for all."

"And Eddie? Doubtless you coached him for his role."

"Naturally. And he did it rather well. Just the right tone to carry conviction."

"But did he believe what he was saying?"

"About Baird's character? I trust so. He shows a true Christian spirit. The minister tells me he is a leading light in the Bible Class and Scripture Union. He has high hopes for him."

"I see. Well, leave it at that." He pursed his lips. "I understand your tale of the imaginary officer marrying Elizabeth, before conveniently falling in battle. It's substantially the same as the cock-and-bull story you gave out years ago. What I fail to grasp is how you managed to alter the birth certificate."

"Ah! My *pièce de resistance*. That was the part I had to carry out myself. The clerk at Register House was most understanding when Lady Hilda Lixmont explained the situation to him."

"You used your title to influence his judgment?"

"Absolutely. I had him eating out of my hand."

"Really?" He shook his head in disapproval. "And what web of fabrication did you spin?"

"That's not quite fair, Edward. I made the account as authentic as possible. I was rather proud of that."

"Ye gods!"

"No need to take exception. Eddie was born in a nursing home – a rather remote location, as you will recall. It was difficult for us to keep in close touch – wartime restrictions, and all that. Anyway, the nurse entrusted with the duty of registering the birth had not been informed of the father's identity. It was to be filled in later, when Elizabeth had recovered from the pain of childbirth. For some reason the omission was overlooked, and the uncorrected document dispatched to the relevant authority. It was only recently that I came across the mistake, and naturally hastened to report the discrepancy."

Lixmont could only gasp in astonishment. "I can hardly believe I'm hearing this," he spluttered when she had finished. "You realise, of course, that it is an offence to make a false statement for the public record?"

"I would imagine so. But in the circumstances," she said coyly, "surely the end justifies the means."

"You know, Hilda, you never cease to amaze me. I think I told you before that you would make an excellent lawyer. It must be the criminal mind." He forced a grin. "Another skeleton in the cupboard. Let's hope it never rattles."

"Why should it?"

"I was thinking of Alastair. It was a stroke of good fortune for you that he was absent this afternoon."

"Good fortune? Where does that come into it? Mrs Harkness happens to be a member of one of my charitable groups."

"Mrs Harkness?"

"The spouse of Alastair's principal in the Department. Do use your imagination, Edward. She was more than willing to oblige me in this little matter."

Oh!" The penny dropped. "To persuade her husband to drag Alastair away to the office this afternoon? So that you would have a clear run? Very good – this time. But Baird will find a way to tackle his brother."

"Hopefully not. But we can always concoct a story for Alastair to tell without offending his high moral code."

"Rather more in your line than mine," he said with a wry smile.

"I'll give it some thought. Look on the bright side. Baird might not believe us, but he can never be absolutely certain. There will always be the shadow of doubt that he might not have fathered Eddie after all."

"In that case it will make him all the more determined to ferret out the truth."

"But what can he do. We've drawn his fangs. You always find problems where none exist." She rose from her seat. It's high time we broke the good news to Eddie and Elizabeth. Then we can take our leave."

Head held high, she marched triumphantly from the room.

* * *

Dusk had already fallen before he was released from the office in Queen Street to make his way homewards. True, the chief had offered a lift in his shiny new motor car, but he was in no mood to accept favours. Now, as if to add insult to injury, the gentle patter of raindrops betokened the arrival of inclement weather. Alastair Baird groaned inwardly as he pulled up his collar and lengthened his stride.

Still, he was fortunate that the storm held its hand as he caught a tram for Stockbridge, and he was glad enough to reach the end of Raeburn Place and turn into the row of houses adjoining the school playing fields before the heavens opened. It was just then that he gave a sudden start. Through the gloom he could glimpse the figure of a woman coming from his house. She appeared to hesitate; then hurried towards him.

"Is that you, Morag?" he called out.

"Sorry. Cannae stop." He caught the strain in the muttered words as she swerved to dart past him. In moments she was lost to view. Puzzled, and a little hurt, he trudged on. Elizabeth was standing by the curtains at the bay window. She gave a wave of recognition and disappeared to open the front door.

"Thank goodness you're home. You must be soaked."

"No need to fuss," he grunted as she ushered him inside. "By the way, was that Morag I saw just now? She dashed away with hardly a word."

"Yes. I can't say I'm surprised." She held up a finger. "But that can wait. Let me help you out of your wet things first." It was the work of moments to slip him out of his overcoat and hang coat and hat on the hallstand. "That's better. Now, about Morag. It's unfortunate, but she was very upset. She was close to tears when she left."

"But how—?"

"She thinks Iain will blame her for what happened this afternoon. You know what a temper he has when roused."

That gave him pause. "I take it things didn't turn out as planned? My brother was out to make trouble?" He looked at her in dismay. "I shouldn't have left you to face him. Unforgivable," he mumbled.

"Don't be silly. We weren't left alone. My parents were here as well." A twinkle appeared in her eye. "And as it happens, things didn't turn out too badly."

He stared blankly. "Parents? Your mother was here? That would set the cat amongst the pigeons, and no mistake."

"You might expect that," she chuckled. "But not in the way you imagine."

"I don't understand." Now he was thoroughly mystified. "I suppose there is some explanation?"

"Naturally. Come and warm yourself by the fireside. And you shall hear all."

"As you wish." He glanced back. "What about Eddie? Did he speak with Iain?"

"Yes, he did. And performed very well. He's upstairs now."

"It must have been something of an ordeal for him. I'd best go up and have a word."

"No. Don't disturb him. He needs a bit of time to himself. He'll come down when he's ready."

"You could be right." He nodded agreement as he eased himself into his armchair and began to unlace his shoes. "Don't mind me. I'll be listening."

"Very well, then. Morag didn't arrive till Iain was long gone. My parents too, for that matter. Apparently she had been sent to buy a present for Eddie's birthday. It's there, on the sideboard." She pointed to a neatly wrapped package. "I didn't get round to asking what it is."

"You had other fish to fry?"

"You could put it like that. She was concerned about Iain – why he had left so soon, without bothering to wait for her. I had to explain that I was out of the room for most of the time. Daddy and mama wanted me to look after Eddie while they dealt with your brother."

Alastair looked up sharply. "You didn't actually witness what went on?"

"No, but they told me about it afterwards."

"And you passed on the information?"

"What else was I to do? Morag flew into a dreadful flap, claiming that she would be accused of plotting against him. Iain would treat it as an act of betrayal. She was terrified he would take it out on her. I begged her to stay, at least till he had time to cool down. But she would have none of it. She was determined to get home as quickly as possible."

"No need to reproach yourself, Elizabeth. It's not your fault. You could hardly hope to detain her by force." He thought for a moment. "I suppose your mother was at the bottom of all this. She found out about the meeting somehow, and went out of her way to scupper any chance of a relationship. And now things are worse than ever."

"I wouldn't say that, Alastair. It's true that Morag will probably bear the brunt of his anger. And for that I'm really sorry. But there is a silver lining – at least for the family. I believe that mama has found a permanent solution to our problem. Your brother will never dare to inflict his malign influence on Eddie again. Call it unfeeling if you like, but there it is."

"I could never believe that of you," he said quietly. "Perhaps if I knew the whole story—?"

"Of course. You've every right to hear it. Mama was magnificent. She dominated the whole affair from start to finish."

"Like a lioness protecting her cubs – or grand cub in this case," he added with a smile.

"If you like. Anyhow, you will recall that Eddie had tea at his grandma's earlier this week. It seems she took the opportunity to break the news that you were only his stepfather."

"Without asking our permission? That was rather presumptuous of her. Still," he reflected, "he had to learn sometime. I was rather hoping it might not have been for another year or so. It must have come as something of a shock."

"Perhaps not as much as you might suppose. Truth to tell, he seemed to take it in his stride. And mama counselled him to say nothing to you. Then she went on to tell him about the army officer, killed in the war. Her old explanation of a posthumous father, as you will remember."

"I certainly do. But why—?"

"Can't you guess? She wanted to get her version in first. That way Eddie would never accept any claim to paternity that your brother might make. In fact, to rub it in, she coached him to repeat the tale in front of him."

"Phew! I bet that would have made the fur fly. He would have been incandescent with rage."

"That he was. But she had anticipated his reaction. She had a pair of private detectives outside, ready to pounce at the first hint of violence."

"How did he respond to that?"

"What could he do? She had him spitting like a caged animal."

"But at least he had sense enough not to resort to violence. I suppose we must be glad of that."

"That's putting it mildly. She called his bluff. He had no hard evidence. And then she produced her trump card. I don't understand how she managed it, but she showed him a birth certificate with an entry for the father's name."

"The army officer, I presume. How did he take that?"

"Badly. Claimed that it was a forgery. But she said he could always go and check with the registrar. He saw the game was up. There was nothing he could do but drag himself out with his tail between his legs."

"Then all's well that ends well? We've seen the last of him?"

"I sincerely hope so. My only regret is that you were packed off on a wild goose chase."

"What on earth gave you that impression?" He frowned slightly. "Oh, I think I see. It was all part of your mother's grand design. Well, things didn't end up quite as expected."

"How come?" It was her turn to look perplexed.

"I'll tell you. The chief was already at his desk when I arrived. He informed me that he had intended to speak to me on Monday, but on second thoughts decided the matter could not wait. Hence my summons today."

"But why the hurry? What was it?"

"Well, as he put it in no uncertain terms, the Minister had taken it upon himself to poke his nose into the Department's affairs. His words, not mine,

I hasten to add. Somehow, he had got wind of my research, and wished to acquaint himself with the findings."

"But that's a feather in your cap, isn't it?"

"Not really. The secretary of state's remit over Scottish education is a grey area. But Harkness didn't want any fuss. As a result, he came to the conclusion that my draft report could see the light of day. It was lying on his desk. He had already unearthed a copy from the archive."

"I see. But it wouldn't have taken all afternoon just to tell you that."

"Not a bit of it. He insisted on sitting me down and going over the detail, almost line by line. Just to polish up the wording, check the facts and figures, and judge if any minor alterations were required That's what he said." He gave a hollow laugh.

"But surely you wouldn't mind that. Some of your figures would be out of date by now."

"I would agree – if that was all. But he demanded wholesale changes, particularly in the costings. He accused me of being unrealistic in assessing what would be required to raise the school leaving age, and provide secondary education for all. The true expense would be much higher; and he had evidence to prove it. I could only blink in disbelief at the amendments in the paper he produced."

"Goodness! That must have been a facer for you. Was the intention to bury your report once and for all?"

"That's about the size of it. On his reckoning, no government could even dream of taking the project further. It was just a ploy to convince the Minister to drop any ideas he might have."

"And you were expected to go along with it?"

"Yes. Just a catspaw," he replied bitterly. "I was instructed to incorporate his workings into my revised draft."

"And you refused?"

"Not in so many words. I said I was reluctant to be party to what I considered to be errors in the calculations."

"How did he react to that?"

"Oh, his usual mixture of charm and bluster. Colleagues would whisper behind my back. Did I wish to be tagged as unreliable? There was no place for disloyalty in the Department. Then he changed tack. Why throw away a promising career on a whim? My principles were praiseworthy, but scarcely practical politics. Finally, he said he would not press me for an immediate answer. I could have a day or two to think things over. Not that it matters," he went on glumly. "I can't bring myself to propagate falsehoods. I shall have to give in my resignation."

"But what would you do?" She gazed at him in horror.

"I don't know." He shrugged his shoulders. "I haven't got that far yet."

"Then don't do anything rash," she begged him. "My father will know what's for the best. Talk it over with him first. Promise me that."

"Do you suppose it will make a difference?" He caught the look on her face. "Very well, then. Though I don't hold out much hope."

Part III: 1931-1935

TEN

Push Forward, Pull Back

Edinburgh
May 1931

"Can you come as well, dad" There was more hope than expectation in the tentative request.

"Tea with your grandmother? His stepfather could not quite resist a wry chuckle. "It's tempting but I'm afraid duty calls. I've my notes to prepare for this evening."

"But I was counting on your support."

"Can't be done. In any case I doubt I'd be of much use to you."

"Then what about mama? She should be home soon."

"Not today. There's a rush of work at her office. It's the advertisements for the autumn fashions."

"Autumn? It's hardly summer yet."

"True. But you know about these things. Preparations have to be carried out well in advance."

"Does that mean I have to go on my own?" It was hard to admit defeat.

"That's about the size of it. But cheer up." He winked and gave an encouraging smile. "I don't see any need to be worried. She can be a bit overbearing, I grant you that, but deep down you're the apple of her eye."

Eddie Baird nodded glumly. There was the nub of his troubles. It was all too obvious that Granny Hilda remained determined to smother him with her attentions, probing and questioning, with the fixed idea of mapping out his future for him. Difficult enough to bear when he was a small child, but almost intolerable now he was on the verge of manhood – or at least about to embark on his final year at school. Why could he not be left to work out his place in the world for himself? The urge to throw off the yoke was growing, but he hesitated to make a direct challenge. Twice already he had resisted her latest invitation, citing prior commitments at school as an excuse. A third rejection was unthinkable. She would be terribly hurt, and he would go to almost any length to prevent that. Little wonder he was in a quandary as what to do for the best.

"Ok, dad." He made up his mind. "I'll be off, then. Grin and bear it, eh?"

"That's the ticket. You'll be just fine. Her bark is generally worse than her bite."

"Let's hope so." They both laughed, before Eddie turned to go.

The smile faded as Alastair Baird eased himself back into his chair. He could sympathise with the boy. No doubt Eddie found it irksome to dance to his grandmother's bidding. But it would take strength of character, and a fine line in judgment, to stand up to her. Still, he was shaping up well elsewhere. His performance in school, both at games and in the classroom, was a source of pride. More important, he had never allowed success to turn his head. There was satisfaction to be had in that – and in the prospect of a glowing university career to follow.

Then there was his own outlook to consider. Reflecting back over the last eighteen months, he was glad he had listened to wiser counsel and stayed his hand. As his father-in-law had pointed out, what purpose would it serve to tender his resignation from the civil service in a fit of pique? What alternatives would be open to him? A teaching post, even in a deprived area, would be difficult to obtain in these times of government penny-pinching and austerity. To uproot his family and seek an opening overseas would be grossly unfair, even selfish on his part. He could never bring himself to contemplate that as a serious option.

It was Sir Edward himself who had come up with a compromise, which he had accepted, though not without reservations. His lip curled at the recollection of how his chief at the SED had jumped at the suggestion of a secondment to the recently established Scottish Council for Research in Education. After all, it would enable him to rid himself of a troublesome subordinate without drawing any repercussions upon himself. At the same time, he was honest enough to admit that he was no longer called upon to become complicit in what amounted to blatant chicanery. No doubt the Minister had been fobbed off, and his report returned to gather dust in the archive. A neat solution to a ticklish problem? That might be the official view. He could not quite see it in that light.

Nevertheless, it was all water under the bridge now. Attached to the SCRE, to some extent he was his own master. The work was congenial, involving the recruitment and training of teachers to carry out research in their own classrooms. And the results were likely to make a practical contribution towards the goal of equal opportunities for all in Scottish schools. That was the purpose of yet another meeting he was to chair that evening – to enthuse willing volunteers to join the grand project.

He freely acknowledged that Elizabeth's father had managed the whole affair rather well. It was his introduction to the country's leading educationist that had tipped the balance. To engineer an interview with Godfrey Thomson, head of the Education Department at Edinburgh University, and principal of Moray House College of Education at the same time, was bound to have an impact. The professor's argument was straightforward: the only fair method of selection for education was by means of measured intelligence, not through the accident of birth, class or money. What was required was the development and application of appropriate intelligence tests, to be administered at regular intervals in a child's schooling. The contention was persuasive, and he had been intrigued by the possibilities. It would have been churlish to spurn the opportunity to offer his services. Since then, truth to tell, it had become a labour of love.

"Penny for them."

"Elizabeth!" Alastair gave a start. "Where on earth did you spring from? I didn't hear you come in."

"That's because you were daydreaming."

"You're back early." He grinned at the mild rebuke. "You weren't expected for a couple of hours yet."

"We buzzed through the final proofs." She glanced round. "Did Eddie get off to visit his grandmama?"

"Yes. Had you arrived a bit sooner, you could have gone with him. He seemed reluctant to go by himself."

"Whatever next? She doesn't bite, you know."

"That's what I told him. But I rather think he took it with a pinch of salt."

"Nonsense!" She pulled a face as she bustled away.

Had she but known it, her husband was much closer to the mark. Eddie's heart sank as he hurried towards his grandmother's house. She was waiting by the gate. Not the most promising of starts, he told himself.

“There you are at last,” she called out. “I was beginning to think you had forgotten again.”

“Sorry if I’m late, granny.” He hastened to explain. “School doesn’t finish till half past three. And I had to go home first. I got here as soon as I could.”

“Never mind, dear. I’m sure you did your best.” She gave a thin smile, as if to assure him it was of little consequence. “I thought we’d take tea outside. It’s such a lovely day.” She indicated the gazebo at a little distance. “Much cosier there, don’t you think? Then we can enjoy our little chat.”

He hesitated as she held the gate open, but only for a moment. “Will grandpa be joining us?” he asked hopefully, following her up the path.

“I’m afraid not. Your grandfather will be at his club by now. He generally goes there for an hour or two on a Thursday. He tells me it gives him the opportunity to catch up with the local gossip.”

Her grandson gulped in dismay. His last chance of a restraining hand on her domineering ways was gone. Had she deliberately planned it like this? It certainly seemed so.

“Shall we sit down?” she went on. “We’ll serve ourselves. Then we shan’t be disturbed.”

Eddie could only gaze in wonder at the array of delicacies already laid out on stands atop a dazzling white tablecloth covering the wrought iron table. To all intents and purposes, it was a meal fit for a king. But he could not resist an inward quake at the image floating into his head – that of a fly lured into the spider’s web.

“And how is your mama?” she asked casually, taking up her napkin. “I gather her business is doing rather well. Though of course I cannot quite approve of my daughter engaging in trade.”

“I believe so.” He smiled weakly. Trust granny to harp on about Victorian values.

“And your father – stepfather, I should say? I cannot help feeling that it was an error on his part to abandon his post in the civil service.”

“But he didn’t leave. It was a secondment.”

“Perhaps. We must trust it is only temporary, and that he receives another chance. To return and make amends, that is.”

“Here, I say—” He flushed with indignation. This was going too far.

“You – you misunderstand me, Eddie. I meant no disrespect.” For a moment she was taken aback, but quickly rallied. She had no wish to be distracted over a side issue. "You must be ravenous by now. I can recommend the crab patties. They're rather good."

In silence he helped himself to a few daintily cut sandwiches. His grandmother watched warily as he began to eat. Reassured, she began on a new tack.

"I must say, Eddie, you're quite the young man, now. I'm informed that you're doing exceptionally well at school. You must be looking forward to your final year."

"Well, perhaps." He wiped his mouth. "I believe I'm in the running to be named as a prefect."

"Not head boy?"

"Hardly." He grinned at her. "But I could have a chance of playing for the first fifteen at rugger. Scrum half."

"That sounds very nice. And your classwork?"

"Well, there's the leaving certificate exams coming up. I'm hopeful of a good group of Highers."

"And then it's on to the varsity?"

"That's the aim. My housemaster tells me I've a good chance of Oxford if I chose to take the entrance exam."

"Oxford?" She frowned, then shook her head. "Oh dear, no. That would never do."

"Why ever not? I thought you'd be pleased."

"But don't you see? The theology course there will be based on the Anglican liturgy. That would never be acceptable to the Church of Scotland. I was under the impression that we had agreed you would attend New College, here in Edinburgh."

"The Faculty of Divinity?" Now he was perplexed, and not a little concerned. "There was never a decision to do that," he protested. "I haven't even really discussed the future with my parents yet. I know you may have mentioned the possibility once or twice in passing—"

"But you think I was talking through my hat?" There was a sharp edge to her voice.

"It's not that, granny." He made a hasty attempt to soothe ruffled feathers. "It's just that I'm far too young to think of training for the ministry. I'm more concerned with the present now, not with the hereafter. I'd like to take a degree in modern history. In that way it might help me gain some understanding of the world as it is."

"Hmm. Following in father's footsteps, eh?" She looked him in the eye. "Would you be prepared to carry on your studies here, in Edinburgh?"

"If you like." He sensed an olive branch.

"Well, there may be something in what you say. You could go on to take divinity as a second degree, if you can promise me you are prepared to consider that as an option."

"Yes, I think I can agree to that."

"Good. Then it's settled." She paused to refill his cup. "Now there is another matter I really must draw to your attention. Not unrelated to what we have already discussed."

"Oh!" He had hoped to avoid the subject he had been dreading. But it seemed there was to be no escape. All he could do now was to face the music, and pray she would understand.

"I'm sorry to have to bring this up, but I've noticed that you are rarely to be seen at the Sunday service these days. And the minister has expressed disappointment that you no longer seem to take an active part in the youth organisations. I appreciate that you may have a lot on your plate at school, but surely this cannot apply to the holidays." She appeared to consider. "Now I'd like you to promise me that you will attend the church's summer retreat in July, as usual."

As a means of taking him to task, he knew it could have been worse; she was contenting herself with a gentle reminder to steer him back into the fold. For a moment he was tempted, before shaking his head. "Sorry, but it's not possible, granny. I've already arranged to go on a hiking tour with some of my classmates. And after that there's the family holiday at Largs."

"But you've always enjoyed summer camp," she insisted. "What can have caused you to change your mind? Surely you cannot be questioning your vocation?"

"If you mean my belief in Christianity, I should hope not." He set his lips. This was the crunch. "All the same it makes me sick to think of the cant and hypocrisy in the church today."

She recoiled in astonishment. "How can you even think of saying such a thing?" Her voice trembled with emotion.

"I knew you'd be cross, granny. If you would only let me explain—"

"Not another word. No!"

"It's just the prejudice and intolerance I can't stand." Anger and resentment could no longer be contained. Caution was thrown to the winds. "God's message is supposed to be about peace and understanding, and respect for other people's feelings. Yet our church has no time for other faiths, especially the Catholics. The pope is demonised as the antichrist. The Irish are treated as an inferior breed of humankind, aliens in our midst. It's even said they threaten the dilution of the Scots race. I've heard demands they should be sent back to Ireland. Need I go on?"

His grandmother slumped back in alarm. She could scarcely grasp he was capable of such unbecoming conduct. "Well, I suppose there might be one or two zealots," she stuttered. "But very few, I should say."

"How can you believe that when I read reports of the very same attitudes in debates at the General Assembly? And it's not just a few ignorant laymen. It's some of the ministers themselves."

"So that's what has brought this on." She made an attempt to stem the tirade.

"Not at all. It's been on my mind for some time. It's just recent events that make me speak out."

She nodded wearily. "You must understand, Eddie, that the church is fighting a battle against the devil and all his works. Remember that the Irish rose up against British rule. They have their own country now. That's where they should stay. It is the Irish who are driving down wages and stealing food from the mouths of our workers. The unemployment problem would be cured if they could be persuaded to return home. And, of course, it is the Irish vote that has enabled this deplorable Labour government to do its worst."

"I say, granny, that's a bit rich." But his passion was cooling. He could feel for the old lady in her obvious distress. And he was responsible. Now he bitterly regretted his wild outburst. "It's just that I think Labour is doing the best it can under difficult circumstances," he added lamely.

"What on earth do you know about politics – about socialist barbarism?" She seemed lost for words. Then a sudden, terrible thought struck her. "You've had no contact with that wicked man, have you?"

"If you are referring to my Uncle Iain, then no. Though I've often wondered why you always tell me to avoid him like the plague. Any time his name is mentioned—"

"But he is a nasty character – a red revolutionary," she broke in hastily. "Any member of the family will tell you that."

"You know, granny, I think I've always sensed a mystery about him, some skeleton in the cupboard. Anyhow, I was curious. That's why I asked Auntie Morag about him."

She stared blankly. This was something she could never have anticipated. "When was this?" she gasped.

"A couple of months ago. When she last paid us a visit."

"And she told you—?" It was little more than a whisper.

"Not much, as it turned out. Just about his political affiliations. He used to be a communist, but he's left them to join the ILP. So you're mistaken there."

"ILP?"

"Independent Labour Party. In fact he's been chosen as a Labour town councillor in Glasgow. And he does good works to relieve hardship in the community."

"I think perhaps his wife exaggerates a little. It's only natural she should wish to support him." It was a crumb of comfort to learn the secret was still safe, at least for the time being. "He's still a socialist, is he not? I can see little difference between that and rank revolution."

"Oh, no. That's simply not true. I got hold of some of their booklets in Stockbridge library. Auntie Morag said I should read about their policies. I was very impressed by their answers to the employment situation, especially by a chap named Maxton. He's leader of the ILP, by the way."

Lady Hilda Lixmont, matriarch of the family, could only shake her head in despair. What else was there to say? She was at her wits' end. What had started as a mild reproof had somehow developed into a violent clash of wills.

"You look tired, granny." He could be tactful. "I've finished my tea. Perhaps I should be off now."

"Yes. That might be for the best." She was not ungrateful for the respite. "Come and say goodbye to your old grandmama."

"Of course." He came round to give her a kiss on the forehead. "Thank you, granny. Shall I help you indoors?"

"That will not be necessary. I'll just rest here and enjoy the sunshine. Your grandfather will not be long now." She needed time to recover from the shock, time to work out a plan of action. Bad enough that he had been led astray to question the good name of the kirk, to show sympathy for the depredations of socialist agitators. But should he fall under the spell of that scoundrel…

At the gate he turned to wave. Mechanically she returned the salute.

* * *

The Edinburgh express was crowded, almost every seat taken. It had been a last-minute dash to scramble into a carriage, somehow wedge himself into the corner of a stuffy compartment. The journey from London promised little in the way of comfort; already the air was blue with the fug of tobacco smoke. No matter; he had endured far worse during his long months of exile. At least his luggage had been deposited safely in the guard's van, or so it was to be hoped.

Time seemed to drag as the train sped northwards. It was difficult to ease his cramped position; the hum and chatter around him was vaguely annoying. Yet the warmth of his surroundings gradually induced a spirit of lethargy; heavy lidded, his eyes closed and he fell into a fitful doze. A tangle of memories filtered through his subconscious – the harsh, unforgiving outback, the unnerving silence of a barren landscape, the endless tracks filled with choking dust.

He woke with a start, blinked, then stared round. Resentment welled up once more. To have been packed off to that godawful fate like some latter-day convict was the ultimate humiliation. And for nothing more than to save his parents' blushes. Anyone could have suffered his bad luck, taken a tumble in the Great Crash. But Australia? There was nothing for him there, nothing but to eke out a miserable existence as best he could. Now the prodigal was on his way back. As to his welcome… well, that remained to be seen. His father had apparently forgotten his existence: there had been no summons back to Blighty when his year was up. But mama had turned up trumps. She had responded to his cable, and coughed up the readies for his passage home. To see her son again would come as a pleasant surprise. Perhaps not so pleasant for the pater, especially if he had not been informed of her good deed.

"Luncheon! Last call for luncheon!"

He looked up sharply at the attendant's call. Dash it all! A square meal would not come amiss: he had not eaten since a hurried sandwich at the station buffet. There was money enough left from the funds sent by the mater. He rose to stretch stiffened limbs, then shuffled into the corridor to make his way towards the dining car. At the entrance a harassed waiter intervened: there were no free tables available, but if he cared to share… He nodded and was ushered to the remaining place at a table set for two.

"Mind if I join you?"

He was rewarded by a glance, followed by a wave of the hand. "Not at all. I've nearly finished."

"Thanks." He settled himself down and took the proffered menu.

"The lamb isn't bad," his fellow diner announced. "And the sherry trifle to follow."

"Thanks again. I'll take your advice." The waiter bustled away.

"Care for a fag?" The man opposite pulled out a silver case.

His eyes narrowed. He was not favourably impressed, now he had the chance of a closer look. There were still traces of a once youthful appearance, but good living had evidently caught up with the man. Now he looked pasty faced, running to fat. And dressed in a loud check suit like someone anxious to be noticed. Not the sort of person he would have chosen for an acquaintance. Still, civility cost nothing.

"Don't mind if I do." He accepted a cigarette, had it lit for him, and leaned back to savour the taste.

"I see you've been spending some time in sunnier climes."

"How on earth—? Oh! I suppose you've noticed the tan."

"Well, you didn't acquire it in this country, that's for sure. But forgive me, I didn't mean to pry. Just making conversation. Are you travelling all the way?"

"To Edinburgh? Yes." He concealed his mild irritation. "I live there. Or at least my parents do. What about yourself?"

"The same. I've some business there. But then I'm going on to Glasgow." He held out his hand. "Here, I'm forgetting my manners. The name's Nick Norman."

"Lixmont – Hugh Lixmont." He was conscious of a slight quiver as they shook hands; a sudden wary look, gone in an instant. Some faint memory stirred within him: the name was vaguely familiar. Their paths had never crossed, he was certain of that. Even so…

"Here's my card, sir."

He frowned as he took the small piece of pasteboard. "Business contractor? What the devil does that mean?"

"Anything you care to mention. I've a finger in a good many pies. Anywhere I can find to turn an honest penny," he added with a sly grin. "And yourself?"

Hugh Lixmont was tempted to damn the blighter for his presumption, but curiosity got the better of him. "Oh, nothing of any significance," he said airily. "Actually, I've spent the last year or so in Australia, looking for investment opportunities."

"That would account for the sun. And you discovered?"

"Nothing but sheep as far as the eye could see."

"And they're a drug on the market. Precious little scope there, I would hazard a guess. Nor in the mines and mineral resources. Not with world trade drying up the way it is."

"So I found out. And that's just what I'm going to report to my father. He may be a big shot in legal affairs in Edinburgh, but when it comes to dabbling in overseas markets—"

"He's not at the races. I quite understand." Nick Norman was prepared to be sympathetic. He coughed politely. "Would you think it impertinent of me to ask if your father is a knight of the realm, and if you have a sister called Elizabeth?"

"How the hell—?" He stared bleakly. Then the penny dropped. "You're the blackguard who diddled my sister after she saved your miserable rag." His lip curled in contempt. "But for her you would have been wiped out."

"Here, I say, that's going over the score." Her erstwhile employer was quick to defend himself. "You've only heard one side of the story. I had an offer no reasonable man could refuse. And I paid back every penny your father lent me. And the interest due. From what I gather," he continued archly, "Elizabeth isn't doing too badly herself these days."

"You stay in touch?"

"Not as such. But I keep my ear to the ground, Mr Lixmont."

"It's Captain Lixmont. I retain my army rank." His tone was stiff, but the flash of resentment was fading. After all, what did it matter? Only his mother showed any concern for him.

"Sorry. I didn't realise." There was a brief silence. "If I might be permitted to give a word of advice, Captain Lixmont. I myself was fortunate enough to avoid the worst of the difficulties, shall we say, a year or so back."

Hugh drew a deep breath. It was galling to be reminded of his own experience. But he would not be drawn again. "I suppose so," he grunted. "What is it, then?"

"Well, I would not be too anxious to dip back into the stock market if I were you. It's my belief shares will take years to recover after such a shock to the system."

"Then what—?"

"For the time being I would place my faith in bricks and mortar. One is unlikely to go far wrong there."

"You're a builder?"

"Scarcely. Though I do commission buildings, and refurbish others, from time to time."

"Houses?"

"Yes, if you like." He gave a short laugh. "Picture houses. That's my main interest at the moment."

"Picture houses?" He blinked in astonishment. "You mean the cinema?"

"Exactly that. It's not a joke, I do assure you. Films have never been more popular, now that *talkies* are all the rage."

"But – I don't understand. You're telling me that audiences are booming. How can they afford it, what with the unemployment and low wages?"

"Escapism." He chuckled. "People can always find a tanner or a bob to forget their troubles for a few hours. I like to think I provide a public service."

"And make money hand over fist, I shouldn't wonder." There was a sigh. "Good luck to you. I wish you well."

"See here, I run a string of picture palaces in Glasgow. Full to the rafters six nights of the week. Punters turned away by the bucket load for want of room. If that's not an invitation to expand, I don't know what is. That's why I've been to the *Big Smoke*."

"London? Any success?"

"A sniff or two, but nothing definite. I rather imagine I'd need to spread my wings before I take on the big boys down south."

"And you'd require plenty of spare cash for that. But I say, Mr Norman, is there any point in telling me all this?"

"Nick, please. Now that we're acquainted. Look, cards on the table. My operation is really too big for one chap to handle, especially with my plans for the future. I could do with some help. Someone who knows the score. Someone I can trust. What d'ye say?"

"A right-hand man, you mean? Is this the offer of a job – for a perfect stranger?" His brow wrinkled in suspicion. "You don't know me from Adam."

"That's not entirely true. I have had a working relationship, you know, with other members of your family."

"And you regard that as a qualification? I know nothing about films, or the building trade for that matter."

"Probably not. But you'll know how to strike a bargain. And turn an opening to advantage."

"Is that what they told you?" He laughed harshly. It struck him where this might be leading. "I presume you'll be looking for a contribution if I decide to join you."

"You're a sharp one. I knew my instincts weren't mistaken." Norman brushed aside the implication. "Yes, that would be customary. A small investment in the company as evidence of good faith."

"Thought as much." He nodded sagely to himself.

"You won't get a better deal anywhere else." The man pointed a finger towards the window. "Look out there. The country is going to the dogs. I've already said as much. This Labour government does nothing but sit on its hands and whine that there's no easy solution. Baldwin and his crew are little better. They can't grasp that the old remedies don't work anymore. What we need is a fresh start, firm leadership – a charismatic figure to inspire change, with the drive and determination to take over the reins, sweep out the old and bring in the new."

"You're talking about someone like Mussolini in Italy?"

"Yes, I don't deny it. Look what he's achieved to modernise his country, make it a power in Europe again."

"A British *Duce*?" He smiled at the thought. "Where are we to find such a heroic figure?"

"Echo answers who. None of the old fogies amongst Labour or the Tories, that's for certain. Till that happy day, we must fetch for ourselves as best we may."

"I don't say you're not right on that score," he conceded. "As a matter of interest – how much were you thinking of asking?"

"Two thousand pounds."

There was a gasp of astonishment. "You call that a small investment?"

"Certainly, in the grand scheme of things. It's the exact amount your sister put into my publication. She had a good salary while it lasted. And, as I already explained, every penny was repaid to your father."

"But surely that was a loan, was it not? This is something different. I could lose the lot."

"Or make fat profits if things go well, as I fully expect. Tell you what I'll do. Treat the cash as a loan, if you must. Then you can convert it into equity at a later date. And make even more money." He stood up. "I'll give you peace to enjoy your meal now. You have my card. Phone me if you're interested. *Bon appétit*!"

Hugh Lixmont was left to make what he could from such an unexpected encounter. He was more than half inclined to dismiss the bounder as no more than a confidence trickster. At the same time… much of what he had to say had the ring of truth. And it was interesting to discover that the pater had helped out Elizabeth in her hour of need. Could he do any less for his own son? He examined Norman's business card once more, before carefully tucking it into his waistcoat pocket.

* * *

Glasgow

Councillor Baird. Councillor Iain Baird. The words could still give a thrill, six months after he had won East Govan for the ILP. Morag had been cock-a-hoop at his victory, boasting to all and sundry that now he was in a position to do great things for the city's working class. Mary Barbour had unbent so far as to welcome him to the council chamber. His star was decidedly in the ascendant. But he was canny enough to know that fortune seldom lasts long. Politics was a fickle beast. Already the ILP was reduced to a small rump within the wider movement. There were strong rumours of disaffiliation, or even expulsion, from the Labour Party. It was only prudent to make hay while the sun shone.

His gaffer at the Trades Council had not been slow to point out the advantages of his new status. No, it went further than that: he had been made abundantly aware what was expected of him. Rab Youngston had not grafted night and day to secure his nomination for the seat, and then his election, just to have his efforts go to waste. Glasgow Corporation had a never-ending supply of business contracts to award: it was only commonsense to ensure a fair proportion was steered in the right direction – to those willing to go the extra mile to guarantee success for their bids. Council members on committees generally lacked the expertise, or were too busy to sift through applications: rather than that, they would rely on the judgment of their departmental officials. Need more be said? Rab would furnish the clients; it would be Iain's responsibility to sound out a sympathetic planning director prepared to give advice in the right quarter. Easy as pie, Youngston had insisted, as they raised a toast to the new enterprise.

Any nagging doubts had been speedily laid to rest. Early results had been promising; and he had no cause for complaint over his share of the spoils. Now he was about to embark on yet another undertaking; and Rab had left him to finalise the details. The City Chambers was, of course, out of the question for a consultation, but there was little chance of being disturbed at the office of Govan Trades Council. The surrounding wasteland, long neglected after slum clearance, had at last been earmarked for urban renewal, for redevelopment as a housing estate. And if all went well, this very building would finally be demolished – to make way for, of all things, a picture palace. The irony was not lost on him.

Standing by the window on the upper floor, he gave a grunt of satisfaction at the sight of an approaching motor car. Vehicles of any kind were rare enough on this stretch of roadway. A black Austin pulled up: the toot of its horn sent him scurrying downstairs to greet the visitor he had been told to expect.

"Mr Norman?" He had no difficulty in recognising the man. Starting to run to seed, flashy clothes – that had been Rab's description.

"Iain Baird?" There was a brief handshake. "I've heard a lot about you."

"Nothin' bad, I hope." He turned to lead the way. "Come away up. Ye'll need to mind the steps. They're a bit wonky."

They clambered the stairs in silence, broken only by the ominous creak of the treads. Reaching the top, the newcomer paused to catch his breath. "Thank God I don't have to do that every day. By the way," he went on, "I've taken the liberty to bring a colleague with me. I trust you've no objections."

Iain frowned. An associate had not been part of the arrangement. And the fewer who knew about the proceedings, the better. He looked back. Following up the staircase was a taller, slimmer figure, more soberly dressed, and with something of a military bearing. He shrugged his shoulders. It was scarcely worth an argument.

"Aye, just as ye like," he mumbled. "It makes nae odds to me. Come away ben an' we'll get on wi' it."

"Good." His nose caught the whiff of the surroundings. "You don't believe in much of the way of comfort here," he commented.

There was a knock at the doorway. "Ah, here he is now. Allow me to introduce Mr – Captain, I should say, Lixmont. And Master Baird. I believe the two of you are not unacquainted." A broad grin danced on his lips at the looks of blank astonishment.

Hugh Lixmont was the first to react. "What the hell—?" Angrily he rounded on the speaker. "So that's the bastard who – Oh!" He had just enough presence of mind to check himself.

"Who has a brother with the temerity to marry your sister? Is that what you were about to say? It wasn't hard to put two and two together. I do know something of the family history. But I'm surprised you should get worked up at such a trifle." His eyes narrowed. "Unless there's something else I should know."

"How can there be?" He would not rise to the bait. "It's just that I refuse to have anything to do with that scum."

"Harsh words." Norman eased himself into the padded swivel chair. "We can't always choose our bedfellows in this line of business. Sure you won't join us?"

"Not if this is the way you conduct your affairs. It isn't decent."

His gesture of disdain was met with a bland smile. "Now there's the pity. I had intended to allow you to cut your teeth on this little venture. As my deputy, of course. You would be working closely with our friend here. But since you are obviously embarrassed by the idea—" He appeared to consider. "What do you have to say, Baird?"

"Me?" Hitherto Iain had remained in the background, a silent witness to the confrontation. It did not take him long to realise he had little to fear. Lixmont's tirade was little more than the futile rambling of a washed-out army officer, lacking the wit to sense he was in the grip of a stronger influence playing him like a fish on the line. A delight to watch, though he was careful to conceal his glee. "I dinnae hae an opinion. I'm just the hired hand."

"You hear that, Captain Lixmont? You insult a man to his face, and he refuses to bear a grudge. You'd do well to follow his example." He turned back to Iain. "Perhaps you would be kind enough to fetch another chair. I think my colleague might reconsider his decision."

"Never!" Lixmont spat out the word. "I'll take myself off – just as soon as you hand over my cheque."

"Ah! I wondered when you'd get round to that." He was totally unfazed. "It's just not possible, I'm afraid. And before you explode, you'd be well advised to hear me out."

The hint of menace in his voice made an impression. "All right, then." It was almost a snarl. "I give you one minute."

"I doubt I'll need that long. In the first place, as well you know, your cheque is locked in my safe."

"I can wait while you fetch it."

He ignored the interruption. "Secondly, you will recollect that the amount is for only half the sum agreed. I was prepared to defer the balance on condition your contribution was to be regarded as an investment, not a loan. I have your signature on the deed."

"I'll stop the cheque."

"In that case it would be necessary to sue for breach of contract. What do you imagine your father will make of that?"

The shaft struck home. The expense of going to law? The publicity of a hearing in court? The old man would hit the roof. Their relationship was already strained, to say the least. It had been made abundantly clear that support of any kind was out of the question. Paying off the debts of his wayward son had drained his financial resources, not to mention the cost to his reputation, or so he had claimed. It was left to the mater to pour oil on troubled waters. She had pressed her own savings on him. Only a measly thousand – but enough to give him a start. And he had let it slip from his grasp.

His thoughts were bitter as he pondered the alternatives. Should he salve his pride and walk away, or throw in his lot with this parcel of rogues?

For long moments he hesitated, his eyes darting restlessly from one to the other – from the greasy cad who had tricked him, to the bounder who had raped his sister. But what choice did he have? He steeled himself to put on a brave face, and eat humble pie.

"I – I apologise. Nick." It was a struggle to get it out. "I shouldn't have lashed out like that. Please forgive me. It's just that it came as a shock to see—" His voice trailed away.

"You've had second thoughts? I knew you'd come to your senses." He could afford to be gracious. "Well, well, never mind. Come and sit down. We've wasted enough time already." He glanced round. "You don't mind, do you, Baird?"

"Nae bother, sir. I'd be glad tae welcome Mr Lixmont. I'm sure we'll get on like a house on fire."

There was a sharp intake of breath. The brute apparently thought he could take liberties, presumably under the impression he could rely on Norman for protection – so long as his services were required. He gave him a fixed look as he took his place.

Forced to squat on a rickety chair, expected to listen attentively as details were hammered out, he found the proceedings tedious in the extreme: it was hard to stifle a yawn as the discussion focused on planning permissions and deeds of disposition. Dry as dust, he thought to himself. Only when the subject of financial arrangements was raised did he stir himself to show some enthusiasm. Nevertheless, it came as no little relief when matters came to an end, and Norman slid over a bulky envelope.

"For your expenses, Baird. I know I can depend on you to seal a good bargain. Anything left you can keep as a bonus."

"Very generous o' you, I'm sure. Thank ye kindly, Mr Norman." The packet disappeared into an inside pocket.

"As for you, Hugh, I hope you've been following closely. You'll be in regular contact with Baird, so you'll require lodgings in Glasgow. Have you found a place to live?" There was a shake of the head. "No? Thought not. That'll be the next step on the programme. Don't bother to thank me. The rent will come out of your salary." He began to gather up his papers. "By the way, Baird, perhaps you could help me out. You're in the ILP, are you not?"

"Aye. Councillor for East Govan. But ye ken that fine."

"Just so. I was wondering if you ever came across a chap who used to be a member. Briefly, I might add. Down south, not your local branch. But with a distinctive moniker. Name of Mosley – Sir Oswald Mosley."

Iain stared blankly. "I might have heard o' him," he admitted, after a moment's thought. "Who could forget a handle like that? Why d'ye ask?"

"Oh, just a casual interest. Then you do know him?"

"Never met the man. But I did see him – just the once, ye understand. It was last year, when he came up for Wheatley's funeral."

"Wheatley?" Lixmont could not resist a mild curiosity. "Never heard of him. Have you, Nick?"

"The only bugger worth his salt in MacDonald's cabinet, Hugh. Died of a brain tumour, I believe. Is that not the case, Baird?"

"Ye could put it that way." He scowled in spite of himself. For all his faults, John deserved better.

"Well, never mind that now. What did you make of Mosley?"

"Ach, a regular Tory toff. Strutted round like he owned the place. I'm no' surprised his ain kind jaloused he was ower big for his boots. That's why he turned tae us. We were the poor saps just waitin' to dance to his tune." He broke into a grin. "And then he took the huff when he didna get what he wanted."

"I see. Was that the general impression in Glasgow?"

"Was it no'? The crowd was baying for blood – jeerin' an' catcallin' outside the cemetery." He hesitated. "Gie the man his due, though. Walked right through them. Never batted an eyelid. Gave as good as he got – good humoured banter, I hae tae say. In the end they gave him a cheer."

"And now he's formed a party of his own, I believe. He calls it the New Party."

"Very original, I don't think. But he's wastin' his time if he thinks that'll help him. Third parties have nae chance. The other two hae it a' sown up atween them. He should have stuck wi' Labour or the Tories an' worked his way up. Now he's blown it. I doubt we'll hear much o' him in future."

Norman sighed. "You could be right. All the same…" Abruptly he turned to leave. "Come along, Hugh. You've a billet to find. And I've a cheque to bank."

ELEVEN

New Allegiances

Glasgow
June 1933

"Baird! Tracked you down at last."

The Member for East Govan looked up stonily. "Captain Lixmont, as I live and breathe." There was no warmth in his greeting. "Ye're quite the stranger these days. So ye've come tae gloat, have ye?"

His visitor smiled faintly as his eye swept round the tiny office deep in the bowels of the City Chambers. "So this is where you hide yourself? Hardly room to swing a cat." He glanced down. "I see you've been reading the evening paper. Anything interesting? Like the report of a juicy trial?" he added with a sly grin.

Iain Baird scowled bleakly. "What's it tae you?" he growled. "It's none o' your business." He could feel the tension rising. For days now he had devoured every scrap of information to be gleaned from the newspapers. Attendance at the trial itself was unthinkable; he could not bring himself to show face on the public benches in the courtroom. The verdict was only to be expected: guilty, on all counts. Not so the sentence, which he had just discovered in the stop press: five years imprisonment, at hard labour. Anxiety gnawed at him. Was that fate awaiting him as well?

"Nothing to say, Baird? I can see I've touched a nerve."

His heart leaped at the cool mockery. "Rab would never clype on me," he muttered sullenly.

"No? Honour among thieves, eh? Perhaps you're right. Time will tell." He flashed a smile. "I must say, Baird, I'd have thought you'd have had more sense."

"What the hell d'ye mean by that? If anythin'?"

"Well, look at it this way. You must admit we got on well enough at the start. In fact, you showed me the ropes, for which I'm not ungrateful." His voice hardened. "And then your chum, Youngston, went and spoiled things. Wasn't happy with his share of the deal, so he decided to set up his own building concern. Took you on as a sleeping partner, I'm led to believe. You should have stuck to what the pair of you were paid to do. As it is, he stirred up a hornet's nest. Did you ever stop to consider why the business came a cropper? Or that no one will touch you with a bargepole now?"

Iain bit his lip. It was true enough. He cursed the day he had allowed himself to be swayed by Rab Youngston. They should cut out the middleman, rake in the real profits for themselves. And he had fallen for it.

"I suppose Youngston diddled you into sinking your ill-gotten gains into his madcap scheme." Lixmont was remorseless. "And now there'll be nothing left."

"Naw." There was no point in arguing. The man seemed to know it all. Over five hundred pounds had gone down the drain – the entire contents of his bank account.

"You should have known vested interests would have something to say. Muscling into their territory? They would never stand for it. You were playing with fire. Literally, as it turned out."

He looked up sharply. "You mean that time at the yard?" The police had suspected arson, but nothing had ever been proved.

"Unfortunate, wasn't it? Pity there was no insurance. And then word going round that you were unreliable – cutting corners, using shoddy materials, and charging over the odds."

"Aye, ye fairly stuck the knife in there. Was that no' enough for ye? You had Youngston arrested on trumped up charges."

"Misappropriation of Corporation property? Attempted bribery of council officials? These are serious offences. He should have taken a warning. As it is—"

"Save yer breath. I suppose ye're here to tell me I'm next for the chop. Take it as read." He jerked a thumb. "Just fuck off."

"Temper, Baird? Your besetting sin?" He shook his head in mock reproof. "Not just yet, I'm afraid. God knows I've no cause to count you as a friend. If truth be told, I've always regarded you as beyond the pale, ever since… well, a certain event. But that's personal. I'm here on business."

"I canna think why. What d'ye want fae me?"

"All in good time. Let me ask you a question first. How are you off for money these days? You must be dependent on handouts from the ILP to keep the wolf from the door. But for how much longer? Membership dropping like a stone? Coffers running dry? They're in dire straits, and how you must know it."

"I get by," he snarled.

"Do you? I doubt that. In any case how do you fancy your chances for re-election in November?" He could not resist a dry chuckle. "Maxton made a big mistake in cutting ties with the rest of the Labour Party. Now it's Dollan who rules the roost in Glasgow. He thinks there's a good chance of winning a majority on the council. He won't want anyone with a seedy background queering his pitch. If you're out on your ear, what's left for you?"

Iain shuffled uncomfortably. There was no denying it. While James Maxton had swanned off to Westminster to spout socialism from the opposition benches, Patrick Dollan had remained behind to build up control of the party machine. When Maxton had split from Labour, his former associate had refused to follow, taking most of the rank and file in the local branches with him. Just like the tussle between Trotsky and Stalin in Russia, he could not help thinking. And most likely with the same result.

"Nothing to say, Baird? I can guess what's on your mind." Abruptly he dropped the pose he had adopted. "For God's sake, man, you're in a hole, and you know it. If that's not enough, there's always the chance of your past coming back to haunt you."

"Ye resort to threats now?"

"Perish the thought." The mask of reason was restored. "I'm only here to see if we can help."

"We?"

"There's a group of us. We'd like you to come to a meeting this evening." He held out an envelope. "The address is inside. And something for your trouble. It really would be in your interests to come," he added quietly.

For long moments Iain hesitated, as though unwilling to commit himself. "I suppose ye can leave the letter," he grunted at last. "Though I'll hae to see how I'm fixed."

Lixmont nodded. "Please do," he said gravely, as he turned to go. "Perhaps Dunlop's journal has its uses after all."

He was gone before Iain could react to the parting shot. Dunlop's journal? What devilry was this? Blackmail? Surely that was impossible – not now after so long. So why dig up ancient history when more immediate ammunition lay to hand? The puzzle was beyond him. What was certain was the barely concealed ultimatum: play ball, whatever that might turn out to be, or share a prison cell with his former partner in crime.

With that unhappy thought in mind, he turned his attention to Lixmont's missive. It was the work of moments to rip open the gummed seal, insert his fingers for the enclosure. He gasped at the sight of a folded slip of engraved paper, even more so when he realised what was in his hand – a five-pound note! If someone was prepared to pay handsomely for his services… well, that was a horse of a different colour. He felt inside once more and withdrew a pasteboard. On the face was an embossed address in Pollockshields – doubtless one of the fine mansions built to house Glasgow's merchant class. Underneath was a scrawled inscription: *7pm*. He glanced at his watch: barely time to dash home for a quick wash and brush up. Fortunately, Morag would be out, as like as not on some errand of mercy to oblige Mrs Barbour. She had already made remarks about his sour mood this past week or two. More awkward questions he could well do without.

It was early evening as he reached his destination, a leafy avenue off the Nithsdale Road. Any qualms that he might arrive late had proved groundless. True, the Southside was far from his usual haunts, but the journey itself had been a doddle: catch a train on the suburban line and seek directions at the local station. The sight of the impressive Victorian villa at the road end was reassuring; much less so the view of two idlers lounging by the heavy wrought iron gates. He had met the type often enough before – big, brawny individuals who looked as if they knew how to handle themselves. He was careful to avoid any hesitation as he marched up with as much swagger as he could muster. But nothing was said; there was no challenge to delay or impede him. He was totally ignored as he passed through, though instinct told him hostile eyes were watching his every movement.

There was a row of motor cars parked in the driveway, a knot of chauffeurs chatting and smoking cigarettes: he gave a brief nod, and hurried up the steps towards the entrance portico. Before he could ring for admission, a door opened to receive him; a figure in a neat lounge suit led him up a grand, curved staircase, and wordlessly pointed to a chair. Obviously not a household servant, he told himself, as the man glided silently away. Iain settled himself down to wait. He could hear the murmur of voices behind the door of an adjoining room. Who could be behind the summons, and for what purpose? It could hardly be for some legitimate end. If so, then why the secrecy – or threat? Was it political, or merely criminal in intent? A growing suspicion began to form in his mind.

Time dragged. Somewhere below a clock struck the quarter, then the half hour. He might have expected this. Leave him to kick his heels; let the suspense prey on his nerves. He stifled a yawn. Rising to his feet, he began to pace up and down to relieve his stiffening limbs.

"Ah, there you are, Baird." He spun round at the sound of a familiar voice. "Taking a little exercise, what? We're ready for you now."

His eyes glittered for a moment. Hugh Lixmont never let slip an opportunity to belittle him. Despite the temptation, he resisted the urge to respond in kind, contenting himself with a scowl as he was ushered into the apartment. Dominating the surroundings was what he took to be a highly polished dining table, now littered with papers, and the dregs of whisky and brandy glasses. On the far side was ranged a group of six or eight expressionless faces. Typical stuffed shirts, he could not help thinking.

There was a polite cough. "Mr Baird, I presume." The speaker looked up from the document he appeared to be studying. "My name is Risdon. Captain Lixmont is, of course, known to you. I gather you are old friends." His lip twitched slightly, as though in appreciation of a private joke. "These other gentlemen hold positions of standing in the community. They are sympathetic to our cause. You may speak freely in front of them. Won't you be seated?" He indicated a solitary chair opposite.

Iain blinked. So that was the ploy. Put him facing the window where the sinking sun's rays would catch every feature. Well, perhaps two could play at that game.

"Cause?" he queried. "You said cause. What in hell d'ye mean by that?"

"A fair question." Risdon gave a knowing smile. "But we should like to hear from you first."

Without warning he launched into a blistering interrogation. Iain could only stammer helplessly as question after question was fired at him. Did Mr Baird subscribe to the view that slum housing conditions were a national disgrace? Did the working class deserve better? Was it right that a fair day's work should be rewarded with a fair day's pay? Should British jobs be reserved for British workers? Was foreign immigration the root cause of depressed wages and heavy unemployment? He tried to protest, to claim there was no time to think, far less give considered answers. But it made no difference: the pace never slackened.

It was torture to endure the relentless inquisition. Did bankers put private profit before the needs of the nation? Had British trade been left at the mercy of international finance? Should scarce resources be squandered in paying off overseas loans? Was there a need for a *Britain First* policy in the war against poverty? Did the solution lie with the imposition of a strong, authoritarian government? Should it have the power to ignore or overrule spineless politicians in Parliament? He found himself nodding weakly to almost everything hurled at him.

"I think we have the picture now, Mr Baird." The tirade ended as suddenly as it had begun. "I take it we are as one on the ends. The only real question is over the means to be pursued." He looked up inquiringly. "Come, come. What I meant is that you people on the Left are fixated on the class war. We, on the other hand, wish to further class cooperation for the greater good – bury differences and collaborate in the interests of country and empire." He broke off sharply. "I assume you know who we are?"

"Aye." He found his voice at last. "Mosley's mob. And yer *biff-boys* at the gate. I worked that out."

"Hmm." Risdon frowned. "Hardly the way I would express it. But we'll let that pass. Our organisation is the British Union of Fascists. And members of our Defence Force exist only to uphold the right to free speech," he added primly.

"Call it what ye please. Anyhow, why wid ye be interested in the likes o' me?"

"Mr Baird, we look to the future. The country must be prepared to resist external foes. Modernization, innovation, technological change: these are essential for the health of the nation. The present regime in Italy has worked wonders. Now Germany has fallen to us, in the shape of National Socialism. The movement is on the march over much of the rest of Europe. Here, In Britain, this so-called National government has no answers to the crisis we face. Only strong leadership can provide us with these."

"Ye mean Mosley. Well, he doesnae stand a chance in Scotland. Look at what happened last year when he put in an appearance. They threw stones at him, sent him packin' wi' his tail atween his legs."

"An exaggeration, I would have to say." He made a mental note that the fellow needed a lesson to show more respect. "Occasional setbacks are part and parcel of the road to power. One only has to look at the German *Fuhrer* for evidence of that. The important thing is to rise above adversity, and pursue our ends with renewed vigour. That is why it has been decided to initiate a recruiting drive in North Britain. We hope to have thirty branches established by the autumn. Captain Lixmont here has kindly agreed to help organise the campaign. His army background will be invaluable."

"But I still dinnae see—"

"How you should be involved? Is that what you were about to say?" He gave a bland smile. "Allow me to explain. You must be aware that former colleagues have become disillusioned with the ILP, and have come over to us. Following in the footsteps of the founder of our crusade, as you will know. We were wondering how you might respond to an invitation to join up."

Iain drew a quick breath. "You're askin' me to stomp around in yon ridiculous outfit, throwin' out an arm tae cry *Hail Mosley*?"

"Blackshirt? You object to the uniform?" He shrugged his shoulders. "No matter. We had something rather different in mind."

"Ye want me to stand for the council as a fascist?" The idea seemed incredible. But what else could it be? "I widnae stand a chance. They'd howl me down – if nothin' worse."

"You may rest assured on that score. There is no intention to put up candidates for any election. At least not for the present."

"Then what?" It was hard to imagine what the man might want, or even who he was. Evidently some bigwig from Party HQ in London, judging by his accent, and how everyone else seemed to kowtow to him.

Risdon appeared to consider before replying. "It is not general knowledge," he said slowly, "but the BUF has two categories of membership. The vast majority make no secret of the fact. However," he continued, "there is a much smaller, secret list. It includes prominent figures in society who prefer to remain in the background until the time comes for decisive action." He looked Iain full in the face. "And in addition, those whose operations on our behalf we would wish to conceal."

"Oh!" The scales dropped from his eyes. Now he knew the significance of Dunlop's diary. It was not seen as a weapon for blackmail, but as proof of his former activities. "Ye want me to spy for you?"

"That's an ugly word. But in essence – yes. Captain Lixmont will explain the details." He nodded towards Hugh, who had not spoken a word since fetching him into the room.

"You would be reporting directly to me," he began crisply. "You will remain a member of the ILP. You may, if you wish, stand for election as a Labour councillor in November. As a matter of fact, it would be useful to us were you to win. Resources can be provided to help you – discreetly, of course."

"Then I'm to be yer eyes an' ears? Let ye ken what's goin' on?"

"For which you will be well rewarded." He glanced back at his chief.

"Thank you, Captain Lixmont. It may become necessary to go a little further than that on occasion, Mr Baird."

"Ye mean stir up trouble?"

"I fear so. Civil disorder? Fighting in the streets? Such occurrences, regrettable though they may be, would serve to show the present government is unable to cope. It mirrors the situation in Germany before Herr Hitler was asked to restore stability and the rule of law. The Blackshirts will always stand ready to give assistance to the civil power in fulfilling its responsibilities."

Ian gulped. Did the bugger really believe what he was implying? He made an attempt to temporise. "Can I hae time to think it over?"

"I'm afraid not. We must press you for an immediate decision."

Desperately he looked round the table. But there was no hope to be read there. For a moment he wavered. Lixmont's steely glower gave promise of the consequences of refusal.

"Then I accept." What else was there to be said?

* * *

Edinburgh

It was meant to be a Red-Letter Day, a grand celebration of his seventieth birthday. But he had tactfully explained that, in his opinion, his wife was making too much of the occasion. Besides, his chambers were planning a function on his final retiral from the legal practice he had founded. Moreover, his colleagues on the city council would mark his service to the community when he stood down at the forthcoming election. Surely that would be sufficient by way of public ceremony. For the moment he would be quite happy with a small family gathering at home. Her initial reaction had been hostile, but he had stood his ground, and in the end she had given way. Now he had been banished to the morning room, while Hilda fussed around, directing operations for his birthday lunch.

The telephone in the hall cabinet began to ring, loud and insistent. With a gesture of irritation, he buried his head in his newspaper. If this was a call to congratulate him or, worse, contact him on some trivial item of business, then someone else could deal with it. This was his day, and he was determined to enjoy it in peace, at least till the family arrived. The ringing stopped; there was a low buzz of voices. Now he could relax.

"Edward!" His wife appeared in the doorway. "Can you not answer the phone? Am I to be left to do everything?"

"Sorry, dear." He laid side his paper. "I'm afraid I didn't hear it. In any case you gave strict instructions I was not to stir from this room."

"Fiddlesticks! That was Hugh. He says he can't come after all. Pressure of business. It's impossible to get away. He sends his apologies." She looked suspiciously at her husband. "If you left the invitation till the last minute—"

"Not in the slightest. I wrote to him a fortnight ago. And he sent a reply saying he would be delighted to come."

"When was that? I saw nothing."

"It was addressed to the office." He gave her a smug grin. "You know what I think?"

"I cannot imagine. Anyhow, I've no time to stand here and listen to idle chatter. There's a host of things still to be done."

"Oh, this is far from idle chatter. Your son was very gracious in his letter. Apologising for past misdeeds, letting me know how well he was getting on, saying he would make me proud of him again."

"So? Very right and proper. I trust you were pleased."

"Not exactly. Reading between the lines, I had the impression he was expecting to walk into my seat on the board. Now I wonder what little bird chirped that idea to him."

"Oh!" She flushed at the twinkle in his eye. "I might have hinted that I'd see if anything could be done."

"Evidently he's had second thoughts on that score." He made an effort to spare her blushes. "Look here, Hilda. I don't blame you for trying. He always was the apple of your eye. And I'm aware you've kept in touch with him."

"But still—"

"It's pointless to go on, my dear. What you wish is impossible, even if it were in my power to grant it, which it is not. As I have already explained, the other partners made it quite clear that they would not tolerate his presence. They insisted I sell out to them, which I have done. And at a more than fair price, I might add. The proceeds will form part of my estate, to be divided equally between my children when the time comes."

"But that might not be for many years," she protested.

"Hugh will not be disinherited. That's the best I can do. And it's more than he deserves."

"I understand that. But in the meantime—"

"You feel I should help him out? For your information, Hilda, I've been at some pains to check up on his activities. You know, of course, that he fell in with that fellow – the rascal who let Elizabeth down so badly. And now they're thick as thieves." He fixed an eye on her. "You should have advised your son to choose his friends more carefully."

"But you can't think he would be a party to any wrongdoing, Edward. I mean, running a chain of cinemas in Glasgow, providing houses for the working class. Surely these are for the benefit of the community."

"Is that what he told you?" He gave a wry smile. "Apparently some of his projects sail pretty close to the wind. Moreover, not content with that, it seems he's taken up with Mosley's crowd – the fascists, you know, like Mussolini in Italy. Or even worse, Hitler in Germany."

"I don't see what's so bad about that," she sniffed. "If it's the only way to keep out those nasty communists and socialists. Extreme situations might call for extreme methods."

"Hilda, you must be aware I have no truck with socialism. But fascists and their brand of violence is no answer to the problem. They're two sides of the same coin, if you ask me."

"How can you say that?" she rasped indignantly. "Sir Oswald is a gentleman. So dashing and charming on the newsreels. And that moustache – it makes him look like Douglas Fairbanks."

"A trifle young for you, Hilda," he chuckled. He was tempted to comment on her naivety, but it would only send her flouncing out in a huff. Fortunately, rescue was at hand. "I think we should call a truce, my dear. I see the family coming up the path."

Her eyes smouldered momentarily, but then she nodded sagely. "*Touché*, Edward. I stand corrected."

There was a knock at the doorway. She whirled round at a timid face peering in. "Yes, Agnes, what is it?" In an instant she was mistress of the house again."

"Excuse me, mum. It's Mrs Elizabeth and Mr Alastair."

"Happy birthday, daddy." His daughter brushed past the maid to embrace him with a kiss."

"Many happy returns, sir." His son-in-law advanced a little more formally to offer his congratulations.

"And Eddie?" Her mother was looking round. "I don't see him."

"Oh, there was a call on the telephone for him just as we were leaving. He'll be here in a few minutes."

"Some friend, no doubt?" She frowned slightly. "No matter. Sit yourselves down while I attend to things in the kitchen."

"Here's your card, daddy." Elizabeth plumped herself next to him on the settee. "I'm afraid you'll have to fetch your present for yourself. In a manner of speaking, that is."

"Thank you very much. But I don't quite understand."

"We've arranged for you to have your portrait painted, silly. It'll look good in the hallway for everyone to notice when they arrive."

"I'm sure that was very thoughtful." He had half an idea his chambers were planning a similar gesture. Two pictures might be one too many.

"What is it, daddy?" She looked at him shrewdly. "Are you put out by the thought of yourself in oils?"

"Not at all. Delighted, in fact." He sighed. "Well, perhaps there is something. I suppose you're wondering where Hugh is."

"It had occurred to me. After all, you did let me know my brother had been invited."

"Ye-es. But at the last minute he found himself unable to come. Your mother is a bit touchy on the subject," he added, putting his finger to his lips. "So don't mention it to her."

"Mention what?" Lady Hilda bustled in, followed by the maid with a tray of champagne.

"Oh, nothing, my dear." He had forgotten how acute her hearing could be. "It's – it's just that I chanced to let slip that the family's present did not come as a complete surprise."

"Did you?" She gave a glare of disbelief, but decided to let the matter drop. "Agnes, please hand round the glasses."

When they had toasted Sir Edward's health, she lost no time in bringing up the subject uppermost on her mind. "Eddie appears to be leaving it rather late. I trust he is coming."

"Naturally." Her daughter waved away the thought. "He would never miss his grandpa's birthday."

"Hmm. How is he getting on at the varsity?"

"Pretty well, by all accounts," said Alastair. "He was quite cheerful about his exams. But we won't have the results till next week."

"Of course. I had no doubts. What about his plans for the summer?" she added casually.

"There's nothing fixed as yet," Elizabeth broke in hastily. "At least there's been no mention of anything in particular. No doubt he'll tell us when he has some news."

"That's what I was hoping to ascertain. We were wondering if we could persuade him to join the kirk's summer gathering again. He's been sorely missed this past year or two."

"You'll have to ask him yourself. Alastair and I would never try to force him against his will."

"Quite so." She rose from her seat. "I thought you might care to help me with the final arrangements for lunch. There are flowers to be sorted for the table. Give the men a few minutes for a chinwag on their own, don't you think?"

Elizabeth made as if to protest; then apparently thought better of it. "Of course, mama," she said quietly.

"Heart of gold," murmured Sir Edward, as the sound of receding footsteps died away. "Though she can be rather wearisome at times." He frowned slightly as he turned to his son-in-law. "Take a pew, old man. I sense you're not exactly on cloud nine. Is it Eddie?"

"Heavens, no. There's no problem in that regard."

"Something you want to get off your chest, perhaps?"

"Well, you'll hear about it soon enough. I've been informed that my secondment is to come to an end. Evidently the SED is unable to bear the expense any longer. I'm summoned back to the Department. Either that, or resign from the civil service."

"I see. Have you made up your mind yet?"

"Not quite. But I can't say I fancy going back to my old post. Life will be hardly worth living under Harkness."

"I think you can rest assured on that score. I've heard on the grapevine that your old chief is leaving for pastures new – in Whitehall, I'm led to believe."

"The Treasury, no doubt. His penny pinching will go down well there." There was genuine bitterness in his voice. "All the same, I'd feel like a fish out of water. I'm probably better suited to the classroom. As I believe I've told you before, my preference was always to be a teacher."

His father-in-law gave a start. This was another attack of conscience. It might be a strength in the boy, but not when taken too far.

"Let's not be too hasty, Alastair. You must be aware of the impending shakeup in the civil service. The Scottish Office is to move its HQ up to Edinburgh. A grand new building is planned for the Calton Hill."

"I know. On the site of the old Calton jail. Can you believe it?" he snorted. "I can't accept it's just coincidence."

Lixmont's head jerked back; then a slow smile spread across his features. "Ha, ha! Very good, Alastair. I'm glad you've not lost your sense of humour. But to be serious, think of the prospects for the future. You've proved your case. There is now wide acceptance of the need to raise the school leaving age. That would mean secondary education for all. It's just a matter of time."

"Assuming you are right, sir, I still don't see—"

"It's staring you in the face, man. What is to go into these extra years of schooling? The shape of the curriculum will be the next big issue. You could have a ground breaking involvement here."

"That's all very well, sir." He was not to be tempted so easily. "But the purse strings will still be controlled from London. Devolution only goes so far. The Scottish Office may have plans for reform, but how are they to be carried out if the money to pay for them is not forthcoming?"

"What are you implying, Alastair?"

"Scottish affairs are rarely debated in Parliament. We have our own traditions of education. Are these appreciated in Whitehall or Westminster?

Of course not. Scotland has to go its own way if it is to maintain its own separate and distinctive system. And that can only be done through a national assembly with its own tax raising powers. It requires political, as well as administrative, devolution."

"Political devolution? Are you proposing a form of home rule?"

"Why not? Elected by the voters and answerable to them."

"It would never work." He shook his head, almost in disbelief. This was a fantasy to be firmly nipped in the bud. "It's not so long since both the Liberals and Labour were chorusing a pledge to home rule. Now look at them. One has all but disappeared at the polls, and the other has thought better of such a hare-brained idea."

"I can't deny that. But now there's a Scottish party with the sole object of achieving self-government."

"Just a fad." He was openly dismissive. "People have more sense. Almost everyone realises that the only way to tackle the problems facing this country is through unity, not diversity." His scorn deepened. "I understand there are two competing nationalist parties now. It seems they're only capable of squabbling amongst themselves over what kind of Scotland they'd like to see."

Suddenly he stiffened. "Hark! I can hear them coming back," he hissed. "Promise me you'll do nothing until we've had time for another chat."

Alastair could only nod weakly as the family matriarch swept into the room, closely followed by an anxious looking daughter.

"You'll never credit this, Edward." She could not wait to get it out. "It would appear your grandson has been making undesirable acquaintances. Elizabeth tells me he has been consorting with another student, a young woman of questionable background. A bluestocking, like as not – a person with the most radical of views."

"That's not fair, mama." Elizabeth felt her hackles begin to rise. "Fiona Handling is far from the virago you seem to imagine. Although I've only met her a few times, I've always found her polite and respectful. Though I must admit she can on occasion present her opinions rather forcefully."

"There, I told you so." His wife's eyes gleamed with triumph.

"Please don't interrupt, mother. I was about to say that you are twisting my words. She is no worse than I was at the same age. When I fell in with the suffragettes, you recall?"

"That was quite different." She hastened to deny the comparison.

"Was it? I prefer to think of their relationship as similar to the one I had with Alastair when we were studying together." She smiled engagingly at her husband.

The master of the house groaned. Here was a first-rate family row in the making. "Ladies, please! Must you always be picking quarrels? This is supposed to be my birthday treat, in case you didn't know."

Elizabeth was immediately contrite. "Forgive me, daddy. I didn't mean to spoil things… Oh!" The bell pealed in the hallway. Seconds later a youthful figure almost bounded into the room. "Here's Eddie now." She could have hugged him for the distraction.

"Sorry I'm late," he called out breathlessly. "Hope I haven't kept you waiting too long."

"No-o." Lady Hilda recovered her composure. "We were just about to go in."

Remembering his manners, he hurriedly gave his grandmother the expected peck on the cheek, before greeting his grandfather rather more enthusiastically with his best wishes. Then he turned to face his parents.

"That was Fiona ringing up to tell me it's all settled. I haven't mentioned the youth camp at Rowardennan before, because I didn't think there would be a place for me. But Fiona managed to squeeze me in at the last minute. It's fixed for the week after next. That means I'll know my exam results before I leave."

"Youth camp?" Hilda was genuinely perplexed. "I thought you might consider our kirk this year, but if it's another church retreat—"

"Hardly, granny." He could not resist a chuckle. "It's mainly outdoor activities. Hiking over the hills, sailing on Loch Lomond, singsongs round the campfire – that sort of thing."

"Has it been organised through the university?" she asked anxiously. "At least given its stamp of approval?"

"Well, there'll be plenty of varsity students there." He caught the look of dubiety. "It's all above board. Separate accommodation for males and females. And no drinking allowed. You've no objections, I hope."

"None at all." His mother looked round, as though daring anyone to make an adverse comment.

"That's a relief. But I say, I'll need to cut things short here. Fiona wants me to go over for the final arrangements. I'll have to get my skates on if I'm to travel to Glasgow and back today."

"Glasgow?"

"Yes. That's where Fiona lives."

As Alastair later remarked to his wife, the expression on her mother's face was worth a guinea a box.

* * *

Stirlingshire
July 1933

First impressions would indicate the Victorian hunting lodge was a prime example of baronial architecture, nestling proudly above the shores of the loch. But that was from a distance. Closer inspection revealed a different picture, with signs of neglect and decay all too evident in the honey-coloured stonework. And the effect was reinforced by the surrounding rows of dilapidated barrack-style huts, probably thrown up during the war as a rest centre for wounded servicemen. Whoever had bought up the estate had not seen fit to have them demolished, but instead had the brass neck to advertise them as holiday lets. Iain Baird shook his head in derision.

It went without saying this was just part and parcel of a pattern throughout the Highlands. The golden age of shooting parties and tartan splendour was crumbling to dust; lairds had been living beyond their means for years. Debt, heavy mortgages, crippling death duties had become the norm; land had been sold off, bit by bit, to keep the wolf from the door. The Great War and postwar depression were the last nail in the coffin, forcing many to face the inevitable, sell for a song, and resign themselves to a life of genteel poverty elsewhere. He could take a grim satisfaction from that.

But had anything really changed? Perhaps it was only to be expected that old money would give way to new – war profiteers like as not, eager to source outlets for their ill-gotten gains. Bankrupt estates were an easy target; vultures would be quick to batten on any opportunity. The big house might be seen as a potential country hotel, or the wartime huts as chalets for trippers from industrial cities. No doubt the economic slump had put paid to that plan, leaving little option but to cut their losses and hire out the premises as and when they could. How ironic that on this occasion it should be chosen as the location for a socialist youth camp.

However, there was little point in idle speculation; his main concerns lay elsewhere. He had come by an early train and registered his arrival. Now he was killing time in a half-hearted tour of inspection. For the moment the place was all but deserted: if so disposed, he could breathe the fresh air while he watched the swoop of the curlew over the still waters of the loch, or listen to the faint bleating of sheep in the distance. But it would not be long before the peace was shattered. Already he had caught sight of the convoy of brakes and traps wending their way up the track from the country station. In minutes hordes of exuberant youngsters would be filling the yard with their excited chatter.

Moodily he began to trudge back towards the main house. There was a refuge of sorts to be found there, in the poky garret allocated to him in one of the turrets. It was all of a piece, he told himself sourly, having to solicit an invitation to attend as an observer. College brats and their ilk, with no experience of real life, held few attractions for him.

Yet Captain Lixmont had decreed he must enrol for the duration, and on the flimsiest of suspicions. It was common knowledge that the Bolshevik leadership in Russia had been badly rattled by the rise of fascism as a political force in Europe. Italy and Germany had already fallen to the forces of the extreme right; other countries might follow suit. Little wonder that Stalin's response had been to demand that parties of the left should band together in a United Front to resist the threat, and rally to the support of the Soviet Union. But to even hint that a youth camp might be used as camouflage for secret meetings, where socialist leaders might draw up their own plans… well, that was stretching things beyond belief. So far as was known, only Jimmy Maxton was booked to put in an appearance, and that only briefly to deliver a keynote address. The BUF had a collective bee in its bonnet, and he had been sent on a fool's errand.

Nevertheless, it would be foolhardy to ignore Lixmont's strictures. His instructions could not have been more explicit: keep his ear to the ground and take note of anything even vaguely open to question. And he had been left in no doubt that a negative report was not an option. But was there any need to confess to failure, suffer the rough edge of the paymaster's tongue – if nothing worse? It should not be too difficult to concoct some story that would pass muster. Perhaps a tale of straws in the wind, arrangements for rallies and protests at some future date… he could work on the details later. In the meantime, the leading vehicles were pulling up in the grounds.

"Uncle Iain!" The call could be heard above the din of excited passengers disembarking to stretch their legs. He gaped in astonishment. A sturdy youth was waving, rushing towards him. "Thought it must be you," he gasped.

"Eddie?" He peered closely. Incredible as it might seem, there could be no mistake; even though it had been nearly four years since their last encounter.

"I came with Fiona. Here she is now." They were joined by a tall, rather slim young woman. The glasses she wore gave her the appearance of a prim schoolmistress. Without hesitation she thrust out a hand.

"I'm so glad to meet you, Mr Baird," she gushed. "My name's Fiona Handling. Eddie was wondering whether you might be here. He's told me you're his uncle. And, of course, I already knew about your work for the Party. I've heard you speak a few times. This is an honour for me."

"Well, I'm damned." Iain still seemed lost for words.

"Fiona is a leading light in the varsity ILP group," Eddie explained. "But she lives in Glasgow, at least during the vacations."

"I see. Well, thank ye kindly, Miss—"

"Please call me Fiona." She looked round. "I'm sure you've a lot to say to each other. I'll just go over and have a wee chat with some of my friends. There's no hurry to check in."

They watched as she disappeared into the throng by the front door. "Is that yer lass, Eddie? She seems to ken what she wants."

"I suppose you could say that. At least we're often in each other's company."

Iain nodded. He was recovering from the initial shock. "How did ye come to meet her?"

"At the university. We were in the same tutorial for European history. She was a bit puzzled over something, and I was able to help her out. Then we got talking. She invited me to a student meeting. And after that—" He gave a wry smile.

"So that's how it all started?" He had few illusions. The poor sap had been easy meat for her. To set her cap at him would be all in the day's work, a small price to pay to entice a new recruit for the cause. Abruptly he changed the subject. "Dae yer folks ken ye're here?"

"Well, they know I'm at a youth camp at Rowardennan. Open air exercise, and all that." He looked up anxiously. "You won't let the cat out of the bag, will you?"

"Naw. Ye're quite safe there. Ye'll mind I'm the black sheep o' the family. I've nothin' to dae wi' them now."

"I suppose so." His face fell. There was something that had to be said. "I'm only sorry I treated you that way the last time we met. I've often regretted saying what I did. To condemn you as a person, just because of your political views, was unforgivable, especially as I now believe you were right."

Iain waved away his embarrassment. "It wisnae your fault. That auld besom put ye up to it. Ye werena to ken any different." He grinned affectionately. "So ye've seen the light. Have ye joined up wi' us yet?"

"Not quite. Fiona's at me to take up membership. I'll probably sign up when we get back in the autumn."

"Watch out, then. Yer maw will hae kittens when she finds out. As for yer grandmother—"

"I know, I know. I'll just have to wait for a favourable moment to break the news." He sighed. "It's not really down to granny. I can't deny she's a bit bigoted. Just the way she was brought up, I suppose."

"Leave it at that. I've a wee job on hand. Catch ye later." He gave Eddie a pat on the shoulder and ambled away.

That at least was true enough. Maxton had left him a draft of his speech, and would be expecting helpful comments. It would be as well to glance through it before he arrived. As for Eddie, the boy had made a rod for his back. Sooner or later a hard lesson lay in store, probably when this hussy grew tired and looked for pastures new. That could not be helped, but for the time being there might be a silver lining for himself. Once Eddie was in the ILP there would be a ready excuse for greater contact with his son.

TWELVE

Hurrah for the Blackshirts

Lanarkshire
September 1934

The straggling column of unemployed miners trudged wearily towards the outskirts of the city, where food and rest would be provided in the local community hall, before the final leg of the journey and rally on Glasgow Green on the morrow. The organizers might have wished for a larger contingent from the coalfield: the route had been well publicised in advance, as had its purpose – a protest against the hated Means Test which reduced family benefits almost below subsistence level. Still, the bulk of the marchers appeared to be in good heart, determined, if not over enthusiastic, to see justice done. They had sluggishly grown in strength as they made their way from one pit village to the next, and now comprised something over two hundred. Not an overwhelming number, but enough to put on a show. Iain Baird stood by the wayside to watch them pass. The poor saps, he thought to himself. None of them could possibly imagine what lay in store before the day was done.

"Look alive there, lads," he called out. "It's no' far now. There's scran an' a hot drink waitin' for ye." He managed to curb a slight nervousness in his voice. It was not by choice that he was there as a steward for the latter stages of the march, though he had volunteered to stay in the rear to chivvy on the laggards.

No doubt news of the hunger march would have come as music to Captain Lixmont's ear. As a consequence, little time had been lost in directing his underling to offer his services as a guide: his background and knowledge of the local area made him the obvious choice for what the fascist leadership had in mind. And he had had little option but to grit his teeth and make the best of it. There was no longer any need to threaten him with arrest and imprisonment; dire financial straits were enough to ensure complete submission. The ILP was now very much diminished as a political force: he had lost his seat on the council at the last election, and there was no place for him as a salaried employee anywhere in the Labour movement. Now he was utterly dependent on his subvention from BUF funds. Naturally, payments had been dressed up for the sake of appearance: to all intents and purposes he remained a dedicated socialist, prepared to adapt to changed circumstances without complaint, and to find employment as a labourer on a building site – but with a sympathetic foreman prepared to turn a blind eye whenever he was called away for other purposes.

The ploy, simple as it was, had proved effective over the past months Snippets of information, passed on at regular intervals, had sufficed to keep Lixmont off his back. But seemingly the leadership was now growing more ambitious. It made the mistake of believing its own propaganda, the lies and humbug churned out in the pages of its weekly rag. *The Blackshirt* could not resist boasting about a tranche of new branches set up in the aftermath of Mosley's triumphal visit to Edinburgh. It only remained for some grandstanding event to set the seal on fascism as a real force in the land.

Such was the intention. But would it work? He shook his head in a weary gesture of resignation. Scotland was barren ground, as he had quickly come to realise. But the *Black House* in London could never grasp that. Membership of the new off-shoots was tiny. It was often impossible to sell copies of *The Blackshirt* on street corners without attracting hostile attention. Even when crowds did gather to hear one of the leaders, it was usually in anticipation of a spectacle, with rowdy scenes of violence, rather than any attachment to the cause. Prejudice and bigotry were no strangers north of the border. But there was little room for other brands of extremism in a country where militant sectarianism and aggressive nationalism were well established. Virulent antisemitism made little appeal since Jewish communities were few and far between, and posed no obvious threat. By contrast, the links with Mussolini and Rome were too stark to be ignored by anti-Catholics. And its version of British nationalism showed scant sympathy for any sense of a separate Scottish identity. Little wonder, then, that the BUF had failed to make much headway.

He cupped his hands to light a cigarette, inhaling deeply as the final group passed by and disappeared from view. It would not be long now. A momentary stab of conscience was ruthlessly cast aside: it was up to every man to look out for himself. His instructions had been to stand well clear and let matters take their course. No more than a few hundred yards ahead, hidden by a bend in the road, the route would be blocked by a carefully prepared trap. Any attempt to force a way through would be the signal for scores of Blackshirts, bussed in from the north of England, to rise from concealment and strike at their opponents from the flanks and rear. He could only hope that the miners would see sense and turn tail before serious damage was done.

Minutes passed. He threw away the stub of his cigarette, strained his ears for the sounds of conflict. At any moment he had expected to hear the shouts of alarm, the taunts and jeers as battle was joined. And there could be little doubt as to the outcome. Surely unarmed marchers, weakened by months of deprivation, would be no match for the bullyboys of the *Defence Force*. Yet there were no signs of flight, of desperate men fleeing the scene in disarray. There was nothing to disturb the quiet of the evening air.

Anxiety grew as he tried to marshal his thoughts. Something had gone far wrong; that was all too evident. Should he go forward and investigate what was amiss? He had been given strict orders to remain in the background. Every instinct cautioned him to give no pretext for any blame to be laid at his door. Yet the suspense was hard to bear. He was still undecided when a lone figure hove into view, swinging along the roadway as though without a care in the world. A single glance told him the newcomer was neither a pitman nor a Blackshirt. Still, it could do no harm to ask if he had witnessed anything untoward on his travels. He waited a few moments as the man drew closer, then stepped into his path.

"'Scuse me," he began.

"Is that you, laddie? Thought it might be."

Iain's jaw dropped at the sound of the voice. An impression had already formed that there was something vaguely familiar. Now the words spoke volumes. It was Stan – Stan Robertson. The bane of his life had returned to plague him.

"Christ!" he gasped. "Ye fair gie a man a fright, Stan. I mean, turnin' up like a will-o'-the-wisp. How in hell's name d'ye manage it?"

"Surprised to see me, eh?" His old mentor chuckled. "I've spent half the day up yonder." He half turned to gesture. "Beside thon big rock ye can see. I've been watchin' the road."

"But why wid ye dae that, Stan?" The initial shock was giving way to bewilderment. "I can understand why ye came back – the Popular Front agin fascism an' a' that. But I never thought tae find ye springin' up here, in the middle o' nowhere. I just cannae see the sense in it."

"No? It's no' that hard tae work out, if ye set yer mind to it. As ye rightly suppose, the Comintern sent me hame to ginger up the fight against the common enemy. Just at the minute I'm attached to the NUWM. That's the National Unemployed Workers' Movement, in case ye'd forgotten," he added with a touch of sarcasm. "The very same that's been happy enough to make use o' your services."

"So that's how ye ken about this march?" Iain ignored the jibe. "Ye found out I was one o' the guides."

"Just so. And while we're on the subject, is it no' a bit strange that ye're hangin' around here by yersel'? Were ye no' meant to be shepherdin' yer flock to their billets for the night?"

"It's no' what ye might think," he muttered. "I was to wait by the roadside in case o' stragglers. Make sure naebody got lost." It was the excuse he had prepared should the question arise. He could only trust to luck that it would pass muster with such a doubting Thomas.

"Is that a fact? It puts me in mind o' the dilution an' conscription rallies durin' the war. A'ways keen to bring up the rear, were ye no'? Now look at ye. Standin' here like a daft gowk this past half hour." He gave a shrug. "Ah well, it's no' likely there'll be any latecomers now. So ye'd best get yer skates on if ye expect any grub left for ye afore ye bed down."

Iain hesitated, but only for a moment. "Then I'll dae just that." There was no point in staying any longer. To delay might well rouse suspicion. Besides, Stan was not there by chance. It was impossible to believe he was not involved in this mystery. "Are you comin' as well?"

"Aye. I'll see ye safe tae journey's end. We can chew the fat as we go."

"Suits me." He decided to take the bull by the horns. "Stan, just why were ye watchin' the road, as ye term it? Are we no' trusted to dae the job on our own?"

"Ye think that's the reason?" There was a twinkle of amusement in his eye. "Well, ye can rest easy on that score. But I've a wee somethin' tae show ye. It's no' far now."

Iain was left to curb his impatience as they walked on in silence. Trust

Robertson to keep him guessing, he thought bitterly. It was only as they reached a sharp bend in the road that his companion called a halt.

"There was a gang o' them just ower there," he said quietly. "Hidin' away so ye widnae see them till the last minute. A wheen o' thae fascist bastards, wid ye believe?"

That much he already knew, though he had the wit to stare blankly, as if bemused at the revelation. "Mosley's mob, ye're sayin'? That cannae be right, Stan. There's been nae trouble so far. Now ye're tellin' me there's been a rammy. Christ, surely we wid have heard the racket. And there's been nothin'. No' a cheep."

"Aye, ye wid expect that, right enough. But what I havnae explained is that they cleared off afore your folk appeared on the scene. Just up sticks an' skedaddled back the way they came." He gave a broad grin. "Must have sussed out that somethin' was wrong and got cold feet. Mind you, there werena ower many o' them – maybe twenty or thirty. No' much chance agin a couple o' hundred, as ye might imagine."

"But I still dinnae get it. Why bother to put up for a fight if they kent the odds were that long?"

"Ah, there's the rub. They were waitin' for their mates."

"Mates? Reinforcements, like?"

"Aye. Busloads o' Blackshirts ordered fae England."

"And they didna turn up?" Light was beginning to dawn.

"Nae fear. No' when we got to hear o' their ploy." He tapped his nose. "It's surprisin' who yer friends might be."

"Then how—?"

"Did we manage to put them off the scent? It wisnae that hard, no' when we found out the routes they would take. It's amazin' what ye can dae wi' a few workmen puttin' road-up signs in their way. We sent their buses scootin' a' ower the place. God kens how long it'll be afore they tumble they've been diddled. And by then there'll be nothin' for it but tae gang back tae England. An' good riddance."

Iain blew out his cheeks as he grasped the implications. Surely that meant he was off the hook. He could scarcely be held accountable in any shape or form for such an unforeseen turn of events. He offered his hand. "That was well done, Stan. It wid have been a poor lookout had ye no' saved us."

"All part of the service, laddie. Ye winnae be bothered by them again. Now maybe ye could dae somethin' for me."

"Anythin' ye like, Stan. Ye only hae to ask."

Robertson nodded. "Ye see, it's like this, Iain. I've been back a month or twa, and it's only now I'm startin' to realise what a hell o' a task they've set me. I hae to admit I could dae wi' some help."

"Really?" This sounded ominous. Already he regretted his hasty promise. "What exactly did ye have in mind?" he asked cautiously.

"We made a good team, Iain – you an' me. We could be that again. Why no' come back to the Party? Ye'd be welcomed wi' open arms."

So that was the shift. To lure him into rejoining the CP. In that case he had a ready answer. "Ye seem to forget that you were the one to throw me out o' the Party. *Not ideologically sound*: was that no' it? What's changed since then?"

"I canna deny it, son." His old boss tried to sound contrite. "Ye ken what it was like back then. It was against my wishes, but I had nae option. There was nae money tae pay ye. But they couldnae admit to that. They had to find another reason." He read the doubt in the younger man's eye. "That's a' washed out now. Ye can work full time wi' me. The same wages as before – maybe a bit more. There's nae shortage o' funds fae Moscow these days." He added a final appeal. "Ye cannae enjoy slavin' as a navvy for a pittance."

Robertson had obviously gone to some lengths to check up on him. He had pitched his offer to good effect; the prospect of richer pickings had its attractions. And Lixmont would be cock-a-hoop at the thought of his agent as a card-carrying member of the Communist Party. The temptation was there; but slowly, almost regretfully, he shook his head. It would be madness to allow himself to be ground down once more, be at his beck and call, day and night. Besides, Stan was a downy bird. Should the slightest hint ever arise of any connection with the BUF... No, the game was not worth the candle.

"Sorry, Stan. It wid lie on my conscience. Maxton an' the ILP took me in when I had naewhere to go. I canna just leave them in the lurch."

"Even though yer chum an' his ilk are a busted flush? No' much influence where it counts now. If they ever had any," he sneered.

"Maybe so. But it's a question o' loyalty."

"Loyalty?" There was a sardonic laugh. "I thought ye a'ways wanted to be on the winnin' side." He was about to add more in the same vein, then appeared to think better of it. "Well, ye're a fool, but I'll no' press ye. Leave it at that."

"Thanks, Stan. I was sure ye'd understand."

"Nae harm done. How's that lass o' yours. I hear she's still in cahoots wi' Mary Barbour. There canna be much profit in that."

"No' a brass farthing. She helps out for love o' the cause."

"Very noble o' her. And what about yer boy?" he added casually. "They tell me he's daein' great things at the university. Ye should be verra proud o' him."

Iain started, then flushed with anger. "What the hell d'ye mean by that? Eddie's my nephew, as I've telt ye often enough."

"Have it yer ain way." Robertson shrugged his shoulders. "Is that why ye're often in Edinburgh? Tae pay him a visit?"

"Ye seem to ken a'thing," he hissed. "So ye'll be aware I'm responsible for links wi' other branches. I only go there when there's a meetin'. In case ye dinnae ken it, he's in the ILP as well."

"That's what I'm led tae believe." He smiled blandly. "Led on by thon firebrand that's got her talons intae him. Now what was her name? Fiona – Fiona Handling. Aye, that was it. I must hae a wee chat wi' her sometime. See if I can persuade her to go a' the way an' join the CP. And if she does, your – young Eddie, I should say – will nae doubt take the same road."

Iain Baird choked, then ground his teeth in impotent rage. Was he ever to be rid of the bugger? A direct appeal had been rebuffed, only to be replaced with the threat of other measures to attain his ends. The implication was all too evident. Eddie must be protected from his malign influence. But how was it to be managed?

Dimly he became aware of a signpost: *Cambuslang*. That was their lodgings for the night. He looked round for directions, but Robertson was already striding away into the gathering dusk.

* * *

Edinburgh

The younger of the Baird brothers adjusted his necktie and hesitated only briefly before knocking firmly on the door at the top of the main staircase.

He had been awaiting the summons for over a week; and now the moment had arrived. He felt a tingle of anticipation as he was ushered into the inner sanctum, and his head of section rose to greet him. Almost at once his eye fell upon the thick manila folder on the desk. It was his draft report on the secondary school curriculum which he had submitted before the summer vacation.

Yet again he had had cause to give thanks for the wisdom of his father-in-law in urging him to return to the SED, and take up an offer to conduct an enquiry into schooling which would meet the needs of a modern society. What part Sir Edward had played behind the scenes he had no means of knowing, but the new chief had appeared sympathetic, listened attentively to his ideas, and handed him a roving commission with broad terms of reference. Naturally he had sought out advice from experts in various fields, but the work and conclusions were essentially his own. Should his recommendations be accepted, or only minor amendments required, then he would produce a final report for the Scottish Office, hopefully to be rubberstamped by the Minister himself, before being issued as an SED Circular to be adopted by schools and colleges.

"Sit ye down, Baird." A slight gesture sent his secretary gliding from the room. "No need for formalities, eh? This is not an official meeting. Sorry for the delay in inviting you in for a chinwag, by the way. Things fairly pile up when one is away on furlough."

"Of course, sir. I quite understand. And how was your break?"

"Oh, fair to middling. I read your report while I was away."

"That was good of you, sir." Alastair leaned forward expectantly. The interview would be challenging, he had no doubt of that. But he would be given a fair hearing, given every opportunity to make his point. Ewan MacArthur had taken up his post with the reputation of a hard, but fair, taskmaster. He had few airs and graces, and treated his staff as colleagues rather than mere lackeys, quite unlike the oily officiousness of his predecessor. It came, therefore, as something of a surprise to find him hesitate, as though uncertain how to tackle the business in hand.

"Baird," he said at last, "I was the new boy in the Department when I was asked to hand this survey to you. I agreed, without reservation. And you have not disappointed me. I have been highly impressed with your efforts, and you are to be congratulated on the quality of your presentation."

"Thank you, sir." He waited patiently for his chief to go on.

"Harrumph." MacArthur cleared his throat. "Bearing in mind the purpose of your research, I have taken it upon myself to communicate the main findings to other section heads. Purely as a matter of information at this stage, I hasten to add."

"You mean there have been objections?" His face fell. His conclusions had not found favour. He could read the signs.

"Well, let's say there have been reservations on a few points."

"But if you will permit me to explain—" His voice tailed away at the sight of a restraining hand.

"I cannot blame you for expressing forthright views, Baird. I have been negligent in not exercising more supervision. But pressure of work…" He shrugged. "Be that as it may, on many issues I can find little fault with your judgment. Your argument that science and technology should be given more prominence in the curriculum is irrefutable. Nevertheless," he added with the faintest of smiles, "no doubt eyebrows will be raised among traditionalists at your treatment of the classics."

"But surely that's of little moment. There's no question of abolishing Latin and Greek."

"And I would concur. The main problem lies elsewhere. There is a chapter which might prove controversial." He thumbed through the folder. "Ah yes, here it is: *Culture and Identity in the Modern Curriculum*."

"I don't quite understand. Surely young minds should be offered the opportunity to appreciate their national heritage. It plays a key role in socialisation."

"That cannot be denied. But your approach weighs rather heavily in favour of the Scottish dimension, Baird. Your emphasis is on Scottish history, on Scottish literature. What about the story of Great Britain, of the British Empire? The study of Shakespeare and the Victorian novel? Are they not worthy of consideration? Did you not realise that your offering would be manna from heaven to certain minority interests?"

That gave Alastair a start. Could anything be known of his mild flirtation with Scottish nationalism? He had attended one or two SNP gatherings, but nothing more than as a spectator in the background. As a public servant there could be no possibility of becoming a party member, but had he been unduly influenced by what he had heard?

"I know nothing of that," he spluttered. "I have never contemplated joining any political party, if that is your meaning. Nor have I any truck with the notion of Scottish independence." That at least was true enough. Then he rallied. "Is it not the case that the SED enjoys autonomy over Scottish education? Surely it should be allowed to decide the best interests of the society it serves."

"Within bounds, yes. But the thrust of government policy over the last two centuries has been to focus on that which unites us as one nation, binds us into a common British identity. By all means include reference to great figures in Scotland's past. There can be little objection to that. But greater emphasis should be laid on the benefits of unionism, how North Britain has flourished as a result of that union. Moreover, it should be coupled with the achievement in building the greatest empire the world has ever known, bringing civilization to countless backward races over the four quarters of the globe. Something to take pride in, would you not agree?"

"But—" He was about to raise the rights of indigenous peoples to their own way of life, but thought better of it.

"See here, Baird. There is no intention to be overcritical. As it stands, your report could not pass muster. But if you were prepared to rewrite the chapter in question, tone down the points we have discussed—"

"Then it would be accepted?"

"So far as I am concerned. But perhaps you might benefit from some help with this task. As it happens, I do have someone in mind. Do you know Dr Green – Dr Ross Green?"

"No." He thought for a moment. "The name is vaguely familiar. Though I'm certain I've never met the man."

"Nor have I for that matter. But I have had a telephone conversation with him. He is at present up here on leave."

"I still don't see—"

"Dr Green holds a post as administrative officer in the SED. However, he has been on long term secondment, attached to the Foreign Office in Whitehall. He is an authority on comparative education. By that I take it to mean he investigates systems and structures in other countries, to discover whether there is anything useful to be learned. He rang to touch base with old colleagues in the Department. I happened to mention your report, and he expressed an interest in arranging a meeting. If you are agreeable, that is."

"Of course, sir. If that is your wish."

"Good." He touched a button on his desk, and the secretary reappeared. "Has our visitor arrived yet?"

"Yes, sir. He's here in the outer office."

"Then show him in." He rose to greet a somewhat short, stocky figure in a nondescript grey suit. "Dr Green, I presume. I am, of course, acquainted with your work. Your mastery of European languages is most impressive."

"You are too kind, sir. Though I must pay tribute to the early training I received here in the Department."

"And then went on to greater things." MacArthur bowed slightly. "Permit me to introduce Mr Baird, the author of our report."

Alastair had to force a weak smile as he took a rather flabby hand. This meeting had obviously been prearranged, sprung on him without notice. Rather a mean trick to catch him unawares, he could not help thinking. But before he could react, find the words to register a protest, his chief hastily made his excuses and hurried away. Clearly, he had no wish to be present at the interview.

"Good of the old boy to make himself scarce, would you not say?" The newcomer was evidently keen to seize the initiative. "But I find his office rather stuffy. Why not take a stroll through the gardens over the way? I found it an ideal setting whenever there was a particularly knotty problem to resolve."

"And I suppose I'm regarded as the latest knotty problem." It was hard to conceal a sense of resentment.

"Far from it, old chap. The very idea," he chuckled, making light of what was obviously ruffled feathers. "I've no doubt we can come to an understanding if we set our minds to it. Something to our mutual benefit, if you don't mind my saying so." There was a fleeting twitch of the lip. "Shall we be off, then? I assume you have a key to the gardens."

"Well, yes. But I'm not sure I can make sense of this. Are you implying you have some personal interest in my work?"

"All in good time. Walls have ears, you know." He turned and made for the door. Alastair had little choice but to follow on. Not even a word of explanation, he grumbled to himself as they left the building to negotiate the heavy traffic on Queen Street. He was none the wiser a few minutes later as he fished for his key to unlock the gate giving entrance to the private grounds sloping down towards the northern edge of the New Town.

"Here we are, then." The heavy ironwork swung back on its hinges. "After you, Dr Green." Carefully he closed the gate behind them. "No need to relock it. I assume we won't be here long. Do you mind telling me what you meant before we left the office?"

"Oh, about walls and ears? Nothing, really. Merely a figure of speech. I only wanted a quiet chat. No need for a secretary to take notes, is there?" He sniffed the air. "Nature in all its autumn glory. Shall we walk on?"

Alastair hid his disappointment. "I don't mind. But you didn't drag me out here to discuss the seasons of the year."

"True." He looked round. The gardens were deserted, which suited his purpose well enough. They had reached an awkward stage of the proceedings. It was as well to tread warily.

"You know something, Baird," he began. "I have a feeling you and I have much in common." He ignored the sudden look of surprise. "Hear me out. We are both men of vision, prepared to recognise the need to move on from the outmoded ethos of a bygone age. The Great War changed everything. New ways of thinking are the key to the future, and society must adapt in its turn. Otherwise, we shall lag behind, become a backwater, while other nations rise to world domination."

Alastair could hardly believe his ears. What drivel was this? "You claim we have things in common? How can you know that? Oh!" A sudden thought struck him. "I suppose they sent you a copy of my report. Is that it?"

"No such luck." Green gave a hollow laugh. "Just a one-page summary. But there was another source open to me."

"Someone in the Department?"

"I'm afraid not. Your brother-in-law."

"Hugh?" he gasped in astonishment. "How on earth do you know Hugh Lixmont?"

"I had the pleasure of making his acquaintance in London last year. On the occasion of his visit to the January Club."

"January Club? I've never heard of it."

"No reason why you should. It's a meeting place where people of influence from many walks of life can discuss pressing issues of the day. But that's of little moment. To return to the point, Captain Lixmont told me about your work in the SED."

"The devil he did!" He spluttered with indignation. "I barely speak to him."

"That's as may be. But he is in close touch with his mother. No doubt she passes on the family gossip."

"Oh!" His spirits sank. Elizabeth could scarcely be blamed for chatting to her mother. Perhaps he might have been a little more circumspect in running his ideas past her. But how was anyone to anticipate such an unfortunate catalogue of circumstances?

"I see. That explains it. But I still fail to understand why my work should be of interest to you."

"Then let me enlighten you. I was particularly struck by your thoughts on *Culture and Identity*."

"That's the section most open to objection."

"Precisely. And that's why I'm here. To help reword it so that it becomes more acceptable."

"Really? Is it possible? I find that hard to comprehend."

"Not at all." His companion waved aside any doubts. "Your basic principle is sound. Direct teaching of values to the next generation is vital, far more so than stodgy scripture lessons. Religion may have been the opium of the people at one time, but is scarcely applicable to the modern age."

"But would there not be strong resistance to such extreme views?"

"Needs must," Green snapped, showing a hint of impatience for the first time. "Vested interests should be made to appreciate realities, by law if necessary. And that includes the influence of the church. European powers place great weight on youth as the future of the state. Programmed instruction in ideology is as important as mathematics or science, perhaps more so. Take Germany as an example. They have compulsory study in what is called *Race Culture*."

Alastair caught his breath. Now he had a glimmer of where this might be leading. "I've heard something of the kind," he said slowly. "The Nazis indoctrinate German children into believing they are the master race."

"Come, come, Baird." He smiled blandly, his good humour apparently restored. "That is surely an exaggeration. False evidence put out by a hostile press. It's not meant to be taken at face value."

"What, then?"

"It's merely a symbol of national pride. Not far different from your hopes for Scottish education."

"I doubt that." He was openly sceptical. "What about persecution of the Jews?"

"My dear man, the Germans have no quarrel with the Jews as individuals. It's the power of Zionism that must be curbed. Once Jews acknowledge they cannot play a disproportionate part in German society, then they have nothing to fear. Far from it. The German government has offered to give assistance to any wishing to return to their ancient homeland. Now what could be fairer than that?"

"I think I've heard quite enough, Dr Green." He was prompt to reject the explanation. To be fed this tissue of lies. To even hint his views were comparable to those of the Nazis… His eyes danced with suppressed rage. "I make no apology for rejecting your premise. Nor can I allow you to corrupt my work and alter that chapter to accommodate your – your warped creed."

Green stared at him, but could only read a fixed determination. He gave a sigh. It was obvious his efforts to suborn the younger man had gone to waste. "You're saying I can't persuade you? Have it your own way, then. I knew it was a long shot, but your brother-in-law thought there was a chance. We'll just have to look elsewhere. You will, of course, not mention this conversation to your superiors."

"And why not?" He recoiled in disgust. "You and your ilk seek to poison young minds."

"A trifle farfetched, Baird. But before you start complaining to others, you should consider your own position. I will simply deny your accusation, and I fancy I carry more weight than you do. A malicious attempt to cover your own misdemeanours. How does that sound? Affiliation to the nationalist movement in Scotland? Attendance at SNP meetings? Hardly an innocent pastime for someone in your position. Need I say more?"

"I see. You resort to blackmail?"

"Not at all. We have a mutual interest in saying nothing. I shall simply report to Mr MacArthur that, regrettably, we were unable to reach a compromise. And then take my leave. You will bear me out on that, and the matter will be closed. Do you agree?"

Alastair pursed his lips. The man was right. He had no evidence. There was nothing he could do. But at least his opponent had failed in his objective. He nodded bleakly.

"Good. I'll be off, then. Give me half an hour before you report back. I should be at the railway station by then."

Alastair was left to sink wearily onto a park bench. But there was no comfort to be had as he slowly recovered from the shock of his experience. His whole world seemed to crumble around him. For a second time the fruits of his labour would be rejected, cast aside as worthless. Not for the first time it occurred to him that he had been shunted off to entangle himself in what was regarded as a hopeless issue – a civil service ploy to neutralise a potential troublemaker.

"Baird!" It was an hour later that he was discovered, still sunk in gloom. "I've been looking all over the shop for you." He looked up despondently, then struggled to his feet. It was the chief himself.

"No, don't get up. I'll sit awhile with you." He coloured slightly. "Dr Green has explained the situation, and is now on his way back to London. I feel I owe you an apology," he went on. "It was not my idea to put you through what was evidently a distressing encounter. But I have superiors too, you know."

"I take it this means my report will never be published."

"I'm afraid so. It will be placed in the archives, along with your earlier submission. However, in years to come they may well be retrieved. The school leaving age is bound to be raised when conditions allow, and quite possibly more attention devoted to purely Scottish items. Till then—"

"No need to go on." He refused to be placated. "Carry on as a bean counter? What scope is there in that? You will have my resignation in the morning."

"Now hold your horses!" The ring of authority was not to be denied. "There may be a way through this. It would be a crying shame to have your undoubted abilities entirely lost to the Department."

"But I don't see how I could be of any further use."

"I was coming to that. There is a vacancy for an HM Inspector of Schools in the Eastern Division. Not exactly my province, but I have no doubt a favourable interview could be arranged. The post would involve some travel, but you would be based here in Edinburgh. In that capacity you would have an influence on teaching and learning, admittedly not on the same scale as you had hoped, but schools and colleges would surely benefit from your input."

"But—"

MacArthur waved away the expected protest. "No need to give me your answer now. Take a few days leave of absence. Talk it over with your family. At least promise me that."

For long moments Alastair stared motionless into the distance. At length he stirred. "I suppose it could do no harm," he muttered.

* * *

Renfrewshire

What did it all mean? He was puzzled, bewildered, and more than a little ill-at-ease at finding himself in such magnificent surroundings. The apartment into which he had been shown was small, though lavishly furnished. Over by the window a table had been set up, with gleaming place settings for a meal. It hardly seemed to make sense.

True, the delay in summoning him over the botched attempt to disrupt the miners' march was not altogether unexpected. Lixmont and the others would be casting round for a plausible scapegoat to carry the can for their own failings. Had a decision been taken to pin the blame on him after all? If so, then why lure him here, to a plush country estate? The axe could just as well have been delivered in a dingy Glasgow office. Adding to the mystery was the manner of his reception at the local railway station. Met by a liveried chauffeur, whizzed off in a powerful limousine, welcomed by a butler at the door of the stately pile, conducted by a footman through the great hall to what he took to be an anteroom, politely informed his hosts would be with him presently. Small wonder he felt bemused.

"Admiring the view, Baird?"

He spun round from the window. "Captain Lixmont. I jaloused I might be seein' ye here. And ye've brought somebody wi' ye."

"Surely you remember your employer, Baird." Hugh Lixmont stood aside to allow his companion to enter.

"Aye." He could sense his heartbeat quicken. "We dinna see much o' you these days, Mr Norman. I was just askin' mysel' why I was telt tae come here."

"You thought you had been called to account for – recent events, shall we say?" Nick Norman smiled faintly. "Well, you can set your mind at rest on that score. We've moved on since then."

"Then why—?"

"You find this impressive, Baird?" Norman cut him short. "It's in places like these that the real decisions are taken. Not in Parliament – nor on the streets. You'd do well to bear that in mind."

"I dinnae doubt it, Mr Norman. So this is where the party bigwigs meet?"

"On occasion, Baird. But not today. This is a country house weekend, to which Captain Lixmont and I have been invited. Most of the distinguished guests will have no direct connection with the BUF. Though it would be true to say they will have sympathy with many of its objectives. His voice hardened. "Now come and sit down."

Iain Baird allowed himself to be directed towards a high-backed chair. At least it seemed he was to escape censure. He could breathe a sigh of relief at that.

"Listen carefully, Baird. We arranged to come early and kill two birds with one stone. You will be gone before the rest of the company arrives. Perhaps," he went on more softly, "your experience here will serve to whet your appetite. Who knows what the future might hold – if you prove your worth." He turned to his associate. "Now, Hugh, would you be good enough to enlighten our friend."

"As you wish, sir. I'll not mince my words, Baird. Some of us are no longer fully convinced that Mosley and his Blackshirts are the way forward. We had high hopes at one stage, but his methods have borne little fruit. As was confirmed by that utter shambles the other week," he added drily. "Street fighting doubtless has its place, but more is required for ultimate success."

"We are taking you into our confidence, Baird." Norman gave him a warning glance. "This is not to be repeated elsewhere. Please go on, Hugh."

"Thank you, sir. In Germany the Nazis came to recognise that the parliamentary road was the only sure pathway to power. That is even more the case in this country. Only when we achieve a majority in the House of Commons can we tackle established institutions, begin to mould society in the national interest. But Sir Oswald Mosley fails to appreciate this. He refuses to put up candidates to serve in Parliament."

"That's because he knows there isn't a cat in hell's chance of winning any seats. Is that not so, Hugh?"

"Precisely, sir. There is simply not enough popular support for the BUF to make any real impact. Nor is there likely to be, as employment picks up again. Rather the reverse, I should imagine."

"Ye're tellin' me that, Captain Lixmont? What does it a' mean?" It came as a surprise to hear any expression of misgivings.

"I should have thought it was plain enough by now, Baird. Mosley has this idiotic idea of provoking the left into insurrection. Then all he has to do is to wade in with his Blackshirts, restore order and bask in the thanks of a grateful nation. And naturally take over the reins of government as well. Ludicrous, is it not?"

"Aye. At least the way ye put it. What's the alternative? Start another political party?"

"Heaven forbid! No, Baird," snapped Norman. "We must exploit the present system to our advantage."

"So how are ye to dae that?"

"Tell him, Hugh." He frowned and sank back in his chair. Superfluous questions were irksome, even without the suspicion of impertinence from a lackey.

"Very well, sir. A general election is on the cards next year, Baird. The National Government is bound to be returned with a thumping majority, leaving the Labour opposition in tatters. Ramsay MacDonald will be eased out of office. He's only a figurehead as it is. Baldwin will take over as PM, but only for a year or two before he retires. His successor will be the key. The Tory Party must move to the right, with a strong leader capable of driving through the reforms to restore Britain's position in the world."

"And what might these be? The same as the BUF?"

Lixmont shot him a dark look. "On the same lines, Baird, since you ask. Reinforcing the bonds of empire, building up the armed forces, dealing with left wing extremism at home, countering the threat of communism abroad." He counted them off, as though to a recalcitrant schoolboy. "And, of course, maintaining the best of relations with Germany."

"I see. And the Jewish problem?"

"Not of any real consequence. Not in this country, I'm glad to say." Norman heaved himself upright once more. "The propaganda aspect can be played down when it becomes necessary. After all, we might need to persuade the bankers to open their moneybags. The changes we have in mind will not come cheap."

Iain nodded slowly. "I hear what ye're sayin'. But ye still havnae explained where I come in. Am I still to report tae Captain Lixmont?"

"That will no longer be possible. He will be stepping down from his position with the BUF. Pressure of work, it will be put out. Instead, he has been asked to search out and recruit suitable Tory candidates to stand for winnable Scottish seats in the forthcoming election. In due course those who are successful will have their part to play when Baldwin's successor is appointed."

"Oh aye. And is there a body waitin' in the wings?" He could not rest the jibe. "Winston Churchill, maybe?"

"Good God, no," spluttered Norman, clearly taken aback. "He's not to be trusted."

"That's quite enough of that." Lixmont hastened to intervene. "Remember where you are, Baird." He broke into a sly grin. "It would appear your past has caught up with you again."

Iain caught his breath. "I dinna ken—"

"We have been approached by the security services." It was Norman who supplied the explanation. "It would seem they have need of you once more. Naturally we are only too happy to give our full cooperation."

"How the hell—"

"Dunlop's diary, Baird. Surely you haven't forgotten? I have told Mr Norman of your work in defence of the realm."

Iain flinched at the barb. "But that was ages ago," he protested. "I thought I was done wi' them."

"It would appear not. They have an interest in a former associate of yours."

"Who have? Police Special Branch?"

"Not exactly. MI5 has overall responsibility for counter-terrorism now. You're going up in the world, Baird."

"Former associate, ye say? I cannae think who that might be."

"Come, come Baird. Don't prevaricate." Lixmont was not to be fooled. "The man's name is Robertson. A communist agitator, agent of the Comintern, recently returned to this country. Has he made contact with you?"

"Of course no." It would never do to confess to an encounter, however fleeting. "It's years since I've seen him, and we didnae part on guid terms. He had me expelled frae the Party. But you wid ken that."

"You haven't seen him?" Hugh Lixmont smiled grimly. "Now that does come as a surprise. Our information is that at present he is involved with the National Unemployed Workers Movement. No doubt as cover for some deeper plot." He let the words hang. "And that is where you were employed as a guide."

"That's as maybe." Iain was alive to the implication. "Ye heard what I telt ye. He widnae be likely to get in touch wi' me."

"Hmm. Perhaps not. We'll let that pass." He paused. "By the way, you asked about my successor. Well, for the foreseeable future you will be subject to official supervision."

"Ye mean a police handler?" He groaned inwardly.

"Just so. An MI5 agent, at any rate. He will be in touch with you presently. In the meantime, you have been requested to locate Robertson and make yourself known to him. That should not be a difficult task."

"Ye think so?" he protested hastily. "Stan wid just smell a rat."

"I doubt that, Baird. How long is it since you lost contact?"

"Six years past. I havnae seen hide nor hair o' him."

"Six years? That's a lot of water under the bridge. The Bolsheviks have changed their tune since then. They can see the way the wind is blowing. This so-called Popular Front is their last chance to prop up their miserable regime. Robertson will be glad to see you, welcome you with open arms. All you have to do is make yourself agreeable."

"I'm supposed tae charm him intae tellin' me what's afoot?"

"Well, offer assistance and gain his trust."

"Look on it as a challenge, Baird," boomed Norman. "If you succeed in unmasking some dastardly conspiracy, it will be a feather in your cap. You will not find us ungrateful."

His head dropped. Evidently there was to be no way out. He had hoped to be able to keep the old fox at arm's length. Now he would have to eat humble pie, kowtow to his every whim.

Lixmont caught the look of dismay. "Cheer up, man. It won't be for long. Not if you play your part." He moved towards the door. "Time we were off, sir. There are still arrangements to be checked."

Norman glanced at the clock. "By Jove, you're right, Hugh. No need to hurry away, Baird. Stay and have lunch. Can't have you complaining we don't feed you."

Iain could only stare as a trolley was wheeled into the room. An attentive footman pulled back his chair at the table, seated him, lifted the silver cover from his plate. The food looked heavenly, fit for a king. He took a sip of the wine poured for him. Delicious, like the nectar of the gods. Now he knew why he had been brought here. See off Robertson, and dazzling prospects lay in wait. Taking up knife and fork, he fell to with a will.

THIRTEEN

A Tangled Web

Glasgow
February 1935

Morag Baird frowned as she took her place at the kitchen table and pulled the basket of old clothes towards her. High time she rooted out the clutter, she had decided, and a rare Saturday afternoon free from Mrs Barbour's campaign against hardship and poverty presented a golden opportunity. Mechanically she began to sift through the contents. Some items were fit only for the rag and bone man, but should bring in a few coppers for the poor fund. Others might still do a turn, if handed in for distribution to the needy. Applying herself to the task, she steadily divided the garments into two piles, but it was hard to work up any real enthusiasm. As usual, her husband had taken himself off with only a mumbled excuse, leaving her to draw her own conclusions.

Not for the first time she reflected on Iain's behaviour. Where once he would have groused about her absences from home, now he raised no objections when she took on yet more commitments. Why the change in attitude? Did he no longer care they seemed to pass like ships in the night? At the outset she had wondered whether he had gone back to his old philandering ways. But there was more to it than chasing other women. She was almost certain of that.

It was not difficult to put a finger on the source of the problem. She could appreciate his feelings at losing his seat on the city council, and the need to find some other means of employment. But to fall in with a pair of scoundrels like Elizabeth's ne'er-do-well brother, and thon greasy Nick Norman… Was that the best he could manage? His excuse would always be that beggars could not be choosers, that it was simply a means to earn a crust to allow him to continue his activities for the ILP. But she had had her doubts then; and they had deepened since. He rarely seemed to do much work on a building site; there was little sign of the calloused hands to be expected from heavy manual labour. True, the housekeeping money was on the table every Friday night – in fact rather more than the usual wage of an unskilled worker. A bloated plutocrat like Norman paying over the odds? That was hard to believe. And then there was the question of all those trips to Edinburgh. Did the local ILP branch really have need of his services so often?

Her brow grew darker. He had closed in on himself, was more guarded in what he said. She could pretend that the lack of communication was only a passing phase, that he would recover his old gallus ways, even though his uncertain moods had now lasted over a year. But for the moment that was the least of her worries. There could be no hiding her dismay at hearing an old comrade had made a reappearance.

Old comrade? Stan Robertson had always been more than that. She had never trusted him, nor ever would. He had come between them, cast a dark shadow over their lives. She had cheered the day they had parted company. So much for that, she thought bitterly. Robertson had only to snap his fingers, and his lapdog had come running. Once more they were inseparable, so far as she could make out, thick as thieves. His half-hearted explanation that Maxton had asked him to liaise with the communists in the anti-fascist Popular Front was laughable. The ILP leader might have made such a request, or more likely had the idea planted in his mind, but Jimmy Maxton would have been appalled that her husband would simply dance to his master's tune.

A sudden burst of light gave her a start; she had scarcely noticed the gathering gloom. For a moment she was dazzled; then her eyes adjusted to the glare.

"Iain? I didna hear ye come in."

"Nae wonder." He advanced into the room. "Sittin' here in a dwam. Why could ye no' switch on the light?"

"Aye, well. That's as may be." She glanced at the mantelpiece clock. "Ye're no' usually back at this hour. Did yer meetin', or whatever, finish early?"

"Meetin'? What makes ye suppose that?"

"It' just that ye a'ways seem to be wi' Stan Robertson these days." She smiled sourly. "Hae ye had a fallin' out wi' him?"

"Is that a' ye can say?" he snapped testily. "We're no' joined at the hip, ye ken. Naw, it was somethin' else."

That at least was true enough. This latest summons to the safe house in the East End had been far from welcome. How was he to account for the lack of progress when there was nothing worthwhile to report? Was it his fault that Robertson had decided, or had been instructed, to play his cards close to his chest? To all intents and purposes Stan was devoting all his energies on behalf of the unemployed. And there was no law against peaceful hunger marches, as he had pointed out. But that, of course, cut no ice with his MI5 handler. The security services were rapidly losing patience with his efforts, or lack of them. It would be in his interest to produce some evidence of wrongdoing before other measures might have to be taken. He could still picture the cold, sardonic leer as he was brusquely dismissed.

"Cat got yer tongue?" she rasped. "Or dae ye think it's none o' my business?"

"Eh?" The scorn in her voice roused him from his thoughts. As though he did not have troubles enough…

"Ye were gawpin' there like a stranded haddie."

"Christ's sake, woman! Gie a man a break. Ye're like a dog wi' a bone." He took a deep breath. "See here, it's no' a secret. There was a dispute wi' the foreman at the Yoker site. I was asked tae help sort things out. That's a' there was to it."

"Really?" She seemed unimpressed. "I didna imagine yer bosses wid thole any interference fae the likes o' you."

Iain flushed at the jib. "Well, ye ken noo," he hissed. "An' while we're at it, what in hell's name are ye daein' wi' a' thae auld claes on the table?"

"What d'ye think? Sortin' things oot, just like you." She made an effort. Trading insults was hardly worth the bother. "Look, there's many a poor soul wid be glad o' somethin' half decent to wear. Some o' this stuff hasnae seen the light o' day for years." She delved into the basket and pulled out a pair of corduroy trousers. "Like these, for instance. I found yer trews at the back o' the wardrobe. Any objection to giein' them away?"

"Dae as ye please. I never much liked them anyway." It was a small price to pay for any diversion into safer waters. He watched impassively as she ran her fingers through the pockets.

"Just checkin' to see there's nothin' left behind," she explained. "Hullo, what's this." Deftly she fished an object from the hip pocket.

Iain gasped, turned pale at the sight. He knew at a glance what it was. Jesus! His lost membership card. It had gone missing ages ago, almost forgotten after he had secured a replacement. Now it had come to light. And his wife was staring at it, as though struck dumb with horror.

"It's no' what ye think," he pleaded desperately. "I can explain everythin'."

"Can you?" Her lips curled in disgust. "*British Union of Fascists*? It's got yer name on it. And a membership number. Ye've even signed it. Are ye sayin it disnae belong to you?"

"No. Of course no'. I was telt – ordered tae join. They wanted me to spy on the fascists, find out what they were up tae."

"Who did? I suppose ye'll say it was Stan Robertson. Well, that'll no' wash. The date on yer card is long afore he came back. And dinnae dare lay a finger on Jimmy Maxton. He would never stoop that low."

"No. Ye're right. It was somebody else. But I cannae tell ye the name. Dinnae ask."

"Nae fear o' that. I'm done listenin' tae yer lies." She spun the card towards him. "Here, take it back. I wouldnae soil my hands on it."

It was the work of a moment to snatch it up, bury it in his pocket. "I hae to go out now. Dinnae wait up."

She sat motionless as he dashed away. A door slammed; she was left alone to dwell on his infamy. How could he have brought himself to live a lie? Iain was guilty of many faults; that she knew well from sad experience. But to go out of his way to deceive her, betray his own kind, sell his soul to the devil… it pierced her to the heart. She might have deluded herself, accepted his excuses, lame though they were. But that look on his face when he saw the card… It told her all.

At length she stirred, made an effort to pull herself together. There was nothing to be gained by wallowing in grief and misery. On another occasion she had fled from his violence. This was far, far worse. He had debased himself, destroyed any relationship they might have. The very thought of his presence made her cringe. Hastily pushing back her chair, she hurried to the bedroom to make herself presentable, and pack a bag.

* * *

Edinburgh

There was a knock at the open doorway, "Mind if I come in, Miss Elizabeth?"

The lady of the house gave a start as she looked up from her typewriter. She had omitted to close the door, and the clatter of keys must have carried to Morag's bedroom. Drat those wretched accounts! To deprive her sister-in-law of the rest she so badly needed was unforgivable. But the work simply had to be done that weekend, and the quiet of a Sunday morning had appeared an ideal time for the task.

"Of course. I'm only sorry you've been disturbed." She managed a wry smile of contrition. "And the name is Elizabeth, as I'm forever telling you. We are related, as well as being good friends, I hope."

"Sorry Miss – Elizabeth, I mean. Auld habits die hard, ye ken. I just looked in tae apologise again for burstin' in on ye last night."

"No need. I'm only glad you chose to come here. No woman should have to suffer the way you've been treated. Little wonder you were so distraught."

"Well, I'm no' proud o' that. But I couldna think o' anythin' else. And now I'm forgettin' my manners." She pointed to the books and papers scattered around the typewriter. "It must be important, workin' on a Sunday like this."

"Not a bit of it." Elizabeth hastened to reassure her. "It's just some overdue figures I have to prepare. The lease on our office is up next month, and the new landlord is sending someone to discuss its renewal. He'll want to know if we're still a sound proposition."

"There's nae doubt about that, is there? Ye said in yer last letter that things were lookin' up."

"True. But you never take anything for granted." She smiled faintly.

And therein lay the worry. She knew little of the new owners, beyond the information that the property had been purchased by an organisation trading under the name of Garnet Holdings. The communication went on to state that a representative would call in due course to inspect the premises, together with the books, with a view to negotiating terms for a possible renewal of the lease. The future of her business could well be determined in the course of the next few days.

"You remember this room, Morag?"

"How could I forget? It's where ye started up the advertising agency."

"And this is where we might end up again." She gave a wistful grin. "Forget I said that. You know you're welcome to stay as long as you like. And Alastair would say the same, were he at home."

"Aye, I was wonderin' about no' seein' him. But I didnae like to ask."

Elizabeth stared for a moment, then burst into a laugh. "No, it's not as bad as that," she giggled. "He's away at a conference of school inspectors."

"Oh, is that the reason?" She looked relieved. "Now ye come to mention it, I mind ye tellin' me how much he was enjoyin' his new job."

"Let's hope he's found his true vocation at last. It's a pity you missed him. He won't be back till the end of the week."

Morag nodded. "Maybe it's just as well," she mused. "I wouldnae like to see him dashin' off to hae it out wi' Iain."

"Well, you know what he's like. Especially when he feels his brother has overstepped the mark. However, we've time to put our heads together, decide what's for the best. In the meantime, don't even think about going back to Glasgow."

"That's verra kind o' you. But it wouldnae be fair, puttin' you to a' this trouble."

"Let me be the judge of that."

"But—"

"Not another word. It's settled," she said firmly. Morag was in no condition to face the world, far less her husband. She needed time and space to recover from the ill treatment she had evidently received.

"Aye, but I was thinkin' o' Mary Barbour. I couldnae just up sticks an' leave her in the lurch. She'll be wonderin' what's happened."

"Always thinking of others, aren't you?" Elizabeth gave her arm a gentle squeeze. "There is the telephone, you know. You could contact her at her office; let her know how things stand. From what you've told me, I'm sure she'll show every sympathy."

"That's a guid idea." Morag brightened. "Shall I ring her now?"

"Better leave it a day or two. Give yourself time to collect your thoughts, decide how you're going to break the news."

"Maybe ye're right. Everything's been spinnin' round in my heid."

"Perhaps it would help to talk about it now." Elizabeth thought she saw an opening. "You were a bit confused last night. It would appear there was no actual physical violence. Was it just mental cruelty?"

"Somethin' like that." A sense of shame swept over her. How could she reveal details of his infamy, even to a closest friend?

"Come and sit down, then. We'll have a wee chat by the fire."

"Aye, I'd appreciate that. Maybe I've been a bit hard on Iain," she said reflectively. "It's no' entirely his fault."

"What on earth do you mean?" Elizabeth could scarcely believe her ears. But then she might have guessed Morag would try to find excuses for his despicable behaviour. "Surely you can't still have a soft spot for him?"

"I'm no' sure how I feel. But that's no' the nub of the problem."

"What, then?"

"Well, since ye ask, it's my belief yon Nick Norman is at the bottom o' it all. Ye'll mind how he used tae take advantage o' ye, then just showed ye the door. He's gone up in the world since then, along wi' yer brother as his sidekick. But ye'd know that already. What ye might no' ken is that Iain fell in wi' them. They've got some hold ower him, and nae doubt involved him in their skullduggery. But what that might be, I've nae idea."

"You never told me this before."

"Naw. I didna like tae bother ye. Truth to tell, I a'ways had a notion Iain wid see sense, and break away frae them. But it wisnae to be. We've been driftin' apart, goin' our separate ways for months now, and yesterday it just a' blew up. He flounced out, and I couldna bear to stay."

"Well, you're safe now. And if that scoundrel dares to show his face, we'll know how to deal with him."

Morag gave a wry smile. "I dinna think he wid dae that."

"No? How can you be sure? He came for you once before. And you went back with him."

"Maybe so. But no' this time."

"Oh!" Her sister-in-law had given her a hint. There was more to this than met the eye. "Leave it at that, then."

"I dinna want to sound ungrateful. It's just that there's things I need tae get straight in my mind first."

"Of course." It was obviously a sore point. "I'm sure Eddie will be pleased to see you again. I heard him go out earlier this morning, but he shouldn't be long. I'm afraid he's rather out of sorts these days. He could do with someone to cheer him up."

"Crivvens! I'd nae idea. And here's me dronin' on about my problems."

She shot an anxious glance at his mother. "He's no' sickenin' for somethin', is he?"

"I don't think so. I wouldn't make too much of it. There's nothing physically wrong, so far as I can tell. Could be his studies are not going as well as he had hoped. Or more likely he's had a tiff with a lady friend. Whatever it is, he refuses to share it with us."

"All part o' growin' up, ye're sayin'? He'll get ower it in his own good time?"

"That's about the size of it. What else is there? Perhaps you—"

"Might hae a word wi' him? I'll dae my best. How long has this been goin' on?"

"Just a week. Last Saturday he never came home. He arrived back the next morning to say he had been at a student party, had too much to drink, and spent the night sleeping it off on the floor."

Morag smiled. "I dinnae see much amiss there. He's a man now. Surely he's allowed to sow his wild oats now an' again."

"There's no objection to that. He's stayed out late before, but he generally lets us know by telephone. He didn't do it this time."

"Well, he'd hardly remember to dae that if he had a drop too much."

"True. But then there's the way he made his excuses. I had a feeling it was not quite the whole story. After that he just clammed up. Hardly speaks a word. And he spends most of his time shut up in his room."

"It certainly sounds out o' character, but—" Was she making too much of it? An anxious mother fretting over a son growing into manhood?

"Hark!" Elizabeth put her finger to her ear. "This must be him now." The doorbell rang, loud and insistent. "Probably forgotten his key," she explained. "Cook will let him in."

They listened to the click of the latch as the front door opened and closed, the murmur of voices, followed by the trudge of footsteps slowly ascending the stairs. "In here, darling," she called out.

"Very kind of you to invite me in," said a wry voice from the doorway.

"Daddy!" she gasped in surprise. "What brings you here at this hour? You're usually at church, aren't you?"

"Not on this occasion, as you observe." Sir Edward Lixmont advanced to give his daughter a peck on the cheek. "I decided to wait till your mother was off the scene before coming over."

"Oh!" She was intrigued. Why make a secret of his visit?

Her father chuckled. "I see you have company. Good to see you again, Mrs Baird."

"Morag, please." Rather nervously she took his hand.

"As you wish." He turned back to Elizabeth. "I'm afraid this is not a social call. I need to speak with Eddie. Is he at home?"

"No, not at the moment." She frowned. The abrupt change in tone indicated that the matter was serious. "He's out for a walk, or something. I expect he'll be back soon, if it's urgent. Why are you so keen to see him?"

"All in good time. How does he seem to you?"

"Not his usual self, since you ask. Rather subdued, you might say."

"Hmm. Hardly surprising, given the circumstances. Has he said anything to you or Alastair?"

"Not really. We think he may have fallen out with his girlfriend. You remember Fiona – Fiona Handling? I have mentioned her name."

"Ah, yes. One of his classmates, as I recall. Something of a bluestocking, with radical views."

"That's the one. I sometimes think she is capable of eating him for breakfast."

"A dominating personality? Now that could be interesting. Has he received any correspondence this week?"

"Not that I'm aware of. But then I'm often away at the office when the postman calls. Something could have come for him without my knowing it. Why do you ask?"

"Bear with me. I need to hear what he has to say for himself." He gave his daughter a meaningful look. "It might be best if I spoke to him alone."

She gave a shrug. Why make a mystery of it? But she knew it would be useless to probe further. "Then we'll take ourselves off. I could do with some tea and toast, and Morag has had no breakfast as yet. Can we send something up to you?"

"Thank you, no." He stood aside to allow them to pass. "Sorry about this – Morag. Family matters, you understand. No need to feel any embarrassment."

He closed the door, and settled down to wait. The presence of a third party in the house had been a momentary distraction, but on reflection he felt there was little cause for concern. The woman would undoubtedly be the soul of discretion, should she hear anything untoward. Meanwhile, there were things to go over in his mind. The case against Eddie, from what he had been told, was damning enough. But was it conclusive? It appeared completely out of character. Much would depend on how he went about tackling the boy, if he was to get to the heart of the matter.

It was a good half hour later that he heard a rather tentative knock on the door. "Come in, old chap." His lawyer's eye took in the obvious signs of distress at a glance. "Take a pew, Eddie." He indicated a chair. "Enjoy your walk? Your mother informed me."

"Not really."

"No? I thought not." He decided on a direct confrontation. "I won't beat about the bush, Eddie. You've gotten yourself into a pretty pickle, haven't you?"

"I – I don't know what you mean."

"Don't prevaricate. It's written all over your face. You formed part of an anti-fascist mob. Your intention was to prevent a leading member of the British Union of Fascists from delivering a speech at the university. The authorities there had resolved that the principle of free speech, however distasteful in this case, must be upheld. You joined a group of students who could not accept this. An attempt was made to physically attack the speaker. You, and others, became involved in a brawl. The police were forced to intervene; you were arrested and held overnight in custody. Did you tell your mother any of this?"

"No." Eddie could only hang his head in shame. "I made up another excuse."

"Just so. The university subsequently had to decide whether or not to prosecute the ringleaders. In the end an alternative was adopted, presumably to avoid adverse publicity. As you will have been notified, a disciplinary hearing is to take place, tomorrow as it happens, and summons have been dispatched to those involved. I assume your mother is not aware of this."

"I – I couldn't bring myself to show her the letter."

"Couldn't? Do you realise the seriousness of your position? You could be sent down – expelled. What career could you expect after that? Have you nothing to say?"

"No." He had to choke back the tears. "I made a promise."

"Ah, now we're getting somewhere." So a misguided sense of loyalty lay at the root of the affair. At least it was a point in the lad's favour.

"Perhaps you may be wondering how I come to be acquainted with the situation. It's simple enough. Yesterday I ran into one of your deans of faculty at my club. Or it might be more accurate to say he sought me out."

Eddie gasped. Was there anyone his grandfather did not know?

"Yes, he outlined the case to me, in strict confidence of course. The evidence against you, as it stands, is irrefutable. Yet he could not help feeling a doubt. Your conduct so far has been exemplary. He hoped there might be some mitigating circumstances which could enable the judging panel to show leniency. Now is the time to speak up, Eddie."

"I'm sorry, grandpa." He looked up, almost in defiance. "I can't betray a trust."

"Even at the cost of any future prospects you may have held?" He sighed, then snapped his fingers, as though finding sudden inspiration. "Tell you what. Suppose I was to give you my impression of the course of events last Saturday. No need to say anything. A nod or shake of the head will suffice."

There was no response.

"I take it you've no objection, then," he continued after a short pause. "Knowing you as I do, it is my belief that you were reluctant to attend this – demonstration, shall we say? Only when a fellow student insisted on going, alone if necessary, did you agree to accompany her. I assume your companion was a young woman. You were concerned for her safety."

He stared back in amazement. It was exactly as his grandfather had described.

"No challenge, eh? Good." He felt in his element now. The affair was as he had suspected. All that remained was to set the scene, followed by the inevitable denouement. "No doubt the speaker would be surrounded by a ring of supporters, at least some of them Blackshirts in mufti. And ready, perhaps eager, to deal with any opposition with a heavy hand. Possibly you might also have noticed a police presence in the background, Am I right so far?"

This time there was a sullen nod.

"Shall I go on? You hoped for a peaceful rally, with as little disturbance as possible. But others would think differently. Bolder spirits would begin to edge forward. Jeers and catcalls would give way to taunts and insults.

Tempers would flare, blows would be exchanged. Before you knew it, a full-scale riot would ensue. Your friend, caught up in the excitement, would break away to follow the insurgents. Naturally you would chase after her, perhaps to see her accosted, even manhandled, by one or more of these Blackshirts. Without thinking, you would wade in to the rescue. In the melee she would manage to escape from their clutches, slip away into the crowd. Then the police would intervene to restore order, with obvious results for you."

He looked for a reaction, and was not disappointed. Eddie suddenly buried his head in his hands. It was not hard to picture the remorse, the harrowing memories cast up – the distraction at the outbreak of violence, his alarm as the girl impulsively took herself off, his chagrin at his negligence as he set off in pursuit, his horror at finding her struggling in the grasp of a brawny fascist thug.

"Don't take it to heart, old man," he said gently. "There was nothing else you could have done."

His grandson wearily raised his eyes. "It was all so confusing," he sobbed. "I remember hitting out, yelling at Fiona to run. Then the police seemed to be everywhere, blowing whistles, chasing people with their truncheons. I was grabbed, hustled away, shoved into a paddy wagon."

"Hmm. Perhaps it was for the best. These Blackshirts don't stand on ceremony. You might have been seriously injured. Anyway, I think we have a case to argue. The white knight charging in to assist the damsel in distress. Foolish, but understandable."

"We? I don't quite see—"

"I have ascertained that legal counsel will not be excluded from the hearing. I intend to represent you. There will be no need for you to give evidence, and your companion's name will not be mentioned. So far as the adjudicators are concerned, you were an innocent bystander who intervened on behalf of a young lady. Close enough to the truth to pass muster, I should imagine. Just look contrite and apologise for any trouble you may have caused."

Eddie gasped, almost in disbelief. There was a good chance he might not be ruined after all. And he had kept to his promise. His eyes lit up. "Thank you, grandpa. You've no idea how relieved that makes me."

"All's well that ends well. There's still life in the old dog," he added with a grin.

"Yes, but what about mama?" A chill thought struck him. "What am I to say to her?"

"Nothing. I'll attend to that. It was a misunderstanding. You were falsely accused by accident. Now it has been cleared up. Not a stain on your character."

"And you think she'll accept that?"

"Well, she may read between the lines. But I doubt she'll press you. She'll be only too happy to see your smile again."

"But what about the others?" he persisted. "They have charges to face as well."

"I wouldn't worry over much on that account. It's my opinion that the authorities will come to a more balanced view. Best to draw a veil over the whole incident as quickly as possible. Fines and written warnings will probably be the order of the day." He stood up. "If there's nothing else, I'll go and have a word with your mother while you tidy yourself up."

"I'll do that. Thank you again, grandfather."

"Glad it's all over? So am I." He hesitated at the door. "I think, if I were in your shoes, I would stay clear of that young lady for a while."

"I – I'll bear it in mind." He knew it was good advice. But could he bring himself to take it?

* * *

Hugh Lixmont felt distinctly peeved as he paid off the taxi outside the anonymous building in a side street leading away from Stockbridge. Carefully placing his attaché case under his arm, he glanced at the brass plaque beside the entrance. *Elizabeth Baird Advertising Agency*: hardly eye catching, he sniffed. At another time he might have derived some grim amusement at the notion of Nick Norman taking over the freehold to the suite of rooms he had once leased as editor of a woman's magazine. But on this occasion he was in no mood for such thoughts.

The task in hand was beneath his dignity, distasteful and demeaning. An underling, a solicitor's clerk perhaps, would have sufficed to carry out the assignment. Yet Norman had insisted he travel through to Edinburgh to attend to the business in person, even though he must have known that relations with his sister were strained, to say the least. His lips tightened. Nick was miffed that he had not been recognised in the latest New Year's honours list. Rightly or wrongly, he had concluded that the omission was due to his fruitless promise to have a notorious communist agent delivered on a plate to the security services. It went without saying that he had subsequently cast round for a scapegoat on whom to vent his spleen. Baird was the obvious choice, but he knew too much to be sacked out of hand. Instead, blame had been passed on to the loyal lieutenant who had made the mistake of hiring the useless wastrel, and therefore must accept the responsibility. And undertake this penance in atonement.

Unpleasant though it was to have to eat humble pie, it could not be denied that Nick's motives in deciding to spread his wings were sound. Investment in the capital's burgeoning property market was an enticing prospect for an expanding business empire. But why choose such a nondescript set of offices as his first venture? Was it simply because Elizabeth was the lessee? A petty act of revenge for some slight, real or imagined, in the past? He had suspected that might be part of the story. And now he knew for certain. Summoned to the main office that very morning, he had been handed copies of two documents, the lease itself, and a separate contract for additional services to be performed, together with very precise verbal instructions. The contract must be signed off first, before the lease was agreed. The terms, as he read them over in the train, could by no means be considered onerous. He could only hope that his sister, as a practical businesswoman, would see them in the same light.

Bracing himself for the encounter, he stepped forward to press the doorbell. He heard footsteps within; the door opened to reveal a rather austere, middle-aged woman.

"Good afternoon, sir. Have you an appointment?"

"I believe so. Is Mrs Baird at home?"

"I'll see if she is available. Won't you come in?" She closed the door firmly behind her. "What name shall I give?"

"No need to bother, Alison." A familiar figure emerged from an inner office. "Brother Hugh, as I live and breathe. This is a rare honour. You've never seen fit to grace us with your presence before." She peered at him more closely. "You've aged since last we met. How many years is that?"

"Too many." He chose to ignore the almost open scorn in her voice. "But you haven't changed a bit."

"Shall we skip the formalities? I do have a pressing engagement."

"Would that be about the lease? A representative from Garnet Holdings?"

"How on earth—?" She gave him a bleak look. "So that's it. You're the errand boy I was told to expect. And your chum, Nick Norman, must be the new owner. I often wondered who it might be. Well, well. Not up to doing his own dirty work, is he?"

"Now don't fly off the handle, Elizabeth." He held up a placating hand. "We do have matters to discuss."

"Do we? For an eviction notice? I chased him out of this office when he sold the magazine behind my back. It's obvious he's nursed a sense of grievance ever since."

"It's not like that at all," he protested. "Nick is not a man to bear grudges. And I do have a proposal for a five-year extension of the lease. Won't you at least take a look at it?"

"Oh, very well." Her initial shock and anger were fading. It would be madness to give up the premises on what might prove to be a meaningless gesture. "I'll listen to what you have to say." She turned on her heel to flounce back to her room, leaving her brother to trail in her wake.

"Close the door," she ordered, seating herself behind her desk. "Now let's see this proposal."

"I think you'll find everything in order." He produced a printed document from his case and handed it over with a flourish. "As you no doubt will be aware, rates on similar properties have increased considerably in recent years, and Mr Norman has been very generous in offering you a continuation of the existing terms."

"That'll be a first, then." She gave him a thin smile. "Find yourself a chair. I may be some time."

Hugh was left to contain himself as best he could, while she passed from one page to the next, carefully scanning every clause, every line. At length she nodded thoughtfully. "As you say, these terms are exactly the same as before. I see there are spaces for two signatures. Are you empowered to sign for your principal?"

"Yes, but before doing so—" He took a deep breath.

"Well?"

"We would like you to read this additional proposition." He slipped a manila folder onto her desk.

She looked at him suspiciously, before dropping her eyes to study the contents. "There's a lot of legal gobbledygook here," she commented. "But from what I can make out, this would appear to be a contract with obligations to provide agency work for Garnet Holdings."

"Only very occasionally. It would in no way encroach on your business with other clients," he hastened to assure her. "And our requirements would be well remunerated."

"Requirements? What would I be expected to do? Write copy for his building projects or cinema chains?"

"Not in the least." He laughed dutifully at the idea. "Nick has little need for commercial advertising. His concern is for the bigger picture. You will observe he emphasises public interest in his submission."

"And what might that involve? Oh!" Her eyes narrowed. "I think I see daylight. Your lord and master has bigger fish to fry. He has political ambitions." She drew breath before spitting out the words. "He wants me to peddle fascist propaganda."

"That's not true," he remonstrated, taken aback by the sudden fury and venom in her voice. "We no longer have any truck with the BUF. It's the National Government we wish to support. There's an election coming up this year, and it's vital to keep out the extremists, whether on the right or left. *Safety first*: that's Baldwin's motto. It's the only path for the country in an uncertain world. Surely there can be no objection to that."

"The leopard changing its spots, eh? There's no mention of providing advertising material for any particular party here. I'm just supposed to take your word for it?"

"But I can show you—"

"Don't bother." She waved away his protest. "In any case it doesn't matter. My agency has never had dealings with any political affiliations before. I don't propose to start now."

"And that is your last word?"

"Yes. You may crawl back and tell the organ grinder he can do his worst. I shall certainly not kowtow to him." She pulled herself to her feet. "How could a brother of mine stoop so low? I can't imagine what the family will think of you now."

Her contempt was palpable. It was clear there was no more to be done. Mechanically he began to stuff papers into his briefcase. Nick Norman would hit the roof when he heard of his failure to come up to scratch. And Elizabeth would pull no punches when it came to telling their parents of his visit. Any prospect of reconciliation with his father could be dismissed out of hand. Even his mother would have difficulty in finding excuses. As for his sister… despite everything, she had made an impression. It was hard not to admit a lurking admiration for her spirit. Her barb had found its mark.

"Elizabeth." He hesitated a moment before plunging on. "Believe me, I understand your feelings. But there may be a way round this."

"You mean a compromise? I doubt that. I doubt it very much. But do go on, brother dear."

"Very well. As I see it, you have no fault to find with the lease itself. Why not just sign that? After I add my moniker, the deed will be sealed and delivered. No changes without your agreement."

"And the other matter?" She was still to be convinced.

"The contract? Bin it, burn it. I don't care what you do."

"What about your Mr Norman? Won't he cut up rough?"

"Very likely. But I can handle him." That was perhaps stretching things, but a risk he had to take. "In any case you won't be affected."

"And that's all there is to it?"

"Certainly. However," he added coyly, "as a personal favour, it would be appreciated if you could at least pretend to consider any requests that might be made. You would not be committed, of course. Anything objectionable could be rejected." It was only a fig leaf, but might be enough to take the edge off Nick's wrath.

She pursed her lips in thought, then broke into a smile. "I think we might manage that. Two copies, I believe. I'll just see if Alison is free to witness the signing."

Within five minutes the business was concluded. Elizabeth was left with a much better impression of her brother. She even unbent enough to bestow a sisterly peck on the cheek as he took his departure. Her assistant set about filing the agency's copy in a locked drawer.

"When you've finished with that, Alison, we'll go and break the good news to the others."

"Very good, Miss Elizabeth. Oh! Before I forget, there was a telephone call for you. I informed the caller you were busy, and asked her to try again later."

"She? Was there a name?"

"Mrs Baird. Mrs Morag Baird. I made a note of it."

"Just as well it wasn't my mother." She gave a faint chuckle. "Thanks for letting me know, Alison. I'll return the call now. You remember Morag, don't you? She worked with us on the mag in the old days. She's staying with me at present. Would you be good enough to dial my home number, and then transfer her through? I'll take it in here."

"Of course, Miss Elizabeth. It's nice to hear from her again." She bustled away.

There was the usual inevitable delay. Why did everything have to go through an operator at the telephone exchange? Still, she could afford to be patient. The phone was undoubtedly a boon and a blessing – so long as connection to a line did not take too long. No doubt Morag would be anxious to hear of the renewal of the lease. She, on her part, was no less keen to find out whether Morag had managed to contact Mrs Barbour. It would be just like old times if she could persuade her sister-in-law to rejoin the agency, if only on a temporary basis. Surely she would see the force in that, and raise no objections.

The bell rang. She snatched up the receiver. "Is that you, Morag? Good. How are things at your end? You'll be pleased when I tell you that we have a new agreement on very reasonable terms."

"That's grand. I ken ye were a bit worried." There was a slight pause. "I phoned Mary Barbour as ye advised."

"Good for you. And you told her about Iain? How did she take it? I bet she was hopping mad when she heard the tale."

"No' exactly. As it happens, she already knew. It seems Iain got his oar in first. He paid her a visit and telt her we'd had a tiff, an' I just walked out."

"And she believed that?"

"I'm no' sure. But wait till ye hear this. He claimed the argument was about the offer o' a new job. And went on tae say that I couldnae stomach the idea because it wid mean him leavin' the country."

"Going abroad? That's preposterous. Surely a barefaced lie."

"No' the way he put it. He telt her it was a waste o' time bangin' his heid against a brick wall in Scotland. We're too hidebound, set in our ways tae make a difference. He was prepared to gang somewhere else where the chance o' a socialist revolution was higher."

"Stuff and nonsense!" She almost snorted into the mouthpiece. "Are you sure of that? Did Mrs Barbour say if he had actually made up his mind to go?"

"Aye, she did that. He was off that very day. Said he might be gone a couple o' years. And I could hae the house tae mysel'. Even left her the key, an' telt her that the rent was settled till next quarter day."

"Does that mean you've decided to return to Glasgow?" She could barely keep the dismay from her voice.

"Nae need to stay away now. I'm sorry. I ken ye must be disappointed. And I'm grateful for a' ye've done. But Mary has need o' me. I said I wid take the train in the mornin'."

"Of course. You must do as you think best." She tried to put on a brave face. "We'll still see something of each other. But I'm curious. Did Iain happen to mention where he was going?"

"Naw. He just said he expected a lot more sunshine there. I'll ring off now. Talk tae ye later." There was a click as the receiver was replaced.

Elizabeth was left to stare, and ponder.

Part IV: 1936-1938

FOURTEEN

Search for Enlightenment

Edinburgh
July 1936

It was the day of Eddie's graduation. First Class Honours in Modern History ran the glowing citation in the programme notes. Following in father's footsteps, as his mother was not slow to point out. The family was out in force at the ceremony to show its appreciation of his achievement, and pay tribute as he was capped and lauded. Morag was there from Glasgow, proud as a peacock for her former charge. Even Hugh had found time to attend, in fact had insisted on being furnished with a ticket. The principal's hospitality at the subsequent reception had been delightful in its way; it was with real regret that the older generation had to take an early departure to superintend the final touches for the private family celebration to follow.

Lady Hilda Lixmont babbled away inconsequentially, as the car sped homewards, but her husband was struck by one remark she let slip. However, he said nothing until they had been deposited outside their house and the chauffeur dismissed.

"Were you serious about that, Hilda?" He opened the gate to allow her to pass.

"About what? Oh! You mean Eddie, I suppose. Yes, I thought it was an excellent suggestion."

"You haven't told me what it is. Have you discussed it with his parents?"

"Certainly not. Hugh wanted his proposal to come as a surprise. He happened to broach the subject the other day. Naturally I felt it would come as a very practical reward for my grandson."

"A graduation gift?"

"Just so. I'm letting you know now as a courtesy. So don't you go saying something and queering Hugh's pitch." She broke off. "Agnes! Be careful with those glasses." The maid was carrying a tray from the conservatory. "Drat the woman. I'd better go round and check everything is in order."

"Just a minute, Hilda." He was not to be put off. "This requires an explanation. Why take the trouble to make a mystery of it – whatever it might be? Is it because no one would have a chance to think of any objections? Is that it?"

"There you go again. Always finding fault with your son. Did he not do Elizabeth a good turn last year? Pulled her business out of the fire?"

"I suppose you could put it that way," he conceded reluctantly. "Otherwise, he would never have been allowed to darken my door again. Mind you, I'm not altogether convinced his motives were entirely altruistic."

"Will nothing satisfy you that he's doing his best to make amends? Did he not explain that he's given up any connection with Mosley and his crew?"

"He's certainly been at pains to emphasise that he's seen the light. According to him, fascism now has no part to play in a democracy. How far the thought goes is another matter. By the way, Hilda, does that also apply to you?" He could not resist a quip. "You always were rather sweet on such an upstanding, handsome figure as Sir Oswald."

"Don't joke, Edward." She knitted her brows. "If you can't say anything sensible, I'll go in and check the champagne is being properly chilled."

"Sorry about that, my dear. My warped sense of humour, you know." He gave a faint smile of contrition. "I must say you seem to be taking things remarkably well."

Her frown deepened. "What on earth is that supposed to mean?"

"Well, it was always your ambition that Eddie should study for the ministry. I haven't heard much mention of that recently."

"No. I gave up that notion some time ago. As a matter of fact, Eddie came to me and confessed he felt unable to devote himself heart and soul to the kirk."

"And you accepted his decision. Were you not disappointed?"

"Of course. But I'm a realist, as you well know, Edward. I admired him for his frankness. No doubt you thought the family could keep up a conspiracy of silence."

He flinched slightly at the rebuke. "Apologies. Did he also inform you of his intentions?"

"To study international relations at Oxford next year? Yes, he did. Possibly followed by an application for a post on the secretariat of the League of Nations."

"How does that sit with you?"

"The course at Oxford is not without merit, so far as it goes. Not so sure about the League, though. It doesn't seem to be much use these days. The Foreign Office might be a better bet. I might be able to persuade him to take the entrance exam," she mused, half to herself.

"There you go again, Hilda. Always planning and plotting."

"Fiddlesticks, Edward." Her ear caught the sound of approaching vehicles. "My goodness! There they are already. And still a host of things to be done."

"Now don't get into a fluster, Hilda. I'm sure everything is in apple-pie order. Let's go and greet our guests."

Hugh's two-seater runabout led the way. His father noted how he immediately leaped out to open the door of the limousine pulling up behind. A small gesture, but it helped create a good impression. Suddenly he gave a sharp intake of breath. An addition to the family group was being handed down from the running board, a rather tall young lady with prominent spectacles. Surely this could not be…

"Daddy, this is Fiona – Fiona Handling." Elizabeth hastened to make the introduction. "Eddie invited her to his party."

"Hope you don't mind, grandpa." His grandson pushed himself forward. "Fiona was at the graduation by herself. Her parents couldn't make it."

"Er, yes." Sir Edward recovered himself. "You are very welcome, I'm sure." He extended his hand. "You have also just graduated, Miss Handling?"

"Yes, but my degree isn't nearly as good as Eddie's," she simpered.

"Good of you to say that. Have you any plans for the future?"

"After the long vac? I'm coming back for a year at Moray House. I'm going to train as a teacher."

"How interesting. You should talk to Eddie's father. He knows all about that. And now you must excuse me." He turned to the others. "Let's all go round to the lawn. Everything's laid out there."

Eddie cringed inwardly as they trooped towards the tables laden with the celebratory buffet. His grandfather had disguised his feelings, but he could sense the disapproval. After the toasts he made a point of catching his attention.

"Sorry about that grandpa," he muttered, when they were left alone for a moment. "I tried to follow your advice. But it's hard to avoid her completely. After all we were in the same class. And I felt for her when I found out there was no one to cheer her on."

"Don't give it another thought, Eddie. Your sentiments do you credit." He smiled benevolently, then looked round. "I think your Uncle Hugh wishes to say a few words."

The buzz of voices died away as his son called for silence. "Sorry for the interruption, but I have something rather important to say. Before I go any further, I should like to ask Eddie if he has anything special planned for the summer."

"Nothing definitely fixed, uncle." He coloured slightly. "I had thought of a battlefields tour of the Western Front. Give me a chance to pay my respects at some of our war cemeteries"

Sir Edward gave a violent start. The very idea was sufficient to send his mind racing. Why this sudden, and totally unexpected, interest in the Great War? Was the skeleton in the cupboard about to rattle at last? He glanced towards his wife: the frozen expression on her face confirmed they both shared the same thought. The prospect of their grandson chasing over northern France in search of a non-existent grave of a fictitious natural father was scarcely edifying. Elizabeth and Alastair appeared none too pleased either; in fact his daughter was staring accusingly at her mother.

Hugh was first to find his voice. "Very praiseworthy, I'm sure, Eddie. But I think we might look to the future, rather than dwell on the past. I have something else to propose." He paused a moment. "How would you like to visit Berlin? Take in the Olympic Games?"

His father's jaw dropped. This was the secret Hilda was at pains to hide from him. He contrived to stifle his alarm. "How on earth can you manage that, Hugh?"

"It's quite simple, dad. I have a connection with the Anglo-German Fellowship."

"Never heard of it."

"Perhaps not, dad. It's relatively unknown as yet." He went on to explain that the society consisted of men of influence beavering away behind the scenes to foster friendly relations with Germany. To this end, it had been decided to accept an offer of hospitality from its German counterpart. A small group would fly by air to Berlin, be accommodated by their hosts, travel daily to the Olympic Stadium, while at the same time learn something of the new *Reich* at first hand. Almost at the last minute, however, one of the intended participants had dropped out. He was now able to offer the vacancy to his nephew.

"I see, Hugh. Or rather I don't see. Won't the others be much older? Eddie would feel out of place."

"It's not like that at all, dad. Sorry if I haven't made things clear. It's a youth group – around Eddie's age. Most of them will be the sons of Fellowship members." He smiled encouragingly. "What do you have to say, Eddie? Most people in your position would jump at the chance."

"I – I hardly know what to say. I never imagined anything like this. I'm very grateful, of course, but—" He looked round for support. "What do you think, grandpa?"

"I'm just as surprised as you are, Eddie." The boy had reservations, as indeed he had himself. Nazi rule had shown scant regard for human rights, but perhaps the regime was now seeking to improve its image. And it would be churlish to reject the offer out of hand, especially if it meant any trip to France would at least have to be postponed.

"What is your opinion, Hilda?" He decided to temporise. "I must confess all this has taken me unawares."

"I'm amazed at you, Edward. Why, this is an opportunity of a lifetime," she enthused. "It will do him good to dip his toe in the water, so to speak, gain some practical experience for the career he has in mind. Hugh is to be congratulated for the efforts he has made on Eddie's behalf," she added, beaming at her son.

"That's all very well, Hilda. But there may be other aspects that merit consideration. At the very least we should hear the views of Elizabeth and Alastair. After all they are the lad's parents."

"Don't mind us, Eddie," said his mother. "It's your decision. We'll support you, whatever it might be."

"Must I give you an answer now, Uncle Hugh?" He blushed with embarrassment. "I'd like a day or two to chew it over, if I may."

"Is that really necessary?" His uncle scarcely bothered to hide his annoyance. "Oh, very well," he snapped peevishly. "I can give you till noon tomorrow at the latest. Time is short, and there are arrangements to be made, applications for passports and visas, as well as your kit."

"Then I'll sleep on it overnight." He glanced at Fiona. Lord knew what she thought of it all. "Gosh!" he exclaimed suddenly. "You'll miss your train to Glasgow if you don't hurry. I'll see you to the tram stop."

For a moment she looked nonplussed, then nodded understandingly. "Thank you all for having me. It's been a lovely afternoon," she chirped to the company, before allowing herself to be propelled towards the garden gate.

On the short journey to the tram terminus Eddie braced himself for the expected tirade of invective against the Nazi regime and its fellow travellers. But it turned out there was to be no fiery condemnation of the Olympic Games as a propaganda tool for Hitler and his minions. To his utter astonishment, Fiona calmly advised him he should take advantage of his uncle's kind invitation. At first it made no sense; then she provided an explanation. Germany was fast becoming a closed society, she argued. Little was known of what was really going on within its borders, beyond rumours of dissidents disappearing into concentration camps, and persecution of Jews steadily intensifying. He should go, and keep his eyes and ears open. Any scraps of information he could glean would be of real value.

Eddie had much food for thought as he slowly trudged back to his grandparents' house. Further up the road the party was beginning to break up, the family saying their goodbyes as they prepared to leave. His uncle was wielding the starter handle for his car. He quickened his step.

"Hold on a minute," he called out. "No need to wait till tomorrow. You can count me in."

* * *

Berlin, Germany
August 1936

Eddie Baird stared dismally through the window in the deserted communal area of the hostel. The *Gasthaus* had been appropriated as living quarters for the duration of the Games: though small, it was ideally situated near the centre of the city, and there could be little complaint about the accommodation. But that was not the point. He now bitterly regretted that he had allowed himself to be persuaded to join the group.

In truth he felt like a fish out of water. He had little or nothing in common with his companions, and they made it clear that he was regarded as a rank outsider. So be it: he could afford to ignore their silent contempt. What need had he for a charmed circle of Hooray Henrys, full of their own self-importance, and slavish praise for Hitler and his works? The group leader was much older, a fussy, weedy individual named Smithson. It did not take long to work out that he was little better than a hanger-on, bowing and scraping, eager to curry favour with power and influence. Consequently, the man had taken an instant dislike to the latest member of the party. And the feeling was mutual. He had shown he was not to be bullied by deliberately folding his arms when everyone else gave the Nazi salute, a courtesy to their hosts as Smithson put it. A minor gesture, but some consolation for all that.

His face clouded once more. That the opening ceremony had been a fascinating spectacle, there could be no doubt. He was half ashamed to admit, even to himself, to being swept away by the exhilaration of the moment. The wildly cheering crowds, the rapturous applause at the arrival of Herr Hitler and his entourage, the giant airship *Hindenburg* hovering overhead... sights that would live long in the memory. But then the Nazis were past masters at bending an audience to their will. Things could look far different when examined in the cold light of day. The sheer weight of the German propaganda machine filled him with repugnance – the glaring display of Nazi symbolism on almost every public building, the cult of personality, amounting to adulation of the little man who bore a striking resemblance to Charlie Chaplin, but could do no wrong and was acclaimed as *Fuhrer*. Try as he might, he found it impossible to blot out the image, to immerse himself in watching the track and field events. It was even hard to raise a cheer when British athletes stood on the podium to receive their medals.

Today, however, marked a break in the routine. The party had returned early from the *Reich Sportsfeld* to attend a reception held at the Ministry of the Interior. He had begged to be excused on the pretext of a slight headache, and had been graciously permitted to remain behind. Doubtless everyone else had been secretly relieved; it would remove the possibility of the occasion being spoiled by some gaff on his part, while giving them full scope to express their admiration for German *Kultur.* And as a result he had been left to kick his heels and amuse himself as best he could. He might have gone out for a walk, but to explore the city on his own, if not absolutely forbidden, was strongly discouraged. Smithson had made it abundantly clear that it would be regarded as an insult to ignore their hosts' wishes.

He threw himself down on an easy chair. What was really galling was his failure to carry out the mission Fiona had entrusted to him. But what opportunity was there to probe beneath the surface, discover what people really thought of the regime? Any attempt would be futile – not least because a squad of Hitler Youth turned up each morning to act as guide and escort.

"Permission to enter, please?" The sudden voice gave him a start. A young man stood in the doorway, dressed in regulation shorts, brown shirt and tie, with a swastika armband to complete the uniform.

"Come in, if you must." It was hard to conceal a glance of disfavour. Evidently he was not to be trusted on his own. One of the Hitler Youth had been detailed to watch over him.

"My name is Hans Hauber. I have been looking for you." The newcomer spoke excellent English, as did most of his troop. No doubt they had been specially selected for their language skills.

"Have you been sent to keep me company, Herr Hauber?"

"Please to call me Hans. Not exactly, to answer your question. You may not be aware that no evening meal will be served today. Refreshment is being offered at the Ministry. I pointed this out, and volunteered to see to your needs."

"Thank you. That is very kind of you."

"Not at all. I am only too glad to be of service. You are very welcome to come to my house, meet my parents and share our food."

His jaw dropped. "Is that allowed?" he asked in amazement.

"I did not mention that option to my superiors. But who is to know?" He gave a broad smile. "Is it permitted to address you as Edward?"

"Eddie – if you don't mind." Their so-called guides had obviously been well briefed. He paused awkwardly, uncertain how to respond.

"You know, Eddie, I think we are, as you say in English, birds of a feather. I observe that the others are not overjoyed with your company. For my part, I am forever being accused of a lack of zeal in the *Hitler Jugend*."

Eddie's eyes opened wide. Was this an indication that not all Germans were fervent Nazis? Of course, it was possible this fellow was acting on instructions, but why would the authorities bother with the likes of him? There was a risk, but this could be his only chance to hear the opinions of ordinary people. Slim though the possibility might be, he made up his mind. "I'll come with pleasure. Is it far?"

"About two kilometres. We have an apartment in Wedding. Not on the usual tourist list, I am afraid, but we do have something of a community spirit left to us."

Was this another hint? He warmed to the prospect. "I say, Hans, I should take a token of appreciation for your parents. I can't go empty handed."

"You British – always so prim and proper." For the first time he laughed. "There really is no need. They will not expect anything."

"But I insist. At least a bunch of flowers."

"Very well, then. I will show you where you may find what you require."

Hans Hauber was as good as his word. A visit to a nearby market provided Eddie with a posy of mixed blooms. Satisfied with his purchase, he listened intently as Hans told him something of his background. His father was a skilled engineer, and his mother a proud *Hausfrau*. He himself had been a Boy Scout, before everyone was pressurised into joining the Hitler Youth. Now, at the age of eighteen, he would shortly be called up for national service in the Labour Corps or Army, though he had hoped for deferment to allow him to go to university. Unfortunately, his application had been unsuccessful: at his interview he had failed to convince the professor of his suitability for the course. His companion noted his wistful expression. It had obviously been a painful experience. They walked on in silence.

There could be little doubt that the district of Wedding was a strongly working-class area, with its shabby streets of rundown tenement blocks, far different from the imposing architecture portrayed in the German media. Its appearance, however, was relieved to some extent by signs of greater affluence in a few scattered rows of houses, and it was towards one of these that they made their way.

"Forgive me", Hans said at last. "I was just thinking… But no matter. This is where I live, where I grew up." He opened a little wicker gate. "My *Mutti und Vater* will be happy to, as you say, make your acquaintance."

The family home on the ground floor was neat and welcoming, with a small garden at the rear. Both parents took his obviously unexpected presence in their stride: his mother expressed unqualified delight at his gift, while his father, after a lingering stare, gripped him warmly by the hand. The meal was simple enough, sausage and sauerkraut, with apple strudel to follow, but tasted delicious. The lady of the house chatted away as they ate, singing her son's praises. He was an only child, but had done them proud, and they had high hopes for his future. Hans crimsoned with embarrassment as he translated for his guest.

By contrast her husband said little or nothing, apparently lost in thought as he concentrated on the food, though Eddie was conscious of an appraising glance from time to time. But once the table was cleared, and Frau Hauber had disappeared into the kitchen, he was prepared to unbend a little, as he lit his pipe and leaned back in his chair. He began with a strict warning that nothing must be repeated to anyone else. He was a Social Democrat, he confided through his son, a supporter of the only political party in the *Reichstag* to resist Hitler's seizure of power. He had also been a staunch trade unionist, till the Nazis banned unions, confiscated their funds and property, and arrested their leaders. He himself knew of several friends who had vanished into the camps, only to reappear months or years later as broken men, too fearful to divulge anything of their experiences. For some reason they had not come for him. He chuckled ruefully at the notion that perhaps his skills were too valuable to be lost to the workplace. It was true, he went on to say, that the Nazi boast of providing full employment for all was not far from the mark, but only at the cost of low wages at a time of rising prices, and the expectation that workmen would be pleased to carry out unpaid overtime in the service of the state. These revelations, and more besides, were staggering, even worse than he had imagined. It was with real regret that he rose when Hans announced it was time to leave.

"We must hurry," he muttered, after they had said their goodbyes. "We should not have lingered so long. That was my fault. The hour is late and you may be missed." He pursed his lips. "I know of a short cut. If we run, we may be in time before the others return."

They put on a spurt, pounding through a maze of alleyways and side streets till Eddie felt fit to burst. He was on the point of calling for a short break to gather breath when there was a faint yelp of pain, a feeble cry for help.

"Did you hear that?" he demanded.

"Yes. But it's probably nothing. We must press on."

"Damned if I do!" Instinct told him something was amiss. He broke away, shooting past his guide.

Rounding a corner, he saw a body scrunched into a ball on the roadway, being kicked and punched by three assailants in the uniform of the Hitler Youth. They looked up, startled, as he rushed towards them, yelling in English at the top of his voice. As Hans followed up, they drew back a little, leaving their victim whimpering on the ground. Suddenly one of them jeered and pointed: "*Hans Hauber! Wir Sie kennen*!" Then they laughed and ran off.

Eddie was puzzled for a moment. "They know you, Hans?"

"Unfortunately, yes," he answered unhappily. "And I them."

"Can't be helped, Hans." He nodded reassuringly. "But look here, he's an old man. Why would those thugs set about him?"

"Because he is a Jew. I thought attacks of Jews were *verboten*, at least for the period of the Games. Apparently not," he mused.

"Well, we can't leave him lying here. Let's try and get him to his feet." Gently they managed to help him upright, where he stood shivering from his ordeal, quaking with fear, his features a mass of bruises. Doors were beginning to open, faces appearing at windows, a few brave souls venturing onto the street. Two women came forward to lead the old man away.

"Best to let his own kind look after him," said Hans. "This is a small Jewish quarter. I would not have brought you this way but for the fact I was anxious to see you home."

"Gosh, yes. I had rather forgotten about that. I suppose we had better get our skates on."

"No need now," he replied sadly. "The damage has been done. We can walk the rest of the way."

The August dusk was falling as they approached the hostel in silence. Eddie groaned. Lights were twinkling from windows; the party had already returned. Hans shook him by the hand, wished him well, and disappeared into the gloom. His companion was left to face the music alone.

It came as no great surprise to find Mr Smithson peering nervously from the doorway. "Where on earth have you been, Baird? We were about to send out a search party to scour the streets for you."

"There is no great secret, sir. I was invited to share a meal with one of our guides. Since nothing had been provided for me here," he added tartly.

"I assume a member of our Hitler Youth escort is above suspicion. He did say he had been given permission."

"Yes, but surely just in the hostel. I presume you were at the boy's home." He thought for a moment. "I suppose we must hope that nothing untoward occurred. You had better take yourself off to your room."

Next morning, he was late in going down to breakfast. Sleep had not come easily; he recalled dawn breaking before he fell into a fitful slumber. No doubt a stiff reprimand awaited him for his tardiness, and for his activities the previous evening: the Germans were sticklers for order and routine. If so, he was prepared to apologise and be done with it.

The clatter of voices suddenly died away as he entered the dining room. Every eye immediately turned towards him, both from his own group and the Hitler Youth who generally shared the meal with them. Some averted their gaze, others stared with unconcealed hostility. He searched in vain for a friendly face; there was none. Then it dawned on him: Hans Hauber was missing.

Smithson was not slow to accost him. He came scurrying forward, clearly agitated. "Whatever have you done, Baird? The police are here. They said they'd wait in the manager's office. I was asked to fetch you."

"Then I'd best go and see what they want," he said icily. Things were evidently worse than he had imagined, but damned if he would show any feeling in front of this lickspittle. "No need for you to come. I know the way."

There were two of them – plain clothes officers. One stood by the door, still wearing his black leather coat; the other in a dark lounge suit sat in the manager's chair.

"Please to sit, Herr Baird." The man behind the desk flashed a card. "*Geheime Staatspolizei*. State Secret Police," he translated in a near faultless English accent. "It would appear that you have been abusing our hospitality, Herr Baird."

"I can't see how you might think that." He resolved not to be browbeaten. "I am simply here as a visitor for the Games."

"Rather more than that, I fancy. You have been making undesirable acquaintances. In particular, you have visited the house of a man whose loyalty to the *Reich* is, to say the least, questionable. Have you been sent by British Intelligence?" He spat out the accusation, as if to catch him unawares. "What information were you to find? Or were you to sow sedition?"

"Absurd! You're making it up," he protested indignantly. "I was invited to supper by one of your own guides. Where is the harm in that? You can ask him. But I notice that he is not here today."

"You need not concern yourself with the boy Hauber. He has been reassigned elsewhere. You have, as you might say, enough on your plate." He opened a file on the desk. "Let us move on. You have also seen fit to commit an egregious breach of the peace. You carried out an assault on a patrol of *Hitler Jugend* going about their lawful business. You repeatedly struck one of them to his severe disfigurement."

"That's a lie!" He flared up. "I never touched him."

"But you admit you were there?"

"Yes. But it was to come to the aid of a defenceless old man. They were kicking and punching him."

"I see. And who was this 'old man'? Did you ask his name? Or where he lives?"

Eddie could only shake his head. In any case it was better not to know. Even to state he was a Jew would probably only provoke more reprisals.

"Not very convincing, is it? As it happens, I have the medical report on your victim. Excessive bruising about the face and head, and a wound requiring several stitches," he read. "What have you to say about that?"

"Only to repeat that it is a falsehood." Now he was beginning to feel desperate. They were seeking to entrap him with their wild allegations. But how to respond? He had no means of proving his innocence.

"I observe you realise your position, Herr Baird. These are serious charges, punishable with a long prison sentence." His interrogator could not fail to note the fleeting glance of dismay. "However," he went on to say, "all need not be lost. The German government wishes to be magnanimous. It would be a pity to sully the friendship and goodwill of these Games with a sordid case of espionage. Accordingly, it has been decided to give you the benefit of the doubt, and show leniency. You are to be deported."

Eddie breathed a deep sigh of relief. Nothing would suit him better than to quit the fetid atmosphere of the Nazi state. There would be awkward questions when he arrived home early, but that could not be helped.

"The prospect attracts you, Herr Baird?" The man smiled faintly "*Gut!* All that remains for you is to read and sign this statement. He pushed a closely typewritten sheet in Gothic script across the table.

Eddie took it up. "This is in German," he protested. "I can't make it out."

"Of course. It merely states that you acknowledge your fault in unwittingly falling foul of the German legal code, for which you offer unreserved apologies. In addition, you undertake to leave the territory of the German Reich without delay."

"There seems an awful lot here just to say that." He was not convinced.

"I have given you the gist. The legalese may be a little long winded, but I assure you it is necessary to satisfy the court. And a written apology is the least that the German people could accept. Should you refuse to comply," he added grimly, "you would face prosecution with the full force of law."

He hesitated, ignoring the proffered fountain pen. It went against the grain to sign something he could not understand.

"Does that not suffice?" The man was growing impatient. "In that case I should inform you that the Hauber family would be taken into immediate protective custody."

Protective custody? Eddie gritted his teeth. Surely that meant arrest without charge or trial. Followed by imprisonment in a concentration camp. God knew what barbarities were perpetrated there. In all conscience he could not allow that to happen.

"Give me the pen." Angrily he scrawled *E. Baird* at the foot of the page.

The Gestapo officer carefully blotted the ink, and grunted contentedly as he added his own name with a flourish.

"And now to the details. You will have no further communication with your fellows. A car is waiting outside to convey you to the *Bahnhof*. My friend here will accompany you." He indicated his confederate. "There is a train for Brussels in one hour. You will take your ticket. Your effects will be dispatched later. Your passport will be returned at the Belgian frontier. Now you may go."

The door was held open for him. Harsh words of admonition rang out as he passed through: "Do not attempt to visit Germany again. You may not be so fortunate next time."

* * *

Edinburgh

"For God's sake, what in heaven's name were you thinking of? How could you have been so stupid?"

"Steady on, Hugh," warned his father. "I'll not have the boy bullied."

Several days had elapsed since Eddie had returned home in the lowest of spirits. But it was a comfort that the family had sprung to his support on learning of his wretched experience in Berlin. His parents had welcomed him back with open arms, followed by the advice to put it all behind him. Somewhat to his surprise, it was his grandfather who had seemed most affected, bewailing the fact that he had allowed Eddie to fall foul of a hideous regime, and bristling with indignation at his treatment by the Gestapo. His grandmother had been a little more restrained, adding a mild reproof that he might have been more circumspect when in a foreign land. It went without saying that he had sought an early meeting with Fiona to make his report. She had been full of praise for his exploits, hinting at the need to convey first-hand information to a wider audience. She had also made mention of how he might bridge the gap before going on to Oxford. Thus far he had not found a favourable opportunity to broach the subject at home. As for the present, it was at Uncle Hugh's request that he had been invited back to his grandparents' house. He had hoped for a word of commiseration from his uncle. Judging by the glare he had encountered on arrival, there was scant chance of that.

"Bullied?" Hugh Lixmont was in no mood to mince his words. "I'm here to demand an explanation. Have you any conception of the damage this young imbecile has caused?"

"What on earth ails you, Hugh?" His father tried to be patient. "So far as I can make out, Eddie has behaved very well in difficult circumstances."

"He would tell you that, wouldn't he?" His eyes glinted. "Only he signed a confession admitting he was a British agent sent to sow sedition. And the Games were to be used as camouflage for his deeds."

Eddie's jaw dropped. "They told me it was just an apology," he gasped. "I couldn't read their old-fashioned script."

"So you just went ahead and did as they asked?"

"Well, I was suspicious. But they threatened to throw the family that befriended me into a concentration camp."

"There was nothing else he could do," said his grandfather firmly. "He acted to save others."

"Very noble, I'm sure," sneered Hugh. "But that's not the view of the Foreign Office. I was hauled down to London for a reprimand. I should have chosen my team more carefully. They think the Germans now have a stick to beat them with in any future negotiations. And as for the Anglo-German Fellowship, I hardly dare to show my face at the door. Your grandson has set relationships back for God knows how long."

"Unfortunate, I don't doubt, Hugh. But that's no reason for adopting this attitude. If there is to be blame, it lies with you, for forcing the boy into a commitment against his better judgment, and with me, for not assessing the risks more fully." He turned to his wife foe support. "Would you not agree, Hilda?"

"Well, I—" she faltered, clearly torn between them. "Perhaps, Eddie dear, it would have been wiser to show a little more tact."

"Nonsense, Hilda." Her husband was not to be swayed. "Eddie has no cause to reproach himself. He accepted an invitation from a Nazi party organisation. He came to the rescue of an old man being attacked by a gang of youths. That's all there is to it, Hugh."

"Far from it, dad." He struggled to contain his anger. "He listened to the grievances of one disaffected German worker. And I suppose he's repeated the tittle-tattle all over the shop."

Eddie reddened. "I did mention it to Fiona Handling."

"Your blue stocking friend? Well, she'll spread it far and wide as gospel truth."

His nephew fell silent. It would serve no purpose to admit he had been urged to address a Popular Front meeting.

"As for your contretemps with the Hitler Youth," he continued, "you would have done better to leave well alone. The Germans are touchy about the enemy within, as they term them."

His father shook his head. "I don't see it that way. So, if you've nothing further to add—"

"But I have. None of this would have happened if Eddie had not told a lie in the first place."

"Lie?" Sir Edward's eyes narrowed.

"Certainly. He informed his hosts he was feeling unwell when that was not the case. He should have gone with the others to the reception out of courtesy, if nothing else."

"Well, yes, perhaps." It was a grudging concession. "But it was of little matter. You intended no disrespect, Eddie?"

"No. It was just that I felt I couldn't stand sucking up to everyone." He took a deep breath. Honesty compelled him to speak out. "I was asked to try to find out what ordinary people thought of life under the Nazis. Perhaps I should not have agreed."

"There, I knew there was more to it." Hugh sounded almost triumphant.

"This puts rather a different complexion on affairs, you know, Eddie," said his grandfather quietly. "It could be construed as a breach of trust."

"Yes, I realise that now. And I'm truly sorry. I'd best take myself off."

"No need to rush away." He felt a stab of remorse. His grandson was a picture of misery. "We all make mistakes. And you were placed in an impossible situation. I'm sure no one holds that against you." He looked meaningfully at his son.

"Yes, indeed." His wife echoed the appeal. "It's all in the past now, Hugh." She smiled at Eddie. "I'm sure you've learned your lesson, dearest. Forget all about it, and concentrate on your future."

His gloom lifted a little. "Thank you. You've no idea what this means to me. Am I forgiven, Uncle Hugh?"

He was rewarded with a bleak stare, then a reluctant nod. "Nothing else for it, I suppose. I can see I'm outnumbered. And family harmony must be restored."

"Quite right, Hugh". Lady Hilda smiled brightly. "Let's change the subject. Have you any plans for the next few months, Eddie? Some good works?" she added hopefully. With a little prodding he might be persuaded to undertake some outreach activities on behalf of her church.

"Good works, granny? You could put it that way. I think I have decided what I'm going to do."

"That's splendid, dear. Can I suggest you offer your services to our church? I'm sure the minister would be grateful for your assistance with his youth work."

"Well, I'm sorry, granny, but I wasn't thinking along these lines."

"Something else, then?" Disappointed, she tried to curb her feelings.

"In a manner of speaking. You will have heard of the civil war that's broken out in Spain. The army and the Nationalists, as they call themselves, staged a coup to seize power, but the Republican government has mobilised the people to fight back. Some are saying that if the fascists win there, the next step will be us. We'll be plunged into a second world war."

"Scaremongering! That's all it is," snapped his uncle. "The best thing we can do is to stay clear, and let them fight it out amongst themselves. That will be the attitude of our government. I believe it's already been decided on a policy of non-intervention."

"Oh, that's very fair!" Eddie was roused. "Do nothing, while the Italians and Germans wade in on behalf of the Nationalists. That will mean the end of democracy in Spain."

"Be that as it may, the only sensible option is not to become involved. Our interests lie elsewhere, in defence of the empire."

"A lot of people don't agree with you. They think a legitimate government should be supported. And so do I."

Hugh laughed. "You're not thinking of going to Spain, are you?" It was evidently intended as a flippant remark, but the frozen look of horror on his grandparents' faces told a different tale. Already there had been calls for the formation of International Brigades to rally to the Republican cause, reports of a growing trickle of volunteers making their way to the conflict.

"No, I don't think so. At least that was not my intention. I shouldn't care to get mixed up with the fighting." He grinned, but could see it had little effect. "The Spanish people will need humanitarian aid," he explained hastily. "I hear there are organisations being set up to collect money and send food and clothes. Knowing her as I do, Auntie Morag is sure to be in the thick of things. I could ask mama to write to her on my behalf, with an offer to help out."

"You're saying you won't go further than Glasgow?" His grandmother wiped a tear from her eye. "I would hate to think of losing you."

"I'll do my best." There was a lump in his throat. "But I can't absolutely promise."

FIFTEEN

Call of the 'Internationale'

Glasgow
March 1937

"Ye seem verra pleased wi' yersel', son." Morag Baird looked up from the kitchen table, "Yer meetin' must hae gone well. Ye've been like a cat on hot bricks these past few days."

"Well, yes," he acknowledged. "You could put it that way, Auntie Morag. Better than I was led to expect." Her nephew took a seat at the other end of the table. Then he looked thoughtful. How was he to explain without upsetting her? It was a delicate issue, and would require delicate handling.

"Come on, then, out wi' it." She pushed aside the accounts she had been studying. "I can see you've got somethin' on yer mind."

He smiled faintly. "Can't deny it, I suppose." There was a pause. "Did I ever tell you how grateful I am for letting me stay with you? Especially since you only have a room and kitchen."

"Aye, ye did. Mair than once," she replied drily. It was evident Eddie was finding difficulty in getting to the point. "But I was glad o' your company," she added more gently. "In any case ye only bide here part o' the week. Ye go hame for the weekend."

He nodded. That was the compromise agreed with his parents. To give Morag a rest, as his mother claimed. At least it gave him the opportunity to badger her into providing free advertising copy for flag days, concerts and rallies to raise money for the people of Spain, though she always insisted on taking a neutral position, supporting neither side in the civil war. Also, it gave him an opportunity to see something of Fiona, who had enrolled at Moray House to qualify for her teaching certificate.

"Ye should take pride in what ye've done, laddie," he heard her intone.

"Nae sense in hidin' yer light under a bushel. But for you, we widnae hae managed half o' what we've achieved."

"A trifle exaggerated, auntie," he grinned. "Still, we've come a long way. You'll remember how we started by collecting contributions in a pram, rattling tin cans for coppers round the streets – and the odd bob or tanner. Then we formed aid committees and relief funds to organise events on a bigger scale. Now there's a Unity Campaign to coordinate efforts on a national basis."

"Aye, maybe. So long as it lasts." There was a note of scepticism in her voice. "A lot o' folk dinnae like the idea o' makin' common cause wi' communists."

Eddie frowned. But there was no denying that the Labour Party and trade union leadership had refused to give official support, though many of the rank and file had not been slow to offer help on an individual basis.

"No need to be so pessimistic. Look how we managed to collect enough to send six vanloads of aid to Spain last December."

"I mind that fine. And you wanted to go wi' them. But they widnae find a place for ye. And thank God for that."

For a moment he flushed at the memory. "That was just a drop in the ocean," he went on. "Now we can do something really worthwhile."

"Ye mean that rusty tramp steamer tied up at the Broomielaw? I hear ye've been helpin' load it up."

"Well, many hands and all that. The quicker we empty the warehouse, the sooner we can be on our way. Whoever thought of hiring cargo space at a knockdown price deserves a medal."

"That wouldnae be you, wid it?" she quipped. Then her brow darkened. "What's all this about the 'we'? You're no' thinkin' o' goin' as well, are ye?"

He flinched at the accusation, then swallowed hard. "Well, yes, actually I am," he confessed. "I was going to tell you anyway," he added hastily. "They were a bit short on crew, so I volunteered as a deckhand."

"And they took you on? Lord's sake, laddie, are ye off yer heid? It's just plain madness."

"There's really no need to worry, auntie. I'll be there and back in a month." He gave what he hoped was a reassuring smile. "Surely you'll agree that someone should be there to check the supplies are delivered safely. Otherwise, it's just possible they might go astray, if you catch my meaning."

"Somethin' in that, I suppose. But why you? Could they no' choose a body wi' more experience?"

"I'm young and I'm fit." He ignored the implication. "The boat's skipper was glad to have me." There seemed no need to add that it was only the sight of two five-pound notes that had persuaded him to overcome an initial reluctance to accept a raw landlubber.

"You might think that, Eddie. But what about your maw and paw when they find out? They'll hae kittens. And they'll blame me for no' stoppin' ye. I couldnae thole that."

"No need to bother yourself on that score. I'll send them a note saying you knew nothing of my intentions."

"But ye dinnae realise what ye're lettin' yersel' in for." She made a despairing appeal. "Things in Spain are even worse than what ye read in the papers. Thae Nationalists hae nae regard for human life. They just trample over anythin' in their path."

"Is that so? How would you know?"

"Well, I wisnae gonnae let on, but—" She hesitated. "Does it ever cross yer mind what became o' yer Uncle Iain?"

"Not really. Out of sight, and all that."

"I cannae blame ye there. But I ken where he is. In Spain. And he's been there these past twa years."

"Not for his health, I presume." He caught her look. "Sorry, auntie. I shouldn't have said that. So that's where they sent him to stir up the workers' revolution?"

"Dinnae joke about it, Eddie. It's a right witches' cauldron, and de'il tak' the innocents who suffer the most."

"I don't doubt what you say. But where does Uncle Iain fit into all this?"

"He writes to me now and again. No' here, for he disnae ken this address. Ye'll mind I had tae flit when his rent money ran out. He sends his letters to Mary Barbour's office, an' I pick them up there."

"And write back to him in reply?"

"Naw. I never ken where he might be. He jumps around a' the time. Never stays long enough in one place."

"I understand. But I don't see how any of this can affect my decision."

"Well, maybe it will when I tell ye. I had some news last week. He says he's on his way hame. Somethin' about bein' more use for the war effort back here. Can ye no' wait an' hear what he has to say? Afore ye dae anythin' ye might come to regret."

"Sorry, but it simply can't be done. I've committed myself already. I have to be on board this evening, to sign on and be shown the ropes. We're off on the morning tide. It's a rush, I know, but there's no alternative."

Morag could only shake her head in disbelief. He was needlessly placing himself in danger, and she was powerless to prevent it. Should anything happen to him… Words trembled on her lips. "I have to go out now," she sobbed. "You'll still be here when I get back?"

"I'll try, but needs must, you know." Her obvious distress cut him to the quick. But there could be no going back, no sign of weakness. It was for the greater good. He watched in silence as she fetched hat and coat, and almost fled from the room.

As soon as she was gone, he hastily set about completing his preparations. Perhaps it was for the best that she had dashed away; it would save further futile argument. It was the work of minutes to thrust clothes into a bag, followed by a couple of paperback books and a framed photograph. His passport he slipped into a hip pocket. Next, he found pen, ink and paper, and sat down to write his letter of explanation. He would leave it on the kitchen table for Aunt Morag to read, with a request to send it on to his parents. Lastly, he dropped his door key on top, before leaving and closing the latch behind him.

Things had worked out no worse than he had expected, he told himself as he caught a tram for the dockside. She had been disappointed, but would get over it, as would the rest of the family. And what a tale he would have for them on his return.

The next day he was not so certain. He had gone aboard as agreed, only to discover that the captain was ashore on business, with no instructions left regarding any new member of the crew. The mate could only advise that he spend the night at the Seamen's Mission, and report back in the morning when he could be properly signed on. There was no danger that the ship would leave without him. Departure had been delayed to allow Customs to search for contraband. Under the recently passed Neutrality Act nothing could be carried to Spain which might be of material assistance to any of the combatants.

Now, as he reached the pier, there was no sign of life on deck, no evidence of customs officials carrying out an inspection. But there were two burly figures standing idly by the gangway. No one could mistake them for sailors; on the contrary they had all the appearance of plain clothes policemen. He groaned inwardly. Were they waiting for him? Was history about to repeat itself? An image of his encounter with the Gestapo flashed through his head. But he faltered only for a brief moment before marching forward, kitbag slung over his shoulder. Nothing for it now but to brazen his way through.

One of the men advanced a few steps to accost him. "Excuse me, sir. A minute of your time, if you please." He brandished a warrant card. "Police. Special Branch. We have orders to check everyone going on board. You have identification, I presume?"

Reluctantly Eddie lowered his bag to fish out his passport and hand it over.

"Thank you, sir." The policeman's eyes narrowed as he scanned its contents. "You are Edward Baird?" He looked up. "Not a particularly flattering likeness, if I may be so bold."

"We're not supposed to smile for a passport photograph," he retorted, nettled by the remark. "I can't help it if it makes me look like a criminal."

"Hmm. I couldn't possibly comment." The detective began to flick through the remaining pages. Then his expression suddenly changed. He turned to his colleague. "Here, come and look at this, Jones." He pointed to an entry. Eddie bit his lip. No need to ask what was amiss. They had found the big *verboten* stamp, lurid in red ink.

"A misunderstanding with the German authorities, sir?" He gave a faint smile. "No matter. But I think we'll hang on to this for the moment, if you don't mind." The passport disappeared into his coat pocket. "Perhaps you might be good enough to state your business on board this vessel."

"I'm a member of the crew."

"Really? Then in that case you will have papers identifying you as such. May I examine them, please?"

"I don't have them yet. I'm due to sign on as soon as I report to the captain. Ask him. He'll vouch for me."

"I'm afraid that will not be possible. The captain and first mate are at the harbourmaster's office."

"Well then, let me go on board and wait for them."

"I have no instructions on that point, sir. In fact I must ask you to come with us while your *bona fides* is established. Should it turn out as you claim, we'll see you're in good time to catch your ship."

Utterly dismayed, Eddie had little choice but to allow himself to be escorted to a waiting vehicle. Once the blinds had been drawn, and the engine started, the senior officer unbent enough to give an explanation. They were duty bound to investigate the possibility that he was attempting to work his passage to Spain, and then to jump ship upon arrival at Alicante. According to the Foreign Enlistment Act of 1870 it was a criminal offence to join the armed forces of another country. His protests that such was not his intention were met with studied indifference. He was still seething with indignation as the car pulled up, and he found himself hustled into a police station, and thence into the austere surroundings of a basement lockup.

Spirits sank as the cell door slammed shut and a key grated in the lock. He had been abandoned in this dungeon to nurse his thoughts while 'enquiries were made', as he was curtly informed. How had the police known where to find him? Could Aunt Morag have betrayed him? Surely not. But she had gone out. To consult Mrs Barbour, perhaps? Or telephone to his parents, or grandfather? Was it a conspiracy? Were they all in it together? There again, he might be barking up the wrong tree. It would be a comfort to know that the family was not involved. Could it be that the ship's captain was responsible? It seemed likely enough. The fellow might have had second thoughts, and decided the risk was too great. Maybe the rogue had always intended to defraud him. Easy enough to keep hold of his money, and tip off the police to rid himself of an unwelcome shipmate. His head spun as he tried to reach some definite conclusion. Eventually he gave it up as a bad job.

Time seemed to crawl on leaden feet. In the background he was conscious of a clock somewhere, striking the hours. God, how long did they intend to keep him a prisoner? Sheer boredom would drive him insane. At long last he heard the clatter of footsteps on the stone floor outside, followed by the jangle of keys. His heart leaped at the sight of the door swinging open.

"Mr Baird, sir." It was the station sergeant. "I am authorised to tell ye that you are free to go. Ye can recover your possessions at the desk."

Eddie gave a start. Was it possible after all? "You mean you're saying there are no charges?"

"None whatsoever. Why would we be daein' that?" The man winked.

"After all, ye havnae actually joined a foreign army." He made as if to leave. "By the way, I wouldnae bother dashin' back to the dockside, if I were you. Thon steamer left an hour ago."

* * *

April 1937

Iain Baird stepped down from the London train and made his way along the platform to join the queue waiting to show their tickets at the barrier. The express had arrived in good time, but that was not the point at issue. Would she be there to meet him? Had she even received the telegram he had dispatched that morning? Anxiously he scanned the crowd as he passed onto the main concourse at Glasgow's Central Station.

"Iain?" He caught sight of her standing by a pillar. "Ower here." She waved a hand.

Thank Christ for that. He could afford a smile of relief as he quickened his step towards her. At least she had not spurned him. For some moments they stared at each other awkwardly, unsure what to do next.

"Good to see ye again, Morag." Her husband was first to break the ice. "Thank ye for comin'."

She nodded. "I wisnae sure it was you. My, how ye've changed."

"Well, it's been mair than two years."

"Maybe so. But ye're thin as a rake. An' brown as a berry. As for that beard—" She shook her head. "Makes ye look like the baddie in one o' thae cowboy films."

He grinned sheepishly. "Truer than ye might think. Ye should hae seen it afore I had the chance tae get it trimmed."

"Aye well, ye've aged. I can see that."

"The penalty o' leadin' a hard life. The sun fair tans yer skin. And ye dinnae put on the beef wi' short commons."

"So ye're glad to be hame?" She tried to sound sympathetic. "Is that a' the luggage ye have?"

"Aye. That's another thing ye learn. How tae travel light." He fingered the valise slung on a strap round his neck. "Look, is there somewhere we can get a seat. A wee teashop, maybe. I could fair do wi' a cup."

"Of course. I'm forgettin' my manners. Ye'll be tired after yer journey. I ken just the place. It's no' far."

Morag was as good as her word. It was not long before they found themselves taking seats in a nearby tearoom. Lunch was over and afternoon teas only just beginning. A waitress took their order and bustled away.

"Cards on the table, Morag." He looked round warily to make sure the nippy was out of earshot. "I dinnae blame ye for bein' angry. Ye must have been in a right tizzy, wonderin' where I was. But I let ye ken I was in Spain as soon as I could."

"That was ages after ye left." It was hard to credit such a feeble excuse. "Is that a' ye can say?"

"Well, ye were gone when I got back that night, and I couldnae thole the notion that ye could believe I was a spy for the fascists."

"So ye thought goin' to Spain was the answer? Did ye work that out for yersel'?"

"No' quite. Stan Robertson wanted me to go wi' him."

"Ah! Now we're gettin' somewhere. I might hae guessed he wid be at the bottom o' this." She gave a little toss of the head. "A fine couple ye make, the pair o' ye," she scoffed.

"Stan's a guid man in his way," he protested. "Saved my bacon more than once, I can tell ye."

"Is that a fact?" She did not bother to hide her scorn. "He managed tae persuade ye? How much effort did that take? No' much, I'm thinkin'."

"That's no' fair," he protested. "I turned Stan's offer down at first, but then I jaloused it might be a chance tae show ye—"

"Where yer loyalties really lie? Is that what ye were goin' to say?" Her lips twisted into a grim smile. "An' then ye supposed I wid take ye back. Is that no' the case?"

Iain flushed. "Can a man no' live in hope?" he muttered. "I ken I've upset ye, but I'm daein' my best. Can ye no' see that?" He broke off as the rattle of crockery announced the arrival of the tea things.

"Thank you, dearie." Morag dismissed the young waitress as soon as she had arranged teapot, milk jug and sugar bowl on the table. "We can manage now." Iain was left to wait impatiently as she stirred the pot, poured the tea over the strainer, before adding milk and sugar. "Three lumps, I seem to remember. Ye always did have a sweet tooth."

"Ye ken that damned fine." He scowled as he accepted the cup.

Morag seemed unfazed, but she could read the danger signs. He would be losing his temper next. The interruption had given her pause for thought. It was time to draw back, especially as she had a special favour to ask.

"Maybe ye're right," she said reflectively. "There's nae need to quarrel. Tell us about Spain," she added as an aside.

"No' much to tell. I help Stan wi' the organisation o' the International Brigades."

"Surely there was mair to it than that. What about before the start o' the war?"

"Well, it's a bit complicated, an' I'm no' sure you would be interested."

He might have been tempted to furnish her with an account of the intrigue and complexities of Spanish politics, the various groups and factions, each with its own agenda, conspiring with and against each other for supremacy in that unhappy country. But in truth he barely understood half of it himself. He and Stan had been sent as agents of the Comintern, not to foment a communist rising as he had supposed, but to rally to the support of the elected government against the forces of reaction and would-be fascist dictatorship. Regrettably, warnings of an army coup had been ignored by the government, and now it was a desperate struggle to resist Franco's forces, aided by Italy and Nazi Germany. True, Brigades of foreign volunteers had sprung to the defence of democracy, including a newly formed British battalion, but they lacked modern weapons, and already huge chunks of Spain were in the hands of the insurgents.

"Well, I'll no' press ye." She sensed his reluctance to explain further. "Did Stan Roberson come back wi' ye?"

"Naw. Nae chance o' that. He's a political commissar now."

She managed to hide her relief. "Political commissar? What's that?" she inquired.

"A sort o' welfare officer, ye might say. Every unit in the Brigades has at least one. They look after the interests of the men, speak up for them." This was far from the whole truth, but she was not to know that. First employed by the Bolsheviks in the Russian civil war, they were the eyes and ears of the Party, responsible for indoctrination, ensuring loyalty to the cause, weeding out any disaffection. It would be a brave army officer who questioned the advice or wishes of his commissar.

"So ye're back by yersel'?" she mused. "Does that mean ye'll be stayin' for good?"

"I've nae idea. I go where I'm sent. The Comintern – the Communist International, that is – they pay the wages, so they call the tune."

"Is that a fact? What dae they expect ye to do here?"

"It's simple enough. I'm tae tramp round the country, drummin' up support for Spain. I've a list o' what's wanted. I'm to get in touch wi' local aid committees to arrange meetings wi' me as the speaker. The voice frae the frontline, tellin' it as it is."

"And what might that be?"

"Is it no' obvious? The fight for democracy starts and ends in Spain. Fail there, and we'll a' be the losers. Fascism an' dictatorship will rule the roost. Only the Soviet Union stands firm in defence o' what is right, while the spineless west does nothin'. It's up tae the workin' classes here to shame the government intae intervention."

"A pretty speech, to be sure." She gave a faint chuckle. "Ye conveniently forget tae mention that Stalin is a dictator himsel'."

"Aye well, ye could hae a point. I'll no' be sayin' ower much about Uncle Joe." He grinned back. "I was goin' to say, Morag, that I'll need a few days to organise things. Any chance o' a bed for a night or two? A shakedown on yer couch wid dae," he added hopefully.

"Oh! That would be a bit awkward. I only hae a wee room an' kitchen. And young Eddie bides wi' me."

"Eddie? D'ye mean my – my nephew?" he gasped in amazement.

"Aye, yer ain kith an' kin." Her mouth twitched slightly. "Dinnae sound so surprised. He's takin' a year out afore he goes back tae the university. That's why he asked to help me out wi' the appeal for Spain." She leaned forward. "But there's mair to it than that. He's set his mind tae get out there – tae see for himsel', he says."

"So that's the way o' it?" He recovered his composure. "And you dinnae want him to go?" The penny dropped. "Is that the reason ye turned up when I sent ye that wire?"

"Aye, partly," she admitted. "But ye must believe how glad I am tae see ye safe an' sound again."

"At least ye're honest about it," he grunted. "Look here, Morag, folk often say they're gonnae dae somethin', and then back out when it comes tae the crunch. I widnae worry ower much."

"Dinnae you believe it, Iain. He's already tried once. Signed on tae work his passage on a ship bound for Spain. Somebody got wind o' it, and the polis managed tae stop him."

"Somebody clyped, ye mean?" A smile spread over his face. "That widnae be you, would it?"

"Naw. At least I dinnae think so. I was in a right flap when he telt me, an' went to Mary Barbour for advice. She said he was old enough to make up his ain mind, and I shouldnae interfere. But—" She shrugged her shoulders. "Ye never ken."

"I see. Does Eddie say anythin'?"

"Only that he thinks it was probably yon sea captain. But I'm sure he still half suspects" She sighed wearily. "One thing I do know. He's mair determined than ever. Gie him half a chance an' he'll be off."

"How can you be so certain?"

"It's that Fiona Handling lassie," she grumbled. "D'ye ken her? She seems to have him in tow these days, near every weekend when he goes hame."

"Fiona Handling? Aye, we have had the pleasure o' bein' introduced. Bit o' a firebrand by all accounts."

"That's the one. I think she imagines hersel' on the barricades, in a red blouse an' black skirt, hurlin' defiance at the evil hordes. She cannae go hersel', so Eddie has tae fill the bill. She wants him to fight as a sodger, no' just deliver supplies. It makes the flesh creep just tae think on it."

"So ye want me to talk him out o' goin'?"

"He'd listen to you." She reached out to pluck his arm. "I'd be more than grateful if ye could speak to him. And so would the family. Maybe it might mend the rift after so many years."

"Wi' that lot? I doubt it." He appeared to consider. "I suppose I could hae a quiet word. Dae nae harm."

"So ye'll come back wi' me?" There was relief in her voice. "It's Friday. He'll be at the flat, getting' ready to catch his train."

"Naw. No' there." He shook his head. "Better just the pair o' us." Things would be difficult enough without Morag present to stick her neb in. "Ye tell me he goes back tae Edinburgh. That means Queen Street Station. I'll wait for him in the buffet there."

She nodded. "Maybe ye're right. I'll let him ken. Ye'll come an' tell me how ye got on?"

"Aye. If ye gie me yer address."

"I'll dae better than that." She fished in her handbag. "I've an auld envelope somewhere. Aye, here it is. Ye'd best take it. That way ye'll no' forget."

He glanced at the handwriting. "I ken the street. No' far from where we used tae bide," he mused.

"Cannae turn the clock back, Iain." She opened her purse and laid some coins on the table. "My treat. Time we were away."

A few minutes later they parted company outside the railway station, she to make her way homewards with a spring in her step, her errant spouse to reflect on his task and fortify himself at the station buffet. He ordered a large whisky at the bar, and carried it to an empty table in a corner of the room. How in hell's name was he to convince Eddie he would be doing more for the cause in Glasgow than he could ever hope to achieve fighting with a ragtag army in Granada or Guadalajara? What if the boy refused to listen? The Bairds could be stubborn as mules, as well he knew.

He drained his glass and contemplated having another. Better not, he decided. That would not help his chances of success. Instead, he lit a cigarette, smoked it, and used the stub to light a second; and a third after that. Morag was right. His own son – his flesh and blood – would be in mortal danger on the Aragon front – or anywhere else in Spain for that matter. He glanced at the clock on the wall. God, was that the time already? The bar was beginning to fill up – passengers dropping in for a quick drink after the week's work. Perhaps Eddie might not notice him in the crowd.

"Uncle Iain!" A voice broke in on his thoughts. A fresh-faced youth was waving, dodging through the crush towards him. "Nearly missed you there, hiding yourself away in the corner."

Iain hastily crushed his umpteenth cigarette, stood up to grasp the outstretched hand. "Sit yersel' down. Nip an' a fag?"

"I won't, thank you all the same." He smiled bleakly as he took his seat. "I can guess what this is all about, so I'll save you the trouble. I'm going to Spain, and neither you nor anyone else is going to stop me."

"But—"

"No need to say anything, uncle. I'll explain why I agreed to meet you here. I want you to show me how best to get to Spain."

Iain's jaw dropped. He had expected resistance, opposition to any plea he might make, but this… It staggered belief.

"That surprises you? You didn't think I would ask you for help?"

"No' in a month o' Sundays. It fair takes a man's breath away." For a moment he sat speechless, before shaking his head "I cannae dae what ye ask. What wid the family think if they found out?"

"Don't worry, uncle. I won't let on." He smiled blandly.

"It makes nae odds." There was a shake of the head. "I'll no' help ye put yersel' in danger."

"No need to get on your high horse. We rather thought you might take this attitude – or at least Fiona did. You remember Fiona Handling? She thinks the real reason you came back was to raise recruits for the International Brigades. Imagine what might happen were it to become known you were prepared to send your own countrymen into action while keeping your own kin safe at home. I'm sorry if this sounds like blackmail, but…" His voice trailed away. "Needs must," he muttered.

Iain blenched. That young woman was too sharp for her own good. If she was to start shouting from the rooftops there would be precious few volunteers to show for his efforts. And the Comintern would not be slow to take action. Stan would be powerless to save him, even if he was disposed to do so.

"Ye cannae rush these things, son," he temporised. "Ye need time to get organised. And ye'll need hard cash."

"No problem, uncle. I've money enough." He patted his breast pocket. Thank goodness he still had the bulk of his monthly allowance. And there were some savings at home, locked up in a tin box in his bedroom. "All I need now is your advice."

Iain ground his teeth in frustration. He was caught in a cleft stick, and the boy knew how to make the most of it. There was a scowl on his face as he groped in his coat pocket and pulled out a handful of cards. "Here, tak' one o' these," he growled. "Make sure ye learn what's on it, an' then see it's destroyed."

A little puzzled, Eddie took the slip of pasteboard while the elder Baird launched into an explanation. There were two addresses where help on the journey could be obtained, one in London, the other in Paris. It was necessary to memorise these, then burn the card; there was always a remote possibility he might be stopped and searched by the French authorities. By the same token he should leave his passport behind. A weekend ticket to Paris could be purchased in London: no identification was required and he could pose as an anonymous tourist. From the French capital he should take the train to Perpignan near the Spanish frontier, and then join a group waiting to be escorted on foot over the Pyrenees. Once in Spain he would be on his own… Suddenly his heart missed a beat. Need that really be the case? Perhaps all was not lost.

"D'ye have a scrap o' paper, Eddie?" There was a new urgency in his voice.

"Why, yes." He scrabbled in his rucksack and produced a notebook. "Here you are. And a pencil."

Iain thought for a few minutes before scribbling some lines. He read over what he had written, then tore out the sheet, folded it over and handed it to Eddie.

"They'll probably take ye to a place ca'ed Albacete," he explained. "That's the base for the International Brigades – where they're trained and equipped afore leavin' for the front. Ye should find my old mucker, Captain Robertson, there. Ask for him and gie him this. He'll look after ye. Better get it sown intae the linin' o' yer coat," he added. "Then naebody would find it if ye're challenged."

"Thanks, uncle. That'll be very useful." He slipped the note into his pocket and shouldered his bag. "Best be off now."

Iain was left to stare moodily into his empty glass. He had often wondered if his old mentor suspected the truth about Eddie. However, that was of little moment now. What did matter was whether Stan would read between the lines when he was asked to look out for the lad. His frown deepened. That was, of course, if he was still in a position to do anything. He might have been transferred elsewhere, or fallen foul of the Russians. Already their Party cadres were strengthening their grip, demanding an ever increasing say in the conduct of operations.

He reached for another cigarette, savoured the calming influence of the tobacco. He had been given a duff hand to play, but there was no use moping over what might be. In the meantime there was his wife to consider. Morag would be expecting a successful outcome; and woe betide him if he reported abject failure. Suppose he simply took himself off, started his mission well away from Glasgow. That would be the easy option, but would also ruin any chance of a reconciliation. Then again, he might spin a yarn that Eddie had been impressed, had faithfully promised to reconsider his decision. But that would only postpone the inevitable. She would soon come to learn the truth of the matter when he returned at the start of the week. No, on reflection it would probably be best to face the music, confess that he had done his best, but that evil hussy had bewitched him. They would have to find some other way to induce him to change his mind. Morag might just about accept that, but he could see his chances of a bed for the night, and perhaps something more, vanish into thin air.

* * *

Paris, France

Church bells began to chime, a few at first, then speedily followed by others, as though in competition to shatter the stillness of a balmy spring morning. Eddie Baird glanced at his watch and quickened his step: it would never do to reach the *Gare d'Austerlitz* and find his train gone. But there was little danger of that, he reassured himself: the walk from the hostel where he had spent the night was little more than a few hundred yards. His main concern was that awkward questions might be asked at the railway station, forms of identification demanded when he sought to buy a one-way *billet* to Perpignan.

As it happened, his fears proved groundless. A bored ticket clerk merely shrugged his shoulders, stamped a piece of pasteboard, and handed it over in exchange for the fare. The man was even good enough to point out the platform where the train was already standing. A few centimes bought him a Sunday newspaper at a nearby kiosk; then it was simply a case of presenting his ticket at the barrier. The guard passed him through with barely a glance. Now he could afford to breathe a little more easily.

Thus far everything had gone without a hitch, he had to admit, as he settled himself in what he hoped was an inconspicuous corner of a third-class carriage. It had all happened so unexpectedly. He had caught the Friday night sleeper to London, followed on arrival by a short trip across town to book the boat train to France. And now here he was in Paris, no more than an eight- or nine-hour journey from the Spanish frontier. Fiona had declared it would all go swimmingly, and it seemed she was right.

The thought of Fiona brought a frown to his brow. Her plan cast a dark shadow, and he still felt a pang of remorse in agreeing to it. His parents had been out when he returned home, and he had lost no time in phoning her halls of residence with news of his meeting that afternoon. She had been delighted; then insisted they must strike while the iron was hot. That he had been dumbfounded by her quick-thinking in coming up with a scheme, apparently on the spur of the moment, was to put it mildly.

She had decided that he must leave a note telling his parents he had promised to attend a youth conference in Stirling that weekend, and would be unable to see them because he would have to return to Glasgow as soon as the event was over. He was then to make his way to the Waverley Station and wait for her there. She would take a ticket to Stirling herself, so as to be out of the way in case of any inquiry, and then wave him goodbye as he embarked on his mission. With any luck it would be days before he was missed, and by then it would be too late to interfere.

At first he had balked at the idea. Telling lies, going out of his way to deceive his nearest and dearest, was despicable, beyond the pale. But she had been adamant; it was for the greater good. And he had allowed himself to be persuaded. He could picture the look of disappointment as his parents read his note. But that would be as nothing when they discovered where he had gone. It would be poor recompense to receive a card saying he had arrived safely in Spain.

A shrill blast on the engine's whistle gave notice of imminent departure. A trickle of latecomers hastily came on board; thankfully no one chose to sit next to him. He opened his newspaper, pretended to be engrossed in its contents. The locomotive puffed slowly out of the station, then gathered speed through the outlying suburbs before reaching open countryside. Only then did Eddie venture to lower his paper and take note of his fellow travellers. It was easy to spot the smattering of stolid French citizenry, but what really caught the eye were four or five solitary individuals, studiously staring out at the passing scenery. Somehow the sight of cloth caps and rough tweed suits gave him comfort.

"*Pardon, m'sieu.*" He glanced up in sudden alarm. A uniformed official was at his side, demanding attention. "*Votre billet, s'il vous plait.*"

Relief flooded over him. It was only the ticket inspector. He fished in his pocket. "Here you are."

The ticket was clipped and handed back. "*Anglais* – English, is it not?"

"Close enough, I suppose," he grunted. It would be a waste of breath trying to explain the difference. "Was there something else?" The man seemed reluctant to leave.

"*Vous aimez* – you wish a place in ze *salle*? *Le déjeuner* – lunch?"

Eddie was tempted. Breakfast at the hostel had been far from substantial, and he had not thought to bring any food with him. But he shook his head. A meal in the first-class dining car was bound to be expensive, and his resources, slender enough at the outset, had been sadly depleted by the cost of the journey. Besides, he might be seated next to some prying busybody. It would be safer to avoid conversation with a stranger.

"Thank you, but no." He waved away the offer. "It's a little early for me. I'll get something at the next stop."

An ingratiating smile was replaced with a scowl of disfavour. The inspector shuffled away, no doubt to try his luck elsewhere. Eddie shrugged and took up his paper again.

There was a dry chuckle behind him. "Gie ye a fright, did he?" He swivelled round at the sound of a voice. "Thon joker took ye for an easy mark. He thought ye were a toff. And nae wonder, dressed in thae togs."

Eddie bristled. It was another of the tweed suit brigade sitting behind him, thus far unseen and unheard. "You can talk," he retorted. "You stick out like a sore thumb as well."

"Aye, well, ye could hae a point. We'll no' quarrel ower it." The speaker gave a broad grin. "Mind if I join ye? Ye look as if ye could dae wi' a bite o' scran." Without waiting for a reply, he came forward, brandishing a battered tin box. "Here ye are," he said, taking off the lid. "French bread an' cheese. No' what we're used to, but it fills a hole."

For a moment Eddie was nonplussed. The chap was evidently disposed to be friendly. And there was something about his open, rugged features that disarmed any ill feeling. "Thanks, I won't say no."

"That's the ticket. Wire in. By the way, the name's Buchanan – Chick Buchanan."

"Baird – Eddie Baird." He gasped as his hand was enveloped in a huge fist.

"Dandy. Bide there a minute. I've some wine tae wash it down. Rotgut stuff, but it's better than nothin'." Eddie was left to munch his makeshift sandwich while his new acquaintance fetched a flask. "This'll put fire in yer belly," he said, sliding his bulk into the adjacent seat.

Eddie took a swig. The fieriness of the liquid left him speechless. It was brandy.

"See what I mean? But it'll dae ye guid. Now if I were a bettin' man, I'd wager ye were fae Edinburgh. Am I right?" He was rewarded with a nod. "Thought as much. We're fae Fife, me an' these lads." He indicated the others in their Sunday best, each apparently with his own paper parcel of possessions. "Pitmen fae Coaltown o' Wemyss. Very appropriate, ye might suppose."

"Miners?" He managed to find his voice. "My grandad was a miner."

"Ye don't say. Was he on the Fife coalfield?"

"No, Lanarkshire. I never knew him. He was killed in an accident years before I was born."

"Aye, it's a dangerous trade, right enough. But what's done is done. Nae sense in dwellin' on it." There was a firm snap as he replaced the lid on his box. "I wouldnae think you were the type tae gang down by. Mair like the golf links, by the look o' ye. Well, ye'll no find much scope here. So just what is yer game? Bird watchin', or some such thing?" He closed an eye knowingly.

"Something like that." Eddie winked back.

"That's all I wanted tae ken. I jaloused we were on the same track. But it's Shanks' pony ower the Pyrenees. Did ye realise that? Ye'll no' get far in that clobber. It can be damned cold on the mountains, I can tell ye."

"I appreciate that." For a moment he looked crestfallen. "I've a pair of hiking boots in my kit. And a greatcoat as well." He indicated a neatly folded garment. There was no need to add that there was a slit in the inside pocket where he had slipped Robertson's letter into the lining.

"Maybe it'll dae at that. It's no' a big deal." He grinned. "See here, what are ye goin' to dae once we're off the train? Any plans?"

"Not really. I was given to understand there would be guides to escort volunteers into Spain. I was hoping someone would make himself known at the station."

"Are you kiddin'? Whoever telt ye that has nae idea. Ye're no' home an' dry when ye get to Perpignan. The place is crawlin' wi' fascist supporters, especially in the polis. Gie them half a chance, and they'd clap ye in jail, or hae ye deported back tae Blighty."

Eddie was mortified. Surely all the risks, the pitfalls, would be known to anyone closely involved with the struggle in Spain. Yet it now seemed advice on how to avoid them had been hazy, not least where it really mattered. Could this be some deliberate ploy to have him stymied at the last hurdle? He drew a deep breath. One day he might have a bone to pick with Iain Baird.

The pitman caught his look. He could feel for the lad's frustration. "See here, Eddie – ye don't mind me callin' ye that? Why no' come wi' us? There's safety in numbers, and I've got an address in the toun. It shouldnae be a bother to find. What d'ye say?"

"But what about your friends?" He sounded doubtful. "Would they not object to a stranger?"

"I wouldnae worry ower much on that score," he was assured. "They usually look to me for guidance on most things."

"They've appointed you as their leader?"

"Aye, I suppose ye could put it like that."

"Well, if that's the case—" He made up his mind. "I accept your kind offer. And I'm very grateful."

"Nae trouble. We're a' in it thegither now. Ye should try an' get some kip while ye can. We'll a' need our wits about us once we're there."

It was useful advice, and he was only too glad to wrap himself in his overcoat and stretch out on the slatted wooden bench. Sleep, the slumber of nervous exhaustion, gradually stole over him. He dozed fitfully, only dimly aware of the train stopping from time to time; people were leaving – few, if any, taking their place.

Suddenly he was wide awake, his ears assailed by a cacophony of noise, men bellowing at the top of their voices. Startled, he threw aside his coat and sat up.

"Come and join us, Eddie," chirped Chick Buchanan. "Ye'll ken the tune."

He looked round in amazement. The carriage was deserted, apart from the little band of Fife miners. And they were singing, belting out the words of the *Internationale*. The spirit was infectious. He found himself chanting the song's refrain.

SIXTEEN

Desperate Times, Desperate Measures

Catalonia, Spain
May 1937

The sound of reveille blared out across the parade ground as the first rays of sunlight heralded the break of day. Men belched, groaned, grumbled and cursed in half a dozen languages for being wakened at such an ungodly hour. But new recruits had been quick to learn it did not pay to carp at their treatment, not with Spanish instructors ready to find fault at the slightest excuse. Blankets were hastily cast aside from makeshift beds, clothes thrown on, boots hurriedly laced; then it was a mad dash to the cookhouse, metal bowl and spoon in hand, for an early breakfast. Each volunteer was painfully aware that food was in short supply, and there was rarely enough to satisfy everyone. The Lenin Barracks in Barcelona was a salutary introduction to the realities of military life.

"Ower here, laddie! I've kept a place for ye." It was Chick Buchanan, beckoning to him. A little out of breath, Eddie Baird joined the scrum round the cooks' urns. "I see ye're still wearin' that coat," he added good humouredly.

"Can you blame me?" He thrust out his bowl for a ladleful of bean stew and hunk of bread. "We've had no uniforms as yet. And it's still damned cold before the sun rises."

"My, my, we are tetchy this mornin'. Come an' sit down while we hae our grub. Then ye can tell yer uncle what ails ye." He indicated a spot away from the crowd where they could squat down undisturbed. "Now get stuck in while it's still hot. It'll make ye feel better."

For some minutes they ate in silence, each apparently lost in his own thoughts. It gave Eddie an opportunity to reflect on what he owed to this man. Chick had gone out of his way to take a complete stranger under his wing: he was honest enough to admit he would never have made it to Spain by his own efforts. Buchanan was surely a born leader, always cheerful in adversity, never slow to chivvy his little band when spirits flagged. Little wonder his companions doted on him.

"You're a good sort, Chick," he said at last, a little shamefaced. "I know I've no right to grouse."

"Sez who?" He grunted in satisfaction as he wiped his bowl clean. "See here, son. A sodger a'ways has guid cause for complaint. So dinnae hold back. I'm listenin'."

Eddie paused. Despite the camaraderie, recent events weighed heavily on his mind. There had been frustration at the week's delay in Perpignan while arrangements were made to join a score of others for the journey across the mountains. And some feat it had been! Was he ever likely to forget the rough slog over the Pyrenees, on foot and by night; surrounded by the haunting solitude of the pine forest as they climbed ever higher on seemingly invisible paths, skirting round rocky outcrops and sudden ravines that spelt mortal danger for the unwary? Mercifully the guides had seen them safely through, and they had been fortunate enough to evade any lurking border patrols. How they had cheered, in relief as much as joy, when their French escorts had wished them '*bon voyage*', and Spanish counterparts had emerged, like wraiths in the mist, to take their place.

At journey's end a waiting charabanc had lifted their spirits, but rather than convey them to find food and rest in the nearest town, as they had been promised, it had sped all the way to Barcelona. Here they had been lodged in the local military barracks, where they still languished; boredom scarcely lightened by daily drills with dummy weapons, and interminable political lectures in broken English. Could he really blame himself for a growing sense of unease?

"C'mon, laddie, out wi' it." The older man gave him a fixed look. "I can see there's somethin' on yer mind. Nae sense in keepin' it tae yersel'."

"I didn't realise I was such a wet blanket." He pulled a face. "It's just this constant hanging around, waiting for something to happen."

"Fed up tae the back teeth, eh? I can understand that. The Spanish are never in much o' a hurry. It's a'ways *mañana* wi' them." He gave a faint grin. "Maybe tomorrow has come."

"What d'you mean by that?"

"Use yer heid, man. Did ye ever stop to consider why they woke us up sae early this mornin'?"

"Well, yes – I did wonder."

Chick nodded towards the closed and barred gateway. "I've a notion we'll be on our way afore long. Nae mair o' these daft wooden rifles. We'll get the real McCoy when we get tae the trainin' camp. And uniforms forbye that."

"That would be good news. But you can't know for certain, can you?"

"Dinnae ask. I've got my sources." He tapped his nose. "Anyway, ye'll be able to send that note ye were gripin' on about tae yer parents."

"To tell them where I am? I'd have done that already if they let us out of this prison. Or at least allowed us to write home." He pursed his lips. "Why do you suppose they keep us cooped up like this?"

"That was explained, ye'll mind. It's for our safety. There's fightin' in the city – a fifth column o' fascists tryin' to seize power. We cannae go out till the civil guard has cleaned up the mess."

"In Barcelona? You believe that? Trotskyists and Anarchists fighting for Franco?" Amazement turned to doubt. "Is that connected with what happened when we were sworn into the International Brigade? They asked who were members of the Communist Party. Card carriers like you and your lads got a pat on the back. The rest of us were advised to claim we had no political affiliations."

Chick reddened "It was for yer ain good," he muttered.

"But I told you I was in the ILP. You said it wasn't important. We were all in the same cause, all part of the Popular Front. Now it does seem to matter. Why might that be?"

"Things are a bit more complicated than I had thought, it seems." He grimaced. "I wish ye could leave things be. But – I suppose ye've a right tae ken."

In the distance a ragged cheer went up. Instinctively they whirled round at the disturbance. The main gates had swung wide to allow a lumbering, open topped motorbus to enter. Chick blew out his cheeks, glad of the interruption.

"Tell ye later," he rasped. "Nae doubt this'll be for us. Ye'd best fetch yer kit. Rouse yersel' now!" With that admonition he was off, calling out the names of his comrades.

It was as well that the Fife miner was quick on the uptake. Eddie was first into the sleeping quarters to retrieve his possessions, speedily followed by his compatriots. "That's the ticket, lads," sang out Buchanan behind them. "Sharp as ye like. Though I jalouse there'll no' be a rush. Just listen tae thae guards, roarin' an' shoutin' in Spanish while a'body else runs round like heidless chickens."

That was something of an exaggeration, thought Eddie, as they marched out. Order had been largely restored; the other recruits were forming up to collect their belongings. An officer caught sight of them, and actually smiled as he waved a hand towards the waiting vehicle.

"Is this no' dandy?" Chick appraised their transport for the journey – a faded, ramshackle affair which looked on its last legs. "Lap o' luxury, wid ye say?" He looked round as the driver dismounted from the open cab and began to gesticulate wildly. "I think he's tellin' us to get a move on." He led the way to the rear of the bus, with its spiral staircase giving access to the upper deck.

"Upstairs?" It was Boab, youngest of the pitmen, who made the suggestion.

"Aye, why no'? Gie us a chance tae admire the view. I see there's naewhere to stow our kit," he went on. "Better take it wi' ye and shove it under yer seat. Mind an' sit thegither," he called out as they scrambled up the stairs.

It came as something of a surprise, as well as relief, to discover that there would be no customary delay before starting off. Within minutes the rest of the recruits came streaming across the square, to be hurriedly directed on board, some clumping upstairs, while others were directed into the saloon. Peering over the side, Eddie could see two armed soldiers follow the last man onto the bus. Before he could raise a query, there was a growl as the engine coughed into life, a screech as the clutch was engaged: then they were off, swerving through the gates, out into silent, deserted streets.

Chick seemed to read his thoughts. "Thae sodgers? I saw them tae. Nothin' to worry about. They'll be our escort."

Eddie nodded, though he was far from convinced. Two men armed with rifles would give little protection against an enemy, but might be considered ample to keep untrained troops in order. Still, perhaps it would be wiser not to press the issue. "It's been quite a rush," he remarked casually. "You gave me the impression the Spanish are never in a hurry to get things done."

"Aye, true enough. This must be an exception. I suppose they wanted us away afore the city wakes up."

"You think there might be more fighting in Barcelona?"

"Buchanan shrugged his shoulders. "Cannae tell. But there's more to it than ye might imagine."

"Really? I thought we were all on the same side."

"Black an' white, eh? Goodies and baddies? Grow up, Eddie. This isnae a film show."

"But – I still don't understand."

"Well then, listen. I'll tell ye as much as I ken. I wid have got round tae it anyway." He turned to the others. "And you lot pay attention as well. Ye might learn somethin'."

The authority in his voice had its effect. "That's better. And I want nae backchat from you, Doug." He singled out the acknowledged humourist of the group. "This is serious."

"Go right ahead. We're all ears." Doug was rewarded with a hard stare. Thankfully Chick decided to let it go at that.

"As I was about to say," he began, "the powers that be think the trade unions and their militias are gettin' ower big for their boots. The government see them as a distraction from the war effort. They're to be disbanded – hand ower their weapons, surrender the areas they've occupied. Once that's done, and the ringleaders arrested, the rank and file can be split up and packed off to serve at the front."

"But it was the trade unions that organized the first real resistance to Franco's invasion," protested Eddie. "But for them the fascists would have won control of the whole country last year."

"Aye, that was then. But now they're fu' o' Trotskyists an' fifth columnists, demandin' workers' control o' industry, redistribution o' land to the peasants."

"But isn't that what the Republican government is all about? The end of class and privilege?"

"No' quite. And certainly no' just now. The Nationalists hae to be crushed afore anythin' else. Stands tae reason, would ye no' agree? Comrade Stalin thinks so, and he ca's the tune. Spain is the frontline in defence o' the Soviet Union. That's what the Popular Front is all about."

"Oh!" Eddie thought for a moment. "It was never put like that to us before. I suppose it means that the Russians don't fully appreciate the contribution made by other leftist parties. They'll never really trust us."

"Ye could put it that way," said Buchanan drily. "And that would include the ILP. Never mind," he went on consolingly. "You're one of us now. We a' stick thegither."

"Thanks, Chick." He smiled gratefully. "I know you'd never leave me in the lurch."

"Nae bother. Get some rest now. We've a long way to go." He looked on as the new chum sank back, wrapping his coat around him. The others were beginning to settle down as well, he was glad to note. Conversation slackened, then died away altogether.

For Chick Buchanan there could be no thought of sleep. He had gathered his little brood from the coalfield; they had followed without hesitation. Now the responsibility for their welfare, perhaps their lives, weighed heavily on his shoulders. Their destination, he had assumed, was the base for the International Brigades, where proper training would be given. This, he knew, was far to the south. Yet no rations had been issued for the journey. And there was no indication that provisions, or even water, had been stored on board. He could only hope that stops had been arranged along the route. Even more disturbing was the thought that they might have to pass through a war zone. Rumour had it that the Nationalists were planning an offensive to the north and east of Madrid. Speculation differed as to whether the intention was to encircle the capital itself, or cut off Catalonia from the rest of the country. In either case heavy fighting lay ahead. He could only trust that they would get through safely before it began.

As the countryside rolled by at a steady, if unspectacular pace, he tried to look on the bright side. Any reservations about the age or roadworthiness of the vehicle appeared groundless. Traffic was light; there were no roadblocks to impede progress. It was even possible to imagine that war was far away. Now the highway was narrowing, climbing upwards, twisting and turning until it reached a plateau. This must be the *mesa* he had heard about – a tabletop landscape of scrub and barren soil, with few signs of habitation. Presently they found themselves travelling alongside a river, fast flowing and swollen by snowmelt from the distant mountains. Ahead lay a viaduct, its metal girders glinting in the sun. The bus slowed to turn onto the bridge; and then abruptly came to a grinding halt.

There was a chorus of invective as men were jolted out of their reverie.

Chick cast an anxious glance over the side. "Nothin' to worry about, lads," he reassured them. "Just the driver goin' to fetch a can o' water. Must be his radiator needs topped up. Might as well make the most o' it," he added, standing up. "Chance tae stretch yer legs."

It appeared that everyone else had much the same idea, as they joined the throng streaming from the bus. Some were already relieving themselves by the roadside, while others made for the riverbank with whatever receptacles came to hand. Eddie alone seemed to hang back, looking round as though unsure of himself.

"What's up, laddie?" His reluctance did not escape notice. "Ye're in a right dwam."

"Sorry, Chick. I say – God, this is embarrassing."

"Ah!" It was not hard to guess the reason. "Ye mean you need the toilet?" Eddie gave a wry nod. "Well, what d'ye expect out here? Away an' join that lot ower there."

"But – it would be undignified. There's no privacy."

"So it's a jobbie, is it? If that's a' ye're bothered about, ye've a lot to learn. Ye cannae expect latrines at every stop." The sight of a woebegone expression gave him pause. "See here, Eddie, there's naebody on the other side o' the river. You could nip across an' hide ahint the bushes. I'll keep a lookout, an' see ye're no' disturbed. I'll even haud yer coat for ye."

"Would you, Chick?" His eyes lit up. "You're a brick." It was the work of a moment to shake off the garment before dashing off.

Draping the coat over his arm, the older man followed more slowly. How peaceful everything seemed. No rumble of distant gunfire, no hint of troops on the move, or defensive positions being prepared. Nothing to indicate the war that was tearing the country apart.

He reached the far end of the bridge. "Are ye about finished, Eddie?" he called out. "The bus'll no wait."

"Just about, Chick." The voice came from behind a clump of blackthorn. "By the way, can you hear anything?"

"Naw. Nothin' but thae damned insects. I cannae mind what ye ca' them."

"I don't mean that. It's faint. High up."

"Are ye sure?" His companion gazed upwards. Shielding his eyes against the sun's glare, he could just make out a dark speck in the cloudless sky. At first he imagined it must be some bird of prey, but as it drew nearer, he caught the unmistakable throb of an aircraft engine. No doubt it was a scout plane out on patrol: now it was dropping down for a closer look. Across the bridge came the shrill blast of a whistle. Glancing back, he saw men rushing to leap on board the vehicle as the driver sought to steer it onto the crossing.

It was only then that he grasped the cause for alarm. The plane had been circling overhead: suddenly it altered course, straightening up, swooping down. Christ! Was it lining up for an attack? For precious seconds he gaped open-mouthed as it hurtled towards the bridge. Almost at the last moment he found his voice. "Get down, Eddie!" he yelled, as he flung himself into the wayside ditch.

He was only just in time. Crouching low, cowering helplessly in the shallow trench, he hardly dared breathe as a machine gun opened up, raking the ground around him before passing on. There was an almighty whoosh, the deafening blast of an explosion, cries of pain and anguish. Then a deathly hush, broken only by the crackle of flames.

For long minutes he lay motionless, scarcely able to believe he had survived unscathed. At length he stirred, brushed off dirt and rubble, before gingerly pulling himself to his feet. The enemy was gone, leaving behind an almost unimaginable scene of horror. The bus was a blazing wreck, churning out clouds of billowing black smoke. Shapeless forms littered the ground. There was no sign of life, nothing he could detect through the carnage. His eyes began to smart, whether from grief or the acrid fumes he could not tell. A bitter anger gripped him as he thought of his friends, comrades and workmates he had known since childhood.

"Are you all right, Chick?"

He swung round. He had forgotten about Eddie in the heat of the moment. His brow darkened. The boy was limping badly, grimacing as he dragged one foot in front of the other. "Ye're hurt laddie. Have ye been hit?"

"Nothing like that, Chick. Just a sprained ankle. I must have twisted it when I dived for cover."

"Aye, well – maybe. Ye'd best let me take a peek." In truth he was glad of the diversion.

"Never mind about me. I've said I'm not wounded. We need to go and help the others."

Buchanan shook his head sadly. "Nothin' we can dae, son. They're a' goners. Besides, ye couldnae get across, no wi' that inferno. Yon bus could burn for hours yet."

"But – we can't just leave them. Surely they can't all be dead."

"It's no' possible," he insisted. "The river's nae use. I cannae swim. Nor can you, no' wi' that gammy leg."

"Then what—?"

"We should get out o' this. That smoke can be seen for miles. But first I'll need tae bind up that ankle o' yours. Have ye anythin' I could use?"

"I – I think there's a scarf in my coat pocket. I'll get it for you."

"Nae trouble. I'll find it." He looked round; then paused, squinting into the distance. "There's somethin' in yon hill yonder. I caught a flash in the sunlight. There it goes again. Maybe there's sodgers up there."

As if in answer to the thought, half a dozen horsemen emerged from the tree line, cantering down the slope towards them.

"Eddie! Gie me yer paybook – what they gave us when we enlisted." He was quick to realise the situation. "They'll want to ken who we are, since we're still in civvies."

As the riders drew closer, it was evident they were indeed troopers – swarthy, stocky fellows in faded battledress. They could only watch as the little group reined in: carbines were unslung as one of their number dismounted and advanced towards them. Chick opened and held out the little booklets for inspection. The man stooped to peer closely, then looked up sharply. "*¿Inglés? Brigada Internacional?*" Without waiting for a reply, he pulled a pistol from its holster.

"My God, Eddie!" His spirits sank. "What have we done? They're Franco's men."

* * *

Edinburgh

The mood was sombre in the Lixmont family home as daughter and son-in-law arrived for yet another council of war. Eddie had disappeared to join the conflict in Spain, or so it had been assumed. But there was only circumstantial evidence to suggest he had actually done so. Now there was just a glimmer of hope that new information might be forthcoming to cast fresh light on his whereabouts. The telephone summons had stressed, however, that it would be unwise to raise expectations too high. The news might amount to little or nothing.

After the usual exchange of greetings Sir Edward began by reviewing such facts as were known. It was a matter of great regret that his grandson's absence had gone unnoticed for several days. His parents had presumed he had returned to Glasgow after his weekend in Stirling, while Morag Baird had taken for granted that he had remained in Edinburgh. It was only when his aunt had telephoned to ask when she could expect him back that doubts had emerged. But by then it was too late. A missed opportunity, he lamented, but no one could be held at fault.

He steadied himself with a sip of water. Enquiries had been put in hand, he continued, and an interview sought with his friend, Fiona Handling. Somewhat to his surprise, she had made no bones about her part in planning the whole escapade, seeing him off on the night sleeper on the Friday, before taking a train to Stirling herself. Police involvement, both in Edinburgh and London, had proved fruitless, as had approaches to railway and port authorities. He had even gone to the length of an appeal to the French consul, again without result. Officialdom was simply not interested.

He shifted uncomfortably, conscious of his wasted efforts. It was Hilda who had insisted there were other channels which might be examined. Her son was an obvious choice. He had contacts in high places, access to more informal sources. It had been for him to swallow his pride, and accept he could see no other option.

"I must pay tribute to your mother," he went on, nodding towards Elizabeth, and studiously avoiding the faint smile on his wife's lips. "She gave me wise advice that I should seek out your brother. You will be aware that relations have been rather strained over these past months, but I must admit he did not hesitate in offering his support. He has spent the last few days in London, and this morning we received a wire to say he was returning immediately." He consulted his watch. "He should be with us within the hour. I suggest we adjourn till then."

Afternoon tea was brought in, but no one had any appetite for refreshment. Conversation was desultory; attempts at small talk soon lapsed. After an interval Lady Hilda rang her little silver bell; the tea things were removed, barely touched. Now all that remained was the waiting.

The sudden hoot of a taxi gave everyone a start. Alastair jumped up to look through the window. "Yes, it's him, all right. He's just coming up the path."

All eyes were on the door as he was announced. "Captain Lixmont, mum." The maid took his coat, curtsied and withdrew, closing the door behind her.

Hugh Lixmont marched in, stooping to give his mother a dutiful kiss, before offering his hand to his father. The presence of his sister and her husband he acknowledged with a casual wave.

"I won't beat about the bush," he announced, seating himself on an easy chair. "The Foreign Office flatly refuses to entertain any representations on Eddie's behalf. Their view is that if he has gone so far as to enlist in a foreign army, then he has broken the law and must take the consequences."

There was a general gasp of dismay.

"Bear with me." He held up a restraining hand. "There is more. I was able to pull a few strings elsewhere. Eddie did reach Spain. He signed up in Barcelona, I was informed. However, the trail runs cold after that. He was part of a draft that left the city for the main training camp of the International Brigades. That's at Albacete – well to the south. But there's nothing to show that he actually arrived there."

"Wait a minute, Hugh." It was Elizabeth who spoke. "Could he not have taken an assumed name when he found he was on his way to the front?"

She was met with a glassy stare. "Why in blue blazes would he do that when he enlisted under his own name? In any case none of the others in his party seem to have arrived either. It's thought they may well have been the victims of an ambush by Nationalist forces."

"I understand that, Hugh." This time it was his father who posed a question. "Could he have been captured or recorded as a casualty?"

"No word of either, dad. I'm afraid lists are far from complete. Sometimes the Nationalists take photographs of their captives and send them to our newspapers. Presumably to deter others from setting off for Spain. I've gone over some of the pictures with a fine toothcomb, but there's no trace of anyone even remotely resembling Eddie."

"What about prisoner exchanges, Hugh? I believe they sometimes take place." His mother was anxious to explore every avenue, however faint.

"On occasion, yes. But I'm sorry to discourage you, mama. I'm told there's little prospect of any more for the foreseeable future."

"Well, thank you for your efforts, Hugh. At least we have confirmation that he actually got to Spain." Sir Edward was appreciative, but it was time to move on. "If officialdom refuses to act, I see only one possibility for a way forward. Someone should go there and find out what actually happened." He looked meaningfully at his son.

"I agree, dad." He was shrewd enough to anticipate the suggestion. "But I'm not the man for the job. I've never visited Spain. You need someone who has spent time there, knows the lie of the land."

"Oh! You have someone in mind?"

"I might have." He turned towards Alastair. "I believe your brother is back in the country, Baird."

"That's true." He was a little puzzled. Why on earth drag in Iain's name? "Morag told us as much. But he didn't stay long. He seems to have gone his own way. No one knows where he is now."

"No? Well, I do, as it happens. I made it my business to find out. The authorities keep an eye on the likes of him. At present he's doing the rounds, drumming up recruits for Spain."

"But – I thought that was illegal." It was enough to raise his father's ire. "Why has he not been challenged?"

"Oh, he's much too fly to be caught out. On the surface his meetings are purely to arrange collections for the downtrodden masses. But there's a sting in the tail. He asks for men interested in taking a more active role to stay behind. Then he interviews them in private – sells them the story, shows them how to get to Spain, gives them money for the journey, for all we know."

"But surely there must be some means to prevent this?"

"That would be difficult, dad. Any attempt to plant a man to gather evidence could be construed as entrapment. Use of an agent provocateur? The case could be thrown out of court. As a lawyer, you should know that."

"Harrumph!" Sir Edward coughed, before hastily changing the subject. "You think Alastair's brother is the answer? According to his wife, he tried to persuade Eddie not to go. But how much weight can be put on that?"

"That scoundrel sent my grandson to risk his life in a war that does not concern us." Lady Hilda had no doubts. "He should be made to fetch him back."

"Hold on, my dear." Her husband was more cautious. "This bears careful consideration." He rounded on his son. "Do you really believe he could achieve anything, even if he was disposed to take on the task – which I would question?"

"Perhaps his chances are not so remote as you imagine, dad. He will have contacts in Spain. And news spreads." His mouth tightened a little. "I'm convinced he would be more than willing to help us out."

"Well, if you put it like that—" He weakened. "I'd pay anything to know what happened."

"I was just coming to that, dad. He must be given the wherewithal for the job. Palms will probably have to be greased. Information costs money in these parts. And that could mean a tidy sum."

"But – can he be trusted? What's to stop him simply absconding with the funds? We'd never see him again."

"It's a chance we may have to take. But remember who it is we're talking about. His own flesh and blood."

"So be it." His father threw in the towel. "I confess I can't see any alternative. Where is he to be found?"

"Not that far away, as it happens. In the Fife coalfield, I'm led to believe. It would appear most of the miners there are communists. Little Moscows – that's what they call the towns and villages in that neck of the woods. A happy hunting ground for a recruiting sergeant, I'm sure you'd agree." There was a gleam in his eye. "And by good fortune I've learned that he's due to address a meeting tonight. A local hall in Lumphinnans, if you're interested. And so, with your permission…"

"You'll go yourself?"

"Of course. I'll take my two-seater. I assume it's still in your garage." He acknowledged the nod, and rose to leave. "One more thing. It occurs to me that it might be as well to have some company. On this occasion two heads may be better than one."

"Good idea, Hugh. Did you have someone in mind?"

"His brother." He gestured towards Alastair. "That all right with you, Baird?"

* * *

The hour was late, very late, when Alastair let himself in on his return to the house in Inverleith. The maid had long since been dispatched to bed, leaving her mistress to nurse her thoughts as dusk slowly turned to inky darkness. Midnight had come and gone before the scratch of a key in the lock announced his homecoming.

"You still up, Elizabeth?" He came into the room, switching on the light. Moments later he found himself grasped in her arms. "Here, I say, steady on," he protested, only half in jest. "You'll have me over if you're not careful."

"You must be dog-tired, darling." She released him, a little embarrassed. "Come and sit down. I've a flask of hot milk and some sandwiches. You must be famished."

"A little peckish, perhaps." He allowed himself to be steered to his favourite chair. "I won't say no."

"How did it go? Did you see him? Is he coming?" She could hardly contain herself.

"Yes. He's given an undertaking to turn up at your father's house at noon tomorrow. That'll be today now. No thanks to me," he added ruefully.

"What do you mean by that?" She paused in the act of pouring his hot milk. "Never mind. First things first. Tuck in." There was a plate of sandwiches on the little table beside him. She handed him his glass of milk. "Then I'll want to know everything."

"And so you shall. We can talk as I eat." He took a sip of milk before selecting a sandwich. "Well now," he began, "the meeting was in full swing when we arrived, so we were able to slip into the back row unobserved. For some reason your brother felt things might go better if I interviewed Iain by myself. He would only make himself known as a last resort."

"The bond of brotherly love, I suppose. Calculated to make your brother more amenable. Strange Hugh should think that."

"Yes, isn't it?" He drained the rest of his milk. "Anyhow, to continue. Iain knows how to make a speech, no argument about that. A heartfelt appeal to the community to strain every nerve in support of the poor innocents in Spain – anything they could afford. At the end the chairman indicated that their distinguished guest would take a few questions from the body of the hall. Furthermore, though pressed for time, he was willing to delay his departure, should anyone wish a personal consultation. Iain walked off the stage to a round of applause. Seemingly that was my cue to follow him."

"And did you?"

"Certainly. Your brother saw to that. I was first in the little room set aside for him at the back."

"I bet that gave him a shock. When he saw who it was, I mean."

"Well, he was naturally surprised, and I think a little alarmed. Then he pulled himself together and asked if I had come to contribute to the cause. Trying to make a joke of it, of course. But he soon changed his tune when I told him Eddie had gone missing in Spain."

"How did he react?"

"Shocked, stunned – and I believe it was genuine. Then he made an attempt to justify himself. He had done everything possible to dissuade him from going. If all else failed, he had been confident Eddie would have been turned back at the frontier. He could not be blamed – the boy was just too headstrong."

"Did you ask him if he was prepared to go to Spain and search for him?"

"That goes without saying. He came out with all sorts of excuses. It would be like looking for a needle in a haystack. If by some miracle he did discover Eddie's whereabouts, probably in the hands of the Nationalists, what was he expected to do next? His work here was of overriding importance and could not be abandoned. All he could do was to write to his contacts in Spain and ask them to make enquiries on his behalf. It all sounded rather lame, and I think he felt rather ashamed of himself."

"So how was he persuaded to come round?"

"That was your brother. As soon as I told him Iain's attitude, he was off like a shot. Ten minutes later he was back, saying it was all fixed."

Her jaw sagged. "You're telling me Hugh worked the oracle? Did you ask how he managed it?"

"What do you think? On the way home he said my failure was probably due to the natural antipathy of an older brother for a younger sibling. He, on the other hand, had an inbred authority which commanded respect in the lower orders."

"What a load of tripe! He was just trying to hurt your feelings."

"Like as not. But for some reason he doesn't want to reveal the truth of the matter. I've been turning it over in my mind. It strikes me that he must have some hold over Iain – something my brother would do anything to avoid coming to light."

Elizabeth snapped her fingers. "I believe you've hit the nail on the head. They do know one another. They must have met when Iain was on Glasgow Corporation, in the planning committee; and Hugh was in league with that obnoxious Nick Norman, helping him with his building contracts. God knows what seedy deals they may have cooked up between them.

Alastair sighed. “Yes, true to character, as always. And now we have to treat him with kid gloves. He’s probably our only hope.”

* * *

Avila, Spain

¡Mañana mueres!

Tomorrow, you die! Such was the usual refrain amid the jeers and catcalls of hostile crowds, whipped up to greet them wherever they might halt for the night. The howl of the mob rang out loud and clear, but did the voice of the local citizenry really count for much? Not so far, it seemed. But the threat could never be ignored. Twice already they had encountered truckloads of cowed prisoners being marched away off the road into secluded forests, followed a little later by the distinct rattle of rifle and machine gun fire, before the vehicles reappeared to speed past them, this time empty.

Nevertheless, there was little to be gained by dwelling on what might be their fate. For the present there was the near certainty of yet another beating for one or both of them. Entertainment for bored soldiers, but there was also a purpose behind the brutality – to wring confessions from them. They had been caught wearing civilian clothes, suspicious in itself; but what was far worse was the note discovered in the lining of Eddie’s coat. Apparently his uncle had given him a letter of introduction to a political commissar in the British battalion. Chick Buchanan swore softly to himself. Had he known that, he would have insisted on the immediate destruction of such an incriminating document. He had taken his young friend at face value – an innocent abroad. Now they were branded as spies.

A swift blow from a rifle butt caught him by surprise. In an instant he flared up in anger; then thought better of it. Retaliation would only provoke further violence. The truck had drawn up on the far side of the hamlet, and this was the invitation to disembark. Silently he assisted his companion down from the tailgate, supported him through a gauntlet of hisses and abuse, with the local priest well to the fore, he could not help noticing. It was a dubious relief to reach the sanctuary of their billet, a mill of some description; then to be forced down a narrow stairway leading into a musty cellar, and the door above slammed and locked behind them.

"Ower here, laddie." Chick led the way to where the fading rays of sunlight filtered through a rusty metal grating set high on the wall. That might bear closer examination, he thought to himself, but first things first. "Sit ye doon on yon pile o' sacks."

"Thanks, Chick. And I'm sorry for the mess I've landed you in. I shouldn't have kept that message there."

"No' your fault. Ye werena to ken." If the boy had apologised once, he had done so a hundred times. "If there's anyone deserves blame, it's yer daft uncle. He must hae kent what a hell o' a risk it wid be. Now put it out o' yer mind," he added. "I'll just take a wee peek at ye."

Even the most cursory inspection confirmed that the youngster was in poor shape. Hardly surprising, given the hardships of four or five days of gruelling travel. Their initial captors had turned out to be a patrol of Moorish cavalry, troops from North Africa, renowned for their savagery. Little time had been lost in carrying them back to the nationalist-held zone, strapped on packhorses like so much baggage. From there others had taken over, conveying them deeper and deeper into fascist territory in the back of horse-drawn wagons or motor lorries. Wherever they halted for the night, conditions were primitive, to say the least. There was little opportunity to shave or wash; sanitation was a bucket or hole in the ground. The short commons served up was almost inedible – watery soup, mouldy bread, rotting fruit and vegetables. Little wonder he looked little more than skin and bones.

And then there were the beatings. It was Eddie who bore the brunt of the rough handling, probably because he was so obviously the weaker of the two. One eye was almost closed, there was an ugly weal on the side of his cheek; below his shirt was a mass of bruises, maybe even a cracked rib. Despite everything the lad showed spirit, had never complained; but now it was a question of how much longer he could hold out. Were he to give way and sign an admission they had been sent as spies, all might be lost. It would make a fine propaganda coup for the Nationalists. And once they were of no further value…

He lifted his head at the sound of a key scraping in the lock; the door above creaked open. A soldier stood at the top of the stairs, carrying a lantern. He looked down, pointed a finger at Eddie, and jerked his thumb.

"Seems like it's me again, Chick. Best go and get it over with. No, don't help me up." He waved aside the offer. "I can manage on my own."

His fellow captive could only bow to the inevitable, and stand tamely aside as Eddie struggled to his feet, hirpled away to climb the stairs, while the guard waited in anticipation. He was only too aware of the likely outcome should he make any attempt to intervene. The door banged shut; the bolt shot home with an ominous thud. Instinctively he clenched his fists, cursed himself for his weakness. But it was only a fleeting gesture. It was not in his nature to give way to despair, he told himself. Surely there must be something…

A final flash of fading sunlight caught his eye, drew him back to the grille set in the rough brickwork. Now he came to notice it, the structure stood forward from the wall, leaving a gap. He gazed up, weighing the possibilities. If the bars could be forced, the opening beyond looked big enough for a man to squeeze through. Hastily he dragged over a few half-filled sacks of mouldy grain, presumably the remnants of the last year's harvest. Clambering up, he found, as he had hoped, rusted mountings in crumbling mortar. Even better was the discovery that the lattice of heavily corroded iron overlooked the roadway, only a foot or two above street level. Another glance to ensure there was no one within view, no voices within earshot, and he took a firm grasp on the bars: a single sharp tug, and the fixture came away in his hands, so suddenly that he nearly overbalanced.

He scrambled up, flushed at such an easy success. Here was an escape route, should need arise. But it could only be as a last resort. They were deep in the enemy's domain, with probably every hand against them. And it was doubtful whether Eddie could travel far in his condition. It was in a more pensive frame of mind that he hefted the grating back into place, pushing the rusty nails into their holes. Once the sacks were replaced in their original positions, he could only trust to luck that nothing would be taken amiss, and hope that the fixings would still bear the weight.

He had barely time to complete the task before there was a fumbling at the door above: a light appeared on the stairs. His heart missed a beat. Had they heard something? Were they coming to investigate? "That you, Eddie?" he called out.

"Who else, Chick?" The light disappeared: the door closed once more. He could afford to breathe a little more easily.

"Ower here, laddie. Watch ye dinnae trip ower somethin'." He could barely make out the figure stumbling towards him. "Sit yersel' down on the sacks. They didnae keep ye long this time. Did they knock ye about much?" he asked anxiously.

"Not so much as laid a finger on me. They even gave me this pail of stew for our supper."

"What?" He stared suspiciously. "Ye havnae signed anythin', have ye?"

"Of course not. You know me better than that."

"Aye, well—" He sniffed, only half convinced. "First time for everythin', I suppose."

"You mean the stew?" Eddie squatted down beside him. "It doesn't smell bad. Better than the usual pigswill. We'll need to eat with our fingers, I'm afraid. They forgot the cutlery. Sorry there's no bread to mop up the juice."

"That can wait a minute." There was more to this than met the eye. "First I want to know exactly what went on up yonder."

"Not much, truth to tell." He was a little taken aback by the sudden demand. "The lieutenant seemed fed up with the whole business. I had the impression he was just going through the motions. He just shrugged his shoulders when I refused to answer the usual questions. I think he was trying to make out that he would be done with us after tomorrow."

"So that's it? Some other lot takin' over as nursemaids?"

"I don't think so. He said something about a *cárcel*. That's a prison, isn't it? Then he mentioned a place called Salamanca. That's west of here, I believe."

"Aye, I think that's right. Could mean we're for the jail at that place?" His brow darkened. "Whatever they've got planned for us, it'll likely happen there. Maybe a show trial. Like the ones in Russia, ye ken. It wid make rare publicity for them." He sucked his teeth. "We darena risk it. We'll need tae make a run for it. There might no' be another chance."

"You mean tonight?" Eddie gasped in disbelief. "How can it be possible?"

"See up there." Chick pointed to the wall opposite. "Yon ugly lump o' rust leads ontae the street. It's easy moved. I've already been at it. Now it's hangin' by a thread. If ye think ye're up for it—"

"Don't worry about me, Chick. As I said, they didn't touch me. I feel fit as a fiddle." There was renewed hope in his voice.

"I wouldnae go that far," said Chick drily. "But there's no' much choice. We'll need tae wait till the wee sma' hours. Gie the guards time tae drown their sorrows. We'll get away while they're sleepin' it off. In the meantime, let's hae the grub. Build up our strength for the morn."

They fell to, sharing the food as best they could. At the end of the meal Chick licked his lips, wiped his hands on the sacking. "At least it filled a hole," he remarked. "Now try an' get some rest. I'll wake ye when it's time."

Sleep was impossible. Each was left to dwell on his thoughts and fears as the long hours crept by. Only when the moon began to rise, casting its ghostly hue, did the older man stir. "Are ye awake, Eddie? Help me shift these bags ower tae the wall." Once in place, he climbed up to pull away the grating. "Now it's your turn, laddie. I'll help ye up, so ye can crawl through the hole. Mind ye keep low when ye're out. Stay in the shadow, if ye can."

His comrade in arms followed on, once Eddie had pushed through the opening. It was a tight fit for a man of his girth to squirm through, but no worse than he had encountered in narrow seams on the coalfield. "What's the plan, Chick?" He heard the whisper in his ear.

"Get the hell out o' this as fast as we can." Heaving himself out, he pointed back. "That'll stick out like a sore thumb as soon as it's light."

"Can't be helped, Chick." He struggled to his feet. "Which way will we go?"

"No' much choice. It would be daft to gang through the toun. And we'll need tae keep off the roads." He paused for a moment. "They'll guess we'll go east, back tae Republican lines, or maybe north for France. In that case it's west for us, tae Portugal. It cannae be more than a hunner miles or so."

"A hundred miles?" He gulped in astonishment. "On foot? Do you really believe we could do that?"

"I ken it's gonnae be hard. But we hae to try. And the first thing is tae find a place where we can lie low in the daytime. Safer tae move at night."

Quickly leaving the roadway behind, they struck out across fields belonging to the village. Beyond these, moorland stretched into the distance, uneven ground where the going was far from easy. It was not long before Eddie began to limp badly.

"That ankle giein' ye gyp again? Never really healed, did it?" Chick looked round anxiously. Dawn was already breaking: high time they found cover. "Here, lean on me. See yon wood ower yonder." He gestured towards trees growing on a hillock. "Think ye can make it. We can maybe rest there."

They ploughed on, towards the mound of pine trees. Eddie was sweating profusely, grimacing with pain. Game though he was, it was clear he could go no further. However, as they were soon to discover, the woodland was far less extensive than they might have hoped. The trees soon thinned, then petered out: beyond lay more open country. There was nothing for it but to retrace their steps, and find what refuge they could.

"Well, this puts us in a bit o' a pickle, laddie." He helped Eddie down onto a bed of bracken, propping him against the trunk of a tall fir. "This is as good as anywhere. Bide here while I see if there's a wee burn. Somethin' tae cool down that swellin'. And wet our whistles." He forced a smile.

It was not unpleasant to sit and take his ease in the stillness of the pine grove, sheltered from the fierce glare and heat of the sun. Presently Chick returned, shaking his head in disappointment. "Nothin' doin', son. No' even a trickle o' water. We'll lie up here awhile, then see what's to be done."

For the next hour or so they took what comfort they could from the peace and quiet of the glade. Suddenly Chick pricked up his ears. "Hear that, Eddie? Sounds like dogs yappin'." He listened intently. "Gettin' louder. They're comin' this way. Must be meant for us. But how the hell—" He broke off. Eddie was staring at him, transfixed.

"Oh, my God!" he groaned. "It's my coat. They must have kept it. That's what gave them the scent."

"Could be," Chick grunted in response. "But there's nae use greetin' ower spilt milk. We cannae stay here now. And they'd soon run us doon." He took a deep breath. "Nothin' for it. I'll try an' distract them. Draw them away. It might gie ye a wee chance."

Without waiting for the expected protest, he was off, dodging towards the unseen foe. After a dozen yards he halted, waving and shouting. "Ower here!" he yelled, then turned to run. Shots rang out. Horrified, Eddie saw him spin, and fall. In an instant he had picked himself up. Another volley, and he tumbled over. This time he lay still.

Now the soldiers were advancing towards him, beating a path through the undergrowth. Dogs were straining on the leash; men were levelling their weapons, ready to open fire. He sank back, closed his eyes in silent prayer. Rough hands dragged him to his feet.

SEVENTEEN

Against the Odds

Glasgow
June 1937

Hugh Lixmont looked up as his secretary marched into the room. "What is it, Miss Harewood? I thought it was understood that I was not to be disturbed. I've a mountain of work in front of me."

"Entirely your own fault, Captain Lixmont." Elsie Harewood rarely minced her words. "Your unexpected absence from the office…"

Lixmont swore inwardly. The dragon, as he thought of her, was no respecter of persons. Willingly he would have dispensed with her services, but Nick Norman had appointed her to the post, no doubt to keep a weather eye on him. She held a privileged position, and knew full well how to take advantage of it.

"I was under the impression I had explained why I was called away," he said stiffly. "There were problems with the new development at Lenzie."

"Strange that it never came to my attention." She gave a distinct sniff. "And you were gone for over a week."

"Do you have to know everything?" he retorted irascibly. God, she was like a leech when she sank her teeth into something. "I'm rather busy at the minute. So, if there's nothing more, Miss Harewood—"

"Ah, but there is, as it happens." She permitted herself the faintest of smiles. "I warned you about the overdue quarterly report. Mr Norman is not amused. In fact, we have just received a telephone call to say he is on his way here. He has arrived in Glasgow by train, and wishes the company motor car to proceed to the Central Station without delay."

"Oh!" It was hard to conceal his dismay. "Then you'd best see to it."

"I already have." She gave a little toss of the head as she turned away, leaving him to glower as she flounced out.

He blew out his cheeks. The prospect of Nick Norman coming to take him to task was a blow, there was no denying it. His excuse for running off at his father's urgent summons had been rather threadbare, but the best he could do on the spur of the moment. And it had seemed to pass muster at the time. Apparently not. She had pretended to accept his explanation, and then promptly informed their employer of a suspected dereliction of duty. Possibly Norman had decided to leave things in abeyance until he had an opportunity to hold him to account in person. It was little comfort that the Harewood woman could have no knowledge of the real reason for his absence, given that the pater had had the sense to contact him at home, rather than at his place of business.

Now there was nothing for it but to cudgel his brains, try to work out something more convincing to deflect the wrath of his lord and master. No easy matter, considering their present strained relationship. Nick had gone up in the world, moving south, opening up an office in London, doubtless in the hope of government contracts now that rearmament was getting under way. But there had been no place for his former righthand man, no offer to take his once favoured lieutenant with him. Instead, he had been left behind in Glasgow, little more than a glorified office boy. Trust had been forfeited; he could acknowledge that. He had put the interests of his sister before those of his paymaster in the renewal of Elizabeth's lease in Edinburgh. What he found difficult to stomach was the role of scapegoat when Norman failed to be awarded his expected knighthood. How could he have anticipated Baird's loss to the security services when he suddenly skipped off to Spain? Perhaps it would be better to bite the bullet, hand in his notice, and be done with his employer once and for all.

He was still wrestling with his options when there was a scraping of chairs and chorus of 'good morning, sir' in the outer office. Hardly had he scrambled to his feet when there was a knock at his door. He braced himself for the inevitable reproach and censure. Much to his astonishment, however, his visitor came bounding in, wreathed in smiles, arm outstretched to grasp him warmly by the hand.

"Glad to see you again, Hugh," he gushed. "It's been far too long. My fault entirely. But sit yourself down," He himself took the chair opposite. "No need to stand on ceremony."

For a moment he was stunned, but only for a moment. Instinctively he was on his guard. He knew Nick of old. Like as not the bonhomie was assumed, masking some deeper purpose.

"First of all," Norman continued, "I should offer you an apology. I was rather sharp with you over that affair with the Honours List, and that rascal, Baird, taking himself off to Spain. I now realise that you were in no way responsible."

"Very kind of you, Nick." What else was there to be said? "You don't mind my calling you that?" he added hastily.

"Not at all, old fellow. Now let's dispose of this – observation, shall we say – from Miss Harewood. I presume you felt it was none of her business to pry. In actual fact it was a personal matter, was it not?" He gave an encouraging smile.

"Well – yes. I suppose you could regard it as such."

"Concerning your nephew? I gather you received short shrift when you called at the Foreign Office."

"How—?" His jaw dropped in amazement. "How on earth could you know that?"

Norman leaned forward. "When I learn that a colleague has gone AWOL, I make it my business to discover the reason why. In all honesty, Hugh, you should have come to me. There are other doors that could be opened, likely to be much more fruitful in a case like this."

"You mean your friends at the German and Italian embassies? I hadn't thought of going down that line."

"Why not? I am always made welcome there. A veritable mine of information, if you know who to ask." He noted Lixmont's scowl. "You can rest easy, Hugh. Your nephew is alive, if not kicking. He is at present a guest of the Nationalists. I might add that I'm due to dine with the German ambassador next week. I'm sure Herr Ribbentrop will be sympathetic if I put in a word for young Edward."

"You mean he could get Eddie released?" Hope stirred within him.

"He could certainly help, were he so disposed. However, you must understand that my powers of persuasion are not limitless."

His heart sank a little. Instinct told him Nick Norman was about to demand his pound of flesh. "Something I can do for you in return?" he queried.

"Well, everything has its price. And it so happens there is a small favour I might ask. I'm sure the boy's mother will take little convincing, given what's at stake."

"Elizabeth? How is she involved?"

"It is in regard to your sister's advertising agency. I would like to purchase it. You can tell her I would offer more than a fair price, and she could stay in charge if she so wished."

"Under your direction." His head shot up. So that was it. Nick's revenge for that business over the lease. "No doubt as an outlet to peddle your pro-German slogans," he growled.

"Come, come, Hugh, you know me better than that." He waved a finger in mild rebuke. "Her copy would be a force for good, extol the virtues of international harmony, help preserve the status of the British Empire. It would be in her own best interests to treat things in that light," he added pointedly.

"Have it your own way." Further argument would be useless. Nick had made up his mind. And he seemed to hold all the cards. "Anything else?" he asked bitterly.

"Possibly. I should deem it an honour if your father would propose me for membership of his club." He hastened to explain. "I am aware that, though retired, Sir Edward is held in high esteem in local society. His influence could be an advantage should I decide to expand my interests in the capital."

"You're not asking much, are you?" This was going too far. "You know my father's opinion."

"An unfortunate misunderstanding. It happened years ago. The world has moved on since. Your family would be wise to accept it." He fished a card from his notecase. "Perhaps you should consult your father and sister. You can contact me on this telephone number when you have an answer. I shouldn't leave it too long." He rose to go. "By the way, your nephew is presently languishing in the city of Salamanca. Conditions in jail there are far from pleasant, I'm led to believe."

Hugh Lixmont was left to curse the day he had thrown in his lot with Nick Norman. The demands were monstrous, and his parting shot laced with menace. It was not difficult to envisage the reaction when his parents and Elizabeth learned of the terms. Already he was in bad odour at his lack of response to heavy hints that he should accompany Baird to Spain.

No doubt they would submit in the end, if no alternative could be found. At the same time, he recalled that Nick had made no definite commitment to ensure his nephew's freedom. What was actually at the heart of his offer? Better treatment while Eddie remained in captivity? Negotiations for a prisoner exchange that might become mired in endless bureaucratic delays? If that was all, it would make a poor bargain for the family. They would feel aggrieved at being tricked. And lay the blame squarely at his door.

Feverishly he cast round for another possibility. At least the boy was alive, and his location known. And Iain Baird should have arrived in Spain by now. He never had much faith in the mission, vague as it was; he had only made the suggestion to save face, rather than confess to total failure. But circumstances altered cases. Baird had said he would begin his search at the Republican training base at Albacete. If word could be got to him there, there was a chance he might just achieve something. If money could secure Eddie's release, he had certainly been entrusted with the wherewithal to grease palms on a lavish scale. Telegraph services to Spain were notoriously sketchy, but a short, innocuous message might reach its destination. A long shot, but preferable to going cap in hand to the family with Nick's proposition.

Abruptly he came to a decision. "I have to go out this afternoon, Miss Harewood," he announced, as he collected his hat and coat.

"Very good, Captain Lixmont. Shall I call a taxi cab to take you to the station?"

"No need." He could sense the knowing look as he passed though the outer office. "I'll find my own way."

* * *

Albacete, Spain

"Here ye are, comrade." The sentry at the gate handed him back his identity card. "Sorry tae keep ye waitin', but we had tae check when ye mentioned the captain's name. He's vouched for ye. Ye've tae go up tae his office. It's ower there on the far side o' the square. Ye canna miss it."

Iain Baird nodded his thanks and hoisted his kitbag. It was good to hear a Scottish voice again, to know he was amongst his ain folk. And, more important, to have it confirmed that his old mentor was still in post. However, that was only a first step. How would Stan react to his unexpected reappearance? And how would he respond to a request for help? There was every possibility that any plea would fall on deaf ears, if nothing worse.

His brow darkened as he tramped wearily towards the jumble of buildings. The journey from the Spanish frontier had been far from easy, taking much longer than he had anticipated. His old uniform of khaki breeches and tunic, his pass as an agent of the Comintern, should have helped speed his travel south. But not this time. He had been met with days of delay, countless roadblocks, endless detours, amid the upheaval and confusion following the latest Nationalist offensive. And, on reaching Albacete, he found the training camp had moved some twenty miles further on. Hardly surprising he had arrived dog-tired, his uniform caked in sweat and dust. The money belt beneath his shirt chafed abominably, stuffed as it was with golden sovereigns and bearer bonds drawn on the Bank of England. Had anyone guessed at the wealth in his possession… But why bother to dwell on that now? He would need all his wits about him if his mission was not to end in abject failure, before it had even properly begun.

"Ower here, laddie." It was a call from the veranda of what appeared to be little more than a hastily built structure of roughly hewn timber. He made his way towards it, suppressing a mild irritation. Trust Stan, still berating him as a mere boy, though he was pushing fifty. "So ye've made it at last."

Before he could even think of a reply, Iain found himself enveloped in a bear hug, before being almost manhandled across the threshold. Breathing heavily, he surveyed the rather spartan quarters: one wall covered in maps, several battered filing cabinets, a desk strewn with papers, with a typewriter that had obviously seen better days. There were also two or three plain wooden chairs. He sank gratefully into the nearest.

"An army marches on its bumf," chuckled Robertson. "Ye look as if ye could dae wi' a drink. I've only red wine. And it's rotgut stuff."

"That was some welcome, Stan," he grumbled, only half in jest. "Thanks for the offer, but I think we can dae better than that." He fished in his holdall. "I brought ye a bottle o' whisky."

The older man whistled. "It's to be bribery, is it? Well, I winnae say no. There's no' much o' the *cratur* floatin' around in this neck o' the woods."

He produced a couple of tumblers from a drawer and opened the bottle. "*Slainte!*"

"Yer guid health, Stan." They touched glasses and sipped the amber liquid.

"My, yon's the real article. I havnae tasted stuff like this for years." Robertson drained his glass. "Anyways, how are things back in Blighty? How was yer recruitin' drive?"

"Fair to middlin', ye might say. Folks are no' sae ready to commit themselves these days, now there seems to be nae end to the war."

"Somethin' in that, I suppose. So ye got orders to come back tae yer old job, Iain? I'm fair pleased to hear it."

"No' exactly, Stan. It – it's for another reason."

"Somethin' else? Somebody at the high command must have forgot to pass on the message. Poor sods like me are a'ways the last tae hear."

"Ye dinnae seem very surprised." For a moment he was puzzled by Stan's quip. The it dawned on him. "Ye've been havin' me on. Ye knew I was comin'."

"Well, I jaloused ye might be on yer way." He unlocked a drawer and withdrew a flimsy enclosure. "Here, it's addressed to you. It's a wire. And ye ken what? It was delivered by a chap from the British consulate in Seville. A bit queer, would ye no' admit? Seemingly he had been a' ower the place lookin' for ye. He was only too glad when I said I would keep it for ye. Sorry I had tae open it. I thought at first it must be some mistake."

Iain unfolded the paper. The contents were short and to the point: EDDIE IN SALAMANCA STOP LIXMONT.

"Mean anythin' to you, laddie?"

"Aye." He recovered from his amazement. This was information he might spend months seeking. "I think I can work it out, Stan."

"Me an' a'. I take it Eddie is thon – nephew, I think ye telt me. And deep in the Nationalist zone as well. So, I presumed he'd been captured. And you've been sent tae bring him back – ye hope. Am I right?"

Iain fell silent. It was undeniable.

"Ye ken, son," he continued, "I a'ways said yer temper would be the death of ye. It seems yer relations come under the same headin'. Just as well I've nae worries on that score."

"But he's my kith an' kin," he protested. "I couldnae just leave him to go tae the wall."

"So that's yer excuse. The powers that be will no' see it in that light. Ye abandoned yer post wi'out permission. That's desertion, pure an' simple. Ye might be a social fascist or Trotskyist saboteur. It would be my duty tae show ye up. And ye ken what the penalty wid be."

Iain gulped. This was far worse than he had envisaged. "Ye're sayin' the cause comes first, and nothin' else counts for anythin'?"

"Of course. Ye accepted that when ye joined up." He appeared to consider. "Lucky for you, yer message came my way. Anywhere else would have meant curtains for you. Especially if it fell intae the hands o' the heid honcho in these parts."

"Honcho? Ye mean the chief political commissar?"

"The very same. Fella called Marty – a Frenchman. He's got a bee in his bonnet about fifth columnists an' defeatists. And he's no' above pullin' out his pistol an' shootin' anyone he takes exception tae. He's no' touched any o' mine yet, but that day will come, you mark my words."

"So ye think I should take care tae avoid him?" His voice shook a little. "Does – does that mean ye're no' gonnae gie me away?"

"Haud on. No' sae fast." Robertson held up a cautionary finger. "There's mair in this than meets the eye. Ye seem to have friends in high places. Yer telegram arrived by way o' the consulate. They widnae get involved, no' without instructions frae London. And yon Lixmont. Accordin' to you, he's a fascist sympathiser, Mosley's chum, hobnobbin' at the German an' Italian embassies. Care to explain the connection?"

Baird could have kicked himself. Did the man ever forget any scrap of information he was told? However, he quickly rallied. "I telt ye I had nae truck wi' the man. I kent nothin' about this message, or how it got here. I cannae help it if my brother married his sister. He just happened to be there when auld man Lixmont asked me tae help find his grandson Ye must believe that, Stan."

Robertson gave a sly grin. "Ye keep yer end up, laddie. I'll gie ye that. But there's still a wee question buzzin' round in my heid. Just how committed are ye? Maybe yer first loyalty is tae yersel'."

Iain went red in the face. "Ye think I've got a foot in baith camps? How can ye make that out?" he demanded. "Tell me when I've ever let ye down."

"I didnae say that, Iain." He waved away the protest. "Nae need tae get yersel' worked up. I a'ways gave ye the benefit o' the doubt."

"Thanks for nothin'. Ye had me kicked out o' the Party. Back in '28, that was."

"None o' my doin'. Ye ken that fine. It was a change in policy fae Moscow. I did my best tae speak up for ye. And mind I took ye back in, afore we set out for here." He sighed. "Maybe I made a mistake there."

An uncertain silence followed. Robertson put a finger to his lips as he pondered what course of action he should take. Baird's protestations of innocence cut no ice with him. At best he had clearly disobeyed orders; at worst he was a double agent, playing off one side against the other. Moreover, it was not as though he had been blameless in the past. What had begun as a vague unease about him at the end of the Great War, had developed into strong doubts at the time of the General Strike, suspicions amply confirmed by recent activities. By rights he should have the man arrested at once, and handed over for summary justice.

Yet he hesitated. They had been comrades in arms for many years, forming a bond which, rather to his surprise, he found difficult to break. Perhaps he had been hasty in branding Iain as a turncoat. Spain was lost; he could see that now. The war might limp on for another year or two, but it was hard to deny the inevitable outcome. Victory would go to Franco and his ilk. Then the recriminations, the search for scapegoats, would begin. He himself might be accused, and suffer the fate of so many others who had fallen foul of Comrade Stalin. Better to cut his losses, and take up the struggle elsewhere, if it could be managed. The fight to crush fascism came first. The triumph of the proletariat would have to wait.

Iain caught the look of indecision. "I can assure you—"

"No' another word." Robertson cut him short. "There's already been ower much talk." He thought for a moment. "Suppose – just suppose ye got as far as Salamanca. What d'ye plan to dae once ye're there? Wade right in wi' guns blazin'? Rescue the lad single-handed?"

"No' exactly, Stan." He gave a thin smile. "I havnae got that worked out yet." It would never do to reveal the existence of a money belt beneath his tunic. Still less the card he had secreted in the hollowed-out heel of his boot.

"Maybe no'. But I bet ye've got somethin' up yer sleeve." He waited in vain for a reply. "Well, I winnae press ye. I could gie ye a pass for safe conduct to the front. But after that?" He shrugged his shoulders.

Iain's heart leaped. "Does – does that mean ye're gonnae help me?"

There was no answer. Instead, Stan rose from his chair. "Come ben. I've somethin' tae show ye."

Curious, he followed his old boss through to the adjoining room. How typical, he thought, as he surveyed the contents. The man never had much regard for creature comforts: the camp bed, some shelving with a few books scattered around, and an ancient wardrobe testified to that. Producing a key, Robertson opened its door and unlocked an inner drawer. He stepped back and pointed. "Take a peek at this."

Iain stared blankly. There was nothing untoward within, only a neatly folded blue garment, together with an officer's cap.

"That might just be your salvation," quipped Stan. "Ever heard o' the Blueshirts?"

The penny dropped. "Ye mean General O'Duffy's Irish Brigade?"

"Got it in one. Irishmen in the ranks o' the Nationalists? Wid ye credit that? Franco has his own foreign legion, no' just the Eyeties an' Fritzes. The priests back home tell them it's a religious crusade for the Holy Mother Church." He lifted the item from the drawer. "Look – no' a mark on it."

"So I see. But how did ye come by it?"

"Ah well, it's like this. Some o' my lads came ower the body after a skirmish near Guadalajara. Shot clean through the heid. His mates had a' scarpered. They went through his pockets an' stripped him o' his sark. Brought it back to me as a kind o' trophy, ye might say."

"And you kept it."

"Aye. Had it cleaned and pressed. Though I never suspected there might be a use for it someday." He opened another drawer. "And that's no' all. Here's his ID – Lieutenant Seamus O' Driscoll, it says. There's a couple o' letters – fae his mother an' local priest in Tipperary. Also, a message o' congratulation on his promotion. Signed by General O'Duffy himself. Ye'd best hae them."

Iain could only gape at the documents thrust into his hand. "I'm to act the part o' this man? Impersonate him?" he gasped.

"Why no'? Ye'll hae evidence tae help ye out if ye're questioned. At least see ye safe tae Salamanca. Ye'll just hae tae hope naebody kens an Irish accent." He closed the drawer. "Though what ye can achieve when ye get there, God alone kens."

"Thanks, Stan. I'll no' forget this." His eyes lit up. The germ of an idea was forming in his head.

"Ah, well, ye'd best take his hat tae. And here's his belt and sidearm." He paused. "I suppose ye'll be needin' some money." He stooped to pull out a tin box from the foot of the wardrobe. "Ye can hae this. There's nae use for it here." He handed over a wad of well-thumbed currency notes. "Now get the lot o' it out o' my sight afore I change my mind. I'm just nippin' outside for a fag."

He had barely time to pack everything away before Robertson came rushing back. "Quick, Iain! Intae the other room. There's a big staff car comin' in at the gate. And I ken who it belongs to."

"But—" There was no time for protest. Iain found himself bundled into Stan's bedroom, and his kit thrown after him.

Breathless, there was nothing for it but to crouch behind the door as the reality of the situation dawned on him. Ears pricked, he caught the sound of a car drawing up; there was the scrunch of heavy boots on the gravel. He listened intently as greetings were exchanged on the veranda. Voices were raised; apparently the newcomer was demanding information. Then they were at it, trading insults, squabbling like Newhaven fishwives. A final curse; then he heard the clump of rapidly retreating footsteps, the bang of a car door, the vehicle speeding away.

He looked up inquiringly as Robertson returned. "That didnae take long, Stan."

"Longer than I might have hoped. I was right, laddie. That was Marty – the heid commissar. He kens ye're back. Somebody must hae clocked ye in Albacete. Wanted tae ken the reason. And why he wisnae informed."

"And what did you say?"

"I telt him it was none o' his business. He wisnae cock o' the walk here."

Iain whistled. "He'll no' appreciate that."

"It's the only way to treat the likes of' him. I said ye were on a secret mission for the Comintern. And I'd nae idea what it was. Ye only looked in tae say hullo. Then ye were off."

"And he believed you?"

"I doubt that. He stomped off in a rage. He was gonnae get at the truth o' the matter. Make some enquiries. He'll be awa' tae phone his superiors. Then he'll be back, ye can stake yer life on it. Ye'd best be gone afore he comes." He took up a paper from his desk. "Thought as much. There's a truck wi' supplies due tae head for the front. I'll try an' speed it up."

"You mean I could get a lift?"

"Aye. If it leaves soon, you could be there by nightfall. Then ye might slip away, nae bother. Cross over under cover o' darkness." He handed Iain his kitbag. "Better dae it now. Afore anyone sees ye."

He led the way to what appeared to be a large shed. Inside, men were loading a lorry with crates of ammunition. Beckoning Iain to stay in the background, he went over to some soldiers. There was a brief conversation before he returned.

"They've agreed tae take ye. But ye'll need tae hide in the back, atween the boxes. They'll put a cover over ye, so ye'll no' be seen. They're just about ready to go, so off wi' ye now." He offered his hand. "Whatever happens, dinnae come back this way. I'll no' answer for the consequences."

He watched as Iain scrambled over the tailgate and crawled under the tarpaulin. The crew tightened the canvas and the driver started up. He waved as the truck jolted down the track towards the gate; then trudged back to his office. His belt and holster hung on a hook behind the door. He took out his revolver, checked it was loaded, and thoughtfully laid it on his desk. Lighting a cigarette, he settled down to wait.

* * *

Salamanca, Spain

The officer in the distinctive uniform of the Irish Brigade straightened his cap as the train rumbled into the city's main *estación*. So far, his journey into the heartland of fascist Spain had gone with scarcely a hitch, far better than he might have dared to hope. It had been a doddle to slip across no-man's land at dead of night: there were no regular lines of trenches, only fixed strongpoints at intervals. By dawn he had adopted his new identity, burying everything that might associate him with the Republican cause, and was standing by a roadside, waiting to flag down a passing army truck. The driver had been more than willing to take him to the nearest railway station. No point in failing to make use of Robertson's money, he had decided.

Naturally his appearance had attracted attention from fellow travellers, but inquisitive stares and snide remarks gave way to smiles and handshakes when they heard the tale he had concocted for himself. He was a soldier on furlough, on a pilgrimage to trace his Spanish lineage. One of his forbears had been an Irish trooper in Wellington's army over a hundred years ago, helping to free Spain from the yoke of French occupation. It was at Salamanca that he had wooed a lady of culture; she had insisted on following him back to Ireland where they had wed and settled down to raise a family. His short leave would be spent in local cemeteries, examining old tombstones, consulting ancient records, before returning to duty at the front.

A story good enough to pass muster for the journey through the seemingly endless countryside, he could tell himself. But would it be enough in a major city, a provincial capital, a hotbed of Nationalist support? That was the worry. Salamanca had served briefly as Franco's headquarters; at present its jail housed hundreds of Republican prisoners, including a number of British captives. There was bound to be a check on new arrivals; Iain Baird had no illusions on that score. Should he be picked out for questioning, he could produce no papers to prove he was on leave. He might be taken for a deserter, or worse. Now there was nothing for it but to put on a brave face, and take his chances.

In the event his fears proved groundless. He had his ticket ready to surrender to the collector at the barrier. There were also two military policemen to inspect papers. When his turn came to present his pass, they merely gave it a cursory glance. One of them queried "*¿Irlanda?*", and, receiving a nod, simply waved him through. Now he could breathe fresh air. At long last he was free to pursue his mission. But how? He could not be sure that Eddie was in prison here, or indeed if he was still alive. One thing was certain: finding somewhere to stay must be his first priority. He would need a base while he cast his net for news of the lad.

It made no sense to stick to the bustling thoroughfare outside the station. What was required was somewhere quieter, where a stranger could come and go unnoticed. Striking out from the main road, it was not long before he encountered a maze of side streets, full of shabby tenement buildings, with any number of signs in apartment windows advertising *habitaciones*. Just what he had been looking for – a district of rundown lodging houses. Selecting an address at random, he knocked on the door. The answering *proprietario* was only too glad to offer what he claimed was the best room in the house, handing over the key in return for a week's rent.

Once the landlord had departed, his next step was to lock the door, and begin a detailed inspection of his billet. There was a grunt of satisfaction as he felt under the bed and discovered a loose floorboard. Screws to hold it in place were missing; it was the work of moments to prise it up. Underneath was a cavity, ideal for his purpose. Unbuckling his money belt, he thrust it into the hole, slid the board back into place. It was a relief to know that Lixmont's hundred gold sovereigns and £5000 in high denomination bonds were safely stowed away out of sight. That done, he dusted himself down, and, carefully locking the door behind him, sallied out in search of a local *restaurante.* Now he could afford to relax a little, eat a badly needed meal, smoke a cigarette or two over a glass of brandy, while he considered plans for the immediate future.

Early the next day, supplied with a grubby map of the city by his host, he bought *tortilla* and coffee from a street vendor's stall, before setting out to negotiate his way towards the open square with the prison at its centre. It was a fair walk, but he was there by mid-morning, gloomily surveying the fortress like structure, with its high walls and iron studded gate, firmly locked and barred against anyone who might be tempted to approach. Somewhat to his surprise, there was a knot of people at a little distance, apparently waiting for some event to happen. A cheer went up as the gate suddenly swung open and a covered truck sped out, escorted by soldiers on motor cycles. The little convoy disappeared from sight, the jeering died down and the crowd began to disperse. A puzzle, certainly. But was it an example of gruesome secrets contained within these grim walls?

It was in a sober frame of mind that he entered a *taberna* in an alleyway just off the square, and ordered coffee and cake. He was the only customer, and the barman was more than ready to pass the time of day with him. In his halting Spanish Iain explained he was a foreign legionnaire, on leave in a strange city, and found he craved the fellowship of brother comrades-in-arms. Did off duty soldiers patronise his establishment? Perhaps guards from the nearby prison, come to unwind after a hard day's slog? The man nodded, and smiled to show he was in luck. If the *señor* cared to return in the early evening, he could be sure of finding congenial company. Thanking the man profusely, and pressing a generous *punta* into his hand, he took his departure, to spend his afternoon pottering around two or three graveyards to add substance to his tale.

Promptly at six o'clock he was back at the inn. As he stood on the threshold surveying the room, his attention focused on a group of half a dozen figures in military fatigues clustered round the bar, drinking beer, exchanging banter. The barman caught sight of him, pointed him out to the soldiers, before beckoning him forward. All eyes seemed to be on him, as though sizing him up; then the ice was broken with handshakes all round. They wanted to know more of their gallant ally. He was congratulated when he mentioned his Spanish ancestry, cheered when he coyly hinted he had learned his trade fighting the English in the Irish war of independence, hailed as a kindred spirit when he insisted on buying drinks for everyone.

This was his opportunity. That morning, he remarked casually, he had chanced to see people in the street gesticulating angrily at a passing truck. What might that be, he wondered? Probably the execution wagon, came the reply. Most days a cargo of miscreants was driven to some remote spot to be dispatched. The jail was grossly overcrowded, and it was a convenient way of getting rid of some of the scum. Were any British prisoners included in this treatment? In the past, perhaps. But not anymore, as a rule. They were too valuable when it came to prisoner exchanges. But of course that could never apply to the young British spy they held in custody, announced one of the men proudly. Not that it mattered anyway. The *bastardo* was in poor health, liable to perish at any moment, before he could be put on trial and shot as he richly deserved.

Iain gasped. This was staggering news. For a moment he bit his lip, choking back despair and horror. Fortunately, no one seemed to notice. The speaker was going on to reveal that guards were sometimes permitted to bring friends and relatives to witness punishment of malefactors. Would his Irish friend care to attend one of these parades? That set him thinking. He was grateful for the invitation, he replied, but was intrigued to hear of the British agent. Would it be possible to see him? Out of the question, came the response. The spy was held in solitary confinement. Only the military governor could authorise such a visit. In that case he would make application, he announced. Where was his abode? He winked to show he spoke in jest. Seriously though, he was reminded that his general had asked him to pass on his respects to the governor as a matter of courtesy He would be failing in his duty if he did not carry out General O'Duffy's request.

An hour later the party broke up amid expressions of mutual esteem, the men to go their separate ways, their new acquaintance to make what preparations he could for the following day. Eddie's whereabouts were confirmed, but it was clear he was in mortal danger. Only an immediate plea to the provincial governor gave him any chance. The funds in his possession would be his main bargaining counter, but, if necessary, he had a trump card which might just swing the balance. Directions to the grand *palacio* on the outskirts of the city were easy enough. A tram would take him most of the way, leaving only a short walk to his destination.

The next morning, he arrived outside a rambling country mansion surrounded by a high wall. As he had suspected, security looked tight, much more so than at the railway station. But this was no time for delay, or hesitation: Eddie's fate hinged on his efforts. He marched straight up to the gatehouse to present his credentials – O'Driscoll's card and his letter of appointment to the rank of lieutenant. The guard did not seem impressed by his request for an interview, nor was his captain, when summoned. It was only after he stated that he had been tasked with asking the governor's advice on the disposal of a generous offering raised by the people of Ireland that he was grudgingly granted admission.

There followed a long and dismal wait in an anteroom before an official came to conduct him to what he took to be the governor's office. Seated behind a huge desk was a short, stocky figure in a rather gaudy uniform, apparently studying his documentation. Without looking up, the man gestured him towards a chair. His subordinate bowed and withdrew, silently closing the door behind him.

"*Muchas gracias, Su Excelencia.*" Iain halted two paces from the table, drew himself to attention and threw out a salute.

"There is no need for formality, *Señor* – O'Driscoll." There was only the briefest hesitation before the last word. "You may speak in English. I understand the language tolerably well. Now please to sit down." He waited till his visitor was seated. "Permit me to introduce myself. I am Colonel Morelos, chief of staff to the general. His Excellency is engaged this morning. He asked me to conduct a preliminary interview. It would save time later. Would you not agree?"

Iain could only nod dumbly. The fellow spoke almost faultless English, with barely the trace of an accent. "I must say I am amazed at your command of my native tongue." He found his voice. "Allow me to congratulate you."

He was rewarded with a smug twist of the lip. "Thank you. I spent some years at the Spanish Embassy in London. That would be in the time of the monarchy, of course." He sighed. "But we must not dwell on the past. I believe there is some mention of a gift from your compatriots."

"That is so." He gave a slight cough as he composed himself to deliver the little speech he had prepared.

"The people of Ireland are angry, angry and disgusted when they read of atrocities committed by the satanists and atheists in Republican Spain. They are sickened by the sufferings and murders of innocent priests. They have not been backward in contributing freely to a relief fund organized for the Holy Mother Church in its hour of need."

"I see. A worthy cause, no doubt. You have been sent to find where aid would be most welcome?"

"Yes. With your help, naturally. The governor and his staff will know where priorities might lie."

"I am certain that would be most gratifying." His smile faded. "A few moments ago, you said you were impressed by my knowledge of English. I wish I could say the same of your attempt at an Irish accent."

Iain groaned inwardly. Morelos had been sceptical. Now he was deeply suspicious.

"You are not Irish, after all." It was a statement of fact. "What are you, then?"

"I – I come from Scotland." Denial would be useless.

"A Scotsman in the Irish Brigade? Now that would be a rarity." His hand strayed towards the bell on his desk.

"Just a minute." His heart leaped in desperation. "I've said I'm Scottish. And I admit I'm not even a Catholic. But the bit about the fund is true." He breathed a little more easily as the hand drew back.

"Then just why have you come here? The truth, remember. Any prevarication…" The colonel left the rest unsaid.

"You don't have to tell me that." He needed time to collect his thoughts. It had been his intention to introduce Eddie as the son of a prominent Catholic family, sympathetic to the Nationalist cause. To their misfortune, however, their only child was wilful, had gone astray, been induced to take part in a youthful escapade. In despair, the boy's grandfather had begged his old friend, General O'Duffy, to intercede on his behalf. Hence his arrival in Salamanca at the behest of his commanding officer. Fat chance that would be accepted now.

"I am waiting, *señor*." The tone was ominous.

"I am sorry, colonel. Please excuse me." Thank God there was still a last throw of the dice. With a few tweaks his story might yet hold.

"You are very perceptive, sir. The truth of the matter is that I have been sent on a delicate mission. I wear this uniform only to facilitate my journey here."

"For what purpose?"

"If you would allow me a moment to explain." He felt in his pocket for the item he had removed from the heel of his boot the previous evening. Silently he passed over a faded and rather dog-eared square of folded card.

It was received with a glance of disfavour. "This is difficult to make out, but would appear to be a membership card for the British Union of Fascists." He looked up. "Your name is Iain Baird? And you claim to be a member of the BUF?"

"Certainly. It bears my signature and that of our leader, Sir Oswald Mosley." His inquisitor was not to know that this was his original membership card which he had thought lost, but which had been discovered by Morag – with dire results. He had kept it ever since.

Colonel Morelos shrugged. "You could have picked this up anywhere. Or perhaps forged it yourself. However," he continued, "let us suppose for the moment that it is genuine. Please to continue with your explanation. I am, as you say, all ears."

He listened impassively as Iain began to weave his tale. A report had been received in the United Kingdom that his nephew, Eddie – Edward Baird – had gone missing in Spain. Naturally, members of the family were distressed, and, as the boy's uncle, he had been tasked with trying to find his whereabouts. Enquiries had revealed that Eddie was imprisoned here in Salamanca, and was in poor health.

"And how is this any of my concern?" Morelos interjected. He sounded highly sceptical.

Iain hastily went on to claim that the purpose of his visit was purely humanitarian. The lad could be headstrong, he would admit, and had defied his parents by sneaking away. But in reality, his action was no more than that of a callow youth whose head had been turned by a girlfriend daring him to show his affection by volunteering to serve in Spain. In mitigation, he would add, his nephew had seen no fighting, in fact had been captured almost as soon as he had arrived in the country. And now it appeared he was being treated as a spy.

"Then he is subject to due process under the law. He would receive a fair trial where he could plead his case."

Iain shuddered. A show trial would be in no one's interest, he argued. Such an event would not go down well with the British public. There were powerful political figures, sympathetic to the Nationalist cause, who would welcome a gesture of Christian charity. There was a second uncle, Captain Lixmont, who was a leading light in the Anglo-German Fellowship, and an intimate of the German ambassador. It had been hinted that an appeal behind the scenes had been suggested by Herr Ribbentrop himself.

"So, you are an agent of the British government?" The colonel dropped his air of amused tolerance.

"No – not directly. But I have been given help." He pursued his advantage. "Eddie's grandfather is a wealthy man. Although now retired, his views still carry weight in conservative circles. He is particularly anxious that good relationships with your government are maintained."

"I take it, then, that he is the founder of the feast. This donation, this gift for the Church that you mentioned earlier—" He leaned forward. "May I ask what form it might take? Surely not food parcels for the poor and needy?"

"By no means. It comes as a financial contribution – eighty golden sovereigns, and four thousand pounds in bonds, cashable anywhere in the world, and in any currency you care to mention." He had already decided to keep back some of the money. Surely he was entitled to a fee for his services. In any case there was no telling what the future might hold. It would be as well to have something in reserve.

"These funds. Are they already in Spain? Possibly in your possession?" There was glint in his eye.

"They are in this city, certainly."

"I believe you. Else you would not have dared to come here today. Perhaps you have lodgings in Salamanca?"

Iain ignored the question. "I thought you might like to take charge of the offering yourself. Then you and your superiors could decide as and when you saw fit. There would be no need to have me followed," he added, almost as an afterthought.

He was met by a cold, calculating stare. This was the crunch. Would the fat bastard take the bait, or have him arrested, perhaps tortured to reveal the location of his money belt. At length the colonel appeared to make up his mind.

"I shall make enquiries." He touched the bell on his desk. "Go back to your quarters. Come again at this hour tomorrow."

The next day there was to be no long wait in an anteroom. Immediately on arrival he was saluted, whisked inside by the captain of the guard, and ushered into the office of the chief of staff. The fly in the spider's web, he could not help wondering. Thank Christ he had the forethought to leave his pot of gold in its lair – though now divided into two portions. But on this occasion Colonel Morelos was all smiles and bonhomie.

"I have good news for you, *Señor* Baird. My superiors have reviewed your nephew's case. They have decided that there are mitigating factors – humanitarian grounds, as you said yesterday. He is to be released into your charge, on condition that you both undertake to leave the country without delay. You will see my government is capable of acts of magnanimity," he added smugly. "I trust this will be made widely known."

As though on cue, a side door opened and two orderlies marched in, supporting a pale, emaciated youth between them. Iain could only gape in horror. It was certainly Eddie. But what had they done to him? His eyes were sunken, fixed in a vacant, glassy stare: he gave no sign of recognition. He could hardly stand unaided; his body began to shake convulsively. There had been some attempt to make him presentable, it was true; his clothes were worn, but clean and mended, his hair roughly cut and his beard shaved. But these only served to emphasise the dark bruising on his head and cheeks.

"Good God," gasped Iain. "I cannae take him back in that condition. He widnae survive the journey."

Morelos himself seemed momentarily taken aback, but quickly recovered. "I take your point. It would not be seemly for the boy to return while he has a fever." Abruptly he barked an order in Spanish. Eddie was promptly dragged from the room.

"There is no need to concern yourself, my friend." He sought to reassure

Iain. "Eddie – I think that was the name you told me – Eddie has simply been escorted to the canteen. He is in need of sustenance, I think you will agree."

"Aye, maybe. But what happens next?"

"Calm yourself. I believe I may have a solution. There is a monastery in the mountains near the border with Portugal. Many of the monks there are skilled in nursing. Arrangements could be made for you and your nephew to stay while he recovers from illness. It would be for you to decide when he is fit enough to travel home."

"That's all very well" Iain was not fully convinced. "But what about his family?"

"I had thought of that. Sit down at this table. Here is pen and paper. You will write a letter explaining that the boy is alive and in good spirits. He has been treated well as a guest of the Nationalist government, but unfortunately contracted a fever which required hospitalisation. There he received treatment which was successful, but has need of a period of recuperation. You will inform them that you will write again when Eddie has recovered his strength."

Iain flushed. It went against the grain, but he could see no alternative. He took up the pen as Morelos looked on, twisting his moustache.

"Good." The colonel nodded approval as he read the result. "Now address an envelope – to the grandfather, I think. I will ensure it is delivered safely."

Hastily Iain scribbled a few lines "Are we done, then?"

"More or less. I shall arrange for an ambulance to transport you and your nephew to the monastery. You will return to your *diggings* – I believe that is the term in English – to collect your effects. You should let it be known that you have been recalled to the front." He held out his hand. "People will bless you for your endeavours, *Señor* Baird. It would not be wise to disappoint them."

Iain bowed slightly and turned away. The implication was unmistakable.

EIGHTEEN

Lessons Learned?

Edinburgh
January 1938

"They're waiting for you at your grandparents' house, Master Eddie."

The words rang in his ears, as he set out along the well-worn path from Stockbridge to Trinity, a route he must have travelled hundreds of times over the years. Strange how the maid had never got round to addressing him as an adult. No doubt she was only following the example of the family; they obviously still regarded him in the same light. That, however, was the least of his worries. They would all be there to sit in judgment. Would he be taken to task, condemned for the pain and anxiety he had caused? Or be welcomed with tears and kisses, all offences overlooked in the joy of his safe return? Probably it would be somewhere in between. He would know soon enough.

Eddie Baird tightened his trench coat against the snell wind blowing through Inverleith Park; already a hoar frost was forming on the ground, glistening amongst the gathering shades of late afternoon. He quickened his pace. His wire sent the previous day had alerted them to his coming, but not the hour of his arrival. Bad enough to face the music at home: a reception party to greet him at the Waverley Station would be too much to bear. But it would be cruel to prolong their wait. It was nearly nine months since he had left for Spain. He had celebrated – if that was the right word – his birthday, his twenty-third, far from home. How would they react to the tale he had to tell?

He could recall nothing of the journey to the monastery, and little of the early days of his sojourn there. But his health and strength had steadily improved, partly due to the skill and care of the monks, partly to the air of quiet solitude in the mountain retreat. Even so, it was a full three months before he was pronounced well enough to leave. The mental scars had taken longer to heal, and he was still prone to the occasional flashback: the cramped, filthy conditions of his confinement; the vermin scurrying around in his cell; the lice and fleas which infested his clothes and hair; the stench of sickness and disease; above all, the death threats and beatings to make him confess. He shivered in spite of himself. Yet he could take pride that his jailers could never break his spirit.

Throughout his long recuperation Iain Baird had remained something of a mystery. That he owed his life to the man was not in dispute. But after seeing him safe and sound he could disappear for days, sometimes weeks, at a time. When taxed about his absences he would only mutter a reference to unfinished business, and refuse any further explanation. After his last trip he had returned with the news that they must depart, before the winter snows made the route impassable. He had sprung another surprise once they had crossed the border into Portugal. This was the end of the line; he had insisted they must part company. He had handed over a purse with five sovereigns, together with a promissory note for £200, enough to cover his expenses and pay for the voyage home. His advice had been to take a train ticket to Lisbon and report himself to the British Embassy there.

The escape into Portugal, however, had been far from marking an end to his troubles. He had attempted to change the sovereigns at a local bank; but the cashier had been suspicious, the police had been called, and he had been arrested. Both gold coins and the bond had been confiscated, and he had been left to languish in custody for a month or more before consular officials arrived to secure his release. Even then, he was treated with scant sympathy at the embassy: only when funds were forthcoming from his parents had he been permitted to book his passage home. To add to his woes, as soon as he had disembarked at Tilbury docks, two detectives had been waiting to escort him to a police station, where he was read a homily on the folly of enlisting in a foreign army, together with an admonition that he was fortunate not to be charged with a criminal offence. Once free to go, he had not immediately taken his train to Edinburgh: he felt a need to collect his thoughts before returning to the bosom of his family. There was a question on his mind – and the answer was to be found in London.

The old, familiar features loomed up through the winter dusk. Nothing had changed; the decorated lamppost on the pavement threw out its customary pool of light. His hand was on the garden gate when he gave a start. No time for second thoughts now; he had been seen from the window. The front door swung open; they were pouring out, hurrying down the path towards him – both parents and grandparents, and Uncle Hugh in the background. He was surrounded before he could catch breath; they were fussing over him, smothering him with hugs and kisses. He was almost overwhelmed by the intensity of their greeting. It was for his grandfather to restore a semblance of order – a sharp word of command not to crush the boy, before shepherding the company indoors. Champagne was poured; glasses were handed round. The head of the family proposed a toast to a safe homecoming.

Once the hubbub had subsided, and they had all taken their seats, Eddie began by apologising for the pain and misery he must have caused. His mother smiled fondly, and waved aside his offer to work his socks off to make amends. Then he launched into his account: meeting up with a group of Fife miners, led by Chick Buchanan; being strafed by an enemy plane, with Chick and himself the only survivors; their capture and attempt to escape; Buchanan's sacrifice to save him. He passed lightly over his ordeal in Salamanca, but was fulsome in his praise of Iain Baird. Lastly, he made a brief mention of his stay at the monastery, before arriving in Portugal and subsequent journey home.

"I learned a lot in Spain," he said in conclusion. "It opened my eyes to things I hadn't really considered before."

"I should imagine you had." His grandfather blew out his cheeks. "You've been through enough to last a lifetime." Suddenly he stiffened. Was there a hint in that last remark? "Your – er, uncle. He was with you at the monastery. Did you talk much? About family matters, perhaps?"

"Not really. He was away most of the time." There was a pause as he seemed to consider. "Oh, I think I catch your meaning. Did he ask me if I knew he was my natural father?"

There was a loud gasp, almost of disbelief: they could only stare at one another in stark horror.

"Well, did he?" demanded his Uncle Hugh.

"Never mentioned it. Though I did sometimes have the impression he was on the verge of saying something about me."

"But never managed to get it out? Was that the case?" It was his mother who gave voice to the thought. "Did your Aunt Morag tell you?"

"My old nanny? She'd never betray a confidence. You should know better than that, mama."

"Then who—?"

"Told me? No one. Worked it out for myself."

"You'll have to explain that, Eddie." Sir Edward noted the general look of bemusement.

"It's not hard, grandpa. I know you all thought of him as the black sheep of the family. You objected to his politics. But your determination to keep him away gave me the notion that there might be more to it. I could sense as much even when I was a nipper. Then there was the story of my supposed father being killed early in the war. It seemed a bit odd at the time. But what really drew my attention was when I proposed a visit to the battlefields, and you persuaded me to go to the Berlin Olympics instead."

"I'm not proud of that," muttered his grandfather.

"No." He shook his head. "It stuck in my mind ever since. That's why I took the opportunity to pay a visit to the War Office in London yesterday. There is no record of any officer of that name and regiment being killed in the first six months of the war."

"Checkmate, Hilda?" Her husband was first to react. He remembered the inquiry agents she had once employed. They had evidently been less diligent in their research than she would have wished.

"Nonsense, Edward." She sailed on, as though oblivious to the revelation. "What we told your grandson was for his own good. So far as I am concerned, there is not a shred of evidence to show that ne'er-do-well is the boy's father."

"No? Do you really believe that, granny? Can you honestly put your hand on your heart and swear he is not my parent?" There was no response. "In any case I can work out the dates."

"What do you mean by that, darling?" Elizabeth gave a wry smile.

"It wasn't hard, mama. You remember when I asked you if you had ever met my other grandmother – the one who lived in a mining village. You told me you had. She was a lovely lady, but died shortly afterwards. You were invited to the funeral. That was in February 1914. Nine months later I was born. Therefore, the deed must have been done then, probably in the family home. If it wasn't dad, it must have been his brother. Stands to reason, don't you agree?" He looked at his mother for confirmation. She gave a slow nod.

"Harrumph!" Sir Edward cleared his throat. "I think that is conclusive.

Give it up, Hilda. I, for one, am glad it's out in the open at last. We've lived a lie for too long." He addressed his grandson. "We owe you a heartfelt apology, Eddie. Can you forgive us?"

"Willingly. You did what you thought best. I can't object to that."

"That's generous of you." He hesitated. "What will you do now?"

"Nothing. I'm very grateful he fished me out of that hellhole, of course. But I could never accept him as my true father. He refused to take responsibility, abandoned me when I was born. I could never regard him as more than a distant relative. My real dad is here, in this room. He took me in, adopted me when he married mama, brought me up as his own."

"Bravely put." Elizabeth squeezed her husband's arm.

"It may be that we have misjudged him, all the same." He felt he could not leave matters at that. "Perhaps we should make an effort to treat him a bit better. Give him some recognition instead of casting him out as a pariah."

"I suppose we could extend an olive branch," mused his grandfather.

"I hear he's back in the country," added his mother. "Morag wrote to tell me. She's taken him back."

"There you are, then. What do you say, Hilda. Let bygones be bygones?"

"Have it your own way, Edward," she sniffed. "Just so long as you don't expect houseroom from me."

"Good. So that's it settled." It would be a relief to move on, now that a degree of harmony had been restored. "What about your future, Eddie? It's too late this year, of course, but you could always reapply for Oxford. It's your ambition to work for the League of Nations, is it not?"

"Not anymore, grandpa. That's what I meant when I said Spain had opened my eyes. There's no reward in negotiating with dictators. Give in to their demands today, and they'll be back for more tomorrow. Appeasement will never work. Sooner or later their aggression will go too far, and we have to be ready for them." He looked round. "That's why I'm going to apply for the air force."

For a moment they were stunned. No one ventured to speak. Then the voice of his grandmother broke the heavy silence. "There's no fool like an old fool, Eddie. Come and give your silly old granny a big hug."

Tears began to roll down her cheeks.